I0823223

ADVANCE PRAISE FOR *IF I DON'T RETURN*

"Every great story rests on character, and General Mark Hertling's character leaps from these pages. With a novelist's eye for detail and a soldier's honesty, he brings to life the realities of war and the timeless questions of love, family, and duty. This is storytelling at its finest—personal, powerful, real, and profoundly human. This is a book everyone should read."

—Daniel Silva,
New York Times best-selling author

"There are no thoughts more profound than the thoughts you have with yourself if you think they may be your last. In this remarkable book, Mark Hertling shares those thoughts with you. This decorated soldier, national security expert, doctor of business administration, and professor of leadership reflects—and encourages you to join him in reflecting—on what's really important in life; in relationships; in leadership; as individuals, families, and teams; and as a country. *If I Don't Return* is a timely and compelling story about hope. If that's something you need, read this book first."

—General (Retired) Martin E. Dempsey,
eighteenth chairman of the Joint Chiefs of Staff

"As a division commander during Desert Storm, I saw firsthand the challenges young leaders faced as they prepared for battle. Mark Hertling's book brings that era back to life with honesty, humility, and extraordinary detail about lessons from both life and combat. This book captures the experience of war and the enduring values of leadership and character that define the American soldier, and it's a must-read for those who want to know more about our military."

—General Barry McCaffrey,
former 24th Infantry Division commander
during Desert Storm, retired four-star general,
and chief military analyst at MSNBC

"*If I Don't Return* is the story every soldier wants to tell but struggles to put into words. Deeply personal, incredibly moving, and storytelling at its finest! Mark Hertling has written a timeless tale of life as a soldier, a father, and a wartime leader, but this book is about more than combat—it is about how we face life's greatest challenges with faith, wisdom, and gratitude. Everyone who is searching will find something of value in this beautifully written narrative."

—Admiral William H. McRaven,
US Navy (retired), former commander of
US Special Operations Command, former chancellor
of The University of Texas System

"Mark Hertling is a natural storyteller. As my dear friend and colleague at CNN, he helped viewers make sense of military operations with clarity and compassion. In this book, he does something even more profound: He opens his private journal to show us the fears, hopes, and lessons of a soldier and a father. This book is moving, accessible, and unforgettable."

—Jamie Gangel,
CNN special correspondent,
Edward R. Murrow Award recipient

"At a precarious moment for our nation, its military, and the world, Mark Hertling has provided an important and captivating book on combat, values, and leadership. Transforming the memories of Desert Storm he gave his sons into timeless lessons of combat, resilience, and family life, this book deserves a place in everyone's library of great leaders' works."

—Thom Shanker,
retired Pentagon correspondent for *The New York Times*

IF I DON'T RETURN

A Father's Wartime Journal

MARK P. HERTLING

Lieutenant General, US Army (Retired)

Ballast Books, LLC
www.ballastbooks.com

Hardcover: 978-1-966786-72-6
eBook: 978-1-966786-73-3

Printed in Hong Kong

Published by Ballast Books
www.ballastbooks.com

For more information, bulk orders, appearances, or speaking requests, please email: info@ballastbooks.com

To Todd and Scott,

The pages that follow contain the random thoughts I had during my deployment of Operation Desert Shield. I arrived in Saudi Arabia today with the knowledge that this would be a significant event in my life that I want to share with two of my three best friends. With the hope that this might give insight into the man you both call "Dad," I'll record my thoughts so that you might share them with me when I return. I love you both.

Dad

(From the front page of the original journal, written 20 December 1990)

And now, with the gift of years and the blessing of perspective, I dedicate this book to Sue—my first and forever friend, whose love has steadied me in every storm. To our grandchildren, whose laughter carries the promise of tomorrow. To our families and friends, who walked beside us in moments of hardship and in seasons of joy, shaping me long after the desert winds ceased and the guns fell silent.

I dedicate it, too, to the soldiers with whom I served—men and women who bore the weight of duty with courage beyond measure, no matter the task. To the doctors who healed both body and spirit. To the journalists who sought truth even when it was fragile and hard to find. To the students who reminded me that learning never ends. Each of you left your mark upon me in the myriad "careers" I was blessed to experience, and each of you has a place in these pages.

And to the readers . . . This book was something I never expected to write, but it came about due to a request from our sons. I hope you'll find this book more than a journal of a war long past. Instead, see it as a testament to growth through experience, to friends who gave more than they asked for in return, and to the potential all of us have for reflecting on our past.

May you be as blessed as I was when you reflect on your own journey.

—Mark Hertling, December 2025

TABLE OF CONTENTS

Introduction i

SECTION 1: Pre-Combat Checks and Inspections 1

25 DEC 1990—Emotions 3

26 DEC 1990—Friendship 7

27 DEC 1990—First Impressions 14

30 DEC 1990—Cultural Differences 18

1 JAN 1991—Appreciate the Small Things 23

2 JAN 1991—A Typical Day 27

6 JAN 1991—Faith 34

7 JAN 1991—Mom 39

8 JAN 1991—Fear 44

9 JAN 1991—Disappointment 50

10 JAN 1991—Near Beer vs. Wiezen 53

11 JAN 1991—Knowledge 58

12 JAN 1991—MREs 62

13 JAN 1991—OPLANS and OPORDS 68

14 JAN 1991—Rock Springs, Wyoming 73

15 JAN 1991—The Deadline 77

SECTION 2: Actions on Contact **79**
17 JAN 1991—The Attack 81
18 JAN 1991—Intelligence in War 84
20 JAN 1991—Heart, Mind, and Soul. 94
21 JAN 1991—Phoning Home 100
25 JAN 1991—Expectations 105
27 JAN 1991—Tactical Assembly Area Thompson. 108
2 FEB 1991—The Bombing 120
6 FEB 1991—Rehearsal, Movement to Contact. 126
17 FEB 1991—Movement Rehearsal to FAA Garcia and Occupation. 127
18 FEB 1991—The Berm .133
20 FEB 1991—The Storm 140
28 FEB 1991—The War .147
1 MAR 1991—Into Kuwait 169
3 MAR 1991—Tunnel Rats 176
5 MAR 1991—The Dead Guys 181
13 MAR 1991—Kuwait City 185
17 MAR 1991—The Iraqi Generals 189

SECTION 3: Having Seen the First Elephant **197**
17 MAR 1991—The Commanding General, Iron 6 199
19 MAR 1991—Misty 207
20 MAR 1991—The Environment 212
21 MAR 1991—The Victims 217
22 MAR 1991—Sensitivity 225

23 MAR 1991—Thanks for Your Service 228
25 MAR 1991—Music. 231
28 MAR 1991—The Media 237
29 MAR 1991—Cursing. 248
31 MAR 1991—Easter 251
1 APR 1991—Iraqi Volleyball. 257
2 APR 1991—War Buddy 263
5 APR 1991—The Human Condition 268
6 APR 1991—Mass Burials .272
9 APR 1991—Unique Personalities and Leadership 279
13 APR 1991—Back in Saudi Arabia 286
19 APR 1991—Camp Kasserine 291
25 APR 1991—My Sons 297

Afterword 307
Giving Back: In Memory of Pete Way. 313

INTRODUCTION

Have you ever had a premonition that you just might die—not the vague worry that everyone has at one time or another about mortality but an official prediction? I did, and it occurred in the late fall of 1990 when our cavalry squadron was ordered to war. It wasn't just deploying into combat that generated these thoughts. It was that our mission, being at the front of 1st Armored Division and going against a premier enemy force, carried a blunt forecast: We might suffer over 50 percent casualties.

That prediction made sense at the time. Iraq's leader, Saddam Hussein, commanded the world's fourth-largest army. His forces were hardened from a long, bloody war with Iran, and he had already shown his brutality by using nerve gas against his own citizens, the Kurds. Facing that kind of adversary, the danger felt real, not abstract, and the predictions of our losses seemed accurate. Today, many Americans forget that Desert Storm was not expected to be easy; back then, many of us soldiers were expecting the worst.

That number—half of us—hung over the squadron like a cloud. As we prepared for what was first called Operation Desert Shield, an operation most of us knew would soon become a shooting war, those in the squadron who had heard these numbers didn't wrestle with panic. We were, after all, soldiers being asked to do our duty. But I had the sober and nagging realization that our two young sons just might grow up without really knowing their father. My remedy was to begin a journal. If I didn't come home, at least our boys would have my words, know my actions, remember some things about me as they grew. Soldiers have done this for generations, and those journals often outlast the battles themselves—frank, unfiltered accounts more powerful than official histories.

But against the predictions, I survived. So did every trooper I served alongside. I returned from Desert Storm in June 1991, then was blessed over the next few decades to stand alongside my wife and watch our boys transform into men, husbands, and fathers.

I kept serving, gathering insights from other wars and from life itself—about leadership, trust, decision-making, and the fragile strength of the human spirit. For years, I kept those thoughts private . . . until one day, I was persuaded to revisit the past and connect it to the future.

That happened on an early, exciting, and energized Christmas morning in 2024. After we survived the early wake-up call from our grandchildren, the joyful chaos that comes with unwrapping gifts, and the subsequent intense and precise building of Lego towns and race cars, our youngest son slowly stood from his chair. He walked across our small living room and handed me one last gift.

His expression told me this wasn't just another present. There was weight in his eyes—this gift was something deeper, something more personal. "I wanted to wait until all the other gifts were opened and the boys were busy," he said, "because this one's just for you."

Inside was something I hadn't expected: a neatly typed and bound version of what had once been a handwritten journal I'd kept more than thirty years earlier during Operation Desert Shield and Desert Storm. The entries in that journal had been written for our sons, Scott and Todd, as a means of providing fatherly advice in case I didn't return home. The entries had also been for my wife, Sue, to remind her of who she married if she found herself a widow.

Now, one of those sons had brought it back to life.

He told me he'd spent months transcribing the ink-smeared pages I had written under a red lens flashlight in the desert three decades earlier. He laughingly told me many of the pages were barely legible because of my extremely poor handwriting—"You write like a doctor," he said—and while the pages had yellowed, they were still readable. He'd inserted old photos into the new Word document while preserving every sentence I had written. He was returning this gift to me as his labor of love.

I didn't say much. I couldn't. Like many older soldiers, emotions flow quickly and I get "misty"—but looking through what he had handed me, what he had worked on for months in his limited free time, left me undone. While silently skimming the pages, the sights, sounds, smells of the desert came back. The dust, the heat, the rain, the tension of rehearsals, the weight of contact with the enemy, and the moments of quiet reflection after the chaos were now part of that Christmas morning memory.

Our youngest son always has a smile on his face, but as he watched me in that moment, he said something with a look of serene seriousness that changed everything.

"Dad, I've read that journal many times," he said quietly. "It's taught me a lot—about war, about you . . . and about me. But you wrote it when Todd and I were the age your grandsons are now. It was for us and for Mom. And as I read it, I came to realize you were writing it in case you didn't come home. But the more times I read it, the more I realized it's incomplete." A long pause. "You should finish it, Dad. Not so much for us anymore, but for your grandchildren. So they will always know you—and *their* children will know you too—when you're gone."

He then reminded me that since writing the words in the journal in 1990–1991, my life hadn't slowed. I had fought in other wars. I had seen friends wounded and killed. I had led thousands of soldiers and civilians—sometimes under fire, sometimes in the delicate arenas of peacetime training and exercises—and connected with others in diplomacy, hospital corridors, or television studios. While doing all that, I had also done my best to show an example of love and devotion to my wife, Sue, even when I failed her or when I wasn't as present as I should have been. And most profoundly, both of our sons—the very boys I had written to—had themselves grown up to wear the uniform. They've served with honor across seven deployments—in Iraq, the broader Middle East, and even Europe during the invasion of Ukraine. They, too, knew the sting of combat and the hope for a better world.

The journal he handed me that day had once been for them. But he was now asking me to add new reflections on those same subjects from a life of service and leadership so others could hear the story. I knew I had to do it.

The journal begins in December 1990, after our advance party had left our base in Europe and arrived in the cold desert of Saudi Arabia, where I served as the operations officer—or "S3"—for a cavalry squadron in the 1st Armored Division. Our squadron was known as the Blackhawks, and my call sign was Blackhawk 3. We had learned of our deployment not through official channels but after being told to watch a secretary of defense press conference on CNN, airing on Armed Forces Network (AFN) that night in November. Secretary Cheney announced that a massive number of units from Europe would go to reinforce the 82nd Airborne Division that had been deployed to Saudi Arabia in August, and that surprise announcement sent all of us into chaos, as we had not known of any such plan. Phones began ringing, and conversations between the squadron commander and me went late into the evening. After we decided what we would be doing the next day, it was well after midnight. Sue and I went to bed, but neither of us slept. It was a strange way to find out you were going to war.

Within a few weeks, we had packed up all our Bradleys, helicopters, trucks, and equipment and conducted dozens of movements from our base in Katterbach, Germany, to the ports of Bremen and Amsterdam. Our stuff was haphazardly loaded onto dozens of ships (back then, we hadn't had much practice in deploying out of Germany to somewhere else), and within a few weeks, I found myself on the advance party for the squadron, landing in Saudi Arabia. Within a day, we were at an assembly area in the middle of the Saudi Arabian desert, waiting for the rest of the unit to join us. By December 1990, all nine hundred of our squadron's cavalry troopers—and twenty thousand other fellow soldiers from the 1st Armored Division—had traveled from various *kasernen* in southern Germany to the sands of the Arabian Peninsula. We began preparing for what would become a swift but brutal campaign. This would be my first of three different deployments over the next twenty years with the 1st Armored Division, often called "Old Ironsides."

For this deployment, our squadron would serve as the advance guard for the division, a mission we knew little about and hadn't trained to conduct, as we had been in a defensive posture for the last few decades in Europe. We studied the doctrinal manuals and began to adjust our approach to this new style of combat. We were postured to lead our division's attack into Iraq for the purpose of engaging and destroying Saddam Hussein's elite Republican Guard. Given that Iraq's army was the fourth largest in the world at the time and that we expected them to use chemical weapons like they had previously against the Kurds in Halabja in the late 1980s, the preliminary 50 percent casualty projection seemed likely.

But here's the spoiler alert: We survived. Thirty-three of our soldiers were wounded during the war, most of them during an errant US artillery strike, but none were killed in action. That wouldn't be the outcome in the units I was with in later wars.

After a last-ditch political effort by the US government to find a peaceful solution failed, we watched all sorts of coalition aircraft fly over our position in the starlit desert nights to wage an air campaign, then crossed the berm separating the Saudi Arabia-Iraq border. In eighty-nine hours, we traversed 250 miles through the Al-Batin alluvial fan, where Iraq's southern border with Kuwait converged in a harsh, fault-lined landscape. We fought across that terrain, then engaged the Republican Guard in what would later become famous as the Battle of Medina Ridge—one of the largest tank engagements since World War II. Along the way, we encountered not just enemy fire but our own humanity. Prayer. Brotherhood. Fear. Thoughts of loved ones back home. Emotions. Tactical decisions that carried life-or-death consequences. The grace of survival.

When I returned home months later, I ceremoniously showed the journal to our sons, telling them it contained reflections on faith, love, planning, rehearsals, combat action, my bond with their mother, the responsibility of leadership, and the burden of leading. But being eleven and eight years old at the time, they were too young to read it or even understand what it held in its pages. They just wanted to go outside with me to play catch. But someday, I hoped it would give them some sense of what we had faced, the emotions we had shared, the lessons we had learned.

Over the following decades, while that journal was tucked away and forgotten in a footlocker, I found myself tested in new ways—different combat zones; complex peacetime assignments; eventual retirement; and new careers in health care, cable news, and teaching. Experiencing moments of victory but also seasons of personal loss. I learned important lessons in every assignment and job, when connecting with generals, ambassadors, allies, partners, and young soldiers. I learned more after retirement from many business leaders, journalists, health care professionals, and students. And always present were lessons on life from my wife and our expanding family. The lessons I learned were about successes, painful failures, human foibles, and the simple experiences we all have in life.

I didn't have a lot of time to reflect on everything I'd learned and experienced until I was handed that typed version of the journal. But over the years, I've come to believe one thing. That life and leadership are forged by one's character. And character is molded by experiences but defined by integrity, shared trust, enumerated values, honest humility, and different kinds of love. Scar tissue and tough lessons also play a part, but there's always a return to joy in service and accomplishments.

That's what this book now aims to share—not just experiences *from* that war but also those lessons learned *before, during,* and *after* that war. Lessons learned from a professional life wearing the cloth of our country and a personal life attempting to provide good leadership in both the military and civilian worlds, all while navigating complex organizations, juggling family responsibilities, addressing personalities and human shortcomings, providing national service, and maintaining integrity. Descriptions of that life and some of the many experiences—professional and personal—are now linked to and a continuation of the entries originally directed at those two little boys. Some deep thoughts, hard lessons, pains and glories, and even some ramblings about nonsensical subjects are in this work. Hopefully, they may now serve as a legacy for my five grandsons and two new step-granddaughters—and, I hope, even a resource for others who may find themselves searching for answers to questions; advice to guide them through difficult moments; and ways to weigh their own character, their own values, and their own actions in challenging times.

Each chapter you'll find in this book includes original entries from that 1991 journal, preserved in italics and presented just as I wrote them: with typos, misspellings, and sometimes a lack of syntax. Some of them have been slightly edited to leave out very personal things that might embarrass or things I just don't want people to know. But most of them are as I originally wrote them. I've included reflections after each of these three-decade-old entries—new stories, memories, thoughts, and advice incorporated in Roman font that add to the context of the journal entries. While these reflections were shaped by what came later, they are related to the journal entries' original subjects. Reflections on values, leadership challenges, my deeper understanding of life, and the encounters with extraordinary people I've met along the way. Oh, and there are war stories to help those who have never experienced deployments or war better understand what our military does since most people today don't choose to serve. I've had lots of questions on those topics while serving as a military analyst on cable TV, so I thought I'd give some insight into how tough it is to go to war, and what lingers after. Finally, there are some things I wanted our sons, grandsons, and new granddaughters to know about me *then* and *now* (that's an inside joke for our daughter-in-law, Lauren, the mother of two of these grandchildren, who is phenomenal in taking me to task!) and about dealing with mortality, with people, with incredibly complex issues.

The journal entries range from the important to the ridiculous, and the reflections will vary in length and seriousness. I have a favorite fiction writer—Daniel Silva, a *New York Times* best-selling author of dozens of books about art restorer and legendary fictional spy Gabriel Allon. During a recent book signing for one of his books, I heard Danny say that his writing process replicated "driving cross country; sometimes in rain, sometimes in the fog, sometimes in very clear weather." I thought that was an interesting way to describe the creative writing process, especially since his books have such complicated and compelling plot lines. That approach has proven to be true, and it now describes how I decided to write about different subjects that occurred over three decades ago for our two young sons, hoping then that my words might act as gifts if something were to happen to me in combat that would prevent me from being there to provide the advice in person. Even though I was writing these entries for boys who would likely be older when they eventually read them (as I said, Todd was eleven and Scott was eight when I left for Desert Storm), I always found myself seeing their current young faces in my mind's eye as I provided these tales for their future selves.

The book is divided into sections, and I hope the reader will find each unique. That's primarily due to the topics I address, the intent of the writing, and the context of the period within the days of the deployment. In the first section, written in the initial phase of the conflict before the war started, I took a few minutes each night to write about a variety of topics. Thoughts on character, ethics, people, life, relationships, and all sorts of other subjects as they crossed my mind. In those early days when I took pen to paper, I would have a thought on a topic during the day: *What would Todd and Scott want to know about their dad's thoughts on this particular random topic if I don't return from this conflict?* I'd give the topic a bit of thought, then write later that night. No polishing, FD=FC (first draft equals final copy). This first section begins quietly, with notes on the ache of separation from home, my myriad emotions, the routines of soldiering, and the uncertainty of waiting.

Section two of the book begins when the war started, when we were in the thick of things. My approach changed. I usually didn't write during the event but rather reported the details days later in some more stable environment when I had the time. I wanted to get the facts on paper. Interestingly, I didn't notice until I reread the journal that the content in those entries had changed from being a rhetorical exercise—father teaching sons—to me relaying historical events as they occurred and describing the intensity of combat—days that stretched into sleepless nights, decisions made under fire, and the moments that lingered long after the shooting stopped. That middle section provides the facts in a simple and succinct way that the boys could understand—what we had done and in what sequence, what I had experienced, and what the outcomes were. In providing reflection on those combat memories first described in 1991, I tried to link events, lessons, and similar stories from later in my life. The commentaries are heavier due to the influence of later combat experiences.

The third section looks outward again, toward coming home, carrying the physical, intellectual, and emotional baggage, the good and the very painful memories as we prepared to leave the combat zone. This third section reverts to rhetorical discourse, almost like an after-action review: a post-war subject, thoughts on that subject, and a reflection that ties post-conflict observations to those I learned later in life.

A caution to the reader: Few of these thoughts are neat or sophisticated. Very little research was conducted, and the thoughts and the reflections are like transcribed "random thoughts while showering," as I once heard a mentor call this approach. But they are real, and some are painful. And I've come to learn that truths, especially the kind found in quiet reflection and random thoughts, are often more useful than certainty, polish, or bravado.

Oh, one last thing.

Like so many soldiers, I once hoped I was fighting so that my sons would never have to. That's mentioned in the journal several times. That hope, noble as it was back then, proved naïve. My sons *did* go to war. Multiple times. Always in Iraq, save two of those tours for our oldest son, Todd. So did one of our daughters-in-law. And for all practical purposes, while they didn't deploy, my wife and the spouse of our other son went to war too. All of them did so with honor, courage, humility, selfless service, and empathy for both their own soldiers and their enemies. Even knowing that, I offer this same hope once again—this time so that our grandchildren, and others who read this book, find that same grace with this wish:

> *May you never face combat. But if you do, or if life ever tests you—whether in war, in family, in leadership, or in moments when character, integrity, values, and personal courage matter most—I hope you'll find strength in these pages. Strength in values. In character. In purpose. In love. In the stories and thoughts of this old soldier who wrote some random thoughts down for his family—now also for you.*

This journal was once a gift to our young sons. It is now a gift to anyone who cares to read it.

—Mark Hertling, December 2025

PRE-COMBAT CHECKS AND INSPECTIONS

Life, Character, People, Deployment Activities, and Preparation for Combat

25 DEC 1990—Emotions

You both planned so that I could receive a Christmas card on this, my fifth day away from you. They were beautiful, and they made me cry. I've always been a very emotional guy—Mom says that I sometimes even cry at supermarket grand openings—and I'll contest that it is a vital part of someone's personality to show emotional swings. I've known people who have always tried to be "cool," and for the most part I've never liked any of them. I've always been drawn to individuals who are trusting and share their feelings with their friends and family. So far, both of you do that; Scott, freely; Todd, with only a little bit of persuasion. Always let your emotions run freely. It will help you work out problems, share your feelings, and it will keep you from getting ulcers. Christmas is usually my most emotional day (next to Easter and the Fourth of July). I think of the greatness of God and all the blessings He has given me on this special birthday, and it always seems to choke me up. From now on, when you're sitting in midnight mass or Protestant services with me on Christmas, and you see the tears in my eyes, you'll know I'm crying because God has been so good to me by giving me your mom and you two. Thanks for the cards.

Dad

Reflection

Reading that entry again after so many years, I smile. Not just because the memory of missing my family at Christmastime many years ago still pulls at me—but because I now understand so much more about what it really means to be emotional. The title I used for that very first entry in the journal.

Back then, I equated it mostly with crying—and yes, I've always been someone who tears up easily at meaningful moments: births, graduations, funerals, retirements, national anthems, and yes, even—as Sue is apt to say about me—supermarket ribbon cuttings. Many have seen my emotions, too, and know that I'm often embarrassed by my tears of joy and pride. But with time, I've come to realize that emotion isn't just about tears. It's about expression—the willingness to let the fullness of life show up on your face, in your voice, and in the way you lead and live.

Few tease me about my other emotions, though! The good ones. The emotion of smiling boldly when you're proud. Laughing out loud at something beautifully absurd. Standing up and cheering because someone you love just crossed the finish line or graduated from a tough course. Listening with empathy to someone who's hurting. Showing anger that's righteous, not reckless. Exhibiting grief that's sacred, not hidden. Emotions also include expressing joy, surprise, awe, fear, and humility.

Here's the deal: Emotion is the full spectrum of what it means to be alive—and to love others more than yourself. For that reason alone, I believe all of us should openly show our emotions. Poker faces should be reserved for card games or high-stakes negotiations!

Over the course of my life, I've read much about the power of emotional expression—especially in leadership. Daniel Goleman's work on emotional intelligence taught me and a whole generation of leaders that self-awareness and empathy aren't soft skills; they're *core* skills. Researchers and psychologists have shown that people who are able to recognize and name their emotions are more resilient, better decision-makers, and better teammates. That's true in combat and in conference rooms. It's true in marriage and in friendship. It's true in life.

In my years as a soldier, I saw leaders who always kept a poker face, who had their command photos taken with a scowl to show their troops how tough they were, who tried to bottle up every feeling. They wanted to project authority or power or control, but what they projected instead was distance. I often found that their teams followed orders but didn't follow *them*. I watched others—noncommissioned officers, company commanders, generals, admirals, and, yes, chaplains (we'll address that in a future reflection)—who shared their hearts, who smiled often and laughed freely, who spoke plainly about loss or pride or hope. They didn't need to shout to be respected. They were trusted because of their presence; they were authentic.

I've always believed that a good leader, like a good father, must be strong enough to feel. If you don't let yourself celebrate others, your encouragement falls flat. If you don't let yourself grieve the soldiers who made the ultimate sacrifice, you can't really honor them. If you never let your children—or your team—see the emotion behind your decisions, then your character becomes a question mark. People don't need perfect leaders. They need present ones. Honest ones. *Human* ones.

Our sons—Todd and Scott—grew up seeing this in me. Since then, they've also served in uniform, and they've both shown that kind of quiet strength in their own unique and very different ways. And now, as I write for others, I want people to know that this doesn't just apply to generals or officers or soldiers. This applies to you and everyone around you. Whether you're on a team, in a classroom, or raising a family, I believe the ability to properly express your emotions is one of the greatest strengths any person will ever have.

Don't let this world teach you that "cool" means being detached. I've never liked "cool" people all that much. I've always preferred people who are warm, who feel things and aren't afraid to show it. It's just as okay to laugh with your whole body, to beam with joy, to clench your fists in frustration when something matters, or to fall silent with awe when it overwhelms you. And it's okay to cry.

Back in 1990, I wrote to our sons that letting emotions run freely would help them work out problems and avoid ulcers. That was true—but now I'll add this: It also helps you connect. It builds trust. It lets others know they're not alone in what they're feeling. And that's where real leadership—and real love—begins.

So when any of us are together in the future at what I might call a "SEE" (or Significant Emotional Event), and you see tears in my eyes, it's okay for you to smile and even tease me openly. Just know that I'm exhibiting a mix of things: gratitude, memory, love, reverence. But mostly, it's joy. It's the joy of knowing that I've been given far more than I deserve. It's the joy of watching members of our family, or someone I love, grow.

And if your eyes well up too? Don't fight it. Get misty. When your heart is full, your body sometimes gets in the habit of pushing water out of your eyes!

26 DEC 1990—Friendship

I'm sure this topic of "friends" and "friendship" will be a reoccurring one in this journal, but it is a topic which necessitates a lot of discussion. What is making this time away from you at least bearable is the fact that I have some very close friends here with me. Those individuals—CPT Scott Milliren, CPT John Dean, CPT Roger Alford, CPT Greg Heck, LT Rich Tunney, LT Mike Ramirez, LT Tim Hanson, SFC Tim Brett—all have shared their laughter, their feelings, and their friendship with me. We've become closer during this short period of time. They are all going through the same things now that I am: missing family and home, fearing what might lie ahead, anticipation of attempting to do their jobs to the best of their ability. They will all do well, and God willing, will support me as I attempt to accomplish some difficult tasks.

Friendship occurs outside the realm of danger in a unique and interesting way; something that both of you should be aware of. My best friend—Marty Dempsey—complements my life much the same way that your mom and you guys do—his shared values, his ability to make all of us laugh, his caring nature and his selfless attitude (this last quality I consider the most important) has made him someone special and someone I truly enjoy being around. What is most interesting is that I can name the qualities that make him a great friend. The term "friendship" is often thrown around like the word "love;" people attach the label without really thinking about what must go along with it. Just like love is something that doesn't come often, friendship—true friendship—should only be shared with a few people during a lifetime. You're very lucky if you can have only a few people who meet your high standards of friendship.

"Acquaintances"—those you meet, like, and usually don't get to know very well—are the people that will make up your daily relationships with others. My advice to both of you is this: you may not want to have all your acquaintances as friends, but you should try to be a friend to all you know. There is an easy way to do this: Be yourself. Don't put on false airs that you think other people want in you (because you'll spend your time being someone else, not a friend). Give of yourself. You do these things, and you'll be a good friend.

I love you both, my best friends—

Dad

Reflection

Friendship. The real kind. The kind that sustains you through war, career changes, deployments, funerals, weddings, victories, and failures. The kind that doesn't need explanation because it's woven into the way you live and lead.

I'm grateful that I wrote those words back in 1990 because I had no idea how rich that subject would become in my life. I mentioned then that friendship would be a recurring topic in the journal way back then. I didn't realize then that it would become a central theme of my life.

I mentioned my friend Marty Dempsey in that entry. I still mention him a lot today. He was a young major then, just like me, and we had forged an early friendship—between us and all the members of our respective families—while living in a triplex during the period when we both had a three-year assignment teaching cadets at West Point. Marty was in the English Department, and I was in the much more cerebral Department of Physical Education, teaching push-ups and "rock squad" swimming. Now, over forty years have passed since we met the Dempseys, and we've forged a lifelong friendship that has seen lots of ups and downs. But he was one of the first people I met who blended brilliance with humor, loyalty with humility. And in our relationship, he always made me better, and I tried to influence him too. Back then, we were both mid-grade officers, learning how to lead and teach. We laughed a lot and slowly built a friendship that deepened before, during, and after that first war in Iraq and across assignments in Germany and in the US. Later in life, when one of us wore three stars and the other four, and now in retirement, we're both still trying to make a difference in other people's lives . . . and our own.

I once wrote in *ARMY* magazine that a best friend can also be your boss and your mentor. That was written about Marty—and it's still true. He wasn't just a colleague. He was (and remains) a grounding force, someone I can be my full self around, someone who sharpens me intellectually, challenges me ethically, and laughs with me through it all. Our friendship isn't an accident. It was built intentionally, over time, through trust and the kind of shared values that make life richer.

But Marty isn't my only true friend. I've been lucky. Truly lucky.

There's Bryan Watson—retired major general, a thinker, a warrior, and a quiet man of immense depth and kindness—who was our chief of staff when I commanded the 1st Armored Division. Retired Colonel Steve Schenk, who was our operations officer in Iraq during the surge of 2007, who was a true strategic planner and leader, who embodied army values and showed genuine care for our troops and for the Iraqis we were fighting to help. My West Point buddy, Tupper Hillard, who does a great Elvis impersonation and who once, as a cadet, sang for President Ford and Secretary of State Haig in the White House (no kidding) and who was there with us in Iraq as the executive officer of the aviation brigade our cavalry squadron was with. My West Point roommate, the best man at my wedding (and I at his), super historian, wonderful human being, and funniest guy who's ever lived on Long Island, Phil Baker. There's Pat Heitert, my high school buddy from St. Louis. We've been ribbing each other for over fifty years, remembering Brewer & Shipley songs and his beat-up Corvair from our high school time together; he still calls regularly just to check in. And I've been privileged to serve alongside command sergeants major like Dave Davenport and Roger Blackwell, men whose wisdom, loyalty, and fierce dedication helped shape my view of true leadership. They weren't just senior enlisted advisors. They were battle buddies, they were partners in command—they were friends I could count on, without question. And a few junior sergeants too. Like Sergeant Andrew Smith, who was my communication chief in Iraq in 2007 and who still calls me "Dad" now that he's retired and doesn't have to say "sir."

Many of these military friendships were forged in combat. And that matters. War, in all its chaos and clarity, forces you to strip away the unimportant and rely on the person beside you. You see people not for their rank but for their soul. That crucible of shared danger and absolute dependence creates a bond that outlasts distance, time, and even silence. These are life-bonds—brotherhoods and sisterhoods born of trust under fire. They are evergreen.

But most people, thankfully, won't need war to discover those kinds of relationships. They find true and trusted friends in the combat of daily life. The crucible doesn't have to be courage shown in combat. Sometimes it's just the courage to give of yourself to others—truthfully and with candor—trusting someone else with your thoughts, sharing the parts of your heart that you can only share with a friend. In my post-army career, there are many others I have come to call friends. In health care, I met professionals like Brian Paradis; Dr. Mike Cacciatore; Dr. Omayra Mansfield; Dr. Mark Shapiro; Dr. Shikha Jain, who was masterful in starting an organization called Women in Medicine and allowed me to participate in and watch her success; and so many others. In cable news, Eason Jordan, Jamie Gangel, John Berman, Kate Bolduan, and Michael Holmes showed me the ropes and helped me provide good information to the American people. In teaching, the bonds with Dean David Allison at Indiana University and with Mike Kazazis, Dr. Keenan Yoho, and Dr. Kim Smith-Jentsch at Crummer School of Business, where I still teach, help me daily in giving the best of what I've got to the young minds of our students, which is now my passion. Also, most recently, in connecting back with the Class of 2025 at West Point—our Class of 1975's fiftieth anniversary class—I was able to see the next generation of leaders, represented by their class president and my newest, youngest friend, Cadet Katherine LaReau. If these graduates are our army's future, we are in damned good shape! A bounty of gifted women and men that make our lives very special.

I'm afraid, as I write this, that some of my other friends who read these words might feel overlooked. If you're reading this and don't see your name—please know this: I am thinking of you. You are part of the pantheon of friends who have blessed my life and the fabric of my experiences. I simply didn't name every one of you because this isn't a roll call—it's a reflection. A tribute to what friendship is, more than a list of who it includes. You know who you are. And I am grateful for you.

The journal entry from December 1990 was some quick scribbling about those I was seeing around me at the time. But since then, I've thought a lot about friendship. Everyone should. Because science confirms what life teaches: Friendship is not just emotionally nourishing—it's physically protective. Study after study shows that close friendships reduce stress, lower blood pressure, boost the immune system, and even prolong life. In fact, some studies show that social connection is an even better predictor of long-term health than exercise or diet. One Harvard study that followed participants for over eighty years found that strong relationships—friendships—were the single greatest indicator of lifelong happiness and well-being.

The Greeks understood this long before the research data came in. Aristotle called friendship one of the highest forms of virtue. He said, "What is a friend? A single soul dwelling in two bodies." Cicero called friendship "the sun of life." C.S. Lewis wrote that friendship is born "the moment one person says to another, 'What! You too? I thought I was the only one that felt this way.'"

Not every person you meet becomes a friend, and that's okay. I've met thousands of wonderful people—students, soldiers, coworkers, reporters, CEOs, politicians, and even strangers who introduced themselves. Many have become acquaintances, colleagues, and companions on a shared mission. They all matter. But they don't all carry the sacred label of "friend."

Here's the difference:

> A friend knows your flaws and respects you more because of them.
>
> A friend tells you the truth when it's hard.
>
> A friend shows up when things fall apart.
>
> A friend remembers—your stories, your quirks, your heart.
>
> A friend keeps calling, even when there's no agenda.

But most importantly, a true friend always makes you a better person and doesn't let you drift from the person you're meant to be.

You only really need a few of those kinds of friends.

I still love making new friends. That's one of the joys of being active and curious, teaching, and traveling—I search out and meet remarkable men and women every day who are hungry to grow, serve, and make a difference. Some of those relationships stay professional. But now and again, one becomes something more—a lasting friendship that adds another layer to a very blessed life.

I called our sons my "best friends" in that entry way back in 1990. That wasn't a throwaway line. It was my way of saying: You and your mom matter more than anything. And now, to anyone reading this—I'd ask you to think about your friends and, more importantly, what kind of friend you are. How do you show up for others? Are you kind? Do you listen? Do you laugh often? Do you give without keeping score? Do you make others better?

Friendship is one of the most powerful forces in life. And if we're lucky, we'll find a few people—just a few—who walk the whole road with us. We should cherish them. Show up for them. Laugh with them. Pray for them. And tell them what they mean to us—before the moment passes. In fact, make a point of calling or writing a true friend right now, just to tell them what they mean to you. It will make their day.

Because one day, if we're fortunate, we'll all look back over decades and likely realize the greatest treasure we carried wasn't titles, medals, or achievements. It was the friends who walked with us through it all.

27 DEC 1990—First Impressions

A man I worked with once said you never have a second chance to make a good first impression. While that may not always be true, I have found that it's worthwhile advice. Know that people you don't know are always watching you. If you're a leader—and I am one of these "things" now in the squadron—there is always someone watching you to see how you're going to deal with different situations and how you'll react to different people. This tells you a few things: you must always be fair, you must attempt to always do the right things, and if you're a leader you need to put other's needs and perception above your own desires. This is tough; sometimes you don't do a good job at meeting other's standards, but that's okay. Try to do well, and you'll make a good first impression.

The reason I'm discussing this area is because I received a special mission directly from the Commanding General today. I like MG Griffith because he is a man, I believe, who wants people to tell him the facts without any candy coating. When he first came to the division and I was the Deputy G3, I was tasked to give him a presentation on how the division did command and control. I did this, with a few other people in the room, and I feel that he asked me some tough questions that I answered straight up and with the best of my ability. I had nothing to lose, and I was as candid with him as I possibly could be. I think he appreciated that (my other boss—LTC Watson—said I was a little too candid with him). In any event, I think I made a good first impression. Since that event he has pulled me into his confidence numerous times and now he trusts me enough to put a very difficult mission on my shoulders. I can't tell you what that mission is right now, but I will someday, and I think you'll find it very interesting. I also think you will see how a good first impression leads to trust and confidence.

Love you guys,

Dad

Reflection

Let me begin with what I now know since I wrote this journal entry so long ago: It's truer today than it was for me back then that you rarely get a second chance to make a good first impression. Because first impressions don't just open doors—they often determine whether there *is* a door to open in the first place. And in leadership, those early interactions often evolve into something far more enduring: trust.

I don't remember the details of that "special mission" from General Griffith, but I do remember the context. I had transitioned from being the deputy chief of operations, or deputy G3, for the 1st Armored Division to the squadron's operations officer, or S3, just a few weeks before we were told we would deploy to Desert Shield/Desert Storm. The general had seen me perform in the division headquarters, where our relationship was built on straight talk, mutual respect, and a shared focus on mission over optics; I, as the chief of operations, had given straight talk with no bluster or hesitancy to a commanding general who needed to know the facts, logic, and rationale for what we were doing. During my year as a key staff officer for him at division headquarters, we had already worked through many tough challenges together in training, in exercises, and in real-life issues. He had seen me under pressure, especially during the few days when the Berlin Wall and the Iron Curtain were coming down across Europe and we had soldiers on the border. During that period, he'd watched me work under intense pressure, and, more importantly, he'd seen me unvarnished and candid, with soldiers . . . and with him.

I guess he remembered that. I learned later that it mattered to him. But I had left the division staff for that new assignment in the cavalry squadron, and now, I was in a different job as the operations officer for another commander, a lieutenant colonel who was my cavalry squadron commander. But even though I had left the general's staff, when the division commander wanted to reach out directly and assign something critical to our squadron, he contacted me directly. Not the squadron commander, who was relatively new to the organization and, frankly, still finding his footing. That squadron commander had taken the route too many do when seeking favor with the division commander—offering flattery, avoiding friction, and performing for approval rather than simply performing—and he hadn't yet garnered trust with the commanding general. So instead of contacting the commander, General Griffiths skipped him and came to me, which was highly unusual. But he wanted clarity, not choreography or sycophancy, and he trusted me. That day, I was reminded that trust isn't given with rank. It's earned through authenticity. And truthfully, experiencing the uncomfortable situation of our general "skipping echelons" and coming to me helped me many years later, when I was a division commander and some of my subordinates were performing that kind of dance to gain my attention. I didn't always skip echelons, but I always knew who I trusted.

Which brings me to my point: Your very presence—what the business world is now calling "executive presence"—is not about polish, posture, or performance. It's not about who talks the most in the room, who has the shiniest resume, or who uses the fanciest language. Those are the trappings of presence. But real presence? It comes from alignment. The alignment that combines your character (who you really are) and how other people see and what they hear from you.

Presence comes from a leader whose character, values, and actions are congruent. Someone who listens before speaking. Who shows care for others without signaling it performatively. Who can be firm without being cruel, decisive without being arrogant, truthful without pause. This is presence rooted in trustworthiness, not theatrics. It depends on our values and beliefs, exhibiting them in all manner of speech and action.

When I teach leadership now, I talk about how presence is less about how you enter a room and more about how people feel when you leave it. Are they calmer? More inspired? More confident in the path ahead? Do they know they've heard the truth, and do they feel seen, respected, included? Because those reactions come not from aura or charisma—they come from credibility. And credibility starts with that first impression. It's that first impression that reflects one's character and one's values.

Psychologists say first impressions form quickly, but trust doesn't. Trust is built when those impressions are reinforced through consistency. Trust is gained in drops, as I once heard someone say. That's why character always wins in the long game. But if our character is like a windsock, bending and swaying with what others want you to say versus what your values tell you is right, then the first impression isn't the right one.

I've seen leaders who try to manufacture presence, who only want to make a good impression, no matter what it represents. They mimic someone else's voice, attire, mannerisms. They think presence is about the show. But presence isn't about show—it's about *go*. About doing the work, being reliable in a crisis, and staying true to yourself even when the room shifts around you. Presence isn't a marketing campaign. It's a reflection of character.

We will meet people along the way who try to impress with style. It's my belief that we shouldn't be like them. We should try to impress with substance. With steadiness. With service.

The first impression we make should be grounded in who we truly are—because if people see that from the start, they'll know we're people they can trust for the long haul.

30 DEC 1990—Cultural Differences

Let me begin this journal entry by saying that although I have been here only a very few days, I've concluded that Saudi Arabians are a very strange breed of people. In just a few days I have seen them do things that would appall people who live in a western civilization. Their dress, manner of driving, eating habits, method of treating women, religious customs are all very strange to me and most of us here. As an example, during a convoy yesterday when we had some Arab men driving for us, during each rest stop the would cook a big pan of rice and animal fat, then five or six of them would squat around the pan and roll the rice into balls which they would pop into their mouth. They would only do this with their right hand, for if they did it with the left (the same hand they use to clean themselves after going to the bathroom) it would be a great insult to their friends.

Granted, this is strange. But think about it. When we all first came to Germany, didn't the Germans have strange customs that were unique to us? Peeing on the side of the road. Eating with their knives and forks in different hands than us Americans? Volksmarches (oh I don't think Volksmarches would go over well here in Saudi Arabia). While you might say, "Yeah, but these are acceptable differences," I would reply by saying that they are acceptable only because they are not that different from what we do. Just as we have made some great German friends and we have loved our time seeing that beautiful country IN SPITE OF the differences, so should we attempt to see beyond any cultural differences to see what is inside the person we meet. All the while, look for the interesting things about a culture, and learn to search out why there are differences. Remember how when we found out why the Germans use their knives and fork different from us it was interesting and made it more fun to do it like them? I wish I had a book entitled Seven

Pillars of Wisdom *by T. E. Lawrence. It was about a man who lived with the Arabs and described their cultural differences. I read it long ago but didn't pay much attention to the intricacies and the details.*

Maybe I'll read it when I return. Or maybe I'll just spend time with you guys.

Love ya,

Dad

Reflection

I wrote this entry in the desert sands of Saudi Arabia in 1990. I was young and experiencing culture shock in real time. Now, with the wisdom of age and the perspective gained through decades of global travel, I offer this reflection to anyone curious about how the world can shape a person if they allow themselves to be open to it.

It turns out, those early observations in the Middle East were just the start of my cultural explorations, and I hope this reflection might influence others to start that same adventure. I had never been to a foreign country before I went to West Point. In fact, I had never been on an airplane until that first journey to LaGuardia Airport the night before I entered the US Military Academy in July of 1971. But since that time, I've had the honor of traveling to over 120 countries—on nearly every continent—and learning something valuable in each. In my two-year tour as commander of US Army Europe, I traveled to thirty-eight of the forty-nine countries in Europe—some of them like Ukraine, Poland, Romania, Russia, and others many times—attempting to build better relationships with military and civilian leaders but also engaging with the peoples and the cultures of each place: their rituals, greetings, food, languages, values, and sense of history.

And the lesson I learned in doing so is this: Cultural differences are not threats to be judged—they are windows into the souls of different and unique people.

For example, in the nation of Georgia, a toast is never just a toast—it is an expression of love, honor, and vulnerability, made complete only with wine and the full attention of your guests, saying what you truly mean. The toast is poetic, often lengthy, and deeply sincere. I've shared toasts in that country that brought tears to my eyes and forged bonds that required no translation. And once, in Tbilisi, I made a horrible mistake of toasting with beer. I learned that when you use that beverage to toast, you must say the opposite of what you truly believe. It is why my host taught me that it would be appropriate to raise the glass of Pilsen and say, "To Putin's health."

In Iraq, a man kissing another man on the cheek is not strange—it's a greeting, a gesture of warmth and respect. I had to learn that quickly as a general officer being welcomed into homes and headquarters. It initially caught me off guard, but over time, it came to feel natural—a reminder that dignity takes many forms. After fifteen months in Iraq in 2007–2008, I came home and was conducting a Christmas reception at our division headquarters. The mayor of the town of Wiesbaden was the first through the reception line, and for a moment, I forgot where I was . . . and I gave him an Iraqi greeting on the cheek. It was a very good thing that we were friends and that he allowed me to explain that "moment of Zen," or he would have thought I had gone off the deep end.

In Germany, where we lived for so many years during very different times, straightforwardness is valued. Germans aren't rude; they are honest and direct. They don't sugarcoat because they value clarity. You always know where you stand—and that's something I came to respect deeply. But even in Germany, the cultural differences between Bavaria and Brandenburg or Rhineland-Pfalz and Schleswig-Holstein, are unique and different.

In the Nordic and Baltic states, I learned that silence is not awkward. It's thoughtful. In Estonia, Finland, Latvia, and Lithuania, people pause. They wait. They consider their words. That approach can teach us to listen more intently and speak with more purpose.

And in places like South Korea, Brazil, Israel, China, Guatemala, Colombia, and Venezuela, I encountered greetings that ranged from firm handshakes to bows to bear hugs. I ate food I couldn't pronounce and listened to stories I could only understand with help—but always, always, I tried to lean in and learn.

That's the heart of this reflection: Seek understanding. Travel when you can. Learn languages if you're able. Taste the food. Learn the arts. Watch how people worship, celebrate, mourn, and love. If you do, you'll find that humans are astonishingly diverse yet fundamentally similar. We all want to be seen, to be safe, and to be respected. It's interesting to me that in the two languages of countries that have many disagreements—Hebrew and Arabic—the greetings of "Shalom" and "Salaam" are similar in meaning: Peace be unto you.

Mark Twain said it best: "Travel is fatal to prejudice, bigotry, and narrow-mindedness." I believe that with all my heart. The more you see of the world, the less inclined you are to judge it. Instead, you begin to appreciate nuance, complexity, and the truth that your way is not the only way.

One book that helped me later in life was Erin Meyer's *The Culture Map*. She describes how different societies approach everything from decision-making and feedback to trust-building and confrontation. It taught me that leadership, especially in a global context, must be culturally agile. You can't lead everyone the same way, because people are shaped by deeply ingrained values, histories, and expectations.

Back in that 1990 journal entry, I referenced T.E. Lawrence's *Seven Pillars of Wisdom*—and yes, I eventually reread it. But I've also tried to write my own version of Lawrence of Arabia's cultural journey, not in published form but in how I live, teach, lead, and love.

So, here's what I suggest to anyone reading this:

Get out into the world. Taste strange food and the local alcoholic delicacies, take part in and try to understand unfamiliar rituals, dance the dance of the culture when they invite you (they love it when foreigners mess it up!), learn to at least say "hello" and "thank you" in languages you don't yet understand. Because each of these things is a bridge. And we should all cross it.

The differences we notice at first—how people eat, greet, drive, worship, dance, and speak—may seem strange. But if we stay curious instead of critical, we'll uncover the *why*, and that's where understanding begins.

It's good to be humble enough to learn. To be bold enough to explore. And to be wise enough to know that culture isn't about comparison. It's about connections.

1 JAN 1991—Appreciate the Small Things

Hi Guys,

Happy New Year. I'm feeling a little bit sorry for myself today, as I realize that while the rest of America is sitting around remembering the party they've been to last night and watching football games with their boys all day today, I'm out here in the middle of the desert planning operations, attending meetings, and choking on the ever-present dust that surrounds us. It makes me want to think of all the things I could be doing and how I know I'll never take those for granted anymore.

Like what, you ask? Well, the warm feeling of water on your back when you take a shower to wake yourself up each morning. I didn't have that this morning; instead, I shaved, washed my face, and brushed my teeth with a canteen cup full of water. Like going to the bathroom on a nice, warm, porcelain toilet. Last night I had to run about 100 yards to a series of "piss tubes" that go into the ground so that my urine (and those of the other Soldiers) wouldn't contribute to sanitation problems. Like sleeping next to your mom, getting warm and cozy with the woman I love—last night my feet were cold all night as the temperature dropped below freezing and I only had my Army sleeping bag. Like eating a meal, relaxing with friends around a nice, well-lit table sitting in comfortable chairs. Tonight, I ate my New Year's dinner standing with my plate on the front fender of a 2½-ton truck. Like just relaxing with my boys, watching TV with one or both of you on my lap. Being comfortable in the knowledge that all is right with the world because my two little guys, a girl named Sue, and a Misty-dog all are safe under a firm roof with me. I didn't have any of that today.

I got to call you last night after driving in my HMMWV with Uncle Tupper (Major Tupper Hillard) to King Khalid Military City, and the sounds of your voices really made me feel good. It was great to hear that you guys are taking care of Mom, and that you're doing fine, but still miss me.

I can't wait till next year, when I can again appreciate the little things.

Love ya,

Dad

Reflection

I didn't know it then, but that would be the first of many New Year's Days our family would spend apart—first because of my deployments and later because of our sons'. Between all of us—Todd, Scott, Lauren, and me—we missed more than a few January 1sts. Over the course of two decades of war that happened beyond Desert Storm, our family missed recitals, birthdays, soccer games, Halloweens, and Fourth of July fireworks. But we, like so many military families, also missed countless tiny hands being held while crossing a street as a family, thousands of lost teeth proudly shown at bedtime, and millions of silly family stories.

When a family is close, missing those things doesn't just feel like absence—it feels like injury. You carry it, and it leaves a scar. The only thing that helps it heal is the knowledge that what you're doing, what you're serving, matters. That sacrifice, even if invisible to most, is part of something greater for our fellow citizens and for our future. Nothing can make you prouder than serving the people of your country, but sometimes it hurts. Pride in your service doesn't make the missed family connections any easier.

That journal entry was written to provide a description of just one part of what we were experiencing in Saudi Arabia while waiting for action, but it's really about something universal: how the smallest comforts in life are often the ones that mean the most—and how quickly we notice them when they're gone. A daily hot shower. A soft bed with clean sheets. The closeness of someone you love. A laugh from a child. A normal, boring day. These aren't luxuries—they're the ground beneath our feet. And we need to be more aware of how good our regular lives are.

But New Year's Day tends to universally bring out the reflective side in all of us. The nature of the day always leads to someone asking, "What's your resolution for the new year?" There's something about the clean slate of a new calendar that invites big promises: *I'm going to get in shape this year. I'll drink more water. I'll write in a journal every night. Maybe drink a little less alcohol. Be a little more patient. Show up better.*

I've made all these resolutions, a few times with success, most of the time not. I've started the year with a crisp plan for self-improvement and found myself three weeks in trying to remember where I put the notebook. But I've come to believe that effort matters—even when the resolutions don't stick. Because what we're really doing with each of those promises is checking in with ourselves. We're taking stock. We're asking: *Am I who I want to be?*

But here's the thing: That shouldn't just happen once a year. Self-reflection shouldn't be seasonal—it's gotta be daily. It's something leaders, especially, must do constantly. After every hard decision. After every mistake. After every victory. During the times when that leader just wants to reflect and take stock.

And there's one more important aspect of all this. Growth shouldn't come from comparison with others. That's a trap—especially now, when it's so easy to measure ourselves against someone else's highlight reel. The real measure of growth is this: *Am I a little better than I was yesterday?* Our army swimming coach, Jack Ryan, used to caution me whenever I told him I had swum a personal best: "Don't tell me your time, Hertling, tell me who you beat." I never completely bought into that. I think who you beat, as well as your shaved time, are both indicators of growth as a swimmer.

Self-assessment, the honest kind, is the root of all improvement. As a soldier, a father, a spouse, and a human being, the only way I've known how to grow is by looking in the mirror and asking tough questions—then doing something about the answers that bother me. And the best leaders I've known weren't the ones with perfect plans or loud voices. They were the ones who could evaluate themselves clearly and adjust.

The philosopher Epictetus said, "No man is free who is not master of himself." And Marcus Aurelius, who led from the seat of an empire, reminded us that "the soul becomes dyed with the color of its thoughts." I think what he was saying is how you think, reflect, and act—especially when no one is watching—shapes who you really are.

So whether it's New Year's Day or just a quiet Tuesday in April, make the time. Sit with yourself. Take mental inventory. Remember what matters. Appreciate the small things. And above all, don't wait for the calendar to remind you to grow. Life's too short, and far too precious, for that.

2 JAN 1991—A Typical Day

Hi Guys,

Not much happened today. A typical day, if there is such a thing out here. I spent the day in the CP (Command Post) and worked with the S-2 and the S-3 (the intelligence officer and operations officer). I helped plan and coordinate some of the convoy routes from the port to our assembly area and rehearsed what I'd say to the soldiers who are arriving on the convoy from the port. I also met with the Squadron XO and the logistics officer (the S-4) to check water, fuel, and ammunition forecasts. Then I went over to check on our maintenance soldiers who are doing some terrific work in the dust and cold. In between, I ate an MRE, went to a brief by the Brigade Executive Officer, and returned to the TOC to check on radio traffic and update the ops board.

It's starting to get colder here in the desert at night, and I may need to find an extra blanket or a second sleeping bag. I miss home, but I'm staying busy. Can't wait to see you guys soon.

Love,

Dad

Reflection

There are moments in every person's life when they begin to believe that they didn't get done what they wanted to, that they were overwhelmed with minutiae, or that they didn't get a chance to make a dent in their work or make a difference in their environment. People sometimes just feel like their day went by quickly and blended into all other days. That the day was just typical. Writing this journal entry to my sons was one of those moments for me.

At the time, I was a staff officer in a cavalry squadron sitting in the Saudi desert, waiting for the rest of the unit to arrive, trying my best to prepare for the unit's arrival and doing routine tasks to pass the time. We were in that strange liminal space between movement and action. The war hadn't started yet. We weren't in the fight. I was doing what majors do: coordinating routes, checking fuel estimates, reviewing plans, and thinking about future events. Necessary work, but forgettable work—or so I thought.

Decades later, I know better. Looking back at things that happened during my life, I've come to realize there is no such thing as a typical day. That's especially true for someone who has chosen to lead or for anyone determined to live with awareness and purpose.

Over the course of wars, deployments, private sector employment, and teaching, I learned that what separates those who drift from those who grow is how they treat the days that don't *seem* important. It's easy to rise to the occasion when the moment is big, the mission is clear, or the stakes are visible. But most of leadership—most of life—is made up of the small, the unseen, the unrewarded.

But I've found that's where good people find their edge. Often, that's even where character is forged and polished.

During later deployments in Iraq after Desert Storm as a more senior officer (first as an assistant division commander, then leading the division as the commanding general), my days became intensely structured: battlefield circulation; planning sessions with staff; briefs from younger leaders; secure video teleconferences with intelligence agencies; battle updates on hundreds of crises; visits with subordinate commanders and their troops; meetings with my commander in Baghdad or a variety of Iraqi officers, politicians, and local officials; condolence letters to loved ones telling about their soldiers who had sacrificed their all. Some days repeated, but they were never the same. A unique conversation with a junior officer. A battlefield innovation brought to my attention by a squad leader. The quiet resolve on the dust-covered face of a grieving soldier. The laughter of other soldiers finding joy in hardship or in Command Sergeant Major Blackwood delivering a box of Twinkies to a patrol base where no one thought anyone was thinking about them.

And yes, too often, a memorial service.

Those days that we held memorial services were some of the toughest because they were the days that shattered the illusion of anything being "typical." We had lost one of our own in the fight. All the friends and comrades of that soldier would stand in a makeshift formation, usually under a blazing Middle Eastern sun, while the name of the person who had sacrificed their life was read aloud. The soldier's rifle, helmet, dog tags, and boots would be on a stand. The chaplain would say a few words, fellow soldiers would provide such poignant insights, then taps would sound, and the final rifle salute would end the ceremony. If you haven't been to one of these events, I hope you never have to. Because they are heart-wrenching. At the same time, it would be beneficial for all Americans to attend one of these, as it would give them a true idea of what it means to make a selfless sacrifice for something bigger than yourself.

My boss during our tour in Baghdad in 2003–2004 was my friend, Marty Dempsey. He was now a division commander, and he—like all of us—felt the weight of any soldier's death. Prior to each of those memorials, his aide would give him, Assistant Division Commander Mike Scaparotti, Division Command Sergeant Major Mike Bush, and me a card with a photo of the soldier we were honoring, along with his family information and the time, place, and other details of the death on the back of the card.

We would all carry those cards in our breast pockets, over our hearts, until we had so many casualties that we could only carry a few. We stored the rest in our living spaces. After one memorial service, Marty pulled his small command team together and said he found it hard to find the words to comfort the friends of the fallen soldier. But he had come to realize the only thing he could say was

"Make it matter." That phrase became a mantra that gave us direction, gave us purpose.

After that tour in Iraq, I was in a cigar store in Virginia Beach and saw a wooden tobacco box. I asked the clerk if they could inscribe the words "Make it matter" on the top of the box, and if so, I would order four of them. Those would be the resting places where I and the others in our four-person command group would keep the over one hundred cards we had at the end of our 2003–2004 tour. As each of us went on additional tours in combat, unfortunately, more cards with photos were added to our boxes. Today, my box, which sits on my desk, holds 253 reminders to make it matter. I pull a few of those cards out each day and reflect on those young women and men who will stay forever young and the families that must still miss them.

Make it matter. That phrase is more than a tribute—it's a charge. It means their sacrifice isn't just to be remembered; it's to be honored in the way we live every second of our daily lives for them. Not taking anything for granted. Not wasting a second. Every day. Especially on the days that some might consider routine or typical.

I later connected the "Make it matter" mantra with another truth, one that I had forgotten until I was invited to speak to the junior class of cadets at West Point on their Five Hundredth Night celebration in 2024. A unique event that only the US Military Academy cadets would be bold enough to celebrate and that had become a unique rite of passage: Five hundred nights until graduation and a marking of a milestone in their cadet careers that demanded a formal dinner with loved ones and a party after!

Understanding the importance of the counting of days requires an explanation of another West Point tradition that is a requirement demanded of all plebes, or first-year cadets. Every day, at different times before lunch or dinner formations, parades, or any other planned events, freshmen cadets stand in the barrack hallways watching the hallway clocks and "report the minutes" until the next formation. Being the target of the upperclassmen in these situations, they also announce how many days there are until key events: the next football game, when Army will beat Navy in Philadelphia, when Christmas leave begins, the graduation date of the seniors, etc. A silly tradition, to be sure, but one that teaches freshman cadets to prepare, to think, to recite, and to be correct for the upperclassmen who are also counting the days to something that is special to them.

While performing that duty during my plebe year, I messed up. I gave the wrong number of days until a key event that the seniors were especially interested in. And I screwed it up, badly, as I suggested there were more than ten additional days until their graduation than there actually were. After I incurred their ire, the upperclassmen swarmed, as they are still prone to do. A herd of sophomores (yearlings), juniors (cows), and firsties (seniors) were in my face and in my ear, reminding me in their unique way that I wasn't as mathematically proficient as I should be—in much harsher terms.

The harassment was relentless and consisted of the upperclassman repeating—politely, energetically, passionately, and with extreme volume—versions of: "Hey, Hertling, get it right! The number of days to our class graduation is extremely important to we lofty seniors," or other words to that effect.

One forgiving upperclassman who was more prone to a transformational leadership style, a rarity when we were cadets back in the dark ages of the 1970s, whispered in my ear when all the others had left, "You screwed up, Hertling. Don't do it again. But remember this: Real leaders don't count days. Real leaders make every day count."

I remembered that line and repeated it often throughout the remainder of my less-than-stellar cadet career and during my army career. I also carried it into command at every level. And I brought it back to West Point, years later, when I addressed the Class of 2025 in the large mess hall during their formal Five Hundredth Night banquet. The purpose of their celebration, I said, was to mark five hundred days until graduation. But I reminded them that while counting days helps them mark the time left until an important event, like their own graduation, passing those days with passion and energy is a much better way to live your life.

I shared with them a story about a young 2nd lieutenant I met in Iraq in 2008. At the time, he had just come out of a fierce firefight on the banks of the Tigris, after an ambush from some al-Qaeda terrorists. When I arrived at the site the following day to see the details of what had happened, he was still there with his brigade commander. He looked worn, exhausted, fatigued—dust-covered, unshaven, and with eyes alive with adrenaline. I asked him to walk me through what had happened.

What followed was a lesson in what it means to prepare like a professional, to make every minute count. He talked about the intelligence his battalion had passed to him about this cache site for the terrorists and how his platoon had conducted multiple rehearsals of how they would approach it. He then described the courageous actions of several of his soldiers, told me how they had approached the site and prepared for the assault. He proudly described how each member of his platoon had known what to do when the shooting started.

And when I asked him what had made the operation a success, he paused, looked down at the ground for a few seconds, then raised his head and looked me straight in the eye. "Sir, we made every day, every hour, every minute count in preparing for this mission. And truthfully, I've been preparing for this moment for years, even when I was back in ROTC preparing for a day like this that I knew I would eventually have. We all got through it alive. And I'm proud of them, but I'm also proud of myself for passing this test."

That's it. That's the whole point.

Many people drift through days, waiting for something meaningful to happen, not really thinking about how they can shape their lives for the better. But leaders—the ones who *make it matter*—are the ones who show up on the most ordinary days, the most routine days, with focus, humility, discipline, and purpose.

And there's something else I learned over time: Our "ordinary" day may be someone else's memory. We never know when our presence, our words, or our actions will shape the course of someone else's life. As I rose in rank, especially when I put on the rank of a general, I noticed that people watched me more closely. As a general, I soon came to realize that I was on a glass pedestal in a glass house, and there are some looking to emulate you but also some who are always ready to throw a rock if you screw up. Sometimes, as a leader, just being there is enough—the fact that the general visits his soldiers at an operating base, or goes with them on a patrol, or climbs up onto their tank to check on their morale when that tank crew is in recovering from a tough fight is enough. Because years later, on many occasions, soldiers would remind me of a moment that I barely remembered—but they did. A moment I couldn't recall being with them had stuck with them. Because to them, that day hadn't been typical at all.

So here's what I suggest all of us carry forward:

Don't waste time waiting for "important" days. They're all important. Don't think your presence only counts in the big moments. It counts in the quiet ones too. Don't drift. Don't delay. Don't wait. Don't count the days.

Instead, make every day count.

And when you make every day count, make them matter as well. Because, as I've learned since writing this journal entry decades ago and in talking to a bunch of cadets from the class of 2025 at West Point . . . there are no typical days, and you should relish in each of them instead of counting them down.

6 JAN 1991—Faith

Church today. Since we're one of the first units to arrive in this assembly area near the town of Al Qasumah near the Saudi Arabian topline road, we seem to be getting more than our fair share of attention. Sometimes that's not so good, because we get visitors from higher headquarters. Sometimes, however, it's good. We had four chaplains visiting the Squadron today to perform Sunday services. I went to church twice—once Catholic and once Protestant (with my all-time favorite Army chaplain, LTC Lehrer). After seventeen days in the desert, it was a good time to stop and reflect, think some more about you guys, and recharge our spiritual batteries. I think it pumped the chaplains up also, as I let them take a ride across the desert in my Bradley.

People look at religion in many ways. It's important to me, because Christ's life gives me an example of how to live my life. Always trying to give of yourself, loving others, keeping yourself separated from sin. I know that you guys may sometimes be confused about "religion" because Mom is a Methodist and I'm a Catholic, and we take you to so many different religious services. We do that because we respect each other's religious upbringing and because we want you to gain something from what is said and done during that religious service.

It's important to us that you gain something now, because we realize how important that base will be to you during the difficult times in your lives. When you're having it tough in school. When something doesn't go right with a friend. When the girl you love doesn't love you. When your dad goes off to war. Prayer, and faith, will help you through.

My prayers, for example, are my time to converse with God. In past months and years, I would thank Him for all the blessings He has allowed me to receive. In recent weeks, I'm only praying that I'll return to you guys soon so we can return to the happy life we've had. I ask Him to give me strength each day so I can face more time away from the woman I love and the two boys I adore. He's listening, I know. He's just making me sweat it out.

Prayer is a big part of faith; for faith is the belief that there is a reason for all the good things we try and do, and prayer is the ability to ask God for the right direction to perform the right act. Faith tells you that there's a reason for living, that some of your hardships, while terribly significant to you at the time, mean very little in comparison to what I believe is God's desire for a world that lives in peace and true brotherhood. Baseball games that are lost, girlfriends that don't like you anymore, even wars in the Middle East don't carry a candle to God's plan. Remember when things seem tough. I used to call it the Hertling ice-ball theory: When the earth is one big ice-ball one million years from now it won't really matter that Mark Hertling spent an insufferable time away from his beloved family in the Arabian desert. What will matter is that someday, because we believe, we'll spend eternity with God.

Love ya,

Dad

Reflection

Faith is one of the few things I've held close throughout every chapter of life, though the way I understand it has changed.

Back in 1991, I clung to it with intensity. In the desert, alone with the unknown, prayer became the place I could take my fear, my longing, and my need for strength. I believed—fully, simply, and sincerely—that I would get through because God was with me. That Christ's life offered a model: of service, of sacrifice, of compassion. That belief sustained me. It still does.

But faith isn't fixed. I believe that if it's real, it grows as you do. And over time, my faith has become less about answers and more about the courage to ask better questions.

I was raised Catholic—fully, deeply, formatively so. I went to Catholic grade school and the Catholic (all boys and military) Christian

Brothers College High School in St. Louis. It was at those places where I learned from nuns, priests, Christian Brothers (the same who make the wine in California), and lay teachers who poured into me the rhythms of liturgy, the catechism, the Gospels, and my first spark of character and ethics. My moral compass was shaped not only by my family but by the crucifix that hung in every classroom I sat in, every nun who hit my knuckles with a ruler, every Christian Brother who taught me that, in the Lasallian tradition, we had a moral responsibility to give to others and were all "brothers for life."

Even when I arrived at West Point, Catholic tradition followed me. In those days—before the US Supreme Court ruling in *Anderson v. Laird* (1972) ended mandatory chapel attendance—I participated in what we then called "chapel formations." Sunday morning, cadets would form up in company areas and march to services: Catholics (affectionately known in cadet slang as the "fisheaters"), Protestants (the "bible thumpers"), and the Jewish cadets (the "chosen ones"). Attendance was required. For many, it was an obligation and a time of spiritual growth. For me, it was a lifeline. We were the last West Point class that had that requirement.

When the Supreme Court ruling changed that policy—and cadet chapel formations became a choice rather than a requirement—I found myself asking, *Why do I go? What is it I truly believe?* That Supreme Court ruling marked the beginning of a personal shift. Faith was no longer a box to check or a rule to follow—it had to be something I chose. And I chose it. But with that choice came responsibility. To ask deeper questions. To listen. To learn. To reflect on my faith and my hope. And to walk into uncertainty with conviction, not arrogance.

I'm still a Christian. Still someone who believes in Christ's teachings, still someone who prays every day. But in the years since that journal entry to our boys, I've walked beside Muslims in Najaf and Karbala who taught me the beauty of submission and discipline. I've sat with Jewish friends at Shabbat tables and learned how memory, tradition, and justice bind a people across millennia. I've worked with Buddhist and Sikh service members who showed me peace in stillness, strength in silence. I've read scriptures not my own and found echoes of truth and similarity in each of them.

Far from threatening my belief, these encounters expanded it.

What I've come to see is that faith, like leadership, is never about shutting others out. It's about living in alignment with values and honoring the sacred in others—even when their path is different from yours. Respecting other people's beliefs does not dilute your own. It clarifies them. And in the hardest moments of life, I've found we all ask the same questions: What gives me hope? What gives me strength? Who do I lean on? Why do I refuse to hate?

That's why I believe that phrase "There are no atheists in foxholes" is both incomplete and misunderstood. It doesn't mean that fear forces everyone to believe in a divine being. But it does mean that, under fire, when the bottom drops out and everything is uncertain, people reach for something bigger than themselves. Sometimes it's God. Sometimes it's brotherhood. Sometimes it's a parent's love or a child's future. Sometimes it's just hope. But always—it's *faith*. In something.

And that something pulls you through.

Even now, I believe in the afterlife, but I admit it's more complex than I once imagined. I used to picture it clearly: heaven, reunion, eternal peace, the great "master of men" floating in a cloud like in the Cadet Prayer. Now, I think eternity may be bigger than we can know—maybe it's presence, maybe it's legacy, maybe it's memory that lives on in those we loved and led. I don't have answers. But I'm no less faithful. Maybe more so. Because my faith now includes mystery—and mystery requires humility. Maybe we don't know all we need to know, and maybe we don't need to.

The Hertling Ice Ball Theory still holds. One day, this whole spinning planet may fade into darkness. The wars, the awards, the heartbreaks—all gone. But what won't fade is how we treated one another. How we loved. How we carried faith—not just in God, but in goodness, in justice, in one another.

If you're questioning what I'm saying while reading this, know this: I don't believe we all need to have it all figured out. We just need to keep asking, seeking, believing, and living like it matters. That's what I've come to believe that faith really is.

Faith is the candle we light in the dark—even if we're not sure what's waiting in the shadows. Faith is the decision to hope, even when we've seen what despair looks like. Faith is the moment we kneel not because we're weak, but because we're strong.

And if there's one thing I still pray for, it's that everyone can carry faith in others—no matter what desert we find ourselves in.

7 JAN 1991—Mom

Sue Schmutz. Nearly 17 years ago I had a blind date with a girl with a funny name. Little did I know when my cadet roommate Mike Burnette first mentioned that name to me would I be eventually meeting the woman I'd spend the rest of my life with. She's my best friend, my love, my comforter, the mother of my children, and the most beautiful woman—inside and out—that I've ever met.

You guys need to know this. Not only because it's important for kids to know that their mom and dad have a great relationship, but you need to know why they have that great relationship. When you start meeting and dating girls, and going through all the things associated with going out and appreciating young women, it's important to know what to look for and what to ignore. Am I telling you to never look at a great-looking girl who has a terrific figure that happens to walk by because it probably won't be the one you spend the rest of your life with? Heck no! Even though your mom is gorgeous, I still look at other girls (much to Mom's irritation) and admire their beauty and God-given qualities. I even, during my high school days, dated girls because they were great looking . . . thought some of them had the brains or personality of a soft piece of elbow macaroni. I could be shallow back then.

What I'm telling you is that when you are thinking that you're serious about a girl, consider the implications of living your life with someone who you like but who has the chance to be your best friend and eventually your soul mate. You've got to know each other's strengths and weaknesses; you've got to communicate openly, you've got to understand each other's quirks, and you must contribute—hear me closely on this one—to each other's growth and developments. This last point may cause a lot of fights and misunderstandings, but if you really want a relationship to work, it is the most important one.

Mom and I loved each other from early on in our relationship (though I was more overt in my feelings). That love has grown because neither one of us is afraid to voice our opinions and to communicate with each other. We know we'll get an honest response—sometimes even an argumentatively honest response—but that happens because we want to let the other one know how we really feel. We don't pull verbal punches. Over the years, that openness and respect have led to changes. Example: I've become better organized; mom has been able to better deal with my spur of the moment ideas.

Mom is the most giving, selfless, loving individual I have ever met. I didn't realize that when I first met her, but as each successive year passes, I realize it more. This is the trait I admire most in your mom, it is a truly amazing characteristic, and I wish I could be less selfish and more like her. In today's world, "giving" and selflessness are traits that aren't found in many people. I'm very selfish in many things—sharing my time with people I don't want to be with, doing things I don't want to do, and not being free to float with the wind bothers me. But Mom will go out of her way to make other people comfortable, feel good, while doing things for them. Amazing.

Mom also has a lot of pride in who she is and what she does. She's in great shape and always will be (I know this about her), she maintains her figure and her looks, and I've never seen her look unkempt (except when she gets up in the morning . . . she always has a bad case of bedhead, which you have both seen!). Even when she's just around us, goofing off, she presents a great appearance. This same pride is exhibited in everything she does.

She makes me feel good. She tells me to straighten up when I'm doing something wrong, she cheers me up when I'm sad, and when I start to get a little haughty because I've achieved minor success . . . she keeps me humble but still relishes my achievements.

Most of all, she has done a phenomenal job as a mother to my other two best friends. For that, I'll never be able to repay her. I guess I'll just try to love her more in return.

Love ya,

Dad

Reflection

When I wrote that journal entry from a desert outpost in 1991, we had just celebrated our fifteenth wedding anniversary a few weeks before I deployed. I was trying to capture the essence of my love for Sue in a few pages of a green notebook so the boys would understand how much I cared for her, how much they should care for their spouses when they married someday.

At the time, we were separated by thousands of miles of sand, war, and uncertainty, but she remained my anchor. I wrote that not only for my boys but as a quiet declaration of how much her presence shaped my life, even when she wasn't physically beside me.

Now, as I write this chapter decades later, we're preparing to celebrate our fiftieth anniversary. Half a century. It's hard to believe—and even harder to express—just how much deeper my admiration for her has grown over the years. The truth is, we still really, really like each other. She's always been my best friend, and she still is. And that is an extraordinary gift she gave me.

Sue has put up with more than most from me—certainly more than she deserved. I could and can be a real jerk at times. And as a soldier's wife, she also endured countless moves (twenty-six as of our current situation), deployments, lonely nights, missed holidays, and the strain that came from holding everything together while I was off chasing the mission. There's a framed saying in our house from army wife Martha Summerhayes, who wrote in 1866, "I had cast my lot with a soldier, and where he was, was home to me." Sue normally finds a special place for that in each of our quarters.

But it wasn't just the army life that she endured; it was also the burden of my own foibles—especially my selfishness, my tunnel vision, my impatience, my defensiveness. Through it all—the good times and the hard ones—she has been loyal, loving, forgiving (especially forgiving!), and ready to bring her best self forward to make me better. She made me a better man. A better father. A better leader. I hope, deeply, that I've given her some of those same gifts in return.

The truth is, Sue has always been the center of gravity in our family—the magnetic pull that kept all of us grounded when the mission, the distance, and the burden of command, school, work, and lives threatened scattered us. In every assignment, in every command, in every house, she made a home. She didn't just follow—she led. She built community, cared for families, held things together while I tried to hold the battlefield and the boys held on to their development. If I was in uniform leading soldiers and they were playing sports or excelling in school, she was in sneakers or sandals leading everything else.

In the MBA classes I teach, I always give an assignment asking the students: "Who lit your fire?" In a room full of students, people usually mention mentors, bosses, coaches, aunts, or a parent. But when I reflect on that question, it's Sue. She lights my fire. She's been the quiet force behind every one of my successes, the one who challenged me when I coasted, who lifted me when I doubted myself, who forgave me when I hurt her, and who believed in me more deeply than I ever believed in myself.

She doesn't just love me. She leads me. By example. With compassion. With conviction. With grace. Her strength is quiet but unshakable, her generosity boundless, her clarity piercing. She knows when to push and when to protect. She holds our family together not by command but by presence, by instinct, by love that's both unconditional and unrelenting.

On the toughest days—whether under fire or in the lonely moments between deployments—I thought of her. Her laugh. Her intelligence. Her way of smoothing the rough edges of our lives. When I stood before angry families back in Germany to explain why their loved ones would be deployed three months longer (that story will come later), I drew courage from the thought of how Sue would handle it—calm, direct, but with compassion. When I taught leadership to future generals and MBA students, I often used stories from the battlefield. But the truth is, the greatest leadership I've witnessed, and many of the stories I tell, have come from watching Sue.

I once told her that she's the best leader I know. She brushed it off with a laugh. But I meant it. She leads through love, through consistency, through sacrifice. She leads by lighting a fire in others—our sons, their families, and, yes, in me. That's the kind of influence that doesn't fade. It glows.

The best decision I ever made was showing up for that blind date with a girl with a funny name. The second best was never letting her go.

She's still the one. And my wish for everyone is that they find someone they like, and love, just like I do her.

8 JAN 1991—Fear

I know you guys saw mom and I having some tough discussions before we shooed you out of the room back before I left. We were talking about "what happens if . . ." The "if" had to do with me possibly not coming home from the war or coming home injured. I know you won't read this until you're much older, and when you do you will understand the anxiety—rather, the fear—that we were both trying our best to overcome, so here's what I'm thinking I want to pass to you on this late and cold night in the desert of Saudi Arabia.

Back before I left Germany, I'll admit, I was scared. And fear is the most interesting emotion. As much as people tell you when fear plays on you to 1) overcome it, 2) don't worry about it, or 3) block it out, all those things are hard to do.

You see, fear is a physiological reaction to what your mind is thinking about. When you're worried about what may happen, or you perceive something bad or scary is going to happen to you, your body releases a certain amount of hormones to help get you ready for what you're about to face, the so-called "fight or flight response," developed by our ancestors when they were fighting saber-toothed tigers. If you have enough time to react to the influences of those hormones, and you have a solution, you'll be in good shape. If not, you might find yourself forcing yourself to do something you may not want to do. This can range from jumping off a high dive when you're not quite ready, skiing for the first time, or giving a speech in front of your class. And those fears increase significantly when you're asked to go to war, leave your loved ones, and perhaps even face death. That's what mom and I were talking about when you caught us a couple of times in our small kitchen; we were having quiet discussions about what might happen to me, and how all of you would then live your life if I was gone. While I'd like to say that all my training and preparation helped me face going to war, I was very frightened at the prospect of leaving my family and possibly facing death.

You will never understand how I felt on the days leading up to my departure from Lehrberg. You probably couldn't understand why I was repeatedly touching your hair, kissing and hugging you more than usual, and watching both of you do the everyday things that seem so normal. I also wanted to kiss and hug your mom at every opportunity because I didn't know the next time I would be able to do that, if ever. The last night at the Gasthaus Kern, I was very quiet, letting you two boys joke and laugh and talk non-stop, because I just wanted to revel in your presence; I wanted to just sit there and listen and look at you as you did the type of things you normally do.

I knew I couldn't face you the following morning as I left so early for the Katterbach airfield, so I told all of you to stay in bed, asleep! None of you listened to me. When I investigated your room, Todd was curled up pretending to be asleep, but he wasn't. Scott was lying flat with just his and his stuffed Theo's eyes uncovered staring at the door. Then, as I was leaving, I looked up at our bedroom window and saw Mom looking out as I was driving away. It was the saddest, and scariest moment of my life. I know now that when I return it will be the happiest, and we will never be apart again.

This fear of possibly dying was a different fear I experienced, and it also contributed to my emotional swings over the last few weeks at home after we were told we were going to Iraq. Quite frankly, I wasn't ready to die. I want to ride bikes with your mom when I get old, and I want to see you boys graduate from college and raise your own families. I know that is going to happen. But I also know that since I believe in God—I have faith—that my life after death will be great and we'll all be rejoined in a better place one day. But I'm just not ready, I want more life with all of you. So, I'm going to do all I can to prevent that from happening while I'm out here.

I pray that you boys never know this kind of fear. For years, men have been going to war so hopefully their children didn't have to—that is part of what love is all about. But I honestly believe that what we're being asked to do is so important, so overwhelming, that if successful, peace will be with our country for some time in the future. I don't want you guys to ever experience the fear I felt prior to coming here. It is also a feeling I never want to have again.

But know this: You will face fear that creeps up on you all during your life. For the things that make you tremble a bit, or the things that you think you can't do so you need to bring about some additional courage, my advice is to push yourself. When you're afraid of trying something new, or you're afraid you might embarrass yourself, or you're worried you might get hurt doing something, think mostly about the rewards that will come from doing it, then try it. Know that your fears will always creep up on you as you face something new or exciting, but there's always a sense of accomplishment when you do it and achieve that feeling of pushing your limits. But also know that sometimes you just might be asked to do something that is very unpleasant, something that every part of your body and mind screams out that you just can't do. But sometimes—if it's important—you might just have to overcome your fears and do it anyway. That's what I'm doing now, and mom helped me overcome those fears. Right now, I'm just focused on completing our mission and then returning to you, Mom, our dog Misty, and our cute little house in Lehrberg, Germany. I guess those thoughts have always been with soldiers who have gone off to war. I'll just have to keep them at the forefront of my thinking, too.

Love ya,

Dad

Reflection

Reading this journal entry again, decades later, I remember exactly when I was writing it (it was after midnight), where I was writing it (it was in the squadron tactical operations center [TOC] , and how I was finding it extremely difficult to explain something that all people face at some point in their lives: fear and how we respond to it. Since writing those words, here's what I've concluded four decades later: There is no courage without fear, and not all fear is bad. Some fear propels you forward. Some fear, if left unmanaged, can freeze you in place. I was trying to explain to our sons the difference between the two and how to react to each.

Fear, as I described it then, is physiological. I'd learned that a few years prior to teaching at West Point when I was getting my master's in physiology from Indiana University. When your brain perceives a threat, your body dumps a lot of hormones, but it mostly releases adrenaline and cortisol. This is the same cocktail of hormones athletes release when they're in a high-stakes athletic event—racing a mile, beating a personal weightlifting record, pushing past limits in training. The heart races, the muscles tighten, the gastrointestinal and cardiac systems become tense, and thoughts accelerate. In athletics, there's controlled exertion, and after the event is over, there's intense fatigue. But in fear—true fear—the body doesn't know whether it's supposed to fight, flee, or freeze. And in war, you often don't get to choose.

The night before I wrote that journal entry, I had felt the rawest version of that fear. It wasn't just about danger. It was about potential loss—of connection, of life, of unfulfilled hopes. I desperately wanted to live. I wanted to grow old with Sue, watch our boys grow into men, see their graduations, weddings, grandkids. While I believed in the mission we were sent to execute, a cause doesn't make leaving your family easier.

Over time during that first deployment—and over several more combat deployments later—I learned how fear evolves. The fear of the unknown during my first combat deployment in 1991 gave way, years later, to the fear of not performing and not being able to control situations so I could protect others. As a commander in Iraq on my third deployment during the surge in 2007, I was no longer a young major responsible for a few hundred soldiers. I was a division commander responsible for tens of thousands of things. During Desert Storm, I was concerned about returning to my family. When I joined the 1st Armored Division in Baghdad as a newly promoted general, I felt a bit of imposter syndrome, wanting to do the best I could for my boss and friend, General Dempsey. During the surge, I was worried about failing our soldiers and not helping them return to their families.

As we were preparing to deploy in 2007, we accomplished all our tasks. But one afternoon, before the planes were staged to take our soldiers to Iraq, I wandered around some of our units and staff sections to get a gut check of morale. Entering our legal center, I found a room full of lawyers and their paralegals talking about the deployment and what it might be like. A perfect setup for a division commander to walk into. After telling them our plans and explaining what it would be like for most of these soldiers who had never seen combat, I started to leave when a young soldier approached and asked me if she could speak to me privately. We walked into the hall, and when we were alone, she asked, with remarkable directness, "Sir, are you going to bring all of us back alive?"

Her question hit me like a punch to the gut. Not because it was inappropriate—it wasn't—but because it was the first time anyone had the courage to ask me that, and it reflected her own deep fear. I saw in her eyes the same anxiety I had carried in 1991. And I also knew something she didn't: *I couldn't say what she was hoping to hear.* We were headed into a complex fight. There would be casualties. I didn't know who, or when, or how many—but I knew it was unlikely we would all come home untouched.

So I gave her the most honest answer I could: "We have great leaders. We've trained hard. You're part of a great team. And we will take care of each other. And I'll do my very best to take care of you, personally. That's all that I can promise." It was true—but I also knew it wasn't enough. She was asking for certainty. In war, there is no such thing. She smiled and thanked me, but I'm not sure I assuaged her fear.

That moment stayed with me through the entire deployment. We lost 153 soldiers on that tour, with many more injured. Each one of those losses still weighs on me. Each one reminds me that fear never disappears. It just transforms—into increasing personal courage, responsibility, vigilance, and remembrance.

But here's the other side of fear: When you overcome it, when you face it and push through, you grow in ways you didn't think possible. That's true in combat, yes. But it's just as true on a stage, in a classroom, at the head of a team, in a hospital room, or when facing a hard truth.

In our own lives, we all feel different kinds of fear. Fear of failing. Fear of disappointing someone. Fear of being seen but not being heard. All of that is natural. But we should also know that fear is often a signpost that we're standing at the edge of something important. And on the other side of fear is often the next breakthrough—increased confidence, more courage, another life adventure accomplished.

When we say someone is "seasoned" or "battle-tested," we usually mean they've faced fear—and they kept going. They didn't allow fear to stop them. Instead, they learned from it; they found something stronger than fear that motivates and inspires them. That's what experience does: It doesn't erase fear; it teaches one how to manage it.

We don't become brave by avoiding fear. We become brave by understanding it, walking with it, and learning to move forward anyway.

But here's something just as important. If we find ourselves asking someone a hard question, like that young legal specialist asked me—know that the courage in asking may be the first step in addressing it, and it may prove more powerful than the answer received.

I did come home. So did that young specialist. I saw her at the welcome home ceremony with her family, where she came up to me again and thanked me for bringing her home. I told her then, in front of her husband and her small child, that her courage and dedication were what had brought her home. She had faced her fears, as had I. And we'd both stared down those different kinds of fears with different types of courage.

9 JAN 1991—Disappointment

Today, many believe, was the last opportunity for a peaceful solution to this Gulf Crisis. Secretary of State Baker met Iraqi Foreign Minister Aziz in Geneva to offer a solution from President Bush to Saddam Hussein. We just heard on the radio that after six hours of discussion it appears that war is inevitable, for Iraq will not pull their soldiers out of Kuwait. When we heard this on the small radio we were all listening to, I know I felt a knot in the pit of my stomach, much like the knot I felt on 8 November when we first heard the 1st Armored Division would be one of the units sent to the Persian Gulf.

There is no room in this situation for compromise. It isn't like Viet Nam, where there were conflicting ideas within a country which "asked" the US for help. In this case, it is an instance of a nation raping another state (Kuwait) out of its freedom and well-being. As much as we all hate being here, and we're all disappointed in war not being avoidable, this type of aggression cannot exist in a peaceful world. Oil and economies add to the reasons for the US being here, but it is not the sole reason. I believe there are some in our nation's government who still believe in stopping vengeful acts. I hope they remain strong.

Love,

Dad

Reflection

Disappointment is the shadow of hope. And for soldiers, it often arrives quietly, in moments like this—when diplomacy died on the radio.

I remember writing this journal entry in broad daylight, outside the tactical operations center, after we had all huddled around the static-filled BBC radio broadcast that gave us the news. I remember that moment with absolute clarity. We had not yet fired a shot, but we knew what was coming. A long, desperate attempt to avoid war had failed. Soldiers usually don't expect peace when deployed, but most smart soldiers still hope for it. That hope can be surprisingly stubborn, even when you know the odds are stacked against a peaceful outcome. After thousands of troops have flowed into a region, as tanks roll and aircraft assemble, the last sliver of belief—that reason will prevail—still stays alive.

I had never before been on the precipice when something like this was about to happen. I'd only read about it in history books. But being there in person, looking at each other as the words came through on the radio, we all felt hope's final breath.

In the years since, I've seen diplomatic missions fail and peace overtures produce little, and I've often reflected—as so many before me have—on what makes war so easy to start yet so excruciatingly difficult to end. Political leaders speak of "red lines," and governments proclaim, "resolute responses," all while armies prepare for action. But the minute a conflict begins, the variables multiply, the damage expands, and the path to an end becomes increasingly unclear. Victory might be defined, might even be achievable, but what comes next? If war is the extension of politics by other means, as Clausewitz alluded, how does a nation get back to the diplomatic track, and can that approach truly secure a future?

That disappointing day in 1991 wasn't just the shift from Desert Shield and the beginning of Desert Storm. It was the beginning of a long American military presence in the region, one that would shape and influence the next three decades of US global affairs and our lives. In places where military leaders would not just fight but would also attempt to rebuild broken societies, improve economic systems in war-torn countries, and engage with foreign governmental and military leaders.

I didn't realize when we were listening to the radio that the broadcast signaled the end of the rational approach and the beginning of a major war in the Middle East. That night was also not the last time, as a soldier, I would experience that kind of disappointment. I'll admit that even today, each time a peaceful off-ramp attempt fails—whether in Iraq, Israel, Ukraine, Syria, or elsewhere—those knots that were present that night return. And each time, I carry the same hard-earned understanding: When soldiers go to war, we don't do it with talking points. We do it with our lives. So we should first work very hard to find a peaceful solution before we resort to war.

10 JAN 1991—Near Beer vs. Wiezen

Hi guys,

A special treat today. The Pabst beer company (I think that's who did it!) has donated several thousand cases of NA (non-alcoholic) beer to the troops in the Persian Gulf. We distributed them to all the troops—one can apiece—and it was amazing how much it meant to the soldiers. But as I drank mine, it brought back the memory of when we go to the Gasthaus Kern at the bottom of our hill. You guys always kid me about how much I'll miss my Hefeweizen when we leave Germany, and you're probably right. There's no finer beer than Bavarian Weissebier!

Well, as great as the "near beer" tasted as I used it to wash down my daily MRE, it wasn't quite as good. That's because Scott wasn't there to ask if he could blow off the foam, as he always likes to do in the gasthaus. And Todd wasn't there to ask me if I was going to order a second one, even as Mom was giving me disapproving looks. I couldn't get a second beer today, but I sure laughed thinking about all three of you when real beer was on the table!

I've already written about the good things I miss since I've been here. But now I want to add one more—our little town of Lehrberg. And that's not just because I can easily get Weissebier there! We've had so many memories together in our little village, walking up to the sports platz and camping that one night near the Kappl that is older than our own country! But add to that the memories of the beer truck delivering our weekly rack of beer and Spezi, and the pond where we swim at the bottom of our hill, and just so many other memories that flooded back when I tasted that Pabst non-alcoholic beer. The four of us have had so much fun during our time together in Germany—the Volksmarches, the festivals, the visits to all kinds of great sites, our time in the gasthaus with all our new German friends like Rita and Wolfgang, and just our time together in our little house near the top of the hill.

I wish I was with you right now to make some new memories. It would be even better if I could drink a Wiezen while doing that!

Love ya,

Dad

Reflection

When I wrote that short note in January 1991, it wasn't really about beer at all. It was about *home*—a home we had made together in just under two years in a small Bavarian town—and about the memories we had already banked, just in case I didn't come back from Desert Storm. All those things flashed in my mind as I tasted a gift of American beer from a well-meaning distillery in Milwaukee. It brought back memories, and that's what I wanted our boys to have if something were to happen to me during that war.

One of my mentors had told me years earlier, "The most important thing parents and leaders can do is create memories for the people they love and the people they lead." Lehrberg had given us plenty of those memories, and I wanted them to stick in the boys' minds when they read that day's journal entry.

Lehrberg sat on a very small river—more a meandering creek—near the much larger city of Ansbach, where our division headquarters was located. Katterbach, where our cavalry squadron was based, was just a few more miles away. Our house was partway up Hauptstrasse—literally "Hill Street"—and the little lane leading to our front door was Ringstrasse, a narrow loop encircling three neat rows of small German townhouses. In those homes lived Germans, fellow Americans, and even a few East Germans who had recently moved west after the Berlin Wall fell.

The mix of neighbors made the place lively, and the neighborhood was perfect for kids: a swimming pond at the bottom of the hill; open fields for throwing baseballs with the boys, which the Germans always found strange ("A sport where you don't use your feet? *Ach du Liebe*, what is that madness?"); and a Lego city built in our attic by two boys who depended on each other and their mom when their dad was away at war.

The history around us was impossible to ignore. At the very top of our hill, a short walk from our house, stood the Kappl—or rather, the tower ruin that was all that remained of a chapel built in 1430 by Friedrich or Eustachius von Lerpauer. The chapel had been erected on a western promontory as a symbol of the lords of Birkenfeld's influence, and hiking up there at dusk provided a magnificent view of the sunset and the surrounding forests. Six centuries later, the stone tower still stood watch over the town, older than the country we served. The boys loved climbing the path to the Kappl, and one night, we even took a small tent and our sleeping bags up there, just us guys.

Life in Lehrberg was rich in small pleasures. Every week, the beer truck would rumble into town, delivering our rack of beer and *Spezi*—the German mix of cola and orange soda that the boys loved. On weekends, we'd walk down to Gasthaus Kern, our favorite restaurant, where the bread-bowl cheese soup and Jägerschnitzel were as comforting as the warm welcome we always received. The dollar was strong against the Deutsche Mark back then, so even a young army family could afford a full evening out. Sometimes our friends Rita and Wolfgang Goehring, who ran the local *friseur* (beauty shop), joined us. They taught all of us some German—Todd would later visit them as a college student when he majored in German and attended the Goethe-Institut in Murnau—we laughed over shared stories, and both boys got their fill of *Apfelschorle* and the attention of every adult in the room.

When I was halfway across the world in the Saudi desert, opening a can of Pabst non-alcoholic beer, it wasn't the taste I noticed so much as the trigger. One sip brought back the sound of laughter in a warm gasthaus on a cold Bavarian night, the sight of the Kappl outlined against the sky, and the feel of my boys' small hands in mine as we walked up Hauptstrasse after dinner. That's the power of memory—and part of why I wrote so often about home in my journal entries. If the worst happened, I wanted my family to have those moments on paper as a reminder of the life we had built together.

Years later, Germany would again be our home base during two more deployments. By then, Todd had graduated from Wake Forest, received his ROTC commission, and was serving in the early days of Operation Iraqi Freedom. Scott was at West Point then, but he came home on a break while I was deployed and brought classmates with him to visit. His friends quickly took to calling Sue "Mutti"—the German word for "mom"—and she wore the title with pride.

In 2004, when Scott and a fellow cadet from West Point, Lauren Harrington, visited us in Grafenwöhr, we made sure they experienced Bavaria the way we had years earlier—a walk through the old town, a meal in a local gasthaus, and a visit to several landmarks in the area. There was something very, very special about Lauren, and we made quite a few memories during her visit. We were so happy when she joined the family after both she and Scott graduated, and we've made a bunch of memories with them and their two boys since. Todd also visited after his first combat tour, and we marveled at the ease with which he used his language skills to chat up the father of one of our German friends, though the Bayern (Bavarian) dialect was a challenge!

When children grow with great memories of a place and a power that has influenced their lives—memories they can return to even when their family is scattered and the world feels uncertain—it's likely because they kept finding ways to make the kinds of memories that would outlast circumstances. For us, those moments were sometimes as simple as Sue arranging a "girls' night" with Lauren while Scott was deployed—a movie, snacks, and conversation late into the evening.

Lauren has said it meant the world to her at a lonely time. Sue still calls it one of her fondest memories.

That's the thing about memories: They're not just souvenirs from easier days. Often, they're built from the difficulties overcome during hard ones—in the pauses between separations, in the rituals that remind us of who we are and who we belong to.

Lehrberg gave us hundreds of those moments. But it was a can of "near beer" in the desert that helped me remember how much they mattered.

11 JAN 1991—Knowledge

I want to pass a bit of philosophy of mine on to you guys about being a "Renaissance Man." As haughty as it sounds, I like to think of myself as an R.M., because all my life I've attempted to learn as much as I can about a variety of different subjects—art, science, literature, film, history, etc. While I've really enjoyed a couple of these areas—especially physiology and history—I've found having a general knowledge of all the areas has helped me a lot: at parties, playing trivial pursuit, and knowing when someone is trying to give you a snow job.

You see, if you have a well-rounded knowledge of a lot of different areas, you tend to have more of an inquiring mind; you tend to question the "whys" and "wherefores" of various actions, and people tend to get uncomfortable and give you more information to clarify their points. This does two things: 1) It opens more information so you can get a clearer picture, and 2) it gives you a better idea of what you need to know. I've always been leery of people who say, "Don't tell me how to build the watch, tell me what time it is." These people tell me that they are not really interested in the whys of what you must say and are only interested in getting only the information which suits their limited needs. In other words, they're selfish. That's the ugliest trait of all.

So, the bottom line is this: Open yourself to knowledge. Dig for information. Take the harder path of learning than the one that will just get you the good grades. And as you go through school, take a subject that is new and different to you occasionally, just to learn something you didn't know.

I'm not sure why the good Lord put us on this earth. But I personally believe he wants us to grow spiritually, emotionally, and mentally. Take every effort to do that. Investigate the other guy's viewpoint. Make it your duty to learn something new every day.

You'll thank me for this advice, I know it!

Love,

Dad

Reflection

One of the things I wanted to leave with my sons in this journal—especially if, for whatever reason, I didn't come back to them—was a desire to learn and grow every day. Certainly, that meant doing well in school, but I wanted them to know it requires much more than that. Good people and great leaders require an informed approach to the world, an intellect that is savvy in a variety of subjects but still curious to learn more. This isn't the kind of intellect measured with and reflected by degrees or test scores. In my view, true intellect comes from three sources: how you see the world, how you incorporate emotional and cultural intelligence into your decisions, and how you develop deep expertise in your chosen field . . . and even beyond. It's about being endlessly curious, willing to learn from anyone, and humble enough to admit you don't know everything.

Even though I had used this as a mantra my whole life, I must have forgotten it when I was thinking about getting a doctorate at the ripe old age of sixty-three after I retired from the army. During a reception for newly admitted doctoral students, I asked my mentor, Rhonda Bartlett—a second-year doctoral student—for any advice she might give me as I started the course, and then I asked what she thought a man my age, with a lifetime of career military and world experience, might gain from this academic pursuit. Her answer struck me as being brilliant, and it has stayed with me: "At this level, Mark, you'll learn just how much you don't know. No matter your age, what you've done before, what you bring to the classroom, you'll be surprised and amazed every day, and you'll be able to put that new knowledge into pragmatic use because of your experience. Just keep your mind open, and you'll be surprised, daily." She was repeating the lessons I'd once given to our sons, so long ago.

And she was right. The deeper I went into my studies and later into my research during that doctoral program, the more I remembered what I always said I believed: that knowledge isn't a possession—it's a continuous pursuit.

And humility is the key that keeps that pursuit alive. I saw that in combat, when I was often surprised by what the enemy did, what the intelligence said, and even by the solutions our young soldiers contributed. And then there were the tactical details, local dynamics, and cultural nuances that if I had just kept my eyes and ears open and my brain engaged, I would have understood better. I saw it most clearly as commander of US Army Europe when engaging with military leaders from our forty-nine allied and partner countries. Each of them operated under different political systems, unique constitutions, and various oaths to deal with national faultlines and defend their nations. I learned to read background notes and ask questions before making assumptions—of embassy teams and my counterparts and their governments—to listen longer than I spoke, and to learn at least a few words of their language. A hello in Polish, a thank you in Romanian, or even a clumsy attempt at an Estonian toast broke barriers fast.

Curiosity, paired with humility, builds trust with others. And trust is the currency of leadership—whether we're commanding in combat or negotiating a contract or introducing a visiting professor to a class. The Renaissance ideal still holds for me: Study art, science, literature, history, and people, not to become an expert in all of them but to see connections we might otherwise miss, to understand people more deeply, and to live more fully.

Like so many other people, one of my favorite streaming shows is *Ted Lasso*. In one moving episode about his childhood and his ability to play darts, Lasso explains that people often judge too quickly because they think they know enough about someone or something.

He mentions a quote he once saw on a wall: *"Be curious, not judgmental."* The rest of the episode doesn't matter, because that's the best advice for leaders. Curiosity keeps you learning. Curiosity keeps you humble. And curiosity keeps you open to the possibility that the next great lesson may come from the most unexpected source.

Sue and I are lucky, as it seems our sons have so far lived this advice. I hope our grandchildren—and anyone who reads this—will also see the advice found in this journal, and this subsequent reflection, to be valuable.

12 JAN 1991—MREs

Meal, Ready to Eat. They've received very bad publicity during this conflict. Lots of reporters have told their readers how terrible the food is, but let ME tell you, it's not all that bad. In fact, compared to the K-rations of WWII (which I tried, once, at West Point) or the C-rations that came of age in Viet Nam (which I ate for the first ten years of my Army career, and which stayed in the force in the early days of the my service in the Cold War), MRE's are . . . not so bad. Maybe eating them 2–3 times a day has caused me to have this viewpoint but let me describe to you what your dad eats every day.

MREs come with a 4–6 oz main entrée in a foil-wrapped package. These entrées range from Chicken à la King (most Soldiers don't like this one) to meatballs and rice, beans and franks, chicken with rice, corned beef. My favorite is Omelet with Au Gratin Potatoes.

The brown bag also has a dehydrated fruit package (just add water, and you have something that tastes a bit like strawberries, peaches, or mixed fruit). Lots of guys experiment with the ingredients, mixing their dried coffee creamer packet with the fruit and coming up with things like Peaches & Cream, or strawberry cream to spread over a pound cake. You get the drift.

The bags also usually include 2 square crackers, about 3½ inches square, with an accessory package of either cheese spread, jelly, or peanut butter. I love jelly, hate peanut butter, don't mind the cheese.

There is usually some type of dessert, like a cookie bar, a pound cake, or a type of candy, and it's a nice treat after the meal.

Finally, there's an accessory packet that has a very short piece of toilet paper (which I have never used as it's too small), some chewing gum (chiclets, which I always chew after the meal), small hand wipes, instant coffee, sugar, salt, and a very small bottle of Tabasco sauce.

It's not a bad meal when it's heated, and soldiers can do that in one of several ways. When we're working hard, we just put the main course pouch, unopened, in one of our cargo pockets and body heat will transfer to the meal. We also sometimes put it in a canteen cup of boiling water for about 5 minutes and that works well. If I'm traveling somewhere, I normally put it on the heater vent against the windshield of my HMMWV—by the time I get to the destination, it's heated to the boil, and I eat it.

I've never really said grace before I ate one of these meals, because I guess I never really thought about giving thanks for this particular type of daily bread. But I think I'll start saying it silently to myself. We ask you guys to pray before you eat, so I guess I should be thanking God for these gifts, as well.

Thank you for making me think about that.

Love ya

Dad

Reflection

I was thinking of eliminating this journal entry when I began writing this book and expanding things with reflections. But the more I thought about it, the more I wanted to keep it, as the description of soldiers' food was an interesting issue—not just for our grandkids to understand but to provide information for any reader so that they might better grasp what soldiers do in a field environment. So let's go with some history and some fun facts.

Providing food to soldiers has always been a combination of science, logistics, military art, and a desire for morale. For instance, the statement "An army marches on its stomach" is commonly attributed to Napoleon, as he understood the strategic role of provisions in a fight. One reason Robert E. Lee suggested the Gettysburg campaign to Confederate President Jefferson Davis was that it would allow the Confederate army to gain a logistical advantage. The Rebels could live off the land in states that hadn't lost their crops and cattle in previous fighting: Pennsylvania, Maryland, and northern Virginia. Those states could sustain an invasion by the Confederates, who had lived through several years of war ravaging their crops!

All commanders know this: What you feed your soldiers—consistently, even in the worst possible conditions—will affect performance and morale as much as any other factor. I've eaten nearly every kind of US field ration since the mid-1970s, and I've shared a few from other armies as well. Some were excellent. Some were tolerable. And some made you wonder how the enemy ever had the nutrition or the will to fight.

My experiences with army chow started when I entered West Point in the early 1970s. The army had long since retired the World War II–era K-ration, as they were phased out in favor of the C-ration. C-rations, which I ate regularly as a cadet and in my early career during field training, were twelve meals with individually canned components—some type of entrée, bread, a dessert, a beverage mix—issued as a daily set. They came with a tiny P-38 can opener, which most soldiers wore on their dog tags. The meals were legendary for both variety and notoriety: Ham and Lima Beans earned the unprintable nickname "Ham and Motherf****rs," while Beef, Sliced was considered a prize and edible by most. While all the meals were dense, heavy, and reliable, the majority were not exactly inspiring.

During my time at West Point, cadets were also provided Long Range Reconnaissance Patrol (LRRP) rations. These were new at the time, designed for the forces serving in Vietnam, and were early approaches to freeze-dried meals that required hot water. They were light and lasted forever, but they tasted like sawdust with seasoning. LRRPs were a godsend for small patrols moving for long distances deep in the field, but nobody would have mistaken them for comfort food.

In the early 1980s, the Meal, Ready to Eat replaced the C-ration. It was lighter and longer lasting and came in a brown plastic pouch instead of cans. At first, soldiers were suspicious—especially when Menu #4, Omelet with Ham, the first one I tried on a tank range at Fort Polk, tasted like a damp sponge. But over time, the variety improved, the taste improved, and MREs became the backbone of army field "dining."

During Desert Storm, MREs were our standard meal, usually twice a day. We also received the occasional T-ration—large tray packs of fully cooked meals (beef stew, spaghetti) that could be heated and served to multiple soldiers. T-rations were bulky and required a field kitchen stove to cook, but after weeks of MREs, they were almost a feast.

Soldiers quickly developed a black-market economy around MRE components, trading crackers for cheese spread or hoarding Tabasco bottles like gold. Some soldiers became "combat chefs," combining components into improvised dishes—beef stew over noodles, peanut butter on oatmeal cookies, coffee mixed into cocoa for a "Ranger Mocha." The Ranger Mochas were a fixed staple in our cavalry operations center before the war.

Combat chefs weren't the only ones finding ways to spice up their meals. I was surprised when I was assigned to the National Training Center as the commander of the observer controllers (OCs), the hundreds of men and women who controlled the training events and provided doctrinal advice to the units, that they refused to even carry MREs. The field-hardened OC teams, different from the training units who were required to execute logistical supply chain operations, had access to the post exchange, just off the training area. These controllers had both pride and their own culinary code: Never eat MREs. Their HMMWVs carried coolers packed with steaks, chicken, shrimp, and fresh vegetables. The OCs would hide in desert wadis during pauses in exercises to dig a hole for charcoal. While the training unit was knee-deep in the orders process, the OCs would be grilling, and the aroma would often allow me to easily find their positions . . . and share a meal. As the commander of the operations group, I was often honored to be invited to one of the many OC teams' evening feasts during the last night of a training rotation, as that was when the coolers would be emptied and the teams would provide a veritable smorgasbord.

I've also had the honor of sharing field meals with allied soldiers at a variety of our allied training sites around the world, and one can learn a lot from another nation's rations. The French rations (what they call their RCIR) come in a twenty-four-hour box with items like duck confit, cassoulet, pâté, and chocolate, plus a small bottle of wine. British rations are hearty: curry, baked beans, plenty of tea bags (their tanks and personnel carriers have what their soldiers call "BVs"—boiling vessels—inside the turret, specifically for heating water for both shaving and tea!), and fruit pudding. Their ration cases also come with enough biscuits to roof a house. The German rations I saw included rye bread, liverwurst, and soup packets, with meticulous packaging that would make any engineer proud.

During a visit to Russia in the late 1990s, I had the privilege of being with Spetsnaz, their special operations soldiers, in the field. I watched them ignore their standard-issue rations entirely, and instead, they waded into a nearby lake, pulled out live freshwater prawns, and cooked them over an open fire. It was fresh, delicious, and utterly unlike anything in my brown plastic pouch. And yes, they did have vodka in the field with them, but I'm not sure if that was issued with a ration pack.

For all the jokes about military food, rations are more than calories. They're comfort food when a soldier is wet, tired, and far from home. They're part of the shared language of service—everyone remembers their favorite menu, their least favorite, and the weird experiments they tried. Interestingly, while writing this reflection, I received an email from my old friend Admiral Bill McRaven, the former special operations command commander who was the leader of the raid that killed Bin Laden. He opened his note by saying, "Mark, it's been too long since we've shared an MRE together." Now, I don't know that I've ever shared an MRE with this American hero, but his message signaled that he was yearning for the bonding over a good, processed military meal!

Back in January 1991, I realized I'd never given a blessing to God for my MREs. But when I think about it now, compared to the meals our allies and foes were eating, the MRE was one of quality and, certainly, durability. And no matter what, gratitude doesn't depend on whether the bread is warm from an oven or from an HMMWV heater vent. In war, the ability to eat—anything—is a blessing.

I've concluded that any "daily bread," even in a brown pouch, still deserves thanks. And I'm glad I kept this entry and created this reflection.

13 JAN 1991—OPLANS and OPORDS

I haven't written to you in the past few days because we've been concerned about the potential for a preemptive strike by Saddam Hussein's Army down a terrain feature called the Wadi al-Batin. The feeling is that as the 15th of January approaches—the day Iraq is supposed to get out of Kuwait—Hussein will try to launch a preemptive strike at either Log Base Alpha (a logistics facility near here where all of VII Corps logistics are stored), Hafar al-Batin, or King Khalid Military City, a town known for its housing of most of the higher Saudi Arabian military officials. While an Iraqi preemptive strike would only seal Iraq's fate in the eyes of the American people, Hussein believes that it could be a psychological victory and a means of making the "Great Satan" (the USA) look bad in the eyes of the Arabs. We have heard intel reports that this attack would come at 0300 hours, 14 January (later tonight).

For the past several days, we've been planning contingency operations to go north from our current locations as a counterattack force. Since we (1-1 CAV) are one of the few forces which have all our equipment here in the Tactical Assembly Area (TAA), we may very well be at the forefront of this counterattack. Here's the plan.

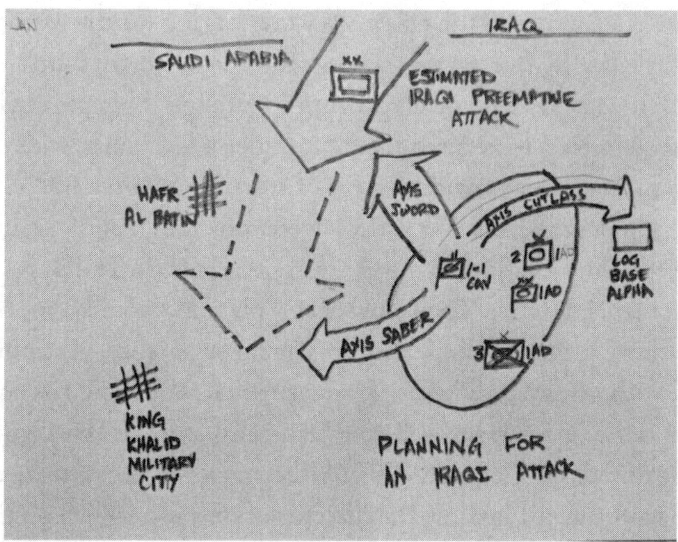

We'll be sweating it a little tonight as we wait to see what will happen. For the past several days we've been on 50% security and conducting recons—the men, and the planners, are very tired.

We heard on the radio news this morning that President Bush was thankful for the declaration of war declared by Congress. He feels that this is the last opportunity for Hussein to realize that we mean business. Unfortunately, the deadline is only a few days away, and he'll have to take some serious action before then.

Write tomorrow,

Dad

Reflection

This entry, written just days before the coalition's air campaign began, offers a glimpse into the uncertainty of planning for military (and, at times, governmental agency) operations.

In this journal entry, you can feel the tension in my words. We had just executed a planning drill with the squadron's young officers and senior sergeants for a possible preemptive strike against an anticipated Iraqi incursion. As I wrote in the entry, we were waiting for the "0300 hours" moment, preparing our cavalry squadron to pivot north, south, or west, if needed. It was gritty, tactical, real-time planning—by captains, lieutenants, and sergeants—executed in a tent under a few lights, with just one portable space heater providing a bit of warmth on a cold desert night. We were under stress, but our actions were rooted in repetition, doctrine, and shared understanding that this was potentially the real thing.

Back then, I didn't yet know how deeply planning would come to define the rest of my professional life. But this small experience—creating hasty graphics with arrows and "what if" movements, something the squadron staff had done often when we'd fought mock battles at the Grafenwöhr training grounds in Germany—would be mirrored decades later at the strategic level, when I became the director of operations (J7) on the Joint Staff. In that role, I became the senior custodian of the US military's global contingency plans. We maintained all our nation's war plans, passed to us by the four-star combatant commanders, all built to reflect national strategy and anticipated global risks. But here's what experience in each rank I held taught me, and what I now teach others: Planning isn't just about generating detailed documents—it's about preparing minds.

There are two primary types of military planning actions. Deliberate planning is a methodical process done well in advance, primarily based on assumptions about potential threats and eventual strategic objectives in different parts of the world. Those plans are aligned with resource allocations, global posture, and whatever any presidential administration guides the military to do during their annual strategic assessments. These are the "big muscle" war plans, and the strength of deliberate planning is in the preparation: It gives commanders options and enables interagency synchronization throughout the government.

Crisis action planning, on the other hand, happens under pressure. The assumptions are replaced by real-time facts, emerging intelligence, and constant change. You must work with what you have, not what you wish you had. And you don't get months—you sometimes get hours.

In both cases, a planning order directs the execution. At the tactical level, the five-paragraph field order remains the trusted structure. In that order, the friendly and enemy situations are defined, the mission is clearly stated, the approach to the execution—with maneuver and movement—is outlined, the sustainment of the forces is described and allocated, and the layers of command and their communication methods are set in place. Whether you're a squadron S3 or a theater-level planner, this structure helps align every element of your actions toward a clear, executable purpose.

What I've learned, and what I hope shows in this reflection, is something even more profound: Sometimes the plans don't matter—but the planning always does.

There's a story I like that captures this lesson. In the early 1960s, President John F. Kennedy suspected the Soviets were preparing some type of provocation in Berlin. Concerned but unsure of what was coming, he asked the Pentagon to develop a series of potential responses, what the military calls an action-reaction-counteraction series of drills. When those potential action-reaction-counteraction plans were complete and briefed to the President, Kennedy—aware of his own limitations as a junior naval officer during WWII—asked the planners to brief someone with deeper experience in strategic decision-making: former President Dwight D. Eisenhower.

So, the planners went to Gettysburg.

In Ike's quiet farmhouse near a battlefield where another kind of crisis had once played out during the Civil War, these senior officers briefed Eisenhower on their assumptions and options. They laid out potential Soviet scenarios: an armored push through the Fulda Gap, economic pressure, nuclear signaling, political propaganda campaigns.

At the end of the briefing, one of the officers asked, "Mr. President, based on what we've told you, what do you think the Soviets are going to do?" Eisenhower, the Supreme Allied Commander who'd planned D-Day and led Allied forces in WWII, and who had been the president for eight years, paused. Then, he reportedly replied succinctly, "I don't really know what they're going to do. But remember—your plans mean nothing, but your planning means everything."

One of the plans the Pentagon officers hadn't considered was that the Soviets would build a wall around Berlin.

That phrase and that story have stuck with me throughout my career. We must plan, but we must always be prepared for the unexpected and find ways to adapt.

The act of planning—of thinking through contingencies, rehearsing responses, identifying critical nodes, and engaging in dialogue—builds mental agility and collective understanding. It transforms uncertainty into readiness. It equips leaders not with clairvoyance but with a point of transition when new information comes. It prepares teams to adapt.

And that's exactly what we were doing in that Saudi desert in January 1991. We were planning not because we knew what was coming, but because we had to be ready for anything.

This commitment to planning continued throughout my career. Whether preparing operations in Tikrit or coordinating cyber defense exercises in Europe, I learned that thoughtful, inclusive, and scenario-based planning saves lives. It also builds trust. When a subordinate sees their teams leaning forward together, sketching possibilities, running rehearsals, and asking for feedback, it sends a clear signal: "I take this seriously. I've thought this through. And I'll lead from the front and be ready to adapt when the time comes."

In the end, the Iraqi preemptive strike didn't materialize. But our planning—those arrows, rehearsals, radio drills, and contingency briefs—weren't wasted. They built muscle memory and sharpened judgment, and the midnight session ensured that when the real execution orders came a few days later, we were confident and prepared.

To my grandchildren who might read this, and to anyone who wants to lead: Don't underestimate the power of planning. Even when plans change—and they will, for as the old military adage goes, "No plan survives first contact with the enemy," or, in the more succinct words of boxer Mike Tyson, "Everyone has a plan 'til they get punched in the face"—the act of planning ensures you won't be caught flat-footed. It gives you something far more important than certainty; it prepares you for what you'll do if you get punched in the face.

It gives you adaptability.

And in leadership, that is everything.

14 JAN 1991—Rock Springs, Wyoming

When people do nice things for you, it makes you feel special—someone has gone out of their way to make only you feel good. Mom and I always ensure you guys send thank you notes to people when they send you gifts because it's nice to show others that you appreciate the things they have done for you.

Well, we've been deluged by letters from children (and some adults) who live in Rock Springs, Wyoming. One of the guys in the S3, CPT Steve Shuster, grew up in R.S. and he wrote to the people there asking them for support. Someone published the request in the local newspaper, and the result has been five or six letters a day addressed to all of us—BY NAME—from people we don't even know. They've sent packages, food, and words of encouragement.

This is special for several reasons. Primarily, it's nice to know someone is thinking about us enough to take the time to write and express gratitude for what we're doing for the country. Secondly, it's very different from the attitude of the people who made up the US's population during our last big war—Viet Nam. During that war, soldiers—those who were willing to give their lives for a cause—were called names and degraded by people who did not know what it was like to spend time away from family and friends.

One of the letters we received was from a man who had served in Viet Nam and remembered the sting of being treated poorly by an ungrateful nation upon his return. He wrote that serving time away from family and friends had to be a 24 hour-at-a-time venture. The trouble was packing those 24 hours into a back-to-back scenario! He's right. I can handle being away from you guys tonight; it's tomorrow that I'm REALLY worried about! I'm not the same, I now realize, when I'm not with your mom. The three of you guys make me complete. Ah, but I digress!

The moral to this day's writing is this: TAKE THE TIME TO MAKE OTHERS FEEL GOOD! Whether it's thanking someone for something they did for you, or doing something for someone else without a reason. It'll make you feel good in the long run, too.

Love ya,

Dad!

Reflection

It's amazing what a letter can do.

That morning in the desert, when a huge mailbag was delivered to our site and we all started receiving letters from Rock Springs, Wyoming, it changed something in all of us. Not just because it was mail—every deployed soldier looks forward to the sound of their name during mail call—but because it was unexpected. None of us had any connection to the people who'd written to us. But they had sent boxes with letters, hand-drawn pictures, hard candy, and words of encouragement simply because someone had told them soldiers were out there doing something hard and lonely. That act—of unsolicited kindness, of human outreach—stayed with me for the rest of my career.

Twelve years later, in 2003, I found myself in a different kind of war. I was assistant division commander of the 1st Armored Division in Baghdad, and we had tens of thousands of soldiers operating in an unfamiliar environment spread throughout that volatile city. One day, I received a strange email from a woman I didn't know. She introduced herself as Carolyn Blashek and said she had started a nonprofit organization called Operation Gratitude. She asked me in the email if I could send her the names of any soldiers who might appreciate receiving a care package.

I smiled as I replied. "Carolyn," I said in the note, "I'm the assistant division commander of a unit with 39,000 soldiers. I can't give you our manning roster over email, but even if I could, I don't think you have 39,000 boxes to send us." As I hit send, I thought that might be the last time I heard from her.

But she replied immediately. "If you can get me those 39,000 names, I'll have 39,000 boxes on the way in a week."

To make a long story short, we found a way. And she sent 39,000 boxes.

That single exchange began a friendship that has endured over decades. While she had started by putting boxes together in her living room, her nonprofit soon evolved to a large high school gymnasium, then a National Guard armory. All done with volunteer workers and donations from a bevy of organizations.

Carolyn and Operation Gratitude remind me again of the quiet power of gratitude. Carolyn's commitment transformed Operation Gratitude into a national movement. Millions of care packages later, today she remains a model of service above self. What she did, and continues to do, is remarkable not because of the size of her effort but because of the purity of its purpose.

But that isn't the end of the story. In 2007, while I was again serving in Iraq—this time as a commanding general during the surge—Carolyn contacted me once more. Operation Gratitude had just prepared its three hundred thousandth care package, and she had a secret. Inside one of those boxes, she told me, was a key to a brand-new Jeep, donated by Chrysler. But Carolyn had a condition: She wanted to deliver that package herself, in person, to a special soldier in Iraq serving in the 1st Armored Division because that was where her actions had gained momentum a few years earlier. Did I have a soldier, she wondered, who had a large family and might need a new car when they got back home?

She'd never been to a war zone before. But she came. She flew into Balad, rode with us into the operational area near Tikrit, and personally handed that milestone package to a stunned and overjoyed private first class with a wife and several children back home. That young man didn't just get a new vehicle—he got a lifelong memory of someone who cared enough to show up.

And Carolyn? She got a firsthand look at the difference her efforts were making. She cried when she saw all the other troops open their boxes.

We speak about leadership, service, and sacrifice. But sometimes, real strength shows up in small ways—a package, a note, a slice of home. These small things matter, especially when they arrive in person. They tether us to something larger than ourselves.

The people of Rock Springs and the passion of Carolyn Blashek taught me this, and I hope you see my point: We don't have to wear a uniform to serve. We just must act on a desire to make someone else feel valued. We should all take that lesson to heart. Make someone feel better today; give them a memory.

Don't underestimate the value of reaching out. Gratitude, after all, is not just something you feel. It's something you give.

15 JAN 1991—The Deadline

It's late on the night of the 15th of January, the day President Bush and the rest of the members of the United Nations have declared as the day Iraq must have all its forces out of Kuwait or face the consequences. We've been conducting reconnaissance missions and preparing various counters to any potential preemptive strike, so we have been busy. We also went to the locally constructed firing range today to "zero" our Bradley's 25mm cannon and Cobra's 20mm Vulcan nose gun.

The range firing went very well. There weren't the usual hassles by range meisters in charge; in fact, we basically did everything we wanted to do in a very short period. The soldiers were on and off the range in short spurts; they knew what they needed to do, they did it, and they now have a lot more confidence; they know they'll be able to hit what they're shooting at.

I'll keep it short today, fellas. But know I love you,

Dad

Reflection

There's something about zeroing your armored equipment's weapon or aircraft's weapon system on the eve of battle that sharpens more than just your sights.

By the time we hit January 15, we knew what was coming. Everyone did. And we were prepared. The politicians had set the deadline, and the soldiers knew the consequences. We'd all been preparing—checking vehicles, rehearsing potential routes through the desert, making maps (yes, making them . . . more on that in a later reflection), scanning for anything unusual, running security patrols. But something changes when you physically raise your weapon and fire it or sight those awesome cannons on the Bradley and Cobra helicopters and see that you can hit the target. It's not just a metal alignment or trigger squeeze—it's a mental calibration.

You stop wondering *if* you're ready and start believing you *are* ready.

That belief is crucial. What was once called Desert Shield was about to become Desert Storm. The stakes were real, the timeline was fixed, and the next time we fired our weapons, it wouldn't be on a controlled range. It would be the real thing.

This journal entry closes the first section of my story covering the deployment, the buildup, the philosophy that I was passing to our sons about a variety of things I knew I might not be able to teach them in person because of the mortal weight of impending war. From that point forward, we weren't preparing for combat. We were *in it*. The next phase wouldn't just be about reflections on life and character. It would be about decisions, actions, and consequences.

As we say in the army, we were about to make contact.

ACTIONS ON CONTACT

1st Squadron, 1st Cavalry Regiment,
1st Armored Division Operation Desert Storm

17 JAN 1991—The Attack

I went to bed at 12:15 am this morning, and LT Rich Tunney—our assistant S2—woke us up by running into our tent at 1:15 am saying we had launched 145 Tomahawk missiles at targets in Iraq. Additionally, the Air Force had put up hundreds of aircraft (we found out later the sorties rate was over 1,400) to strike targets ranging from SCUD missile sites to airfields and strategic C2 centers (where commanders of armed forces units go). As I shook myself from sleep and had the stark realization that I was in the middle of a new war, my first thoughts were of those doing the fighting and how we would be a part of it soon. But a close second thought was of mom, you guys, and the Blackhawk soldiers who were here with me, all asleep in their tents, not knowing what was happening. I was instantly awake.

We listened to both our BBC feed and the tactical radios in the TOC, both providing information about the missile strikes and the success of the Air Force fighters and bombers and the Navy rounds and missiles hitting their targets, and we soon found out about the Army Apache hitting key targets that paved the way for an opening for the Air Force to fly through in the opening battles. There wasn't a lot of conversation as we listened intently. The mood was very somber and serious. I remember looking at the faces of each of our squadron leaders as we were huddled around as we all listened to the reports. I will remember those faces as if they were ingrained in my brain with a hot iron.

I love you guys. And I miss you all.

Dad.

Reflection

That wake-up call on the night of January 17, 1991, wasn't a surprise in the grand sense—we'd been expecting the attack for days—but the way it happened made it feel like the ground had suddenly opened beneath me. One minute, I was in a warm sleeping bag, and the next, I was in the cold desert night, pulling on my unauthorized Israeli tanker boots with the straps and rubbing my head, trying to process what I'd just been told. We were at war. Not preparing for it. Not talking about it. In it.

As the operations officer, I felt the weight settle immediately on my shoulders. I knew we'd be moving soon and that our part of the fight was coming. But that night, there was no detailed picture, no crisp briefing slides. Intelligence about the air campaign was almost nonexistent at our level. We got bits and pieces from the BBC radio station that we were able to pick up in our remote location in the desert, but we heard almost nothing from our brigade and division—not because they were holding anything back, but because they didn't know, either. The start of the air campaign was a masterpiece of operational security.

Only later, long after the war, would I learn about the army Apache helicopters and special operations teams that had slipped across the border in the opening minutes to destroy air defense radars and observation posts all the way to Baghdad. That night, all we knew was what the BBC reported and that the war we'd been training for had begun. Nobody in the TOC slept again until sunrise.

It wouldn't be the last time I was pulled from deep sleep into the middle of a fight. In Iraq in 2003–2004, it would be errant terrorist rockets striking our logistics base. In 2007–2008, it would be incoming rounds landing near our division headquarters at Camp Speicher outside of Tikrit. Other times, it was the special operations liaison from either LTG McChrystal's or Vice Admiral McRaven's headquarters waking me at 0200 or 0300 to report the outcome of a night raid—*jackpot* if the target had been captured or killed, *dry hole* if not. And sometimes, it was simply a staff officer reporting that one of my priority intelligence requirements had been met and the battle staff couldn't wait until morning to let me know.

But that night was the moment when the war shifted from an abstract possibility to a lived reality—when all the maps, plans, preparations, and briefings gave way to the raw fact that people were already fighting and dying. That night, in the cold Saudi desert, I understood in a visceral way that nothing would be the same from here on out. What followed in the days ahead would test everything I thought I knew about war—and about myself. The philosophy of leadership I had carried into the desert would now be measured for the first time of many against the reality of combat. And as I would learn in those years to come, those lessons don't stay on the battlefield; they follow you, shaping every decision, every moment, for the rest of your life.

Over the next two decades, I would become very familiar with those middle-of-the-night wake-ups. It would become part of the life of a commander, part of the reality of leadership in combat or in peacetime. War, and information, don't wait for you to get a good night's sleep or even for you to get your boots on.

18 JAN 1991—Intelligence in War

When I went to the School of Advanced Military Studies (SAMS) at Leavenworth, we studied the writings of a man named Clausewitz who wrote about war. To the uninitiated, his works are long and very boring: a deadly combination! But one of the things I remember he wrote about was receiving accurate information about the enemy. He said that the smart Soldier does not put any faith in the intelligence generated by staff officers about the progress of the battle because most times it's just flat wrong!

We're not getting any info about what is happening with the Air Force's mission in Iraq right now. The best "intel" we're receiving is by listening to Peter Jennings and Ted Koppel on an ABC news report from an Israeli radio station during the day, or a BBC broadcaster beaming in from one of the Gulf States on an AM radio feed at night. In fact, this morning we received info about a SCUD launch toward the ports, and before the intel nets could tell us what was happening, a very young Wolf Blitzer of CNN was reporting from the ports in Saudi Arabia that both SCUDS had been shot down by Patriot missiles. Amazing.

The moral: Don't put a lot of trust or faith in people reporting any important information—it tends to be embellished by their own prejudices. And that doesn't just happen in warfare.

Love ya,

Dad

Reflection

Ready for a long one?

When I wrote that journal entry in January 1991, I was sitting in a cold Saudi desert assembly area with a cavalry squadron that had one captain for an S2 (intelligence officer), a lieutenant as his assistant (the guy who had awakened me the night before when the attack began), and a single enlisted soldier who wasn't even an intelligence analyst. On that day, right before I wrote this journal entry, we were all sitting in the TOC, trying to figure out what was going on. We knew we were about to play a critical role as the advance guard for our division's attack into Iraq. Our mission was to "gain contact with the enemy, develop the situation, and find the Republican Guard forces." In practical terms, that meant we were expected to feel out the front lines, determine where the enemy was and in what strength, report information to the division headquarters and the tank brigade that was following about ten kilometers behind us, then conduct a battle handover to the fighting force. Scouts—cavalry—kill with their radios and their reports; back then, they didn't have the firepower or armor protection to defend themselves against larger enemy armored forces, so they tried not to get engaged in big fights.

Much like a cavalry "screen" in the defense, a cavalry "advance guard" mission in the offense harkens back to the traditions of centuries past: Scouts push forward, sometimes taking fire to confirm where the enemy is, send couriers (or voice communications on the radio) back to their superior commanders to describe what they found, then get out of the way so the main force of infantry (and armor) can engage the enemy. The cavalry is then sent to conduct reconnaissance elsewhere.

Our intelligence collection and analysis capabilities while sitting in the assembly area were sparse. There was no "unblinking eye" like we see with the drones and overhead platforms that are a mainstay of modern reconnaissance. Our "intel" came from maps, aerial photographs (sometimes weeks old), and the occasional intercepted radio chatter. We didn't have satellite imagery piped directly into our command post or real-time feeds from drones overhead. And in that vacuum, rumors—"rumor intelligence," or RUMINT, as we call it—could become as powerful as any formal report.

Clausewitz, I remembered from my time at the School of Advanced Military Studies (SAMS), said that "many intelligence reports in war are contradictory; even more are false, and most are uncertain." That wasn't just a quaint nineteenth-century observation from a Prussian colonel—it was our daily reality. We filled gaps with our best guesses, and bias crept into our assessments each time. Confirmation usually only came through contact.

But on that cold January afternoon after the bombing campaign started, those estimations were the only intelligence we had.

Our army learned a lot from Desert Storm. Throughout the 1990s, we adjusted our organizations, and "intel-based operations" became a catch phrase. As a colonel placed in charge of a huge tank-heavy brigade combat team (BCT) with over eight thousand soldiers, I was ordered during the last six months of command to "transform" that unit into what would be the first of the newly designed Stryker brigades. This brigade, the brilliant brainchild of General Ric Shinseki, the chief of staff of the army, was heavy enough to fight but light enough to move anywhere in the world on no notice. The twenty or so soldiers who made up the S2 section of that armored brigade—our intelligence staff—were soon reinforced with over two hundred additional soldiers in a newly designed reconnaissance, intelligence, surveillance, and target acquisition (RISTA) squadron. This new brigade had lighter vehicles and a lot more infantry than I'd had previously, with vehicles that could be loaded quickly onto C-17s (tanks, not so much). But the key to this new form of fighting was what we gained from increased intelligence. This transformed, lighter brigade of Stryker vehicles—which had sprung from the roots of Abrams tanks, Bradley Fighting Vehicles, and Paladin artillery pieces—would make a difference in the early days of the twenty-first century, operating across battlefields in Afghanistan and Iraq.

Later, in the spring of 2001, I was the commander of the operations group—the COG, call sign "Outlaw 01"—at the US Army's National Training Center (NTC) in California. My job was to produce, direct, and manage large-scale training rotations for brigades undergoing their capstone training event in the Mojave Desert of California. The NTC is famous for its opposing force (OPFOR)—the 11th Armored Cavalry Regiment—that makes life miserable for any visiting units by exploiting their every weakness. That year, we conducted a main event called the Division Capstone Exercise, or DCX. A specially equipped brigade, loaded with the army's newest gear, sensors, and technologies specially tailored to utilize intelligence, was put to the test against our seasoned OPFOR. Army expectations were sky-high. With "perfect situational awareness" springing from massive amounts of intelligence feeds, they believed this brigade would certainly dominate the battlefield.

But that didn't happen.

In the first mock battle, the visiting training unit committed nineteen incidents of fratricide. Nineteen. All that advanced gear couldn't compensate for poor soldier skills, bad communication, and the chaos of battle. My boss at the time, Brigadier General JD Thurman, stood next to my HMMWV on a hilltop surveying the carnage and, in his Oklahoma twang, said to me, "Outlaw, these troops sure have a lot of fish finders. But it seems no one taught 'em how to fish."

That line stuck with me. Intelligence, no matter how precise or abundant, is useless if you don't know how to act on it—or if your people aren't trained to operate in uncertainty. Technology doesn't win wars by itself; trained, disciplined, adaptive soldiers who know how to use intelligence to their advantage do.

When I joined the 1st Armored Division in Baghdad in July 2003, I was stepping into a formation with a storied history. For decades during the Cold War, the "First Tank" had been forward deployed in Germany, preparing to fight the Soviet Union in massed armor battles using AirLand Battle doctrine, an approach developed to overcome the quantitative advantage the Soviets possessed. As part of that doctrine, intelligence would identify echelons of tanks and track follow-on forces that were heading to reinforce the front lines of the enemy. Our air force brethren would strike deep to attrit the enemy before they reached the front, while frontline friendly forces would destroy those Russians in contact.

What we found in Baghdad in 2003 was nothing like that.

Instead of tracking tank regiments and motor rifle divisions—what we had been preparing to do for years—our intelligence sections had "network charts" on butcher paper taped to the secure compartmented information facility (SCIF) walls, showing the composition of insurgent and terrorist cells—the financiers, local imams who blessed the attacks, bomb-makers, and the triggermen and fighters who carried out the attacks. Each cell operated independently, loosely connected by ideology or tribe. There was no front line, no deep battle—the fight was everywhere, and it was as much about mapping human relationships as it was determining follow-on forces and terrain. We had been an army focused on being at the leading edge of technology, on having complete battlefield situational awareness—seeing first, understanding first, responding first. In Iraq and Afghanistan, we would learn that we had begun to rely too much on technology and not enough on the will or capability of an immature and "third-rate" enemy.

It was in that environment that our division commander, then–Brigadier General Marty Dempsey, said something that became a mantra to Old Ironsides soldiers: "Every soldier is a scout, every soldier is a sensor." In a city where an IED could be buried in any pile of trash and an attack could come from any alley, situational awareness was key, and intelligence reporting became everyone's job.

We also guarded against "single-source intelligence." Too often, we'd get a tip—RUMINT—about a supposed weapons cache or high-value target, only to find it was a wild goose chase, a piece of intelligence that was designed to settle a personal score between rival families or mislead our action. Good intelligence had to be corroborated before being acted upon.

Over the years of fighting in Afghanistan and Iraq, the military expanded and exploited a vast ecosystem of intelligence disciplines. Human intelligence (HUMINT) is the information gathered from human sources, whether through interrogation, debriefing, or informants. In Iraq, this could mean talking to a shopkeeper who noticed unusual activity, cultivating a source within a hostile group, or using information gained from various sources outside the military chain of command. Signals intelligence (SIGINT) is the intercepting of various communications, from radio chatter to, eventually, cell phone calls. This was invaluable for tracking insurgent coordination but required careful filtering to avoid overload. In the later stages of the fight, the most important information was gleaned through SIM cards collected from terrorists' cell phones after they were captured. Geospatial intelligence (GEOINT) involves imagery and mapping from satellites, reconnaissance aircraft, and, eventually, small and large drones. This gave us patterns of life, compound layouts, and movement routes. Measurement and signature intelligence (MASINT)—the highly technical collection of data like heat signatures, chemical traces, or unique radar profiles—was usually invisible to the layperson but when properly interpreted became critical for spotting hidden threats. Then there was the unpredictable open-source intelligence (OSINT), intelligence gathered from publicly available sources, including newspapers, radio broadcasts, and social media. In Baghdad, in 2003, we created a cell we called the "Baghdad Mosquito," which consisted of local journalists scanning open-source newspapers, radio broadcasts, and even rumors generated by taxi drivers (a technique Saddam Hussein had cultivated during his reign). Later would come cyber intelligence; this was not a formal "INT" during my early career but would become essential for tracking online propaganda, recruiting, and even operational coordination by adversaries.

These disciplines were supported by a constellation of agencies—CIA, DIA, NSA, FBI, CISA—and, at the tactical level, by military intelligence units embedded in brigades and divisions. In practice, no single source told the whole story. The best intelligence came from fusing multiple streams, cross-referencing, and looking for patterns that held up under scrutiny. In 2008, then–Lieutenant General Stan McChrystal took all this to another level in our northern area of operations when he drove the establishment of intelligence fusion cells, using the power of computers to coordinate, collaborate, and combine the collection, analysis, and dissemination of intelligence that was used to rapidly strike terrorist targets.

During the time I commanded the 1st Armored Division, and later Task Force Iron during the surge in 2007, our intelligence capabilities grew tremendously. Our intelligence staff sections were providing actionable intelligence that drove operations daily, and they coordinated in an effective and efficient way with subordinate headquarters for tactical effects. As I conducted visits to units, I would take the intelligence analysts who were responsible for that area with me, and those young sergeants and specialists would have face-to-face coordination with those in the fight. Special compartmented programs that handled the highest of classified information also drove action . . . but even now, I can't say anything about what those programs did. As a division commander, I would tell Congress that our intelligence centers—along with our brave fighters—were the primary reason that attacks by terrorist and insurgent groups dissipated during our time in northern Iraq. During the fifteen months we were in northern Iraq in 2007–2008, attacks declined by more than two-thirds.

But as we transformed our intelligence collection and analysis, the challenges evolved too. One of the more interesting threats we faced in northern Iraq was the use of suicide bombing by the widows of al-Qaeda members in Iraq.

In a society where women couldn't be searched by male soldiers and where female police officers were nonexistent due to cultural dynamics, an abaya worn by the wife of an al-Qaeda member killed in combat could conceal a deadly explosive vest. The traditional military solution—a checkpoint search—simply wasn't viable, as Iraqi soldiers would not search any woman entering a crowded marketplace. We needed a different approach.

Drawing on earlier innovations, at a women's conference in Erbil, the female soldiers of our division brought together female Iraqi political leaders and cultural influencers. My wife, Sue, even opened the conference via satellite link and shared her perspective through an interpreter. From that conference came the idea to recruit Iraqi women into the police force. Within days, we had hundreds of volunteers but a noncompliant chief of Iraqi police. After some persuasion, the first class graduated within weeks, and soon, female officers were deployed in markets and at events to screen women for explosives.

A breakthrough came when the human intelligence gleaned from a rookie Iraqi policewoman helped Iraqi police capture a fifteen-year-old named Rania, a widow who had been persuaded to avenge the death of her al-Qaeda husband but surrendered when an Iraqi policewoman noticed her suspicious action and approached her before she could detonate her vest. She revealed to the policewoman that she had been drugged and coerced and even said during later interrogation that her mother was complicit in the plot. Her testimony not only led to more arrests as the network was compromised but also helped shift the public narrative. Iraqi media—not us—told her story, and those reports generated more HUMINT and SIGINT, which helped eventually bring down the cell.

By the late 2010s, as commander of the army in Europe and later a military analyst on CNN, I saw the vestiges of a new front emerging—one where the weapons weren't bullets or bombs but manipulated narratives.

Disinformation, misinformation, and malinformation became tools of state and non-state actors alike. Russia's *maskirovka*—the techniques of deception that the Soviets generated during WWII—evolved into sophisticated digital influence operations, amplified by social media and, increasingly and most recently, generative AI. I watched deepfakes and fabricated audio sow confusion and distrust across Europe and in my intelligence feeds in ways that would have made Cold War propagandists envious.

During the war in Ukraine, anchors would sometimes ask me to walk them through a battle map as if it were a chessboard—as if I or any other military analyst had full knowledge of where every unit was, what they were doing, and how the fight would end. I often had to remind television anchors that real war isn't a video game, and I wasn't privy to classified information in retirement. But even with today's incredible intelligence capabilities, uncertainty remains. The fog and friction of war—Clausewitz again—never go away.

Long before most Americans had heard of artificial intelligence, US Special Operations Command was experimenting with AI tools to process vast megabytes of information and huge amounts of sensor data so they could identify patterns and accelerate targeting decisions. These early systems could flag likely insurgent safe houses or track the "pattern of life" of a high-value target across multiple data sources. While all this was a leap forward, even AI wasn't perfect. A false assumption in the data could still lead to the wrong house, the wrong person, and the wrong conclusion. Technology could speed up decision-making, but it didn't eliminate the need for human judgment.

From that cold night in 1991 to my last years in uniform, and even into my civilian role analyzing conflicts for the public on cable news, one truth has remained: Intelligence is never perfect.

It certainly has gotten better, faster, and more detailed than ever before, and the way we analyze has separated the important from the mundane, but intelligence will always be incomplete, sometimes contradictory, and often filtered through human bias. The key is not to wait for perfect clarity—because it will never come—but to act with discipline, to verify relentlessly, and to adapt when the situation changes.

Clausewitz wrote, "War is the realm of uncertainty; three quarters of the factors on which action is based are wrapped in a fog of greater or lesser uncertainty." That hasn't changed, no matter how many satellites we launch, how many drones we deploy, or how sophisticated our algorithms become.

What has changed is our ability to pull together multiple strands of intelligence, share it rapidly, and put it in the hands of soldiers on the ground. But even the best intelligence is only as good as the training, discipline, and judgment of those who use it.

That's as true for a cavalry squadron probing the Iraqi desert in 1991 as it is for a Ukrainian unit today using a tablet to call in artillery on a Russian position after spotting it with a tethered drone.

And that is my very long reflection on the state of battlefield, or board room, intelligence today.

20 JAN 1991—Heart, Mind, and Soul

Chaplain Steve Thornton came to provide a worship service, and it was just what we needed. Steve is one of those individuals who is totally selfless, and he completely relates to the Soldiers. We needed his words today, as we ponder what may happen soon.

But Steve is also undergoing a lot of pain from an old back injury; it's so bad that it often paralyzes his left leg for periods of time. A few days ago, a doctor said he ought to be Medevac'd back to the States, and if he doesn't, there is a chance he might lose his leg. Steve took the case to a senior doctor and told him he wanted to stay here with the unit as we prepared for combat. And he's still with us.

His sermon was on prayer and the different forms it can take. Prayers of the heart are those that are made with love in mind—the wanting to be close to God so you attempt to let God guide you in the direction that he wants you to go. Those are used during the times when you're confused or need guidance on a problem, and by dwelling on the Christian way to address the issue, you allow God to come into your heart.

The second type is a prayer of the mind, where you talk to the Lord and "pray" as we know it. I've been doing a lot of that lately as I pray my rosary every night to allow peaceful thoughts to come into my mind, and I hope the mantra of those prayers may cause an intercession in this war, delivering a miracle.

The final type is a prayer of the soul. By pondering the glory or greatness of a supreme being, we become filled with grace—we better understand the role of God in our lives, guiding us as we live. I've always felt very close to God when I've experienced beautiful things in nature: a beautiful sunset, an unspoiled beach, a bike ride with your mom on a warm day in Germany. Those, to me, are prayers of the soul.

Interesting concept, this prayer stuff. Talking to God in many ways helps us become better people, better Christians, better human beings.

We hope you both continue your faith journey, and you both use prayer to ask for God's help and guidance and comfort throughout your life. He'll never forget to answer, in one way or another.

You're in my prayers!

Dad

Reflection

Chaplain Steven Thornton was an incredible man of courage and faith. I wanted to tell the boys about him in a journal entry, hoping they would understand that people of faith very often help us through the tough times in life.

But rereading this journal entry so many years later caused me to reflect not just on Steve or his message that day but on all the powerful chaplains and people of faith I met throughout my career. They all came from a powerful history; they represented a phenomenal legacy of service; and they were each extremely quiet, humble, and courageous in the performance of their duties.

The chaplain corps is one of the oldest branches of the army, formally established on July 29, 1775, a little more than a month after the army was formed on June 14, 1775. They remain incredibly important to our army. Soon after their formation, the Continental Congress authorized one chaplain for each regiment. Since then, chaplains have served in every American conflict—unarmed but always in the thick of it—as ministers to soldiers' spiritual needs, counseling them through crises, risking their lives alongside them, and, all the while, providing advice to their commanders.

That's because chaplains have a dual mission: to provide religious support to soldiers and families in accordance with their faith and to advise commanders on moral, ethical, and spiritual matters affecting the unit. In doing that, army chaplains serve in two professions at once—their calling as a minister of faith and their commission as an officer in the United States Army. Balancing both is no small task. There's also a sacred trust between chaplains and their commanders, as well as between the chaplain and his or her troops.

Their history of courage is impressive too. In World War II, four army chaplains—George Fox, Alexander Goode, Clark Poling, and John Washington—became known as "The Four Chaplains" when their troopship, USAT *Dorchester*, was torpedoed in the North Atlantic. They gave up their life jackets to save others and went down together, praying arm in arm. In Vietnam, chaplains routinely went into combat zones to minister under fire. In Iraq and Afghanistan, they conducted battlefield memorials in the open, often still within range of enemy attack. To date, eight US Army chaplains—none of whom ever carried a weapon—have been awarded the Congressional Medal of Honor, the nation's highest award for valor.

That legacy of devotion isn't confined to the pages of history. I've seen it firsthand.

This journal entry was about Chaplain Steve Thornton. Steve was a humble man of deep faith and even deeper commitment. When that doctor told him he ought to be medevac'd home, he told me that his place was "with the soldiers as we prepare for combat. You'll never get rid of me." And he stayed. That kind of devotion doesn't show up on an officer evaluation report, but it sure did get etched into my memory.

When Steve preached about the three forms of prayer on that cold January day—of the heart, mind, and soul—he was able to describe prayer with a sense of awe and gratitude that rises simply from being alive. I'll never forget that sermon, and I've found myself leaning into all three kinds over the years.

Steve wasn't the only chaplain who left a mark on my life and leadership. Military chaplains come from all different backgrounds and denominations. While it seemed Protestant chaplains were the most ubiquitous—and even they represented the various faiths within the Protestant denominations—I was lucky enough to serve with and learn from Jewish, Muslim, and Buddhist chaplains. Each one of them was terrific, but still I often found myself measuring all of them against Steve's example.

When I took command at Fort Knox after Desert Storm, our squadron chaplain was LTC (Chaplain) Tony Torrer, a Catholic priest who absolutely loved soldiers and the army equally, with an extrovert's great sense of humor. When I once asked him to provide details about the Order of St. George and why we used Saint George as the patron saint of armor and cavalry, he provided a staff paper on how many groups were supported by the patronage of that saint. One thing that surprised both of us was that Saint George served as the patron saint of prostitutes, which I ordered him never to tell the soldiers in our squadron! We kept that inside joke between us! Sue and I once hosted a "no shop talk" party for the troop commanders and staff at our quarters. The rules were simple: We wanted to get to know people for who they were and separate them a bit from their army experiences. We also told everyone that anyone who violated those rules would have to stand on a chair and, in their best David Letterman impression, deliver a "Top Ten" list after we had given them a topic. Father Tony was the first violator, and his penalty was to provide the "Top Ten Things You've Heard in a Confessional." He kept it clean, but we made him stop at number five.

Later, in brigade command at Fort Lewis, our unit had a great Protestant chaplain, Wesley Smith. Wes became a family friend, and he also masterfully led a team of six battalion chaplains, all new captains, for our subordinate units. Wes was a superb leader, organizer, and preacher, but most of all, he was a gifted counselor. I watched him guide struggling couples back toward each other, often under the strain of repeated deployments. Wes saved a lot of marriages in our nine-thousand-soldier brigade in a two-year period.

Later, as a division commander, my chaplain was LTC (Chaplain) Terry Meek, with MAJ (Chaplain) Lou Del Tufo as his deputy. They were an awesome team, and under their mentorship, one young captain—Chaplain Bill Green—would eventually become the army's chief of chaplains in 2023.

But it was one night in Iraq that allowed me to remember Terry forever.

We were conducting a division-wide operation called Iron Harvest. On one day during the first week of the operation, we lost eight soldiers in four separate actions across northern Iraq. I had been moving across the battlespace all day, monitoring the operation and getting reports over the radio. Late in the afternoon, I was at a location just a few hundred yards away when three of our men were killed by a booby-trapped house. While getting back on the helicopter to fly to another location, I learned about the other KIAs.

Late that night, I flew back to Tikrit and our headquarters. The weight of those losses—and the knowledge that the losses were the result of missions I had ordered—settled hard on my shoulders. I told our chief of staff, Colonel Bryan Watson, that that revelation was weighing on me. I had always executed the orders of others, not personally created the orders that resulted in someone's death. I was internally debating the difference, and Bryan knew I needed someone to talk to about it all. He called Terry Meek.

I was surprised to see Terry when he showed up at my door so late, but he came into my office, pulled up a chair at the side of my desk, and casually asked how I was doing. He got my automatic, "I'm okay, Chaplain. How are you tonight?"

He shook his head and responded, "No, sir, you're not okay. Don't try to BS me. You're carrying a heavy load. I'm not just the division chaplain—I'm your chaplain too. Would you like to talk about it, and would you like me to pray with you?"

We did both.

From the Four Chaplains on the *Dorchester* to Steve Thornton refusing to leave his unit to Father Tony's humor to Wes Smith's counseling to Terry Meek's quiet prayer and consolation, I've seen chaplains serve heart, mind, and soul in ways that transcend rank or circumstance.

The technology, the tactics, and even the nature of the fight may change as I provide my reflections throughout this work. But the chaplain's role has not. They remain the ones who walk toward the hurt, who stand between despair and hope, who carry no weapon but somehow fight on the front line of the human spirit.

And sometimes, even an old division commander will learn that the most important thing a person of faith can hear is "I'm your chaplain too."

We should all rely on them—and each other.

21 JAN 1991—Phoning Home

What a bittersweet occurrence. It was so good hearing your voices, and it was a special surprise for me, as I forgot that it was Martin Luther King, Jr. Day and you would be out of school. Mom sounded terrific, and a little bit scared, as I am sure she and Mrs. Dempsey were perceiving the worst with the news of the SCUD launches going into the same port MAJ Dempsey was at when they hit, helping get his unit to the tactical assembly areas.

Your voices all sounded so good. Scott seemed so excited and wanted to tell me all the things he had been doing over the days since I left: cursive writing in school, sending me my field dinosaur, etc. Todd sounded like he missed me—really missed me. That made me sad, because I miss you guys so much, too. Mom sounded scared. That made me very upset.

When the peace of your family life is undergoing such an upheaval, it's something you just can't get out of your mind. I thought about that phone call all day today. As much as I wanted to make the call—and I truly did want to hear all your voices and see how you were doing—I knew it would be tough, on me and you. I miss you guys so much. I hope I can make another call before we depart TAA Thompson and go forward to our new FAA's.

Love ya/Miss ya

Dad

Reflection

I can still hear the first voice that day—Sue's. She wasn't expecting me to call, so there was a pause, then that surprised, delighted tone she always gets in her voice. Then, I heard her yell, unexpectedly, to you guys: "It's Dad!" In the background came the sound of two boys rushing to the phone, eager to grab the receiver and cram as much news as they could into what we all knew would be a short conversation. Scott's voice was bubbling with excitement—school updates, his new cursive writing, the field dinosaur he'd sent me. Todd's voice was quieter, more reserved, but full of longing. For a few minutes, the cold, damp air of the desert gave way to the warm chaos of our home that I knew so well.

During Desert Storm, that phone connection was a special treat, and it was made possible by something new to us—the Thuraya satellite phone. Our squadron had been issued three of them, officially for "morale purposes" but also for critical coordination with our home station in Germany. As the S3, I asked our squadron commander if we could rotate them through the units so every soldier might get five minutes to call home. It was a small thing, but it mattered. As leaders, though, we were also working our way through the uncharted territory of what that kind of instant access could mean.

A few weeks later, during the fighting, I was wounded, along with a couple of dozen other Blackhawk soldiers, in an artillery attack. Thankfully and luckily, the injuries weren't life-threatening, our medics and combat lifesavers sprang into action, and only one soldier had to be medevac'd to an aid station. But an aviation unit in the rear, far from the fight, learned about the incident. They meant well, but with no guidance in our standard operating procedure (SOP) on what was helpful versus potentially harmful information to share, they used their Thuraya to call a soldier's wife in Germany: "Major Hertling was wounded, but not seriously, and he's still in the fight." That wife immediately called Sue to pass along that I was okay. The intention was kindness; the effect would become something else entirely.

Several days later, our rear-detachment officer—a brand-new 2nd lieutenant eager to "do the right thing"—received a message with a list of names of all those in the squadron who had been wounded in that artillery strike. With good intentions, that lieutenant decided he would make the rounds to family housing to visit all the quarters of the married soldiers who had been wounded in the event. When he showed up outside our front door, Sue's heart sank. In that moment, she thought she was about to hear more news, this time devastating. Only after a few anxious seconds did she realize the rookie lieutenant was delivering old news she'd already heard. It was another reminder that speed in communication, without coordination or clear thinking, can sometimes do more harm than good.

That incident was my first real lesson in how communication technology could outpace the systems we had in place to manage it. That's part of a bigger story—the evolution of how soldiers have kept in touch with the people they love over the years.

My mother-in-law, Betty, was part of the generation that relied on letters from the front. After she died at the age of ninety-five, we found two shoeboxes under her bed filled with letters from my father-in-law, Lou, written during World War II and later during the Korean War. They were stacked neatly by date, the edges worn from being opened and reread. Those letters, containing such beautiful words, had taken weeks or months to arrive back then; those delays could soften the edges of fear or exacerbate disturbing news about the front lines.

During Desert Storm, letters were still the backbone of communication, and our mailrooms in combat were busy. But those satellite calls we were making hinted at a future where connection could happen instantly. By the time 1st Armored Division got settled in Baghdad in 2003–2004, that future had arrived. Our division set up internet cafés on forward operating bases (FOBs), and suddenly, troops could send an email or call home after conducting a patrol. The sight of a soldier walking out of a plywood hut with a huge grin after an email session was a morale boost for everyone.

But with speed came new problems. Facebook groups sprang up, connecting families back home. Those were great for keeping families informed, but unfortunately, before the army figured out how to shut down internet connections during specific events, those pages often passed news of casualties before official notification teams could reach next of kin. Operational security was harder to protect, and emotional security could be shattered in an instant.

By 2007, internet cafés weren't a novelty; they were expected. Most every FOB, combat outpost (COP), and command post (CP) had them. Care packages still came in bulk, smelling faintly of home, perfume, or chocolate chip cookies, but handwritten letters had almost disappeared.

And yet, some things never change. Whether it's a letter in a shoebox, a voice on a satellite phone, or a quick "I love you" over email, wartime communication has always carried the same dynamics. No matter the method, messages draw families closer even as they remind them of the distance. They bring joy and reassurance but can also deliver the hardest news a family will ever hear. That balance—between connection and consequence—is as much a part of soldiering as the uniform itself.

One more thing. I learned something from several terrific mentors about the power of a written note. Not an email, not a text, not a phone call, but a handwritten note on a tangible piece of paper that the receiver can hold in their hand, tack on the wall of their office cubicle, or put in a frame—one little note can mean the world to someone. It has amazed me how many small handwritten notes of thanks I've written to someone, delivering them by mail in the old-fashioned way or personally putting them on their desk, that have made it home to parents, spouses, or scrapbooks. They're gifts that don't take much time to deliver, and they always show someone has taken the time to say thanks. They're gifts, as someone once said, that keep on giving.

In 2008, when I was deployed to northern Iraq, Sue came up with the idea of having roses delivered to all the spouses back home on Valentine's Day. While it initially seemed like a major project—and truthfully, a distraction—this project created a positive rumbling among the staff in the headquarters at Tikrit. Sue told me I could announce the effort, and she and a couple of other spouses back in Germany would make the arrangements with a local florist. All the soldiers had to do was contact the participating *Blumenhändler* (German for florist) via email with their credit card, but there was a caveat: The florist would not send the flowers unless they had a personal note attached for the recipient. That requirement took the soldiers by surprise. "You mean we have to include a love letter, sir?" But interestingly, we had hundreds who participated in that event. The flowers were nice, but it was the soldiers' handwritten notes that made the difference.

One more time, communication is important. But the way one communicates is what really matters.

25 JAN 1991—Expectations

When we first were notified that we were coming here to the desert, all the advice we received told us to prepare for the heat, dust, sand and lousy climate. Those were the expectations; in fact, you guys have been continuously writing me letters about how I should compare the "sand down here" to the "rain up there." Well, like many things in life, expectations did not match reality.

For the last several days, it has been cold, wet, rainy, and muddy. In fact, it is very much like any field problem I've ever been on in Hohenfels or Grafenwöhr. Our uniforms are soaked, our boots are covered with mud, you can't find a dry place to sleep, eat, or stand, and—for the most case—all of us are miserable. Don't get me wrong, there are still the jokes and lightheartedness—indications that this is a very good unit and conglomeration of individuals—but we all wish that the sun would come out and make this a real desert.

So much for expectations.

Love ya—

Dad

Reflection

When I think back to that day, I remember the damp chill in my bones. The rain had soaked everything we owned, our clothing, the equipment bags that were on the racks on the side of our vehicles, the dirt floor in our command post. The rain had turned the desert floor into sticky clay that clung to boots, vehicles, and our morale. It certainly wasn't the "heat, dust, and sand" we'd expected. With the rain sloshing out of the wadis around us, it was more like a wet winter training week in Bavaria.

This mismatch between what we often expect and what we eventually get is a recurring theme in a soldier's life. Years ago, when I was a young lieutenant on my first trip to Germany's Grafenwöhr training area, I had one of my boots sucked off as I walked through the mud on a tank range; my company commander saw me attempting to pull it out while balancing on one foot to keep the sock on my other foot dry, and he yelled down from the range tower, "Embrace the suck, Lieutenant!" I didn't know it then, but the marines had their own more profane version of this expression, which is where my Vietnam veteran commander had first heard it. Even years later, when I commanded initial entry training as a three-star general, my drill sergeants loved shouting another mantra at the new recruits when they experienced downpours at Fort Jackson or Fort Benning: "If it ain't really raining, we ain't really training." Beneath the humor was the hard truth that soldiering is certainly an all-weather sport that's never played in a covered stadium.

As we played that sport in every kind of climate Mother Nature could throw at us, leaders and their soldiers experienced all sorts of uncomfortable situations. I've led troops wading through torrential rain at Fort Polk, Louisiana, where the red clay trails turned into deep brown rivers. I've seen soldiers endure winter REFORGER exercises or border patrols between East and West Germany, where the snow blew sideways. Once, when the heater in our tank failed—as they so often did during long field problems—we joined our infantry brothers around the tank exhaust just to thaw our hands. In Korea's mountains, where the kind of cold that seeps through every layer and makes even the simplest task feel like a test of will, I thought back to the soldiers who fought in that war at places like Chipyong-ni and wondered how they did it. Even at the National Training Center in California, I've watched the desert bake at ninety degrees at noon, then plummet to near freezing once the sun went down.

The weather doesn't care about the mission or a soldier's comfort. It doesn't wait for soldiers to be ready, and it isn't all that concerned as to whether we're happy and comfortable or not. And that's why leaders cannot allow the elements to become an excuse. Leaders don't get to moan about the mud or the cold if we expect our soldiers to push through it. Instead, leaders must keep their team focused, find small ways to lift spirits, and lead like the conditions don't matter—even when they do.

That day in January 1991 was less about the upcoming combat we would soon face and more about patience, discomfort, and mindset, just like all the other similar situations that we experience. On January 25, 1991, we were waiting for the order to move and fight. And until it came, our job was simple: Embrace the suck, keep each other going, and stay ready for whatever came next—rain, mud, or fire. But that was awfully hard to explain to our two young sons in that journal entry.

27 JAN 1991—Tactical Assembly Area Thompson

It's funny that we've been here in TAA (Tactical Assembly Area) Thompson (don't really know who named this place Thompson!) for almost a month now, and I haven't told you anything about it. We received a warning order to move today, so we'll likely be going to a Forward Assembly Area of an Attack Position somewhere closer to the Iraqi border, so I better describe TAA Thompson to you before we leave.

The TAA is near the towns of Hafar al-Batin (to the northwest of us, about 25 miles) and Qaisumah (to the north, 20 miles). The Trans Arabian Oil Pipeline and Tapline Road border the TAA to the north. To the west is King Khalid Military City, which is a gaudy, Disneyworld type city that houses an airfield and a major Saudi Arabian military base . . . I've been there twice. The TAA itself is probably about 30 km in circumference, and all the units of the 1 AD are spread throughout the area. There is a main circular tank trail, and a north-south/east-west main supply route. 1-1 Cavalry is located on the far west side, right off the main east-west MSR.

Our guys in 1-1 CAV are spread out over five different nodes within that small circle of ground. There is a node for A Troop, B Troop, the air troops of C/D/AVUM, or the two helicopter Troops and their aviation support and maintenance unit (which we call the trinity), which is closest to our Aviation Brigade headquarters, the field/combat/unit maintenance collection point and the supply trucks which we call the "trains," and the tactical operation center (TOC)—which is where I am.

The nodes are made up of tents, field sanitation areas, vehicle areas, defensive perimeters, and operation centers. You'll find it funny that we have latrines that we've built (and where our waste is collected in half of a 55 gallon drum that we've built wooden toilets over, and which has to be burned every day by details of soldiers who mix diesel fuel with the waste and then stir it), and what we call "piss tubes" that are basically pipes driven into the ground that gets rid of our urine.

We always have guards walking around each unit, and for the most part the NCO's keep the soldiers disciplined, clean and the living area in pretty good shape.

You can see for long distances because the ground is so flat—we can see A and B Troops clear as a bell and they are almost 1½ miles away to the west.

Every morning, we wake up at 4:30 for stand-to—an army tradition that goes to the belief that if the enemy is going to attack, they will do so before dawn—and all the leaders go to the TOC to receive a battle update from the night shift as to what went on the night before. Then, a few of us leave camp to go do our daily duties, while most of the Soldiers stay in the area to prepare, train, or conduct exercises.

There are details every day. As I said, we must burn our waste products (feces) and trash daily, so we don't cause diseases. Since we eat two C-Rations for two meals and receive only one hot meal a day, the Soldiers don't have to pull KP that often. There is maintenance of vehicles, posting of maps, planning, training, and conducting exercises. All of this makes for a full day. Luckily, so far, the days are going by quickly.

I miss you guys and my real home with you.

Love ya—

Dad

Reflection

When I reread that entry, I can see (and smell) the burn barrels and JP-8 fuel and feel the crusted dust in the creases of my eyelids. A tactical assembly area sounds clinical on paper, but in Desert Storm, it was a living organism: canvas tents and concertina wire; maps clipped to cargo straps inside our M577 vehicles and their extensions; a perimeter defined by machine guns, chem lights, and the shared understanding that this patch of desert was where we'd knit ourselves together before stepping off.

I remember the small quartering party that drove to that location on the very first day. The area had a wooden sign that said "1-1 Cav" to mark the location, and we had an order that outlined the approximate size of the location we should occupy as our troops continued to roll in from the airfield and ports in Saudi Arabia. This was the one key memory I had after I received direction from the brigade planner: "Follow the Tapline Road to the intersection of the main supply route, which is marked by a sign; go right and follow the MSR for about one mile until you get to two dead camels, make a right, and that's your piece of ground." The "two-dead-camel" intersection was the only terrain feature in that featureless desert, and sure enough, the carcasses of those two "ships of the desert" were exactly where I turned.

Back then, the process of occupying a TAA wasn't a suggestion—how to do it was in our doctrine, our squadron's SOP, and in our muscle memory. We had done this many times in Germany during REFORGER (Return of Forces to Germany) exercises, and we had done it most recently in our unit's rotation at the Hohenfels training area before we had even been alerted for Desert Shield, so we all knew how to do it. But in Europe, the TAAs were mostly hidden in the trees; here, we were in the wide-open desert, where there was no camouflage or concealment.

In army doctrine, a tactical assembly area is a temporary location where a unit assembles to prepare for future operations—to disperse, refuel, rehearse, issue orders, and move forward as one ready unit. It sits back from the forward edge of the battlefield, protected, deliberately organized, and designed for quick onward movement. You can find the definition in the training lexicon: It's where you close your ranks, check your kit, conduct pre-combat inspections (PCIs), and align the plan with the ground. In this directional playbook, an assault position is often mentioned in the lexicon as the last covered-and-concealed halt before you cross the line of departure and commit to contact—a final pocket of order right before the mess of combat begins. Those words may sound sterile, but they capture a rhythm that soldiers have known for generations: stage, step, strike.

In that January of 1991, TAA Thompson worked. The division massed, prepared, synchronized, and flowed. We did the things armies do before a mechanized fist swings: leaders reconned; crews maintained; medics checked aid bags; staff typed (on typewriters) the plans and orders that were then reproduced by an evil-smelling, hand-rotated, blue-line diazo printer (no computers, laser printers, or reproduction machines were in the field in 1991). We honed our processes, rehearsed, then rehearsed again. There was, to be frank, nothing else to do, and soldiers must always be kept busy. Then, when the orders came from on high, we moved as a whole.

It was interesting to experience the changes that occurred in our army—brought on by a lot of new technology—in the years right after Desert Storm. Everything we learned and everything that became available as we faced the enemy in the Balkans, then Afghanistan, then Iraq again, was on fast-forward, on double speed, like the center of gravity was continuously shifting under our boots.

Our doctrine was built for echelons; the war gave us networks.

For most of the Cold War, the 1st Armored Division's doctrine was AirLand Battle. We learned to think about our Soviet enemy coming at us in echelons: first, second, follow-on—what we described as the close, deep, and rear fights. Aviation and long-range rockets would attrit the enemy's deep echelons that were preparing to relieve the close forces, and the rear areas, that were providing logistical support to the Soviet hordes. All the while, our tank, infantry, artillery, and attack aviation battalions chewed up the front line in what we called the close fight. The plan was briefed to troops with arrows and phase lines; intelligence analysts counted the destruction of the enemy regiments, divisions, and second echelons as they were depleted; the fire support plan was a geometry problem addressed with steel, air force, and long-range attack helicopters. That doctrine—described in the 1980 editions of *Field Manual 100-5*—sharpened us for a very specific kind of war: defense of Western Europe. But in Desert Storm, we were now applying that doctrine—and the training we had conducted around it—to a different kind of maneuver in a very different kind of place against a very different kind of army, which was, at the time, the fourth largest in the world.

But even that early adaption changed with the 9/11 attacks and our retribution that would become known as the Global War on Terror, or GWOT.

When I once again joined the 1st Armored Division in Baghdad in 2003 as the assistant division commander for support, the battlefield didn't look anything like what we had become used to for years, either applied against the Soviets or the Iraqi Republican Guard. There were no echelons of T-72s rolling down a corridor for us to attrit "deep." Our G-2's walls weren't covered with Soviet order-of-battle overlays and range fans or the known locations of Republican Guard units like the Medina, Tawakalna, and Hammurabi divisions. They were instead stitched with butcher paper covered in webs of names, photos (if we had them), phone or courier networks, mosque locations, financier names, bomb-maker names, and descriptions of what were essentially independent street gangs who wore no uniforms. The enemy was a network, not a formation. General Dempsey, our division commander in the 1st Armored, applied what had been a cavalry mantra—"Every soldier is a scout; every soldier is a sensor"—to every single one of the thirty thousand troopers who were in our division. We were building intelligence from the ground up, fusing tips from patrols with HUMINT sources, SIGINT cuts, and a lot of hard-won pattern recognition. Dempsey had experience in Saudi Arabia, as he'd been stationed there to work with the Saudi Arabian National Guard right before he took command of the division, so he was steeped in Arab culture and language, which gave us an advantage. But it still was a fascinating, and sometimes painful, mental pivot. The TAA model—stage, step, strike—gave way to a city-wide lifeguard rotation: Pick a place to live among the combatants, protect yourself, get out among the population, realize you're never off duty or "in the rear," absorb information, gather intelligence, put together snippets of information, and constantly adjust.

That shift changed how—and where—we lived.

While we used "staging" during Desert Storm, in later wars, during rotation of forces, we just "fell in" on what the previous unit had developed, initiating the left-seat/right-seat process, and took over as the unit that had been there departed. In this new era, units replaced one another in a multiyear counterinsurgency. Unlike the years our army fought in Vietnam, when individual replacement soldiers joined units that had been in country for years, the GWOT saw units deploying together and replacing other units that had been there twelve, sometimes fifteen months.

During Desert Storm, we built Tactical Assembly Area Thompson out of nothing. In 2003–2004, the 1st Armored Division, after their attack north through Iraq, found the most convenient place to institute a base using available buildings in the largest city in Iraq after a long attack through the southern part of the country and set up shop. Then, in 2007–2008, the 1st Armored took over those same types of base camps, forward operating bases, and patrol bases that had been established in northern Iraq by the division that had been there for twelve months before we arrived and had replaced the unit that had been there before them.

In September 2007, we mostly fell in on places other units had already built. The army formalized these relief-in-place/transfer-of-authority (or RIP/TOAs, as they would be called) as a left-seat/right-seat process: The incoming unit rode with the outgoing for seven days, watching, seeing the ground, learning about the enemy, and taking lessons from the unit that had been there. Then, after seven days, the roles were reversed; the new unit took charge while the outgoing unit watched, correcting mistakes and reinforcing information. Finally, the new unit took the keys and the old unit redeployed home. It was efficient and—let's be honest—lifesaving. You learned the routes that were "hot," the neighborhoods where people would smile at you and the ones where the local men would give you the "stink-eye" and plant improvised explosive devices (IEDs) along your route of travel. You learned which sheikhs, local political leaders, and even imams you could trust and which ones you couldn't. The army's Center for Lessons Learned (CALL) was working overtime in publishing observations and so-called lessons learned, and units were learning those and practicing them at training centers before they deployed.

But there was a cost. Over time, we stopped practicing the expeditionary skills that had built TAA Thompson from bare desert: establishing a TAA or an assault position from scratch, planning field sanitation and bulk fuel processes from zero, instituting an efficient flow of supplies and logistics, creating an air medevac point and an ammo transfer holding area with nothing but engineer tape and sweat. Our soldiers who'd served most of their time in the GWOT knew how to occupy an established FOB or COP, how to sign for a containerized housing unit (CHU), and where the morale, welfare, and recreation (MWR) tent was; fewer knew how to site a perimeter on a barren hillside or lay out a dispersed laager by doctrinal diagram. We had traded some expeditionary muscle memory for rotational efficiency. In fact, even our lexicon had shifted: FOB—forward operating base—became the default noun for "home," and COP—combat outpost—was now the small node that pushed security into a neighborhood. Patrol bases were truly the austere exceptions.

In 2003–2004, the division headquarters sat at Baghdad International Airport (BIAP). Brigades were scattered like thumbtacks on a city map—one in a former palace near the Green Zone, another in the husk of an amusement park in northeast Baghdad, another near Abu Ghraib. The division support command (DISCOM) and my ADC-S team started at a place we called Muleskinner on the outskirts and later moved into old Iraqi Army barracks on the south side of BIAP, across the runway from division headquarters.

But there were still some sporty moments. One morning, just after first light, as my team was in an HMMWV driving from our living areas to the division headquarters for a battle update, we watched a civilian airbus taking off from the runway that was near our base camp and headquarters. Suddenly, a comet tail of flame stretched across the sky and hit that slow-moving commercial aircraft. A terrorist-launched, surface-to-air missile from outside our perimeter had struck that DHL cargo plane as it took off. The crew somehow got that crippled bird back on the ground, but having seen the attack, we reported what we'd seen when we arrived at the 1AD TOC, and everyone in the operation center stood still for a beat. Another reminder that our division headquarters, a place that had once been closer to the "rear areas" than to the front, wasn't at all safe in an urban insurgency.

The places we lived were as eclectic as the fight. FOBs ranging from city compounds to converted bases. COPs tucked into alleyways or inside police stations. Patrol bases that were truly spartan. We tried to make them safer, smarter, and—when we could—more livable. The army's base camp doctrine matured; the engineers and sustainers learned how to run water, power, waste, and force protection like a small city. We brought in CHUs because they could be shipped, stacked, wired, and even air-conditioned. We built dining facilities (we called them DFACs) that could serve a brigade and small PXs that could sell you a pair of socks, a phone card, and more. In Afghanistan, there was even a debate about whether fast-food concessions belonged on big bases—General McChrystal famously told some of them to pack it up so lines of effort could prioritize supply lines for warfighting needs. All of it was part of the pendulum swing between expeditionary and enduring.

By 2007–2008, as the division commander during the surge, I watched this at scale. Our headquarters at Camp Speicher near Tikrit was a near-perfect division HQ platform—runways, helipads outside the CP, comms, a defensible perimeter, and space to stage many forces. But most of Task Force Iron's thirty thousand soldiers lived and fought on more than thirty different bases, from Baghdad up to Mosul and Tal Afar, east to Kirkuk, and west toward Samarra. Some were mature FOBs with CHUs, T-walls, and established life support. Others were COPs with HESCO barriers, plywood, and a place to store boxes of Meals Ready to Eat. In visiting our marine contingent, who were manning a critical communication node on top of Mount Sinjar, on Thanksgiving Day, I marveled at how they made their own gym using tank parts for weights and how they were delighted to just get a marmite can of turkey and a case of near beer on that holiday.

My battle rhythm in Baghdad in 2003–2004 was driving in a convoy of three HMMWVs to different parts of the city and our various forward operating bases. I'd get updates on units and what they were experiencing, finding ways to support them with equipment, parts, fuel, and ammo and sometimes going on mechanized patrols with their younger soldiers. Later, in 2007–2008, I flew to the different outposts and bases that were scattered all over the northern part of Iraq, leaving from our headquarters at Camp Speicher in Tikrit and roaming an area that was larger than the state of Pennsylvania. That steady, daily diet of what we called "battlefield circulation" included many things: getting updates from commanders I'd never served with before (the downside of what the army was experimenting with the "plug-and-play division" concept tested during the surge), patrolling neighborhoods with lieutenants and their small units, watching young leaders engage with imam and local sheikhs, looking into the eyes of both our soldiers and the Iraqi military-aged males who watched us as we patrolled the streets, and learning about the kinetic fights the US soldiers were experiencing at their level. In 1991, I could walk across the TAA and find every brigade commander I needed to talk to. In 2007, I was on a helicopter day and night to do the same thing across a battlespace about the size of the Keystone State.

It was doable. It was necessary. But it changed the way we built teams and the way we taught the army to communicate, move, and fight.

Emerging doctrine is useful precisely because it gives you a starting point for all this. The TAA and assault position are still there in the glossary and in the collective memory—staging points with roles, layouts, and controls. FOB is now there as a term of art for a forward operations base. The patrol base is still the austere, tactical overnight spot, as it always has been. Those are the bones.

But the last two decades forced us to learn a second language. We learned relief in place/transfer of authority (RIP/TOA) for an area of operation with left-seat/right-seat rides (one unit welcoming an incoming unit by providing them advice, then watching them conduct operations to ensure they get it right) because the war didn't pause for exchanges of personnel and equipment. We learned to fall in—to inventory what the last unit had left, keep what worked, fix what didn't, and continue moving. Those CALL handbooks were right: Our processes saved time, lives, and momentum. Over time, though, we would soon need to be intentional about reteaching the expeditionary basics: how to pick ground, build from scratch, and depart with nothing but footprints.

When I commanded US Army Europe in 2012, I saw how much we had lost during a training mission we planned in Europe for the 173rd Airborne Infantry Brigade that was stationed in Italy.

The 173rd's training mission was to seize an airfield (at Grafenwöhr Training Area) and operate from it. Tactically, they were sharp—no surprise for these airborne sky soldiers. But years of falling in on established bases had dulled the instinct to plan the unsexy parts: arranging fuel bladders and water points, caring for waste management, laying wire, emplacing aid stations and standby medevac pads, building forward arming and refueling points.

In talking with their terrific commander during the first after-action review, he admitted his and his staff's shortsightedness in planning. He told me that his S4, after being caught short on some class of supply, had reported that he was going into the garrison of the training center to requisition needed equipment; he'd quickly learned the garrison supply center was off limits to training units. The commander also told me their operation section hadn't thought to bring paper for generating and passing orders, expecting it would be waiting for them on the ground as part of a transfer, like they had experienced in their many tours of Afghanistan.

None of this was negligence; it was an ingrained new culture. We had to retrain the muscle associated with those skills across the force—at Hohenfels, Grafenwöhr, the National Training Center in California, and the Joint Readiness Training Center in Louisiana.

The places we lived shaped the leaders we became. And we had to change some of that.

Back to Saudi Arabia in 1991. TAA Thompson was primitive and pure: sleeping on the ground and later on army cots, burning the waste, eating a single hot meal every other day and a whole bunch of MREs. There was a map board with an acetate covering that picked up more dust each night to the point you almost couldn't see through the plastic overlay.

In 2003, the division headquarters at Baghdad International Airport (BIAP) and our logistics base, "Muleskinner," outside of Baghdad taught me that "the rear area" is a myth and that an IED along a route, a missile streak tracing the sky over your morning coffee, or an incoming insurgent rocket would make you—at first—run to the bunkers. But as we became used to them, these new ways of combat made us realize that if it was our day to go, the rocket would find us . . . and there was nothing we could do about it.

In 2007, Camp Speicher taught me how to run a division from an established operating base, but that platform had myriad spokes reaching out to trusted commanders in seven different provinces.

Each one had different threats, dynamics, successes, and operational requirements.

And if I had to explain to someone who's never worn boots, I'd say this:

- The TAA is where a unit becomes a single mind before a big punch.
- The assault position is the last breath before you throw it.
- An FOB is an enduring foothold; a COP is the forward knuckle. They face all kinds of different challenges.
- A patrol base is a foxhole with friends.
- RIP/TOA and left-seat/right-seat rides are how you keep momentum when the team changes at halftime.
- CHUs and creature comforts don't win wars, but they keep people human enough to keep fighting.
- And no matter how good your "finders"—sensors, feeds, blue-force trackers, drones—are, you still must teach people to decide, to coordinate, to lead under pressure.

That day in January '91, I was living the doctrine the way it had been written for past generations. In the decades after, I watched—and tried to help—the army rewrite parts of it in real time. If there's one thread through all of it, it's this: The place you stage shapes how you fight. And the way you live together before the first round is fired has everything to do with whether you can live together after.

2 FEB 1991—The Bombing

I'm gonna buy all the Air Force guys I ever see in a bar a drink. Over the last few weeks—since Jan 17—the pilots have been taking it to the Iraqi fighting positions. The more damage they do in this close air support, interdiction, and operational bombing campaign, the less work we will have to do when we cross the border.

One of these Air Force types, a CPT Yamamoto, writes a daily intelligence summary (we call it INTSUM) that he calls the "Yam's Gram." This daily message provides, with a little bit of humor, the daily targets for all the Air Force bombers/fighters that are going into Iraq/Kuwait. Reading this report is often the highlight of my day.

Yam normally begins his INTSUM by talking about what the BUFFS (B-52s) are doing. For the most part, these bombers have been hitting the Republican Guards Divisions (Tawakalna, Hammurabi, Medina, 10th, 16th, 17th Armored Divisions). They normally drop cluster bombs and big (750–2000 lb.) iron bombs. As a "ground" Soldier, I know I wouldn't want those things continuously pounding me daily. It not only affects the units in terms of casualties, but it also deprives them of sleep and makes them realize they are helpless in fighting back. One trick they use is to drop leaflets telling the Iraqis to surrender and come across the border or the next thing that will reach them will be a large bomb dropped right in their face. Then, the next day, the Air Force follows through with some positive reinforcement on the same people they dropped the leaflets on. The day after they bomb, they drop more leaflets saying "see, we told you we'd be back." They repeat the same process throughout the theater.

Yam then talks about what the other fighters/bombers (F-16, F-15, F-111) are doing in the theater that day. The mission number for these types of aircraft daily usually runs into the hundreds. It is unimaginable for me to understand how they can put so many fighters into the air in one day. It is also unimaginable that Hussein allows his Soldiers and his entire Army to be destroyed.

Yam calls the F-117 Stealth aircraft the "cockroach." Usually, he only talks about their missions after they have completed them. They evidently own the sky over Baghdad and Kuwait.

He then discusses what the "Hogs" (Warthog, A-10, air-to-mud) guys are doing. These are the aircraft that are the main tank/artillery killers, and the ones that we'll depend upon most when we kick off into combat. Today, for example, 158 A-10's will fly in southern Iraq, arbitrarily knocking out tank and artillery positions. These are the same positions we would have to fight if they didn't get them first.

Thankfully, we haven't lost very many pilots yet. Considering the massive number of sorties (over 24,000 so far) we have had relatively few (12) losses thus far. I pray every day for these guys, and I hope they continue with their success.

There is a massive wind/sandstorm today, so I'm not sure many aircraft will be out. It's unfortunate this Sunday, the day of the Lord, to say this, but I hope the weather gets better.

God, please help this killing to stop.

I love you boys—

Dad

Reflection

The "Yam's Gram" was one of those little treasures of the Gulf War—daily packets of insight from a young air force captain who had a knack for combining operational detail with just enough humor to make it readable. What I didn't realize at the time was how valuable that kind of communication was for soldiers on the ground. Yam wasn't just telling us where the bombs were falling—he was translating the air tasking order (ATO) into something we could visualize, something that connected the dots between what the air force was doing overhead and how it would shape our fight when the ground war began.

The ATO is the air force's equivalent of the army's operations order. It's the daily plan for every aircraft in the theater: who's flying, where, with what ordnance, on what mission, and at what time. It's an extraordinary feat of coordination, and during Desert Storm, it was the backbone of the air campaign. It could also be inflexible. Ground commanders sometimes chafed when they needed to adapt to changing conditions, and the ATO couldn't—or wouldn't—shift quickly. But in January and February 1991, we were in awe of its scale and precision.

We'd studied air power theory back at Leavenworth and in SAMS. I'd read about the great campaigns: The Doolittle Raid of April 1942, a daring strike on Tokyo after Pearl Harbor, when army air corps bombers took off—for the first time—from a navy aircraft carrier. Militarily minor but strategically powerful in lifting American spirits and shaking Japanese confidence. The Schweinfurt–Regensburg Raids of 1943 that targeted German ball bearing factories inflicted heavy damage but at a huge cost in B-17 crews and aircraft, which showed both the potential and the vulnerability of unescorted strategic bombing. The controversial fire-bombing of Dresden in 1945, intended to disrupt German logistics and morale, was remembered as much for the civilian toll as for military impact. And, of course, Operation Linebacker I and Operation Linebacker II in Vietnam in 1972 were the heaviest use of air power in the Vietnam War, aimed at bringing North Vietnam to the table. Linebacker II's eleven days of concentrated bombing helped push Hanoi toward agreement—but at significant cost. Each taught its own lesson: Air power could shape the battlefield, break supply lines, and influence enemy decision-making—but rarely alone.

Desert Storm's air planning cell believed this campaign might be different and sold their thoughts to General Schwarzkopf. Precision-guided munitions, stealth technology, and the sheer volume of sorties created effects we'd never seen before. From my tent in the desert, with

Yam's Gram in hand, I looked up day and night to see the streaks of aircraft heading north, making it seem like air power might deliver on its most ambitious promises.

Years later, as the assistant division commander for support in Baghdad (2003–2004), I saw a more intimate form of air-ground integration in the closer coordination of air and ground forces and the transformation of the joint terminal attack controllers. These JTACs, embedded with smaller tactical army units, could call in strikes within minutes, with a speed and accuracy that was unimaginable in 1991. By the time I later commanded the 1st Armored Division in 2007–2008, the precision and responsiveness had only improved—but so had competition for air assets.

That's when I remembered something Marty Dempsey had taught me back in '03: If you gave your ground operation a strong name, corps air planners would take notice. A "named operation" seemed to carry more weight than a generic engagement. As MND-North commander, I put that to work—Iron Hammer, Iron Strike, Iron Resolve. The results? More aircraft were assigned to support our fight. Of course, by then, other division commanders had caught on, and the naming game was in full swing across Iraq.

At the National Training Center, I watched our observer/controller "Eagle Team" at Nellis Air Base evaluate how well brigades planned and executed synchronized air operations, and my time and experiences in the deserts of California provided me more respect for my air force brothers and sisters when I served with them on the Joint Staff in DC.

It was at the NTC that I got one of the most memorable invitations and hands-on experiences of my career. The lieutenant colonel in charge of our Eagle Team—the separate team of airmen who coordinated our aircraft at Nellis and would later provide after-action reviews to the training units—asked me during one of our down days, "Would you like to fly in one of our two-seat F-16s during a training mission over Fort Irwin? It'll give you a better feel for the pilot's perspective of what's happening on the ground." Of course, I said yes.

On the day of the mission, I drove to Nellis early for a few hours of training on wearing a G suit, breathing techniques for high-G maneuvers, and what to do if I had to eject. When I asked the pilot who would fly me on the mission what I should eat as we broke for lunch before the flight, he said, "Bananas."

"Why bananas?" I asked

"Because, Colonel, they taste the same coming up as they do going down."

I realized this was going to be more of an adventure than I had bargained for.

On the flight to the training area, the young captain let me take the stick. I learned quickly that small hand movements created radical changes—fine motor skills were essential if you didn't want to find yourself in a dive or drifting into the flight path of your wingman. Once over the training grounds of the NTC, he took control and asked if I was ready for maneuvers. Before I could answer, he pulled us into a six-G dive. I wasn't breathing the way I'd been taught, and within seconds, I blacked out—only for a moment—before waking up in yet another dive.

After a few cycles of passing out, coming to, and feeling increasingly sick, I held on for what felt like the world's most extreme roller coaster. When we finally landed, I was exhausted from both the maneuvers and the constant pressure of the G suit. As I climbed down the ladder, the captain grinned and said, "Sir, I proudly present your air force call sign! It's nothing like 'Maverick' as you had probably hoped—it's 'Three-Bags.'" That was the number of air sickness bags I'd filled, and it would become my enduring legacy with my air force friends.

My respect for the air force—their effectiveness, professionalism, training, and sense of humor—only grew. That was especially true during my final assignment in Europe, when I had the pleasure of working with General Mark Welsh, who was my counterpart as service commander of the US Air Force in Europe. Every six months, we brought our staffs together—army and air force—to find new ways to train and operate jointly. Those sessions built a level of trust that mattered, and when Mark became chief of staff of the air force, I knew his character and that same spirit of cooperation would shape the whole service.

The air force itself evolved after I left the army. In 2019, part of it became the US Space Force—a separate service for the domain where satellites, GPS, missile warning, and space-based intelligence all converge. It's a recognition that the next big joint fight will depend not just on air superiority but on space superiority too.

And yet, some things haven't changed. Every fall, Army plays Air Force in football, and for those few hours, much like it is when Army plays Navy, we're mortal enemies. The other 363 days of the year, we're partners—relying on each other in ways that matter far more than a scoreboard.

Looking back, the "Yam's Gram" was more than a clever name on an intel sheet. It was my first real window into the complexity, precision, and reach of modern air power—and the start of a four-decade respect for the men and women in blue who take the fight to the enemy from above. The motto of the air force is "Aim High!" I think it should be, from our enemies' perspective, "Don't Make Me Come Down There!"

6 FEB 1991—Rehearsal, Movement to Contact

Very long day yesterday. Woke up at 0300 to put together a road march of over 20 miles for all the Squadron's vehicles so we could practice a movement to contact with the 1st Brigade. We went to a training area on the eastern side of TAA Thompson, and probably for the first time in recent history assisted in practicing a brigade-level attack with the cavalry squadron out front. It was an awesome display of combat power. Bradleys, tanks, artillery pieces, supply trucks—over 1,500 vehicles spread over 20 x 16 kilometers to replicate an attacking brigade. The Squadron had a big piece of the action—our helicopters were all up attempting to find the "enemy" (in this case, a couple of Hummers and some M113s in the expanse of desert we were playing in), and our guys were very successful in finding the enemy and assisting an infantry battalion from 1st Brigade as they actioned on the bad guys.

This was a rehearsal for combat. After viewing the speed and capabilities presented by the Brigade, I would not have wanted to be the enemy. I hope he feels the same way when he sees us coming—it would be easier on both of us if he were to just surrender.

Love,

Dad

And . . .

17 FEB 1991—Movement Rehearsal to FAA Garcia and Occupation

Well, as you can tell I haven't had time to write in your journal for the past ten days. Lots of things going on, but most importantly we moved yesterday from TAA Thompson to FAA (Forward Assembly Area) Garcia, about 15 kilometers (about 9.32 mi) from the Iraqi border. On the 15th of Feb, Saddam Hussein did a "head fake" by implying to the world that he may pull out of Kuwait. He did that, we believe, because he detected our VII Corps movement and felt we were about to attack, and he wanted to cause us a stutter step to delay the attack. He came out at the end of the day, tying the peace initiative to other things (President Bush calls it linkage) and it was obvious to everyone that it was just a ploy. We continue toward a ground war (or G-Day), which many believe will be on 21 Feb. I'll be sure to let you know!

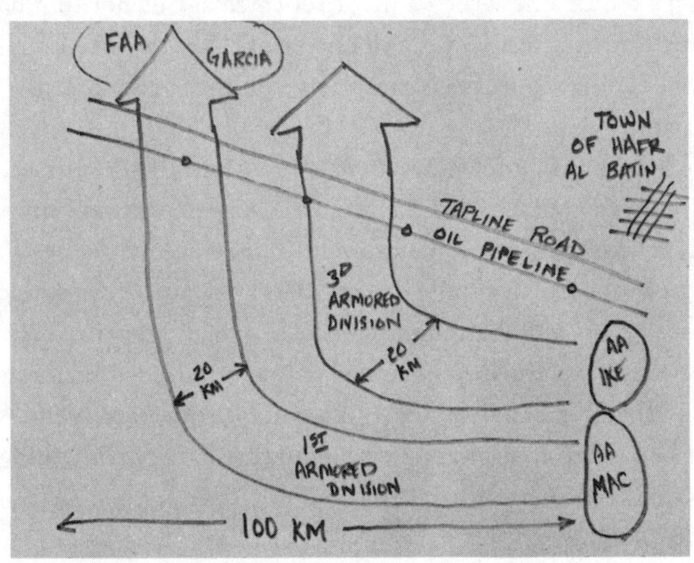

The movement here was extremely exciting. 2 Divisions (us—1st Armored Division—and Uncle Marty's [Dempsey's]—3rd Armored Division) along with 2nd Armored Cavalry Regiment conducted a practice move with over 20,000 tracked and wheeled vehicles. Something like that had not been conducted since WWII.

The Blackhawk squadron led the way for 1AD, and I think we did a very good job.

The plan is bold; it was a little exciting and awe inspiring. We're in a new place, and I'll write more later.

Love ya,

Dad

Reflection

When I look back at those two journal entries from two days in February 1991, I realize they were the first times I saw some truly astonishing events. I had been in rehearsals before—many of them—at every echelon, from a platoon clearing a building to a brigade commander walking his team through an ROC drill on a taped-out map in a dusty tent. I knew the value of rehearsals. But nothing had prepared me for the scale, scope, and power of these two events. The first was large enough to impress me; the second was so massive it defied comparison.

On February 6, a few days after we received the order to rehearse a movement to contact with the armored brigade we were supporting, I understood it would be a major event. I knew we would be out front, our cavalry squadron leading Colonel Riley's brigade, locating and fixing the enemy so his tank battalions could dash in and destroy them when we gave them the word. I imagined a few hundred vehicles at most, some simulated enemy contact, and a solid day of hard work. What I did not know was that our exercise would be part of something much bigger—an eventual rehearsal that would connect to a division-wide training effort. And that effort itself would be nested into something larger still: the VII Corps rehearsal overseen by General Fred Franks, a man whose approach to preparation was as deliberate and meticulous as any commander I had ever known.

General Franks wasn't just another corps commander. Before taking command of VII Corps, he had led the 1st Armored Division, where I had served as his chief of operations. He was quiet but unshakably confident, a man who had lost a leg in Vietnam but never lost his stride. A master tactician and operational artist, he believed in deep preparation—not just in knowing the plan but in making sure the plan could be executed when the enemy inevitably did something unexpected. He would later design, plan, and lead the "left hook" that broke the back of the Iraqi Republican Guard during Desert Storm. But during those rehearsals, what I saw was a conductor with a symphony of armored formations at his fingertips, determined to make sure every section knew its part and how it fit into the whole.

Our own part was clear: Lead the advance guard twenty kilometers ahead of the brigade, find the enemy, and set conditions for their destruction. That meant our two ground cavalry troops—Alpha and Bravo—were spread across the desert with their Bradleys at three-hundred-to-four-hundred-meter intervals, and our two air cavalry troops—Charlie and Delta—with Kiowa scouts and Cobra gunships overhead, were looking far out. The squadron commander and his crew, the air liaison officer and fire support officer and their team, and my crew and I were all in a small tactical command post in the center of the formation, controlling the maneuver. Behind us was our main tactical operations center, then our squadron's logistical tail—a lifeline of fuel, ammunition, and recovery assets that had to keep up without slowing the formation.

Even during that first rehearsal, some challenges we hadn't considered revealed themselves quickly. Communications, for example, looked good on the planning chart but were strained during the movement. Distances that seemed trivial during a map exercise now stretched our radios to the edge of their range. We found ourselves able to talk to division headquarters but not brigade, and vice versa. Sometimes our air troops could hear us, but our ground troops could not. That's when our operations sergeant, SFC Tim Bretl, improvised a solution: He lashed a forty-foot camouflage pole to our antenna, mounted it on top of an M577 command post vehicle, and secured it with guide wires. It swayed like a fishing pole in the wind, but it worked—and it would work later in combat.

We also practiced the forward passage of lines—one of the most dangerous maneuvers in armored warfare. When we fixed the enemy in place, the follow-on brigade's tank battalions would race forward through our positions to deliver the killing blow. It required precise timing, coordination, and nerve. In daylight and under fire, the risk of confusion or fratricide was always there. The rehearsal allowed us to refine our visual signals, radio calls, coordination, and positioning. And we needed that refinement—because when we did it for real weeks later, one of Riley's tank crews, seeing a "hot spot" through thermal sights, nearly fired on one of our recovery vehicles. Only bad aim and sheer luck prevented tragedy.

Logistics was another focus. Refuel/rearm on the move (R-ROM) is one of those operations that sounds easy until you try it. In theory, vehicles peel off to a resupply point, top off fuel and ammunition, and rejoin the line without slowing the advance. In practice, it's like trying to gas up and reload a NASCAR while the race is still underway. Every second counts. Every delay can ripple back and stall the formation. We rehearsed it until we could do it smoothly because we knew the advance into Iraq would cover hundreds of kilometers and likely involve multiple engagements, so we would need a sturdy supply and fuel chain.

Those were the lessons of the first rehearsal. The second rehearsal—the movement to FAA Garcia on February 17—magnified everything. Now, we were not just part of a brigade exercise, or even a division exercise. We were part of a corps maneuver involving two full armored divisions, a corps cavalry regiment, and thousands upon thousands of vehicles. From horizon to horizon, the desert was filled with armor, artillery, logistics trains, and aviation assets. It was the largest mounted movement I had ever seen, and something that, in scale and coordination, had not been attempted since the Second World War.

That second rehearsal set the conditions for movement to forward areas. In army doctrine, a forward assembly area—or FAA—is more than just a parking lot for combat units. It is the final staging ground before the attack, the place where units complete last-minute preparations, refit, redistribute ammunition and supplies, conduct final briefings, and ensure every soldier and vehicle is ready to cross the line of departure. It is also a place of deception and security: concealed from enemy observation—which was difficult to achieve in the open desert—defended against attack, and designed to allow the force to launch on short notice. In many ways, the FAA was the place to coil the spring before it was released.

After the long maneuver rehearsal, when we reached FAA Garcia, we could feel that tension. Everyone knew that once we left the FAA, the next stop was combat. The rehearsals were about building confidence and ironing out flaws. Now, we were in the place where the final adjustments would be made before the real thing. You could sense it in the way soldiers moved, in the way commanders walked their lines, in the way maintenance checks and rechecks were conducted, in the way conversations shifted from "if" to "when."

Those two rehearsals—and the movement into the FAA—taught me more than any ROC drill or map exercise ever could. They showed me the value of finding problems before the enemy found them for you. They proved that no plan survives contact without adaptation and that rehearsals are where you learn how to adapt.

Years later, when I commanded the operations group at the National Training Center, I saw brigade after brigade go through their own rehearsals. Some treated them as vital, make-or-break events. Others treated them as a box to check. That assignment was, in many ways, the place where I earned a warfighting PhD. I could see instantly which commanders were serious about preparing their formations and which were bluffing themselves. And when I became a division commander, I knew exactly when to trust a subordinate's plan and when to send them back to the rehearsal field.

Because the truth is this: Rehearsals are not just for the military. I have seen the same principles apply in medicine, when doctors walk through how they will run an operating room during a hurricane. I have seen it in business, when CEOs rehearse their strategies for a tense board meeting. I have seen it in the classroom, when MBA teams that rehearse deliver with confidence and those that don't falter. In every field, rehearsals are the bridge between planning and execution, the place where theory meets reality.

And as we settled into FAA Garcia that evening in February 1991, I knew reality was about to arrive. The war was coming, and when it did, the enemy would get a vote. The rehearsals we had conducted were how we made sure we were ready to cast ours.

18 FEB 1991—The Berm

Linked up with a MAJ MacGregor, S3 of 2nd Squadron, at the 2nd ACR command post today. 2-2 Cav will be the unit directly to our front during the first 10 kilometers of the move toward Objective Python, which is our first day's objective inside Iraq. After talking to my old SAMs Director, COL Holder, for a short period of time, Major MacGregor and I did a reconnaissance together of the area from the 2ACR's Forward Assembly Area to the Saudi Arabia-Iraqi berm. It was an interesting ride, and it was remarkable to realize I was the first member of the 1st Armored Division to go this far north.

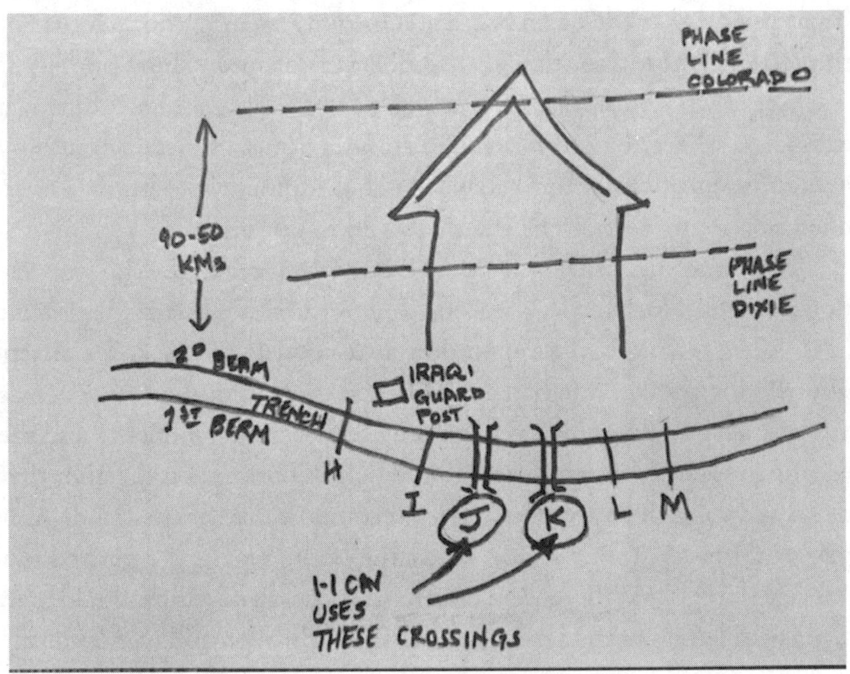

The land was marked by plateaus and escarpments as we drove across the desert and was free of any form of life. Even the Bedouins were nowhere to be seen. I guess they are leaving the area due to fear of the war that will soon take place in the area.

Our two HMWWVs traveled north to about 1 kilometer from the border, then we got our binos and looked at the berm, which is the man-made boundary between the countries of Iraq and Saudi Arabia. The berm was about 12-15 feet high, with another berm just on the other side of it. This will be where engineers will make the cuts so all the combat vehicles will be able to roll through. It's so peaceful now; in a few days, it will be filled with all types of machinery, which will be used for killing.

Thinking of you guys,

Dad

Reflection

That quiet day at the berm is burned into my memory not because of the action—there wasn't much, just observation and a short ride—but because of what it represented. It was one of those moments during a campaign where the ground you're standing on will mean something very different in a matter of days. At that moment, the berm was an obstacle. Soon, it would be the threshold to our attack.

That morning, I met with MAJ Doug MacGregor, the S3—operations officer—for 2nd Squadron, 2nd Armored Cavalry Regiment (2-2 ACR). Doug had a reputation as a good tactician and a sharp, unorthodox thinker. He had a confidence about him that came across as brusque, but it was rooted in a deep understanding of tactics and the way he thought armored forces should fight. Our mission together that day was straightforward: Conduct a reconnaissance of the Saudi Arabia-Iraqi border in our sector, study the berm, ensure we plotted our passage points (and there were dozens of those, all of which would have signs with letters of the alphabet), and think through and communicate how the breach would unfold when the ground war began. Because 1-1 Cav would follow behind 2-2 Cav on the same breach points, we wanted to ensure there was no bunching up at the narrow crossing points.

The 2nd ACR was a very different animal from my own 1st Squadron, 1st Cavalry. As I've mentioned, a divisional cavalry squadron like ours had two ground troops of Bradley Fighting Vehicles, two air troops with Vietnam-era AH-1 Cobras and OH-58 Kiowas, and a small but necessary headquarters and logistics elements. We were optimized for reconnaissance and security in support of our division; we were not built for slugging it out. The 2nd ACR, the corps' cavalry, by contrast, was built for independent, sustained combat. Each of its three ground squadrons had tank platoons embedded directly in their cavalry troops, giving them an armored punch in every element. Each squadron also had a pure tank company for concentrated shock power. And the aviation squadron was reinforced and robust, with the brand-new AH-64 Apaches—each bristling with Hellfire missiles and a 30mm chain gun—plus an impressive number of scout helicopters. They were a reconnaissance force, but they could also hit like a sledgehammer. They also had a huge support squadron to care for all their ground and air assets. 2nd ACR had about ten times the number of soldiers we had in our Blackhawks. They were, in effect, a small division.

This difference in organization mattered. In the coming fight, 2nd ACR would be the spearhead and the eyes of VII Corps, and their reporting and action would drive General Franks's decision-making as to how he would maneuver the divisions against the Iraqi Republican Guard. Our divisional squadron would be tucked in behind the 2-2 Cav for the first ten to fifteen kilometers, using their lead to open our own route toward Objective Python. When they peeled away to continue the corps' deep thrust, we would diverge into our own fight toward a more northeasterly approach. That meant our timelines, communications, and situational awareness had to be tied together seamlessly for the opening phase—and that's where Lieutenant Mike Rodriguez came in.

Mike was our squadron chemical officer. Tall, lean, stoic, and with clean-cut good looks, he had been trained to prepare the unit for chemical, biological, or radiological threats. But that morning, I handed him a very different mission: Pack your stuff and come with me because you're going to be our liaison officer to the 2nd ACR headquarters. His task was to plant himself in their TOC, keep a secure radio link open to us, and send timely, concise reports on location, movements, and any enemy contact. LNO work requires a mix of patience, tactical acumen, and interpersonal skills—you're a guest in someone else's house, but you're there for your own boss. Mike did it superbly. He stayed with them through the breach, tracked their movements with precision, and rejoined us exactly when I needed him in the open desert.

The LNO role is one of those things civilians rarely see in military history, but it's a quiet linchpin of large-scale operations. When you're coordinating the movement of thousands of vehicles across hundreds of kilometers, with multiple formations converging on a single point of breakthrough, there is no substitute for a set of human eyes and ears on the other headquarters' floor. It's the difference between "we think they're here" and "I just watched their lead company turn left at this location."

Mike came with me for the recon when Doug and I drove north through terrain that was all muted tans and browns, the sky pale and empty. The land was broken by occasional small desert escarpments and low plateaus that led to wadis—nothing dramatic, not flat like we had experienced so far, and enough to mask movement in places. What struck me most was the absence of life. Not a single Bedouin tent, no herds, no dogs trotting after trucks. It was as if the land itself had held its breath, anticipating our invasion.

The berm loomed across the horizon as we approached, a man-made ridge of earth, maybe twelve to fifteen feet high, stretching beyond the horizon in both directions. On the Iraqi side was a parallel berm, forming a narrow trough between them. We later learned that in the 1st Infantry Division's sector of attack, the ravine between the berms would be filled with diesel and set on fire. 1st ID soldiers smartly let it burn off before crossing. But in our area, there was no defense. Guard towers were spaced at regular intervals, but there were no guards. We couldn't see any indications of minefields on either side of the border. And there were no tank ditches, but even if there were, the plows that would break down the berms would fill them up. All this could mean the Iraqis had pulled back to stronger defensive positions, that they were setting the stage for something we hadn't anticipated, or they just didn't expect us to be this far west. No matter, the berms would need to be breached and then traversed with speed, coordination, and a clear plan for what came after.

Breaching, at the corps and division level, is one of the most choreographed forms of combat. It's not just a matter of cutting a hole in an obstacle. The breach must be secured, kept open, and fed with a constant flow of combat power without creating a traffic jam that strands forces in a kill zone that any good enemy would emplace behind an obstacle. Engineers lead the way—dozers, mine plows, and explosive line charges fired from what the army calls a "MICLIC"—and artillery suppresses any enemy who can fire on the breach site with both smoke and artillery. Once lanes are cleared and marked, the assault forces—that would be us—surge through, fanning out into their designated sectors to counter any hasty enemy defense. It's an operation where knowledge of the terrain is imperative, understanding of the enemy you're up against is critical, and timing is everything. Lose momentum, and you risk turning the breach into a choke point that invites artillery, air strikes, or a counterattack. A killing zone.

Our reconnaissance that day was part of shaping where and how we would breach. "Shaping," in military terms, means creating conditions for the decisive operation to succeed. Sometimes it's about positioning forces. Sometimes it's about degrading the enemy's ability to fight and blinding their observation through smoke and high explosives. Sometimes it's about gaining information that will let you make decisions at speed once the shooting starts. That morning, it was about understanding the ground, the routes, the visibility, and the gaps in our communications because the enemy didn't seem to be present. We were even so bold (and stupid) that we both drove all the way up to the berm, climbed the mountain of dirt, and investigated Iraq. There was nothing we could see.

I've carried the idea of shaping into every leadership role I've held since. When I worked with Ukrainian forces in the years after 2008, shaping meant building their capacity before a crisis—joint exercises, shared doctrine, candid talks about readiness. In NATO, shaping happens in the quiet grind of staff work: aligning budgets, setting training objectives, rehearsing responses to crises. In the civilian world, I've seen shaping in hospitals running hurricane drills in their auditoriums, CEOs red-teaming tough board presentations, and MBA students spending hours rehearsing their pitch before stepping into the classroom. The difference between those who shape an outcome and those who wing it is the same difference between a clean breach and a stalled column under fire.

There was another kind of shaping at work that day—the shaping of careers and relationships. At the war college, after studying strategy for over a year, a professor suggested that in the real world of strategy, "personalities matter." Who one dealt with and how influential leadership was applied would often determine an outcome. Years later, the names from that quiet reconnaissance would surface in very different contexts throughout my career. Doug Lute, my classmate and good friend and the 2ACR S3 during that fight, would reach three stars, serve as "War Czar" in the White House to both President Bush and President Obama, and would end his government career as the US ambassador to NATO. The squadron S3 Doug MacGregor, who was my partner in our reconnaissance of the berm, would retire as a bitter colonel, write books on armored warfare, and become a Fox News commentator and senior advisor in the Trump administration. HR McMaster, one of the troop commanders who was also on the recon, would lead his cavalry troop during the Battle of the 73 Easting and eventually serve as national security advisor to President Trump. And I would sit in television studios for CNN, sometimes sparring with

MacGregor over policy, often finding fault with McMaster, and always aligning myself with Lute on strategy around NATO.

Our fights in the Gulf—the Battle of Medina Ridge for us, the Battle of the 73 Easting for 2nd ACR—would be studied by future generations of soldiers and shaped, in part, by the reconnaissance and coordination we did that day.

The berm was ominous that afternoon. The sun was low, the air cooling, and more rain began to fall as we headed back to our respective FAAs. We could imagine in our minds the roar and smoke that would soon pour through those engineered gaps. War has a way of making even the most peaceful landscapes temporary. But at that moment, on February 18, the berm was an obstacle. Within days, it would be a starting line. And once you cross a starting line in combat, nothing is the same.

20 FEB 1991—The Storm

We have been working on the final order all day yesterday, which issues the guidance for our attack into Iraq. But late last night, I told the staff that they all looked beat, and they should all get some sleep, and we'd complete it in the morning. But even as we worked on it all day, our short-wave radios kept giving us the news that the peace plan proposed by Mikhail Gorbachev "did not meet the expectations" of President Bush. While this was disheartening, that statement was followed by one from Bush right before I told the guys to hit the rack that he would wire Moscow telling them what improvements could be made before it could be considered. At the same time, there were no flat refusals from Hussein—that could be a good sign. I vowed that I would not let myself get optimistic; my hopes have been crushed too many times already.

I went to bed, as did the rest of the staff, leaving only the night watch officer in the TOC. But we were all awakened by the most fascinating thunderstorm you can imagine. The violence of nature's event was devastating winds, microbursts of energy, lightning that would last for minutes and torrential rains that seemed to go on forever throughout the night. Many tents were blown down; mine, surprisingly, stayed erect. Many soldiers were soaked to the skin. In the morning, we all woke up wet, to a windy, but beautiful, sunshiny day. What a bizarre adventure and strange ending to a long day . . .

Love ya—

Dad

Wrestling with Scott and Todd at West Point in 1987, before Desert Storm. I'm wearing my Department of Physical Education shorts and a jacket—the best uniform I ever had!

Iraq in 2003. Todd was with the 3ACR on the Iraq-Syria border at al Qa'im; I was in Baghdad as an assistant division commander of 1st Armored Division. I had the chance to promote him to 1st lieutenant in front of his platoon.

With youngest son, Scott, in Baghdad in 2007. I was in the process of coming back to Iraq as the commander of 1AD and Multinational Division North, and Scott was about to leave Iraq after a fifteenth-month deployment.

Scott's wife, Lauren, was a brigade intelligence officer in the brigade I once commanded in 1998. We had a chance encounter in 2007 at a fusion cell meeting in Diyala.

Embracing Sue in December 2008 during the division's welcome home ceremony in Wiesbaden, Germany.

Sue and me in better times—post-retirement in Napa, California, 2019.

The exhausted and unshaven crew of HQ 33, still in our mission-oriented protective posture (MOPP) chemical suits, the morning of the ceasefire. In the distance, burning Iraqi Republican Guard tanks.

Sergeant Daugherty, our crew's gunner, out of the hatch in "Sasquatch," bumper number HQ33, 1-1 Cav.

Behind our Bradley Cavalry Fighting Vehicle, coordinating a rearm-refuel on the move (R-ROM) with our squadron executive officer, Major Bob Hnat. Bob was an aviator by specialty; he had a unique plan to deliver fuel and ammunition to both the ground and the air troops.

Supply trucks and other vehicles moving through the berm on D-Day, Feburary 1991.

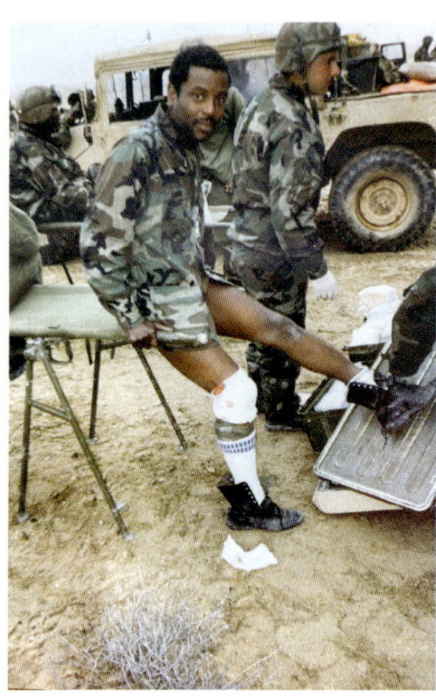

A 1-1 Cav NCO being treated by our medics after the night's cluster bomb attack, in which twenty-eight soldiers were wounded and several vehicles were damaged or destroyed.

Soldiers with the task of burning human waste in the barrels pulled from our wooden latrines. Those morning rituals became a place to exchange the latest gossip, or "RUMINT."

During our "destruction mission" after the ceasefire, we had captured ammunition that was stacked and later destroyed.

Traveling in the back of our squadron's UH-1 Huey aircraft, conducting reconnaissance for our future move back to Saudi Arabia. We got a sense of the environmental disaster from burning oil wells in northern Kuwait.

With Fire Support Officer (FSO) Captain Scott Milliren. This photo was taken at noon, but the smoke from the oil well fires turned day into dusk.

An interview during our extension in 2004 with dogged CNN reporter Jane Arraf. We developed a trusted relationship, even though she was "height challenged."

With my battle buddy, then–Brigadier General Mike "Scap" Scaporrotti, and our public affairs officer, Captain Dave Gercken, outside the 1AD tactical operations van in 2004. If I remember correctly, this was right after the announcement that we would be extended during the Sadr uprising.

After our extension in 2004, 1st Armored Division was sent to southern Iraq to counter the Sadr revolt. As I recall, this picture was taken in the town of Najaf with the "Bandit" battalion commander LTC Garry Bishop and one of his platoon leaders.

A Red Crescent ambulance that al-Qaeda had turned into a vehicle-borne improvised explosive device (VBIED) that could kill hundreds of Iraqis.

With battle buddy and close friend Division Command Sergeant Major Roger Blackwood. On that Thanksgiving Day in 2008, we visited every one of our FOBs, COPS, and patrol bases to bring near beer and Twinkies to the troops. This picture was from the top of Mount Sinjar, where a small team of marines was operating one of our communication sites.

Speaking with a group of Iraqi *jundi* (soldiers) as they were preparing for their first night air assault into an al-Qaeda-held village in Kirkuk province on our US CH47 helicopters. I would go with them on that operation, and I was impressed with how effective they were.

A tense meeting with a provincial police chief. I had just told him that we would be establishing a police training site for women, who would join his force to thwart the female suicide vest scourge.

On a combined US-Iraqi patrol with a commander from the 3rd Iraqi Division. They were one of the better of the five Iraqi divisions that were part of Multinational Division North.

US Ambassador Ryan Crocker and Iraqi Deputy Prime Minister Barham Salih (who would one day become president of Iraq) at our headquarters in Tikrit. I had asked both for assistance in bringing Iraqi ministers from Baghdad to our northern sector to meet with leaders from the seven northern provinces to address their concerns.

Flying into Samarra. Our area of operations in the north was as big as the state of Pennsylvania, requiring me to spend a lot of time in the back of a Blackhawk.

On several occasions, I traveled from Tikrit to Baghdad to give televised briefings to international and US national press. Information is critical during an insurgency campaign, and the press wants to hear from commanders.

In his role as acting CENTCOM commander, then-LTG Marty Dempsey visited Iraq several times. On this occasion, he found time to head north to visit his old command of 1st Armored Division. He and I went on a "market walk" of Mosul to get a feel for the situation. Since Iraqi soldiers were contributing to our security, I had an Iraqi flag on my left shoulder (with the US flag on my right) and my Arabic nametag on my front.

Pre-combat map reconnaissance and discussion with soldiers from the 2nd Stryker Cavalry Regiment. This was my first combat patrol riding in a Stryker, with the unit that I helped bring into the force back in 1999.

With General Fred Franks, General Marty Dempsey, and the late General Ron Griffiths—all former 1st Armored Division commanders—at the 25th VII Corps Jayhawk Desert Storm reunion in 2016. General Franks established this event, with all proceeds going to the education of the children of those who fell in Desert Storm.

With three WWII veterans at the D-Day drop zones and later in the town of Sainte-Mère-Église, France. Their stories and their camaraderie speak to the evergreen connections of veterans.

My friend and father of the modern Ukrainian army, the late Colonel General Henadii Vorobiov. When he presented me a list at Yavoriv Training Area, Ukraine, in 2010 explaining how I could help him transform his army, I knew we would be stalwart partners. He died of cancer in 2016.

The sacred "make it matter" box holding the photos of the 253 men and women who made the ultimate sacrifice during my time as an assistant division commander and later the commander of 1st Armored Division.

Reflection

My journal entry was not quite descriptive of what we all went through on February 19–20. The night that storm rolled through the desert was one of the most unforgettable episodes of my life. We had spent the better part of the previous day on reconnaissance to the berm, returned late, and pushed deep into the evening of the 19th to refine the final attack order. The plan was almost complete, but I could see the fatigue in the staff's faces. We'd been pushing hard for days. The political news coming over the radio—Gorbachev floating proposals that weren't going to sway either Bush or Hussein—was background noise, but the uncertainty of it all was its own kind of distraction. I finally made the call to stop for the night; we would hit it hard tomorrow with fresh minds.

Not long after, the real storm came.

The squadron commander and I shared what was called a general purpose (GP) small tent—a sturdy canvas shelter big enough for two cots and a heater. Our troopers were in GP larges, the long, high tents that could fit thirty to forty soldiers in rows of cots, with boots, gear, and drying uniforms lashed to straps along the walls. Those tents were functional, but they were also vulnerable: side flaps not always tied down, entryways that caught wind like sails, wooden crossbeams that could crack under the right force.

The first thing I noticed was the sound—wind-driven rain hammering our small tent in bursts, each gust stronger than the last. But it was holding. Then came the low hum that built into a roar, followed by the shouts outside. The GP larges were coming apart, their flaps snapping violently before collapsing in, sometimes falling on the men inside, sometimes sending the canvas flying into the darkness.

The squadron commander and I jumped up when we heard the shouts. We pulled on our boots, grabbed our flashlights, and waded into the chaos. We worked alongside other soldiers to wrestle tents back into place, secure loose gear, and haul cots and personal items into the few small tents still standing. By morning, our GP small and two or three others were miraculously still upright. The rest were down. We crammed as many soldiers as we could into those still-standing shelters, and our squadron logistics team began sending urgent requests to the brigade for replacement tentage.

The storm scattered equipment across the desert. Some of it we found hundreds of yards from where it had been tied down. The damage was more than physical. In the days before an offensive, soldiers were already on edge, so we were attempting to give them the opportunity to feed off rhythm and predictability. This storm shredded that rhythm. For twenty-four hours, our focus shifted from preparing for the attack to recovering from nature's ambush.

"I guess they didn't call it Desert Storm for nothing," I remember a soldier saying. In the back of my mind, I wondered, *Will this delay the attack? Were other units hit worse? Are there casualties from lightning or flash floods in wadis we haven't heard about?* And more pragmatically, as we were doing our final planning, I thought about Eisenhower postponing D-Day due to the weather. Would this be the thing that could force higher headquarters to change the timeline?

The memory of that night stayed with me for decades because it wasn't just about the weather. It was about unpredictability. It was about seeing in real time how quickly momentum can be lost, how fragile the sense of forward motion is, and how recovery requires immediate, decisive leadership.

Years later, in 2004, I saw another kind of storm—one made of politics, ideology, and violence. The 1AD had been in Iraq for months, grinding through counterinsurgency operations, and the situation began to look like it might finally be slowly turning. Insurgent activity was down. Tentative local leaders were engaged in talks. Some areas that had once been unsafe for a convoy were starting to see nascent Iraqi police, "sons of Iraq," and coalition patrols working together. It wasn't peace, but it felt like we were at least climbing in the right direction.

Then came the uprising of Muqtada al-Sadr—the Shia firebrand whose militia ignited a wave of violence across the country. Almost overnight, the fragile stability evaporated. Sadr's forces struck across multiple cities in coordinated attacks that killed civilians and soldiers alike, erasing months of hard-earned progress.

The order to extend our deployment, one that we were dreading but expecting, came down in the early spring of 2004, not in some grand speech or formal ceremony but in a short, clipped message from higher headquarters: mission change, duration indefinite, prepare forces for continued operations. General Dempsey called me back from the ports in the south, where we'd been preparing the shipment of our equipment and soldiers. He gathered his commanders, explained what he knew, and said something I've often quoted:

"Hey, none of us want to stay. But we have new orders. Kick some stones if you want, be upset, then pull it together and tell your soldiers the news, give them the best explanation you can. But remember this, when we leave this meeting, none of us leaders have the right to have a bad day. Because when we show our anger, our emotions, and continue to kick stones, our soldiers will too. None of us have the right to have a bad day once we leave this session."

Commanders and leaders then went from unit to unit, telling the soldiers face-to-face. There is no easy way to deliver news like that—no clever phrasing that can soften the blow. You just say it straight, answer questions honestly, and make it clear you will be in it with them every day until the mission is done.

That night, the small leadership team of the division huddled, and General Dempsey gave me a new mission. He asked me to fly to Germany and tell the families what was happening. A few days later, I boarded a plane to face the other half of the storm: the families. I half-kiddingly told Sue that this would be the worst combat tour I have ever experienced. But those family members deserved to hear from someone in leadership directly, not through a newsletter or a carefully worded e-mail. General Dempsey was spot on with his plan. I walked into base theaters and community halls filled with spouses, children, and parents. Some held notebooks of questions; some held hand-drawn posters that were not too complimentary. Others just folded their arms defensively and waited. I first validated their emotions (a tip given to me by my wife, Sue), then explained the why: that the mission was critical, that the threat had escalated, that pulling out now would undo everything we had fought for over the last year. I made the promise that we would be committed to keeping their soldiers as safe as possible, but there would still be dangers, and every commander knew their personal stakes. Then, on the advice of my wife, I answered questions until there were no more questions asked. In some places, these town halls lasted over three hours.

Some understood. Some were understandably angry. Some cried openly, especially the young spouses of the nineteen-year-old soldiers who had come to Germany before the war and hadn't expected to be left alone for so long. In one meeting, a mom said their daughter desperately wanted her dad to take her to the high school father-daughter dance, and what would she do now? Thankfully, one of our rear-detachment soldiers yelled out from the back of the theater, "I'll take her, ma'am . . . We're all in this together." Another mother stated her small son had been taking M&Ms out of a jar to count down the days until his dad's return. A woman across the room yelled out, "Put some more M&Ms in the jar when he's not looking." I will carry those moments with me forever.

That extension brought dark days. Right after I returned to Iraq from the emotional three days in central Germany, a vehicle-borne improvised explosive device detonated in a crowded area, killing eight of our soldiers. They were all from the same community back home . . . Three of them lived in the same stairwell of an apartment building, so their families were close. These were men whose families had been expecting to see them walk off a plane in a matter of weeks. The grief in that community was raw and unrelenting. There is no storm like that one—no wind or rain or lightning that can match the damage of that kind of loss.

Then, later in 2012, back in Europe, we fought another storm—this one in Washington. As commander of US Army Europe, I had made the case to retain two of our armored brigades on the continent. The intelligence we had on Russia's ambitions was clear to me. Moscow was probing, planning, and preparing. I argued that pulling all our heavy forces back to the United States would weaken our deterrence and invite exactly the kind of expansionism we'd later see in Crimea and Ukraine.

In briefings after briefings to members of Congress, I laid out the strategic necessity, intelligence indicators, and historical context. I pointed to the Baltic states, to Georgia, to the patterns in Russia's military exercises. I stressed that armored formations on the continent have always been a deterrent, and they are not something you can surge into a crisis overnight—they take weeks to move and years to train, and when they're gone, you also lose trust from your allies. You can never deploy trust.

But in the political climate of the time, the label "Cold War general" stuck too easily to me. Many of our representatives saw the fight for those brigades as me clinging to an outdated posture, not as preparing for the future. The administration had announced a "pivot to Asia," Congress wanted defense cuts, and the public was tired of hearing about Europe's security needs. I was told, more than once, that my perspective was "rooted in the past."

Congress had already made up its mind. I lost the fight. The "heavy" brigades left, leaving no US tanks in Europe, and two years later, Russia invaded Crimea and the Donbas region.

That failure to persuade remains one of the most bitter memories of my career because it wasn't about proving myself right—it was about preventing what I believed, and still believe, was an avoidable disaster. The storm had been forming, and it was a storm I couldn't steer around, no matter how many charts, briefings, or intelligence reports I put on the table.

If there's a lesson in all of this, it's that storms come in many forms. Some blow down your tent. Some rip through the center of your unit.

Some unfold in hearing rooms under fluorescent lights. Many are unpredictable, but some you can see coming. You don't get to choose when they arrive. And you don't get to choose what kind of damage they cause.

What you can choose is how you meet them. Secure your people first. Protect what matters most. Recover what you can. Fight to get back to normal. And when the winds finally die down, get back to building for the future.

Because storms don't last forever—but the way you lead through them will be remembered long after the skies are clear.

28 FEB 1991—The War

So, when you read this journal someday, you might ask, "So dad, where have you been for the last few days?"

Guys, I've been involved in what was a most demanding, stimulating and simultaneously frightening event: The attack from Saudi Arabia into Iraq as part of VII Corps main effort. In four days, our Cavalry Squadron led the 1st Armored Division over 250 miles across two countries (Saudi Arabia and Iraq) against 5 enemy divisions, all the way to the border of Kuwait, which simultaneously was being liberated by Marines, Saudi Arabian Royal Land Forces, and the Kuwaiti Martyr Brigade. I couldn't write during those periods for a few of the following reasons: 1) I was busy executing orders, 2) I wasn't getting a lot of sleep, 3) I was firing on enemy vehicles, 4) I was taking enemy prisoners of war, 5) the vehicle that this book was in—my wheeled vehicle that was near the TOC while I was in my Bradley—was the victim of artillery fire and had to be towed someplace for repair, and 6) there just wasn't the time. It's not that I wasn't thinking of you guys—in fact, the picture of Mom and you two and Misty standing outside the front door of our home in Lehrberg was pasted to my hatch and you were constantly in my mind even as I was engaged in some of the strongest physical and emotional battles I have ever felt.

I'm going to do a few things before my memory starts fading of the events. I'm going to describe exactly what we did starting on 24 Feb until today (28 Feb—After the call of the cease fire) and then, over the next few days, as I get some time, I'll go into more details of things as they occurred and my memory serves me. Here goes:

G-Day, 24 Feb

Our plan was to lead the Division up to just south of the Saudi Arabian Iraqi berm, the man-made obstacle which we knew we would have to cross to invade Iraq. 2ACR had cut the berm the day before (2LT Ramirez, my crew and I went up to watch this breach—it was an awesome display of firepower and engineer work from 1315-1600 on 23 Feb). I had reported to the Division and 1st BDE exactly where the 18 Berm cuts were from the previous day, and the Squadron was going to put Bradleys through all openings on the 25th (G +1).

As we approached our staging area south of the berm, we received a warning order that Marine forces in the east were proceeding very well, the breach by 1st Infantry Division and the 1st UK Armored Division near the Wadi al-Batin was going very well, so we should be prepared to cross into Iraq immediately upon reaching the berm—we would not wait until the next day to cross the Line of Departure. While the Squadron was prepared to do this, I don't believe the rest of the Division was, so we waited just south (2 kilometers) of the berm for the 1st BDE to come out of FAA Garcia and march the 30 kilometers (about 18.64 mi) to the berm crossing site. We finally crossed the Line of Departure—LD—at about 1430—we were in Iraq. We immediately took three casualties when two of our chemical recon platoon members and one engineer stepped on an anti-personnel mine. We marked that minefield, Medevac'd the three Soldiers who were only slightly wounded and continued north.

We proceeded to move north that day, following behind the 2nd ACR. They pulled off to the east at a Phase Line they called PL Dixie, and from there until we stopped that night at PL Colorado, 1-1 CAV was leading the Division into Iraq. We received no enemy contact on that first day, but all our Soldiers were somewhat nervous. We established a screen line which was 20 kilometers wide and we waited for the rest of the Division to refuel their tanks and prepare for the attack into Objective Bear.

Attack into Bear, 25 Feb

Approximately 60 kilometers into Iraq we reached our first Objective. This location, which the Division G2 said would contain about 2 companies of mech infantry and several tanks, was thought to be our initial test of fire. The CAV's job was to poke the area, find out what was there, and if a major enemy force was at that location, we were to hand over the battle to the 1st BDE's infantry. We reached the objective at about 0900 in the morning, and our scout helicopters told us that there were many soldiers in the town waving the white flag of surrender. As the helicopters hovered in the area, more soldiers appeared waving the white flag. We had already taken several prisoners earlier in the morning as we rolled north, but they were in groups of ones or twos. We suspected a trap, like that which had occurred at Khafji just a few weeks earlier, so we were very leery of lurching headlong into the objective.

The soldiers started walking toward the hovering helicopters, and they left their trenches and buildings that were in the area. As the helicopters monitored their approach, COL Riley, the 1st BDE Commander, stated that he wanted to launch artillery and MLRS (Multiple Launch Rocket Systems) into the area. We persuaded him to delay the strike until we could develop the situation. After about an hour of prisoners coming out of the trench work, and it appeared they truly wanted to surrender, we sent a ground Bradley Platoon to secure the enemy soldiers. All counting, there were approximately 150 POWs collected by the CAV from that objective. We established a POW cage and continued our mission to the north while the 1st BDE pounded Objective Bear with artillery for approximately 1 hour. If there was anyone in that trenchwork that had not surrendered, I'm sure they were killed.

We didn't get far. Traveling about 5 kilometers to the north, we began meeting more Iraqi soldiers in trenches. Two of our helicopters destroyed a BRDM (a Soviet-style armored personnel carrier with a 12.5 mm gun) and as soon as the Iraqi infantry saw the accuracy of the helicopter guns, more began to surrender. Alpha Troop fired two shots as at a cargo truck, and it exploded about 200 meters to my flank—excellent shooting! As our line troops passed, we met hundreds of surrendering Iraqi soldiers. We did not want to stop, so we took their weapons, told them to put their hands in the air, and told them to walk south. They did this without question.

At one point, after the line troops had passed, we received a call that an MP unit needed assistance in destroying a BRDM that was to our rear. We did not want to turn any of our troops around, so I told the SCO that I would get it. HQ-33 (SASQUATCH!) went to the location, found the MPs with a bunch of prisoners and a BRDM. I could not shoot at the vehicle because there were too many "friendlies" around, so SGT Daugherty and I threw some hand grenades inside. There were MANY secondary explosions from the ammo inside, and we got the heck out of there as fast as we could.

We continued to move north, in the rain and dark, to a phase line right in front of the next objective, Obj Python, which was the town of Al Basiyah. This town was a major logistics crossroads for the Republican Guards, and the 1st and 2nd BDEs came online to attack it the morning of the 26th, while we screened to the southeast to prevent any reinforcements from coming in and attacking them. We did that until the early morning of 26 Feb.

The Attack of Python and Movement Toward the Republican Guards, 26 Feb

Early in the morning, the Maneuver BDEs began their attack against the logistics center at Al Basiyah. We watched loads of MLRS rockets go into the town, and we watched and listened as the tanks began firing. As that battle raged, we began moving to the north and then directly east, again about 15 kilometers ahead of the closest unit. At the time, although we didn't know it, we were also the lead element in the Corps, for 24th ID and 3ACR (to our northwest) had been bogged down in bad terrain, and the advance of 3AD (Uncle Marty's brigade) and 2ACR had slowed in the south because of enemy contact. We lost any security to our north or south, and we were moving far forward of our division. It was not a comforting thought. Our helicopters, moving ahead of our ground Bradleys, spotted a tank column and proceeded to call air attacks against the Iraqis. We were credited with killing 27 tanks, and B Troop avoided running right into this Iraqi tank brigade. At about dusk, after moving about 120 kilometers, we continued to move, more slowly, through an Iraqi training area. We saw many dud rounds of ammunition—Air Force bombs, arty shells, etc. As it became dark, we continued to move toward the anticipated Adnan Brigade location of the Republican Guards.

The two ground troops set up a screen about 4 kilometers short of where we thought the Adnans were. Both troops started firing at trucks, BMPs (a Soviet-style personnel carrier), and enemy soldiers who were not surrendering. Our training paid off, as troop commanders used mortar fire and direct fire from Bradleys to destroy enemy vehicles to our front. It appeared that there was a road several kilometers to the east of that position, and a lot of traffic was moving north. We used OH-58Ds and Apache helicopters to attack that convoy, and it was very effective.

As we were sitting on the screen line along Phase Line Spain, the SCO and I were in the TAC, moving directly behind A and B Troops, about 1 kilometer to the rear of the screen line. At about 10 pm we received a call from the TOC—another 3–4 kilometers back—that they had dismounted enemy soldiers, 2 tanks, and a BMP in the rear. Since the TOC doesn't have anything that can protect themselves against tanks, I told the SCO I would go to that location to ensure the safety of the TOC. I linked with the LRS (Long Range Surveillance, who were in HMMWVs) teams that had seen the tanks and looked through their night sights to find the targets. To my surprise, there were 2 tanks less than 400 meters away in dug in positions. We positioned our Bradleys to take the best shot, and we fired several 25mm rounds in the hull—we thought that would scare the tankers into surrendering. Much to our surprise the 25mm rounds penetrated the tank turrets, and they began burning. We engaged the second tank in the same way and then shot High Explosive rounds at a nearby building that looked like some type of headquarters. There were no prisoners who surrendered.

After this encounter, our Bradley moved back to the screen line, where the ground troops were still engaging targets. The night observation helicopters (OH-58Ds) were extremely helpful during that period.

27 Feb

At about 0130 in the morning, we received a call that not just 1st Brigade, but the entire Division was going to pass through us and attack the enemy to our front. A night passage of lines is a very difficult operation, and there were already several instances of friendlies shooting at our vehicles—a tank from 2nd BDE shot at and barely missed one of our Bradleys at about midnight, another one shot at our M88 recovery vehicle in B Troop and missed. Not very funny. The thermal night sights in the Bradleys and tanks only give a "hot spot," so it's tough to distinguish enemy from friendly at night when they're more than a couple hundred meters away from you. Anyhow, I suggested to the SCO that we pull everything tight in the center of the sector to avoid any possible future fratricide, turn out our red taillights in the vehicles, and message our actions to the brigade commander behind us. He agreed.

We pulled the ground troop in and put them on a screen line about 7 kilometers wide, with Bradleys about 150 meters apart (different from the wider distances they had been on in the march since crossing the berm). We put our support guys together and turned their rear lights on, told the 1st Brigade we were doing that so the forces coming up behind could pass through without firing on us, and we relocated the TOC and TAC behind B Troop—about 500 meters. We completed this action by about 0130, and just as I was climbing up on and lowering myself into the commander's hatch in our Bradley after coordinating with the LRS team and B Troop Commander, I heard several explosions to the west (we were heading east) and overhead a popping sound right over our heads. I thought it was the sonic boom from an MLRS initially, but then all hell broke loose.

Canisters began popping overhead, and hundreds of small bomblets were falling all over our position. I couldn't get the hatch on my Bradley closed, and every time I tried to close it another hundred—thousand?—small explosions that appeared to be hand grenades went off all around us. It was a roar of sound and senses and light. All I could think of were all the Soldiers less than 50 meters from my Bradley who were in wheeled vehicles—especially my OPS NCO, SFC Tim Bretl, who was with my HMMWV driver, SPC Harold Palmer. What was happening to him? When the explosions stopped, I jumped out of my Bradley and ran to my HMMWV, the one SFC Bretl and SPC Palmer were in—and found no one there. People were everywhere, many of them lying on the ground screaming in pain. I ran into SFC Nonnemacher who told me it appeared no one was killed or seriously injured, but quite a few had shrapnel wounds.

As I walked/ran toward HQ 30, CPT Egan (the S4) stopped me and told me to get back to my Bradley as there were folks from Division trying to get me on the radio and there were a lot of unexploded rounds around that made the whole area like a minefield. He also told me that no one in the TOC could run the battle right now since the Squadron Commander had not been heard on the radio. I ignored CPT Egan's advice and instead ran to HQ 30 (the S3 Command/radio vehicle, part of the TOC). Inside there were several wounded individuals—none seriously—but our assistant S3, CPT Steve Shuster, told me all was okay, and they had communication with both the ground Troops.

I then started running toward my Bradley, which was about 200 meters from the TOC. On the way back to my Bradley, I ran into Dr. Putnam in his HMMWV—how did he get there so fast from the supply trains?—who told me we had about 20 wounded, but none of them needed immediate Medevac. Thank God!

As I was climbing back on my Bradley, the first group of tanks from the Brigade began their passage of lines and were screaming past us. We pieced our TOC/TAC together in a circle as the tanks went past and waited—prayed—for morning to come. Hundreds of tanks rolled by our position between 0400–0500 hours, going into the attack against what we would later learn were two divisions of the "elite" Republican Guards forces: the Medina Division and the Adnan Brigade. The vehicles running to the north were those of another division, the Hammurabi, who would be engaged by the US 24th ID the following day.

We remained set on the screen line for the rest of the day and monitored a very large tank battle to the east. We had done our scouting—we had been "cowards and tattletales," as the division commander told us what he wanted us to be when he warned us not to get into a heavy fight in front of the Division. We had reported where the enemy was and become decisively engaged with the enemy forces only when it was required; we had given the Brigade behind us and the Division time to prepare to roll into the fight. Now it was time for the big guns—tanks, arty, MLRS, Apache, etc.—to do their jobs.

Over the next few hours, it sounded like they were doing it well. Behind us was an MLRS battalion. Throughout the day we watch hundreds of rockets soar into the gray skies over our heads (there was a light rain all night and into the next day) toward Iraqi positions. There were still reports of surrenders, but not as many as there had been on the first two days. We all concurred that what was taking place was a slaughter of the Republican Guards. We found out later that was exactly what was happening.

We remained vigilant through that day, but all of us were totally exhausted with the strain of constant movement, fears of potential contact with the enemy, extended hours of little/no sleep, and a few bites of food, and the remembrances of the artillery attack on our position.

The attack against the Republican Guards continued. The three ground Brigades continued to engage enemy T-55, T-62, T-72 tanks, and BMPs, BRDMs, and trucks (most of them new Mercedes) as the dawn started to break. About 0430 we received word that there may be a cease fire at 0500; that was later changed to 0800. MG Griffith, the Division Commander, wanted to push as hard as he could until that deadline in order to destroy as much of Hussein's war machine as we could. There was no one who disagreed with him.

On the 27th, we received change of mission orders from Division; our squadron was put in the Division reserve. I believe this was done because we had: 1) done such a good job of finding the enemy for the rest of the Division and leading the Division over 200 kilometers into Iraq, 2) because we had received so many casualties (of the 2 KIAs and 45 WIAs taken by the Division during the war, 1-1 CAV had 26 WIAs).

28 Feb

As we were "relaxing" in our hasty defensive positions, we received another change of mission from the CG—destroy all the vehicles that we could find in our area of operation. There were plenty of Iraqi dug in positions that had been bypassed by the tanks, and our job was to find them and destroy anything that was left in those holes. We performed that mission with a vengeance, destroying literally hundreds of cargo trucks, ammo dumps, motorcycles, and other "soft" combat equipment that were left in the prepared defensive positions. I went with A Troop, the SCO went with B Troop, and for approximately eight hours on 28 Feb we put a major dent in the Iraqi war machine. It was good gunnery practice for our scouts, good demolition practice for our attached engineers (they had not done much for us to that point in time). I even "monster trucked" a BMP with my Bradley by running completely over it and crushing it. Quite frankly, that was fun. It appeared that the war was over.

We slept very well on the evening of the 28th, although we were still very vigilant. Again, most of my thoughts were on your mom and you guys as we conducted this operation and thank goodness this war will go down as the fastest, most violent one-sided affair in the history of warfare. For now, we're all safe. I hope that continues so we can be rejoined as soon as possible.

Love,

Dad

Reflection

Leadership, like war, is a cumulative endeavor. You don't arrive on the battlefield—or at any new job—with a blank slate. You bring everything with you—the training, the scars, the questions you asked and the ones you were too afraid to. And if you're lucky, you bring the wisdom earned through experience and some of the scar tissue you've endured.

I hadn't seen this entry in over thirty-five years. Not since the day I wrote it. But in reading this remembrance from my journal that our son typed up for me, I was immediately transported back to the tabletop flat deserts of southern Iraq, feeling my face being struck by rain; seeing various Iraqi units on the horizon, either with their hands up or shooting at us as we approached; hearing the chatter on the ear piece of my CVC (combat vehicle crewman's) helmet from the squadron, brigade, and division radio nets simultaneously as well as the voices of my crew members—my gunner, SGT Sean Daugherty; our driver, SPC Darrin Izer; and our JAFO (an informal acronym for "Just Another F**king Observer," reserved for the youngest scout in the vehicle at the very back), Private Brent LaJoie; and smelling the unique smell of vehicle fuel, machine gun grease, and human sweat. It's amazing how the memories come flooding back.

I had forgotten a few of the details listed about that very short fight, but one thing that did strike me as a more experienced and mature veteran was this simple thought: How did we do that? How did we make that continuous move, with just one pause, with almost no sleep, through a monotonous and featureless desert? We leaned over the side of our Bradley and held on to the turret handles, relieving our bladders as we moved so we could keep up with the vehicles to our left and right. We stood in the hatches, snacking on crackers from our MREs, while maneuvering through a barren and level land and checking our move and location with LORAN and boat compasses strapped to the turret (there was no GPS back then). We took hundreds of prisoners in very short periods of time and processed them for the military police to take care of as they came up from the rear. We engaged enemy vehicles while continuously on the move, hitting them with our first shot on almost every occasion. We coordinated with our own helicopters, the air force aircraft when they came into our sector, and the artillery that was constantly firing after we gave them the targets and a grid coordinate to strike. We treated our wounded quickly after what some would call a mass casualty, then began moving again. Looking back now, through the lens of three deployments with the same 1st Armored Division across two decades, I realize that each role prepared me for the next, but in war, even with experience, you'll never feel completely adequate.

During that fight in 1991, I was a young major controlling and helping lead a nine-hundred-soldier cavalry squadron in an advance guard mission for the rest of the huge 1st Armored Division. We were spread across a frontage of twenty kilometers, feeling out the enemy over 250 miles for eighty-nine intense hours. After training and preparing for years in a static defense in our home of Germany against a Soviet threat, we were now the lead element in a fast-paced armored offensive thrust that crossed hundreds of kilometers, and our division would eventually shatter three Iraqi Republican Guard divisions. We were the division's scouts, advance guard, and vanguard. And in the process—succinctly covered in my journal days after the fight—we took fire, returned it with precision, took prisoners, cleared objectives, saw our teammates from other units perform magnificently as they passed through us to continue the fight that would later be called the Battle of the Medina Ridge, and watched as the Republican Guard crumbled in front of us. The war was violent, one-sided, and quick—but it didn't feel that way when you were in the turret, feeling each action and decision in your chest.

I read further and was reminded of the chaos of the nighttime movement, the sheer uncertainty of each engagement. After firing on and destroying two tanks that were likely outposts for the Republican Guard, my Bradley was hit by artillery later that night. The squadron took over thirty casualties when our unit was struck by friendly fire during a nighttime MLRS barrage. We were constantly out front, sometimes too far out. But we adapted, conducting several refuels on the move and a forward passage of line (two very complicated actions). We relied on each other, and I learned that even in fast wars, leadership is about many things, but it's most often about endurance.

That campaign—to those who lived it—was anything but simple. From our G-Day crossing of the berm on February 24 to the final ceasefire on February 28, we were in near-continuous motion. I remember the cautious approach to Objective Bear, where hundreds of enemy soldiers emerged from trench lines waving white flags when we had expected them to fight. We suspected a trap, and it took hours to confirm it wasn't, even though at a critical point, two or three Iraqi soldiers of the hundred we had rounded up decided to fire on our Bradley as we were gathering the prisoners together. That proved to be a mistake for them. Throughout our move, there were instances of firepower—we had to decide whether to hold back or strike with either Bradleys or our Cobra helicopters. I watched as our troops, trained for conventional tank-on-tank warfare, became impromptu custodians of prisoners of war, logisticians, and negotiators in the chaos.

We engaged armored columns, dodged minefields, and outpaced our own division and corps to find the Adnan Brigade of the Republican Guard. I vividly recall the encounter with dug-in tanks behind our lines, where we fired our Bradley 25mm rounds against two tanks at close range, perhaps five hundred meters, expecting only to frighten the enemy and cause them to surrender like so many of their comrades had already done—but instead watching as our small shells penetrated their Russian-supplied turrets and ignited the ammo that was stored inside. The enemy was everywhere, but we could see them at night with night-vision goggles and outrange them with our fire.

Then came the friendly fire. A misfire from friendly MLRS canisters in the dead of night rained cluster bomblets—what I called "small hand grenades" in the journal entry—over our TOC. The opening of the shells and the cascade of small munitions led to hundreds of explosions . . . it was like being in a popcorn popper. We were all momentarily paralyzed by the sound—my crew and several of the Bradleys from A Troop that had stopped as we planned the forward passage of the tank brigade that was following us. Soldiers screamed in pain. Two of our TOW launchers on different vehicles had been penetrated and cooked off, and one HMMWV with light anti-tank weapons (LAWs) was hit. They all exploded. Shrapnel injuries spread across the football field–sized area where we had stopped, but miraculously, there were no fatalities. Our medics and combat lifesavers (CLS) took over, bandaging the wounds, and we began to regroup and continued the mission. As I drifted to see about each casualty during those hours of darkness, PFC Marty Coon from our S3 shop—a soldier who had taken the CLS training classes—was in the thick of it, bandaging his fellow soldiers along with the medics. Interestingly, I heard a female voice . . . and found a medic I didn't know about who had volunteered to be part of the cavalry before we'd left the assembly area. PFC Tammy Reese was part of the support battalion, and when she'd heard the cav might need more medics, she'd volunteered. That was my first experience with women in a combat unit alongside me; I've since had a bias that that's where they belong if they want to be there, because they're damned good, and we need them.

By the 27th, our unit had taken more than half of the division's casualties. Two had happened right after we'd crossed the berm into Iraq when a couple of troops got out of their vehicle and stepped on a cluster bomblet from a US Air Force strike, then twenty-eight on the night when the cluster bomblets had come raining down. We'd advanced over two hundred kilometers and destroyed or captured massive amounts of enemy equipment. On the 28th, we were given a final mission: Destroy any remaining Iraqi vehicles left behind. We were later informed that this was due to an anticipated ceasefire that would occur the next morning. That day became a surreal mix of combat demolition and grim satisfaction. We flattened vehicles. I ran over an Iraqi BMP with my Bradley like I was at a monster truck rally. And then the quiet came. It was over. We had all survived.

But after reflecting on those eighty-nine hours of Desert Storm, my thoughts drifted to twelve years later, when I returned to Iraq with the same division—this time as the assistant division commander for support under my friend, then–Brigadier General Marty Dempsey. The contrast was stark. In 1991, it was conventional maneuver warfare: large-scale formations, clear objectives, and high-intensity contact.

In 2003, as I joined the division in Baghdad after they had completed their march to the capital, our large division faced the chaotic aftermath of regime collapse. We weren't just killing enemies—we found ourselves in a complex counterinsurgency, trying to build a functioning society out of ruin.

That time, instead of being part of a Bradley crew, I was one of the four members in the "command group": the commanding general; me; another assistant commander, BG Mike Scaparotti; and CSM Mike Bush. Dempsey had given us all a written document with our specific responsibilities. I was responsible for sustaining the force. That meant coordinating logistics: food, fuel, ammo, water, maintenance, and all the other classes of supply across a vast battlespace, encompassing most of Baghdad and a few outlying areas. But my job went beyond logistics. The CG also gave me the task of overseeing the engineers, who were tasked with all sorts of projects and would later be magnificent at clearing roads of IEDs, rebuilding bridges and culverts that the enemy had destroyed, and constructing dozens of bases and combat outposts across the city. I watched those masterful sappers fortify sites, repair schools, keep our routes clear, and reconstruct electrical grids. They were warriors and builders at once.

Our logisticians became fighters, too, because supply routes were part of these complex war zones. What had once been a rear-area function for these kinds of soldiers now required mounted patrols, route clearance, overwatch, and resilience. I watched as maintenance sergeants became convoy commanders. Truck drivers became gunners. Logistics battalions adopted the mindset of infantry companies. They adapted because we had no choice.

Our civil affairs teams—a function that is difficult to practice in peacetime—were also ubiquitous. They were everywhere, coordinating the rebuilding of war-torn areas, standing up civilian functions, dealing with retired Ba'athist leaders, and providing coordination with civilians from various US agencies to bring a functioning government to what had once been an authoritarian regime filled with corruption.

One of my lesser-known but significant roles was leading the division's information operations and public affairs efforts. Baghdad was flooded with US, Arab, and a multitude of international journalists, and their cameras were often our best—and worst—messengers. General Dempsey had given me the task of speaking regularly with media outlets, shaping strategic messaging, and balancing transparency with discretion. Our troops, and the citizens of the world, needed to understand what we were doing beyond the explosions and the too-plentiful car bombs.

Then came a test of moral leadership. Just when we were preparing to redeploy to our home stations, the radical cleric Muqtada al-Sadr stoked a Shia uprising. The secretary of defense surprised everyone on one of the Sunday talk shows by saying the 1st Armored Division was the best choice to extend for several months to quell the insurgency. When we were extended by three months—just weeks before our scheduled redeployment back home to our base in Germany—General Dempsey sent me back to Germany to explain the extension to our families. Over three days, I traveled to installations across Europe, addressing thousands of anxious, frustrated, and war-weary spouses and families who only wanted their soldier home, the reason for us staying be damned. Some cried. Some shouted. Some listened. I told them the truth: that their soldiers were making a difference and that we were all ready to come home, but we had been given a new mission. It was one of the hardest things I've ever done—and one of the most important.

My tasks were now very different than when I'd been a major serving with a cavalry squadron in an eighty-nine-hour war in 1991, but they were difficult, nonetheless.

In 2007, I returned to Iraq once again, this time as *the* commanding general of that same 1st Armored Division. At the height of the surge, the US sending the division I had just taken command of to Iraq was one option to provide additional soldiers for the fight. But the mission was broader, murkier, and more politically fraught. My commander,

General Petraeus, told me our division's mission would primarily be giving the nascent nation of Iraq room to breathe after the recent threat of a Sunni-Shia civil war by conducting tactical operations. But there were other missions as well. Working with Joint Special Operations Command in our area to thwart al-Qaeda and other terrorist networks. Building, training, and conducting operations with five nascent Iraqi Army Divisions that would eventually take our place. Recruiting and training thousands of new Iraqi police officers, as well as improving the actions of the Iraqi border patrol along the several-hundred-mile borders of both Iran and Syria on our eastern and western boundaries. Improving the economic conditions in the north and working with the provincial governments of four Arab provinces and three Kurdish provinces. Yeah, it was an extensive mission set.

We would be called Task Force Iron. Our area of responsibility stretched from Baghdad to the Turkish border, surrounded by Iran to the east, the Kurdish autonomous region to the northeast, Turkey to the north, the Syria to the northwest, and the volatile Anbar Province to the east. The enemy was everywhere and wore many faces: Sunni extremists, Iranian-backed Shia militias, Ba'athist insurgents, tribal gangs. Each province had a different context, and each was, in effect, a different war.

In the Ninewa province and its capital city, Mosul, we walked a tightrope between Kurdish ambitions and Sunni Arab frustrations. AQI operated in shadows. Intelligence was fragmented. In the Diyala province, just north of Baghdad, we hunted Shia militias who had Iranian support and wrestled with violent sectarian fault lines. In the Salah ad Din province and Tikrit, Saddam's home province and hometown, we worked with tribal leaders to establish a semblance of order while being undercut by former Ba'athists in the shadows of government. In the "rat line" of the old spice road from Syria to Tal Afar, we watched smuggling networks feed violence. In Anbar, the "Sons of Iraq"—many of them having once been insurgents themselves—became our allies in a fragile reconciliation along a shared western border.

The 1st Armored was tasked with what the military calls "lines of effort." As I mentioned, our mission was to continue to fight the terrorists, insurgents, criminals, and gangs but also to continue to build an Iraqi Security Force out of the five different Iraqi Army Divisions in our areas, as well as recruit and train tens of thousands of police officers and border patrol soldiers. We embedded partnership teams into every Iraqi unit. We flooded neighborhoods with combat outposts. We conducted thousands of combat patrols and hundreds of kinetic operations. But we were also tasked to help rebuild the economic system and strengthen the political machinations of an emerging government in four Arab provinces and three Kurdish states. And our soldiers were rebuilding schools, reopening health clinics, restoring markets, brokering ceasefires, and mentoring local appointed government officials (some good, some not so good).

Our brigade commanders were statesmen and warriors. The battalion commanders were both fighters and ambassadors in camouflage. Everyone was stretched. But in 2007, everyone believed in the mission. And the results, though not perfect, were measurable. During that fifteen-month deployment, violence across our battlespace declined by over 70 percent. The Iraqi Army's capabilities and operational tempo increased significantly; they were fighting for their new country. We oversaw elections, helped generate employment for disenfranchised young men, reduced sectarian displacement, and rebuilt a core of legitimacy around the Iraqi government. It was gritty, granular, and often thankless work—but it mattered.

The experience of leading that division in combat—after having been its deputy for sustainment and one of its cavalry scouts a long time ago—was humbling. Like anyone who has been in any business for a long time or who purposely finds ways to increase their knowledge of an organization, everything I had learned came to bear. I had to draw from every lesson I'd learned from combat in this same nation and in this same unit in both 1991 and 2003. I saw the limits to firepower and the power of expanding trust.

When I reflect on this arc—Desert Storm's decisive mechanized assault; Operation Iraqi Freedom's post-invasion chaos and the shift to the counterinsurgency and counterterrorism fight of 2003–2004; and the deliberate, population-centric grind of the surge—I see more than a continuum of warfighting. I see a need for constant adaptation and a required continuum of learning. Each conflict added a new layer. Each role forced new growth. We were all changing.

During Desert Storm, I was a major—an operations officer helping lead a cavalry squadron on the left flank of the VII Corps assault. Our mission was clear. The enemy wore uniforms. The battlefield had defined boundaries. We trained to close with and destroy a known force on open terrain. I can still see the sands of the Wadi al-Batin, the red arrows on our acetate maps, and the linear battle plans that guided our movements. Our five-paragraph operations orders gave structure to chaos. Our rehearsals—though often dry—prepared us for almost every possible contingency. We knew where the friendly units were, where we thought the enemy was, which friendly units were to our left and right, and what success was supposed to look like.

Later, I returned to Iraq under two very different conditions. The lines were gone. The enemy had no uniforms. The battlefield was urban, rural, tribal, political, and asymmetrical. We were no longer fighting a state's army but instead a network of insurgents, terrorists, foreign fighters, and criminal gangs, each with different motives. There were no front lines—just a sea of overlapping conflicts in Diyala, Ninewa, Salah ad Din, Kirkuk, and parts of Al-Ta'mim and Erbil. The terrain was complex: ancient cities, sectarian fault lines, economic grievances, and external influences from Syria, Turkey, and Iran. Our tactical battles from Desert Storm evolved into campaign plans that were a chessboard of phased, sequential clearing and holding operations—moving across the Za'ab Triangle; conducting hard urban fights in Mosul and Samarra; and pursuing remnants of fighters across valleys and mountain ranges back toward Tikrit and later Mosul, their ideological heartlands.

Unlike Desert Storm, there were no unifying moments of crossing a berm, rolling over phase lines, taking or bypassing terrain objectives on a map, and rolling to an eventual ceasefire. There were no singular "culmination" points, no lines drawn across a map where we could coordinate movement and places where the guns fell silent. Instead, we fought and rebuilt at the same time. Continuously. We mentored fledgling Iraqi security forces; counseled local tribal sheikhs; ran operations with State Department- and USAID-led provincial reconstruction teams; and tried to fuse political, economic, and security efforts—what we called the "full-spectrum" approach.

Our mission in each of the three conflicts I was involved with was to "win." That was easy to do in the first war, but winning in the second two was much more complicated. During Desert Storm, we had the luxury of deliberate planning and tempo, and the fight was resolved quickly. Later, in the surge, we lived in the gray zone of crisis action—dealing with evolving intelligence, constantly shifting resources, and a battle rhythm that rarely allowed for second-guessing and sleep. As we departed in late 2008, when gaining the trust of the citizenry was a key to victory, the battlefield was quieter. Not stable, not resolved—but quieter. Iraqi institutions were standing, insurgent leaders were on the run, and local populations were, for the first time in years, beginning to trust again. I remember getting on a plane in December 2008, leaving Iraq once again, looking out the window to an emerging Iraq below with more lights on and people moving through the streets, and realizing that the toughest part of my life had been lived in that country, under three different conditions. And truthfully, I hoped to never come back.

But as I reflect, I realize a lot stayed the same over those years.

On all three tours, it was the soldiers who carried the weight. Young men and women who served not because they sought glory but because they believed in each other and the mission. In all wars, planning mattered. In 1991, I learned the value of rehearsals and synchronization. In 2001, I saw a change in approach. Terror and insurgent networks were posted on the walls of the intelligence cell, and human targeting became an approach that led to soldiers experiencing a radical mindset change. In 2007, adaptability—the ability to rapidly revise, rethink, reframe—became more important than ever. My time as the Joint Staff J7 helped me understand the difference between deliberate planning and crisis action planning. In Iraq, we did both simultaneously, every day.

Our soldiers patrolled by day and executed by night. And those men and women I served with? In all three iterations, they remain etched in my memory—their courage, their mistakes, their resilience. From cavalry major to deputy commander to division general, I didn't just fight in Iraq—I grew up there. And that growth continues still. Some nights in my dreams.

I've neglected to mention the families and what they were doing during all this change. I learned when I returned home from Desert Storm that on the day the ground war had commenced, Sue had pulled away from the news, jumped in our car, and taken the boys to a Volksmarch in the German town of Rottenburg. Her stress levels were high, and she knew a combination of exercise and the bucolic scenery of Germany would bring distraction and a sense of peace, even as the world was in turmoil. That pattern of exercise for stress reduction only intensified for her with each deployment, partly because in later tours to Iraq, our two sons and daughter-in-law were often deployed as well. Yes, having a partner or offspring wear the uniform is your greatest pride. It also, at times, induces your worst fears.

Looking back across the arc of my tours, as well as the continuous wars we fought at the beginning of the twenty-first century, I'm struck by how much changed—in me, in our army, and in our families. And how much good leadership and caring for each other mattered. Desert Storm taught me how to fight. The time in Baghdad taught me how much I didn't know. The surge taught me how to lead through complexity—how to integrate force with purpose, how to trust partners, how to adapt daily to the terrain of war and the human terrain of recovery. Those conflicts also taught military families a lot. It was the most challenging thing in my life and in the lives of most of the soldiers and family members I know. And it remains the most defining for all of us.

All this taught me something about trust, about purpose, and about the quiet burden of leadership. But I also learned a lot about resilience and the power of families. During Desert Storm, Sue and our two sons remained in Germany, praying every night for my safety. During later tours, in later years, those two boys and one of our daughters-in-law served alongside me, at different times and in different places.

Our oldest son, Todd, would serve in Iraq from April 2003 to 2004, in places like Ramadi, Falluja, Hit, and Iraq's borders with Jordan and Syria. I flew out from Baghdad to promote him to 1st lieutenant on the Syrian border in front of his soldiers, and it was a proud moment because I not only got to see him but was also able to engage with his cavalry troopers. It was obvious they all admired their lieutenant. He would return in March 2005 and serve again with the 3rd Armored Cavalry Regiment, this time in Mosul and Tal Afar. He returned in November 2009 to Rasheed Air Base, near Baghdad. Then another tour, this time not in Iraq but as part of the Central Command reserve force based in Kuwait. While there, he would be sent to the Sinai for several months during some increasing tensions, and then to Kazakhstan. His last deployment wasn't to Iraq, either. This time it was Poland, during the Russian invasion of Ukraine. Then, as a lieutenant colonel and the G3 of the 1st Infantry Division, he would travel to many NATO nations that were supporting that fight. He still serves proudly.

Our youngest son, Scott, and his wife, Lauren, would serve in the brigade I'd once commanded at Fort Lewis, Washington. The former armor brigade combat team had transformed into the very first of the Stryker brigades. In June of 2006, that 3rd Brigade of the 2nd Infantry Division (the "Arrowhead Brigade") would see combat not in the hills of South Korea for which they had trained but in the palm groves of Diyala and the Dora neighborhood of Baghdad. They would later fight the insurgency in Al-Diwaniyah, then go back to the restive Haifa Street in Baghdad. On our youngest son's second tour in 2009, he would begin at a small forward operating base near the Iranian border, then move to another base in southern Diyala, then go on to a very tough fight in both Jalawla and Baqubah. His wife, Lauren, joined that same unit as a new 2nd lieutenant in February 2007; she was based at the Baghdad International Airport, where I'd been quartered back in 2004. She served at Baqubah while her husband was in the eastern Diyala province during the 2010 tour. They saw each other for a few hours during that fifteen-month deployment, even though they were in the same unit.

The four of us overlapped several times, all of us fighting at different locations in the same faraway land that I had wished twenty–plus years earlier they would all avoid. All the while, Sue—my wife, their mother, their mother-in-law, the bravest member of our family—bore the biggest burden of being at home, worrying and praying for each of us. If a Fitbit had been available during that time, I'm sure her daily step count would have been off the chart. It remains very difficult to describe the emotions, the anxiety, and the love that went into those tours of duty. Yes, a spouse or a child serving is a family's greatest pride, but a deployment to combat is a family's greatest nightmare.

We all sincerely hope that we contributed to the growth of and a new beginning for the Iraqi nation.

1 MAR 1991—Into Kuwait

We stopped our combat just short of the Kuwaiti border. While the maneuver brigades were in Kuwait for their final tank battles, the CAV found itself lingering in Iraq, waiting to be called forward. We got that order today and very unceremoniously crossed a north-south road and a wadi in the middle of the desert which marked our entry into Kuwait. It felt safer.

We moved into some low ground. There was a little bit more grass in this area of desert, so they must have received more rain recently. No difference, except tonight we had a fabulous view of a bright orange glow to our east. The glow, we found out later, is the fire generated by over 200 oil refineries in Kuwait that Saddam Hussein torched as he was pulling his troops out of the country. Those fires are expected to burn for the next two years. The guy was a true thug. I'm glad we stopped them, so you guys don't have to.

Love ya

Dad

Reflection

I remember writing that entry on the morning of March 1, after most of us had collapsed in the turret or on the observation deck of our Bradleys. We were exhausted . . . almost near comatose.

When we'd crossed into Kuwait the day before, the engines in our vehicles had been running almost nonstop for nearly eighty hours. The first seventy-one hours were a steady, deliberate advance—a maneuver we had rehearsed countless times and executed before the age of GPS or onboard navigation aids. We guided ourselves with a Loran navigation system, a boat compass strapped to the top of our vehicles, and the faint glow of a chem light taped to the end of the gun tube on the vehicle in front of us to keep us on the path during darkness. We covered ground, made contact with scattered Iraqi second-tier units, captured prisoners, and finally located the main body of the Republican Guard. For hours, the calm choreography of our advance unraveled into the chaos of combat. The Iraqis had not expected us to arrive from the west—intelligence later confirmed one of their generals had admitted, "We always get lost out there in the desert." They were scattered, some fleeing, others fighting desperately.

For the Blackhawks—the 1st Squadron, 1st Cavalry Regiment—this was a modern echo of an old legacy. The "1-1 Cav" designation wasn't just a set of numbers and letters painted on our vehicles; it represented a lineage stretching back to the Civil War. Then, our squadron had been a regiment, a cavalry division that was part of a cavalry corps. All those Civil War cavalry formations fought mounted on horses and adapted quickly to changing battle conditions. One of the division's most famous leaders during that Civil War period, John Buford, commanded the 1st Division of the 1st Cavalry Corps at Gettysburg. On the first day of that three-day battle in 1863, Buford's troopers rode hard into the fields west of town and made a stand that shaped the course of the campaign. Many Civil War prints hanging in military offices today show Buford's horsemen under a fluttering set of cavalry flags—red over white, emblazoned with a large, gold "1" at the top and bottom. Those were the same colors we carried across the sands of Iraq, a tangible link across more than a century, binding the smell of wet Pennsylvania hay in 1863 to the smell of oil-soaked desert in 1991. Buford's cavalry had set the stage for the fight on McPherson's Ridge to the west of Gettysburg town; we had done the same thing in finding and fixing the enemy in this place in the desert. In 1863, Buford's men had been relieved at the end of the intense fight on the first day and sent to a small area to the south of the battle to rest, recover, and prepare for the next mission. We had done the same.

Much like Buford, as the fight developed, we knew at our level only fragments of what was unfolding in other sectors. Just like Buford didn't know how the various Army of the Potomac corps were flowing into the fight on the hills of Adams County, Pennsylvania, we were also blind. We didn't know what the 1st Infantry Division, under Major General Tom Rhame, was encountering in their final battles or how the 3rd Armored Division, under Major General Paul Funk, was pushing forward. We had no idea what the 2nd Armored Cavalry Regiment was doing after their own hard fight or where the 1st Cavalry Division, under Major General John Tilelli, was positioned. The British 1st Armoured Division, commanded by Major General Rupert Smith—a charismatic tanker beloved by his troopers—was somewhere to our south, and we assumed they were in the thick of it. Nor did we know what was happening to the XVIII Airborne Corps, where Lieutenant General Gary Luck had the 24th Infantry Division, under Major General Barry McCaffrey, executing their own wide, fast hook farther west in Iraq.

Later history would reveal that tense conversations were underway at the highest level—between Desert Storm Commander General Norman Schwarzkopf, Chairman of the Joint Chiefs Colin Powell, and President George H. W. Bush. Schwarzkopf pressed the fight, wanting VII Corps to close the noose on the Republican Guard and the air force to obliterate retreating Iraqi forces. Powell, with the president's backing, saw a different picture: The war had achieved its objectives, the Iraqi Army was shattered, the American media was already reporting a slaughter, and continuing the attack risked turning victory into a massacre. The images of the soon-to-be infamous "Highway of Death"—littered with the burned-out shells of fleeing Iraqi vehicles—were already raising profound moral and political questions.

In that moment, none of that information filtered down to us in the low ground where we laagered that night. To our east, the glow of over two hundred burning oil wells lit the horizon in an angry orange, the smoke thick enough to smear the moonlight into a dull haze. The smell was acrid and clinging—a mixture of burning vehicles, jet fuel exhaust, and scorched oil. The sight was mesmerizing in scale, horrifying in its implications. Saddam Hussein's forces had committed a final act of vandalism against the land and people they had already brutalized—and the environment was paying the price.

We had done our job. We had found the enemy, fixed them, and opened the door for the hammer blow that followed. But as always in combat, the end of a battle is not the end of the story. The questions lingered: What came next? Did we hold there? Push deeper? Redeploy home? None of us knew. We were left with a familiar mix of pride, exhaustion, and uncertainty.

We had "won" Desert Storm in just eighty-nine hours. But we would be back, years later. And those next wars would not be measured in hours. They would be measured in years, with questionable gains and devastating losses that we would sometimes describe as "three steps forward and two steps back." These counterinsurgency and counterterrorism actions looked very different from the clean maneuvers and the eventual end of conflict we delivered in 1991.

Looking back now at Desert Storm, I see how *trust* was the thread running through it all. At the unit level, trust was instinctive and immediate. We built it in our squadron, and President George H.W. Bush generated it in our citizens. Chairman Powell and Secretary of Defense Cheney reinforced it in their conversations with politicians and the American people. We often didn't have the same in our later conflicts.

In combat, you cannot hedge or calculate trust—it must be whole. On a Bradley or Abrams tank crew, drivers trust commanders to navigate through the night; gunners trust leaders to identify targets; wingmen trust each other to cover their flanks. Once proven, that trust became indestructible. That was what carried us through exhaustion, confusion, and chaos. Desert Storm also enjoyed broad trust at home: Its objectives were clear, the coalition strong, the war short. That was due, at least in part, to the fact that Desert Storm was a quick war, and Americans like quick wars, with a lot of explosions shown on TV.

By contrast, trust would not be as stable during our later counterinsurgency and counterterrorism wars. Soldiers in combat zones continued to trust what they could see: their buddies beside them, their leaders in the field, their sense of mission, and their practiced competency. But they couldn't personally affect the shifting political calculations in Washington, the support of the citizenry of the country, or the intelligence that shaped actions. The disadvantages of long wars—counterinsurgencies and counterterrorism fights that took much longer to generate success—and the fleeting attention span of our citizenry caused a loss of interest in what the professional military force (less than 1 percent of our nation) was accomplishing. And the results of Operation Iraqi Freedom (and Operation Enduring Freedom in Afghanistan) stretched that trust thin, often to the breaking point. The false intelligence about chemical weapons, the changing conditions and mission creep, and the president's advice to citizens to keep going to the malls contributed to that deterioration of interest and trust.

This contrast reminds me of something I later learned outside of the army. After retirement from the army, while working in a large health care system, I taught physician leadership courses. In one of those programs, I met a young emergency physician, Dr. Omayra Mansfield. Bright, energetic, and committed, she absorbed leadership lessons quickly and began applying them in one of the most stressful professional environments imaginable. She went on to become a chief medical officer at the largest hospital in one of the most respected health care systems in America. She later wrote a book called *The Trust Transformation*.

In her book, Dr. Mansfield relayed a core message that is simple but profound: Before you can build trust in others—your patients, their families, your colleagues and leaders—you must first trust yourself. Leadership requires clarity of individual values, consistency of action, and authenticity of presence. She knows this is true in an emergency room, and I know it is true in a combat zone. It is something that must also remain true for citizens and policymakers. When trust is absent—when leaders are inconsistent, opaque, or self-deceiving, and when employees or citizens don't feel a part of the team—trust quickly collapses.

Many of those who study trust often revert to a model called the "Johari Window." It's a rhetorical tool used to explain self-awareness and trust between individuals. In combat, soldiers operate almost entirely in the "open quadrant" of that theoretical window—we depend on what we know about each other, gained from close connection, shared hardship, and repetitive experiences that all lead toward trust. There are no illusions about fear, courage, or capabilities. But in other groups—larger teams in different situations—the Johari Window posits that participants often exist in the "hidden" or "blind" quadrants. Some individuals often withhold their full motives (hidden), fail to see their own limitations (blind), or are misled by information that is just not true. The result is a breakdown in trust. As someone who is a student of leaders in the private sector, I'm convinced that trust is the building block of relationships, leadership . . . and life. Trust is gained in myriad ways, and, as I once heard someone say, trust is earned in drops but lost in buckets. Trust is relatively easy to build in small teams, if one knows what it takes to build it. But it is much harder to sustain when hidden motives, blind spots, egos, and personal agendas that are often present in larger teams enter the equation.

Interestingly, military theoretician Carl Von Clausewitz described something similar in broader terms for warfare. He wrote of war as a paradoxical "trinity"—a balance of passion, chance, and reason—that found its practical expression in the relationship between the government, its army, and its people. Each had to trust the other. Citizens had to believe their government's cause was just. Armies had to believe their political leaders would use their sacrifices wisely. And governments had to trust their soldiers to execute with discipline and competence. If one leg of that triangle fails or is even oft kilter, if confidence collapses, the nation that goes to war will suffer significant consequences. Ukraine's resistance to Russia's invasion in 2022 illustrated this perfectly: Ukraine's people trusted their government, its army trusted both the people and their leaders, and the government trusted the army enough to unleash it with broad support. That synergy sustained Ukraine when the odds seemed impossible. Trust, in that sense, is not just personal—it is strategic.

As a nation—as a government, as citizens, and as an army—we were successful in building the trust needed to execute Desert Storm inside our units, between the government and the people, and between the people and the army. But during later wars, we found ourselves in a place where no military leader, and certainly no government, wants to be. Despite tough fighting by courageous soldiers, competent diplomacy of the State Department, and the desire of governmental officials to achieve stated goals, three of the other wars—Vietnam, Operation Enduring Freedom in Afghanistan, and Operation Iraqi Freedom—were failures. In my view, a big part of the reason boiled down to an unbalanced Clausewitzian triangle. A lack of trust.

To me, the lesson is simple. Trust is critical between people, between the citizenry of a nation and its government, and between governmental officials and their army. Find ways to build trust—improve communication, eliminate misinformation, define the mission, maintain humility, ensure competency and integrity, create understanding—and it will bring you closer to success. All seemingly easy, but to paraphrase Clausewitz, the simplest things are often the most difficult.

3 MAR 1991—Tunnel Rats

Had a busy day yesterday. We're currently located in an area which, I believe, may have been an Iraqi battalion headquarters CP complex. Three days after the war has ended, there are still a lot of Iraqis coming out of their holes and surrendering. Yesterday, 18 guys came out of a bunker complex we didn't even know was about 300 meters away from our command post. After giving them food and water (they wolfed down some MREs—probably had not eaten in days), we talked to one of the guys who spoke very poor English. He claimed he was not a member of the Republican Guards, but you could see where he had ripped his red triangular patch off his shoulders. He took us to his bunker, and we found a series of others that even he didn't know about.

There were weapons, food, and radios in all these underground tunnels. And they were all a mess. That's understandable, knowing all these Iraqi soldiers had lived in these mud huts underground, under constant bombing and lack of food and other necessary supplies. It was simply unbelievable.

I wanted to be out there with the soldiers that were scouring these bunkers; it was important to me to see what they were like, and the conditions. Early on, the entire crew of HQ 33 would drive up to a location, and then we would all enter, one after another. In later wars, that would be called a "stack," though we had not practiced that skill. On a few occasions, I entered first into bunkers with my pistol drawn. But soon, the "stack" fell apart, since we hadn't found anyone inside any of them, and we became complacent. We each started looking into the bunkers without any help from others in our crew.

Doing that to one bunker, I received the shock of my life when I encountered an Iraqi soldier huddled in the corner in the darkness. I shot once toward his feet, and he immediately jumped out in the open and surrendered. I started thinking about how stupid I was for going, face first, with only a .45 caliber pistol, into a dark hole that had once been the headquarters of an "elite" army unit. I vowed never to do that again.

These holes were very barren—a few steps down into the earth, a blanket for a bed in the middle of an earth floor, a place for a weapon and some dishes, and some type of overhead protection. They all smelled like mildew and wet dirt. It was disgusting!

We found a lot of "stuff" that we could take back as "war prizes" for our museums and personal collections. The war rules say we couldn't take weapons for personal use, but if we make them unserviceable, we can take weapons back for the Division's use in our museum. I, personally, don't even want to see any of that stuff again. I just want to see you guys, and I really would like to be with you tonight.

Love ya,

Dad

Reflection

I lied in that journal entry. Not just a small omission but a deliberate choice to write one version of events while having lived another. I lied because even then, three days after the war had ended, I knew this was something I couldn't admit on paper—not to myself and certainly not to the sons I imagined one day reading these words. Some truths are too heavy to hand to your children, especially when they're still too young to understand.

The truth is that before that moment, we had been clearing bunker after bunker, each one foul and lifeless. In reading this journal entry, I remember the sights and the smells. We descended into dark, earthen caverns with rotting food scattered in corners, rusted weapons stacked like firewood, and discarded uniforms. The air was thick with mildew but also the rank odor of sweat, urine, and feces. These were not just shelters; they were tombs-in-waiting, where soldiers had huddled underground for months under relentless bombing, never sure if the next explosion would seal them inside forever or just make their lives more miserable than they already were. In every bunker we found, there were no men—just the evidence of how they had tried, and failed, to endure.

That pattern made us careless. We separated and moved to individual bunkers so we could clear more of them in a shorter period. I stepped into one bunker alone, expecting more of the same: silence, filth, abandonment. Instead, in the shadows, a man leaped up. His weapon was already coming to his shoulder. I had the angle and the surprise, and in that instant, my body reacted faster than his. I fired three times. He dropped.

When his body fell forward, his helmet tumbled away, and when it did, I could see a picture inside the headgear. A wife, two children, smiling in a sunlit moment of better times. I've carried that image with me for a long time.

That single act—the only time I killed another human being at such close range—haunted me in ways the destruction of Iraqi tanks, brigades, or divisions never did. From our Bradleys and Abrams, and from our fighters and bombers flying overhead, the US military had unleashed devastation at a distance, impersonal and overwhelming. But this was not distant. This was intimate, visceral, and undeniable. It wounded something deep inside, and I've carried the scars since then.

Scholars now call this *moral injury*. It is distinct from physical wounds and even from the flashbacks of post-traumatic stress. It is the psychic cost of crossing a line your own moral compass told you not to cross, even when you had no choice. A friend and journalism instructor at West Point, Professor Elizabeth Samet, wrote a book called *Soldier's Heart*. In it, she traces how medicine struggled to name this affliction. In World War I, it was thought to be a cardiac problem and was called "soldier's heart." In World War II, it was termed "battle fatigue." But by the time science analyzed those who'd fought the war in Vietnam, it became post-traumatic stress disorder, or PTSD, or PTS, a lesser variant, not a true disorder, without as much baggage. Different names for the same rupture of the human spirit when confronted with things no person is designed to endure.

Iraq and Afghanistan later showed this truth again. Most of the killing there wasn't done with tank cannons or aircraft bombs. It was infantrymen entering houses, often face-to-face. And many who weren't trained as infantry—engineers, logisticians, artillerymen—and were not prepared for, as a friend of mine termed it, "coffee-breath close assault," also found themselves fighting at close quarters, killing or being killed. For some, the memory of those moments never leaves, and they replay in dreams and in silence.

It's not only soldiers who carry such burdens. A psychiatrist in Orlando once told me that railroad engineers have a very high rate of PTSD because they sometimes have to watch helplessly as a child or a car lies on the tracks ahead, knowing they can do nothing to stop their trains. Police officers forced to pull the trigger on a dark street and physicians who watch too many patients die night after night also experience it in high numbers. Survivors of sexual assault, who bear memories no one should ever bear, also experience this trauma. Different professions, different circumstances, but the same wound: human beings placed in situations that overwhelm the natural order of human experience. And, interestingly, in combat, it isn't just the fighters who carry these scars. Sometimes it's the sergeant in the operation center, who isn't on patrol but feels guilty for not being with his buddies. Or it's the truck driver, who may see the carnage and the combat detritus after the fight is over. Or it's the parents who have offspring in combat because when their child comes home, those parents see the loss of innocence that is present when someone returns from war.

I know for years I locked away my experience in that bunker, never telling anyone, even my wife. Silence was my armor, but it was also my prison. Sue finally broke through, seeing my mood swings and some of my sleepless nights, and urged me to talk to a counselor when she knew there were some things that I just could not admit. That is what loving family members do—they notice, they persist, they help you face what you cannot face alone.

The truth is that the scar remains. The dreams still come, though less frequent and less intense, and I know the photograph of that Iraqi soldier's family will be forever etched in my mind. Scars are different from open wounds, though. Partly because they remind you of the injury, but also because they prove that healing, however imperfect, will occur if you treat the pain correctly and if you have a little help from your friends.

5 MAR 1991—The Dead Guys

This was a long-range war. The Air Force was bombing from well over 5,000 feet; never saw their targets. Even the A-10s—the ground support "close air" aircraft—would launch Mavericks from over 3,000 feet at tank targets. When tanks and Bradleys met the enemy, they could engage from anywhere between 2,000–4,000 meters. The result was we won decisively—one Iraqi soldier, when asked when he knew US tanks were approaching his position, said he knew it when the tanks on each side of him blew up. He didn't even see what hit them. That was good for us, bad, very bad, for the Iraqis.

The result of this has an interesting twist for those of us in the Army. We didn't really see the people we were killing; we only saw equipment blow up. There was no personal attachment to some of the things we were doing.

That changed for me today. I saw several dead Iraqi soldiers near a destroyed tank. I'm sure my Bradley crew didn't know what was going on when I told them to pull over and got out of my vehicle. I stared at the faces of the tank crew for several minutes and saw different things in each one. In one, total agony, eyes open, mouth gaping. The driver was sloped over the front of the driver's hatch, and his face looked almost peaceful. The tank commander had been thrown several hundred yards from the tank. His body was twisted but not burnt like the other two. Flies were all over him. His corpse was the only one that made me feel sick, and I almost threw up as I looked at him, but for some reason I couldn't pull away. The war had not been real for me up to the time I saw those Iraqi soldiers. After I looked at them and realized how many other like them—tens of thousands—were spread over the Iraqi countryside, I realized what this war's toll really was. It was a grave price to pay by the Iraqi nation.

Up to today, I thought Saddam Hussein was a mean, evil man who had to be stopped. We were the ones to do it. Whatever price it took, no matter how many Iraqi tanks we had to destroy, no matter how many Iraqi soldiers we had to kill. But when I saw the faces of those three Iraqi tank crewmen, all I could think of was how they might have two sons like me, how they may have, the instant before their death, wished they could be home with their wives. How they would miss all of life's best in the future because a political leader had asked them to fight for something that was as simple as power or stature. It was at this point I learned two things: 1) I hate Saddam Hussein, not only for who he is, but for taking me away from my family and for permanently separating many Iraqi mothers and wives from their men, 2) That war, beyond all its glory and flag-waving and patriotism and medals, is a very ugly thing. I will sincerely pray, for the rest of my life, that neither of you two boys will ever experience the horrors of war.

Every time I put on my dress uniform—my dress blues—in the past, I felt very patriotic and proud of what I was doing. I think from now on, I will also always remember the faces of those three Iraqi tank crewmen that I met, but never knew, up close and personal.

I'll be praying for you tonight,

Dad

Reflection

In a previous reflection, I talked about the term "moral injury," how close-range killing leaves scars different from distant destruction. This reflection may seem repetitive, but it was also based on the coincidence of what happened on the ground on two separate days in early March 1991. This journal entry was several days after the ceasefire, the end of the war. What this moment added for me was permanence—the awareness that long after wars end, it is the loss that endures. I carried the memory of those Iraqi soldiers with me, and years later in Baghdad, I walked up to wreckage caused by a vehicle-borne improvised explosive device (VBIED)—a suicide car bombing—and saw nothing left in the burned-out car but a pelvic bone resting on the driver's seat. I was instantly back in 1991. Death has a way of linking itself across decades, stitching together memories you wish you could forget.

The army tried to address the unseen costs of war with programs like *Battlemind* and resilience training, trying to help troops recover and get "back to normal" before their next deployment, but nothing truly eliminates those images or prepares you for the future. These are not abstractions, not "casualty figures," not "boots on the ground." No matter that they were the enemy, they were also sons, daughters, fathers, mothers—each one loved, each one with a story they never got to finish.

I mentioned earlier the "make it matter" box that is on my desk. There is other information on those cards with photos of soldiers I served with who never came home. On the back of each card is a lot of personal information, like places of birth, birthdays, how old they were when they died. All a reminder of the life that was cut short. I take out a few every day and think about who they might have become if war hadn't ended their lives when they were young men and women.

One card I looked at today was a young private who died in 2003. He'd be in his early forties today. He could have been an army command sergeant major, shaping the next generation of soldiers. Or maybe he would have left the army and become an insurance adjuster, a schoolteacher, a doctor, a lawyer, a minister. He might have married his high school sweetheart and raised three kids. Or maybe his first marriage would have failed, but he would have found love again, and with it, stability and joy. The possibilities were endless—except they were not to be. That particular soldier's story ended at eighteen, and he remains forever young in the photo I hold. The promises of life didn't come to fruition.

When I've spoken to the American people as a CNN analyst, I've tried to bring that truth forward—to convey the insight provided in historian John Keegan's wonderful book, *The Face of Battle*, that war is not just about strategy, arrows on a map, and objectives taken but also about what happens to human beings in the mud and the fire. I despise when the uninitiated use the phrase "boots on the ground." Boots don't bleed. Boots don't laugh. Boots don't write letters home. People do. And when people die, it is not only their lives that are lost—it is the families they would have built, the careers they might have pursued, the communities they might have shaped.

War is always about people, those who sacrifice for a cause or who are thrown into a mix. The faces of those we fight beside and the faces of those we fight against. The faces of the families left behind, on both sides. To ignore that is to mistake war for strategy alone, when in truth, it is always, inescapably, about people and what they believe in or what they are asked to defend. For that reason, if for no others, we ought to be very careful when we sound the war toxins.

13 MAR 1991—Kuwait City

The SCO asked me to conduct a recon of a route we'll be taking back into Saudi Arabia from where we were now near the northwest border of Iraq and Kuwait, near the town of Al Basiyah, so I had a chance to fly toward, and over, Kuwait City on the way to that location. The flight made me vow to become an environmentalist when I return to you guys and civilization.

The sky for the past few days has been a depressing gray, and the sun has simply been a white ball in the sky. It's been dark here at four in the afternoon. All this was due to the soot coming from the hundreds of oil well fires that Hussein lit prior to the end of the war in Kuwait. As I flew toward the city today, it got much worse.

The sky was black, and visibility was limited to a few hundred feet (in a helicopter, that's not so good). On a stretch of side lane highway near Al Jahra (a suburb of Kuwait City) was a stretch called suicide alley. Hundreds of destroyed tanks, trucks, personnel carriers, etc. were all pushed off the side of the road. What I saw were the remains of what at one time was probably the prettiest city in the area. It will be many years before it is restored. What a shame.

Dad

Reflection

That flight in one of our squadron helicopters over Kuwait City toward what would become our planned redeployment assembly area back in Saudi Arabia was my first real look from above since the war began. That aerial view offered a haunting reminder of what war can do—not just to armies but to the land itself. First, there were the tracks of thousands of armored vehicles that marked the route of attack of so many units in the wet sand of southern Iraq, moving north and then turning to the northeast. Then, in the distance, hundreds of oil wells set aflame by Saddam's orders were belching smoke into the atmosphere, and the sun at that altitude was like a flashlight behind a dark gray blanket. In the days that followed, the skies would increase in their blackness, and the sun, when it appeared, would be a white disc. Later in the day, when I returned in the early afternoon, our laager site already looked like it was dusk. The smell of burning crude would increasingly cling to us. I later learned that some estimates indicated more than six hundred wells had been torched, and it took an international effort nearly a year to extinguish them. Saddam had lost on the battlefield, but in his army's retreat, he ensured the environment and Kuwait's economy would suffer long after his army fled.

That raised a dilemma I would encounter again, years later. Destroying infrastructure may achieve military advantage, but it exacts an enduring cost on the land and, more importantly, the population and infrastructure you may one day have to govern and rebuild. In 1991, the destruction was largely Saddam's doing. In 2003, the next time I came back to Iraq, we Americans inflicted it. The "shock and awe" campaign toppled Saddam swiftly, but the damage to Baghdad's power grid, sewage systems, civilian buildings, and government ministries left a broken city. I remember driving around the capital in a Humvee during my next tour in 2003 and seeing the ruins of Saddam's palaces but also the rubble of schools, hospitals, high-rises, and government offices that Iraqis depended upon. What looked like precision war from the air and on cable news was, at ground level, a source of daily misery for civilians who had to live among the wreckage.

The problem wasn't confined to Baghdad. In 2007, when I returned a third time to another area as the 1st AD commander in northern Iraq, we faced the same destruction. I remember my first visit to the Baiji Oil Refinery (BOR), which was once the economic engine of the Salah ad Din province, Saddam's home turf and where his tribe and most of its people lived. The BOR was no longer a modern complex; it had once provided a jobs program for Saddam's tribe when Saddam had ordered the diversion of Kurdish oil to the south. But Baiji had been bombed in 2003, and by the time I walked through its grounds, Iraqi workers were still struggling heroically to patch it back together. Even half-functioning, it was vital for the livelihoods of thousands, so we assigned a young captain by the name of Joe DaSilva, who was a company commander in one of our brigades, to help the plant come back to life. What Joe soon learned was the ultimate paradox of a counterinsurgency and counterterrorism fight: Every attempt we made to help restore Baiji was shadowed by terrorists siphoning fuel for the black market in Syria, where they would funnel the profits after sale back to al-Qaeda in Iraq. Infrastructure was not just an economic lifeline for normal citizens—it was also a target, a prize, and a weapon for the terrorists.

Baiji was only part of the story. Tikrit, Mosul, Tal Afar, Kirkuk, and every other town in our area of operations bore scars of destruction from our earlier actions and the more recent conduct of the terrorists—bridges dropped, markets leveled, roads cratered. When we poured money into reconstruction projects, through USAID and State Department teams, what Iraqis often saw was not our generosity but our guilt: We were fixing what we had broken, and the terrorists further undermined our actions until we could stop them. Trust was hard to earn in places where people remembered the US bombs and artillery shells before they saw our engineers attempting to help them rebuild.

The lesson is one that still resonates: Victory on the battlefield cannot come at the cost of the society that survives it. Destroy too much, and the peace you hope to build becomes a peace built on resentment. Destroy too little, and you prolong the fight. That's what the Israeli army wrestles with every day with their Hamas and Hezbollah enemies after the October 7th attack. The middle ground is the hardest to find, but it is the essence of strategy.

What I learned flying over Kuwait City in 1991—seeing the tracks of our conquering army, feeling appalled at the roads below filled with death, watching a nation smothered by black smoke—was that the human and environmental costs of destruction linger far longer than the celebrations of military victory. And what I saw in Iraq after 2003 only reinforced all that. Wars are not just about tanks destroyed or enemies defeated. They are about whether societies left behind can someday again live, breathe, and rebuild. If attacking forces—governmental and military elements—fail to plan for that, they will likely win the war but lose the peace.

17 MAR 1991—The Iraqi Generals

Hi guys,

Saw a report today that summarized a prisoner of war interview with nine captured Iraqi general officers. Very interesting. A series of topics were addressed, and though the document was secret I think I can sanitize the contents in this book to make it "unclassified." Here's the summary:

Regarding Kuwait: There was the feeling, and it was obvious in the interview, that Iraq feels Kuwait is the snob of the area. The Kuwaitis are better fed, wealthier, and did not realize the "sacrifice" that Iraq made in fighting against "Iranian" expansionism during the eight-year war. The impression was that Kuwait got what it asked for, since she would not help Iraq clear her nation's indebtedness by increasing oil prices for the world.

On the Iraqi Army's Role: Saddam's gamble was not widely discussed prior to the invasion with the military—most Army officers learned of the invasion on the Baghdad evening news (much the way we learned of our call up). Saddam did not trust the regular army and hence did not consult them as would have been done in our country. All the generals, even the hard-core Ba'athists, said they would have counseled Saddam against the confrontation with the Coalition. Hence, while the takeover was believed to have been just, the consequences and Saddam's reaction to them, were considered foolish and unwise.

The Air Campaign: War weariness, harsh conditions, and lack of conviction as to the justice of the cause caused widespread desertion in the Iraqi Army. The bombing campaign significantly contributed to their problems. All the generals said most of the psyops campaign was extremely effective—the pamphlets told the Iraqi soldiers to stay away from their vehicles, and then the next day they came in and destroyed the vehicles very efficiently. While the A-10 was the big tank killer, the B-52 was the most feared.

Intelligence: The generals said the defensive strategy that worked so well against the Iranians failed against the Americans because of our satellite intel and our collection management of data, combined with our precision weapons systems. One said, "I know about your intel systems—I saw their products during our war with Iran." All the commanders also said the Iraqi tactical intel was terrible—they did not know where our units were or what we were equipped with—one said he did not know what a British Challenger looked like until one pulled up outside his command post. Others did not know the Americans were attacking until our units overran them.

Logistics: The generals said the ground campaign was unnecessary, for if the air campaign would have lasted two or three more weeks, it would have effectively strangled the Iraqi army's capability to wage war. They had plenty of ammo, but they only had days of water, food, petroleum, and parts. This was backed up by what we saw on the ground and what we heard from the E-POWs.

The American Soldier: Without exception, the generals expressed their admiration for the American Soldier they encountered on the battlefield and in their captivity. They commented on the discipline, professionalism, and expertise, and the kindness the Soldiers showed when POW's surrendered. All said they would take the story of American magnanimity in victory home to fellow Iraqis.

It was an interesting report, and I thought you guys might find it interesting at some time in the future (you probably won't understand a lot of this when you first read it—but as you study history, it might be fun to reflect on it).

Love,

Dad

Reflection

The report from those Iraqi generals was confirming and humbling at the same time. They noticed our strengths—precision, logistics, intelligence, discipline—and they were right. But their words were the tip of an iceberg that had all begun when I was a young captain, when we had terrific general officers who wanted to rebuild the army and transform the force, which took us fifteen years. After Vietnam, and with lessons we learned from the Israelis, we rebuilt the force, rewired our training, and, with the prodding of the Goldwater–Nichols Act, forced ourselves to fight as a joint team. By 1991, the army, air force, navy, and marines could choreograph a conventional and high-intensity campaign at a tempo and clarity our adversaries simply couldn't match. What these Iraqi generals sensed on the receiving end was the product of doctrine hammered at the training centers, staffs drilled on planning and targeting, new equipment acquisition, a focus on leadership and doctrine, a professional force with great NCOs, logisticians who could move mountains, and a culture that had put learning and growing at the center of their actions. All of those had been coordinated and refined at our newly established training centers: The National Training Center (NTC) in California, the Joint Readiness Training Center (JRTC) in Louisiana, and the Combat Maneuver Training Center (CMTC, later Joint Multinational Readiness Center, or JMRC) in Germany.

Our own assessments after the war—coming from the CALL collections from the desert, RAND studies, the *Gulf War Air Power Survey*, and even individual unit after-action reports—added nuance the POW interviews couldn't. They praised what worked but also noted where we were lucky or vulnerable. Airpower was devastating, yes, but damage claims were optimistic before assessments, and many Iraqi units survived bombardment in numbers that required further clearing and destruction of their equipment. The logistics and supply chains were magnificent but thin in places; communications, while mostly superb, could still get saturated by too much traffic. Those reports were not glamorous readings—charts, annexes, "observations"—but they mattered because they kept us honest. They created some scar tissue. They reminded us that one quick win does not confer a lifetime warranty.

That's a leadership lesson I wish I could bottle for anyone running any organization, in the military or in the private sector: Victory is a terrible teacher if you let it flatter you. The Iraqi generals' respect only fed our hubris. The better response was to treat their praise as a baseline and ask, "How will the next fight be different—and are we reorganizing now to meet it?" In uniform, in a hospital, in a classroom, the same rule applies. When the scoreboard looks good, leaders are tempted to spike the football, freeze the roster, and frame the plan. That's precisely when you should revise and build your next playbook.

I tried to translate those insights into habits. The first habit is humility with structure. In Desert Storm, we ran deliberate after-action reviews at every level, from our combat reports to our time at the training centers, then fed the results up to CALL. The point wasn't to admire success; it was to capture what continued to show up as broken and fix it before the next rep. Years later, as a division commander, then in health care and as a professor, I tried to keep that muscle alive—after every mission, every project, every course, I asked, "What did we intend? What happened? Why? How can we polish the diamond on good things, and what can we do differently in areas that aren't so good?" That's the AAR process. It's amazing how quickly an organization matures when humility isn't a feeling but a process and when thick skin prevails.

The second habit is dissent on purpose. We won fast in '91, and it would have been easy to surround ourselves with people who told us why we were brilliant. The better path is to seat a red team at the table—smart skeptics empowered to poke holes in our plan or what we were considering. As the J7 at the Pentagon, that was my drumbeat. When the concept for the 2003 invasion began to take shape and was discussed in the Joint Staff, many of us argued the "troop-to-task" math didn't work, especially for what would be needed after the fight to stabilize the broken Iraqi nation. I also provided information on what opening a second front—our army was, after all, fighting the main effort in Afghanistan—would do to our security. But others offered the counterargument of opportunity, speed, and "economy of force" in this second theater. During the eventual attack, our forces fought through southern Iraq with relative quickness—but with some issues we hadn't anticipated—and eventually rolled into Baghdad—but without enough civil affairs, engineers, military police, or governance capacity to hold what we took. And then occupation policies—de-Ba'athification and disbanding the army—poured gasoline on the fire. On one occasion, we had arranged a meeting with a room full of retired Iraqi generals, trying to enlist their help to shut down a growing insurgency and assistance in building a new Iraq, when my aide passed me a note that Ambassador Bremer had revoked all military pensions for Iraqi generals. They received a note from a courier simultaneously, and I had the privilege of watching trust evaporate in real time as over three hundred men stood up and walked out of the center. In the years ahead, some of those officers provided skills to the insurgents who were fighting us. But a few, like LTG Riyadh Jalal Tawfiq—who later became my operational counterpart in northern Iraq as the commander of the Mosul Operations Center (or MOC, as we called it)—chose a different path and became a trusted partner. That day in Baghdad taught me what happens when leaders suppress dissent: Reality supplies it later, at a higher cost.

The third habit is to plan for the day after as hard as you plan for the first day. The day after we finished Desert Storm was clean: drawing boundaries, doing cleanup, meeting end states, conducting redeployment. But later, in 2003, there was no single "day after"—it was months and years of security and nation-building while simultaneously fighting terrorists and insurgents. If there's one through-line from those Iraqi generals' post-conflict comments to our later frustrations, it's this: We excelled at defeating an army, but we were underprepared to midwife a polity. That's not an indictment of the army leaders or our soldiers; it's a reminder to civilians that clear political end states and the resources to achieve them are the non-negotiables of any strategy.

The fourth habit is reinvention. After I retired, an entrepreneur guest speaker told a class of MBAs I was teaching that every three years, leaders should reinvent some part of their organization—the structures, skills, or tools—before the market forces them to. That stuck. The US military's 1980s reinvention resulted in victory in Desert Storm. The 1990s didn't deliver quite the same intensity of change, and we stutter-stepped as we learned and adapted post-9/11. The fix isn't a perpetual revolution; it's disciplined cadence: Keep what works, sunset what's dated, experiment on the edges.

In Mosul, while working with Iraqi LTG Riyadh, we reinvented together—combined map rehearsals during the "Mother of Two Springs" operation (introducing him and his subordinate leaders to what I described earlier), shared networks, integrated patrol bases—because the enemy and the fight in that city demanded it. Reinvention was not a slogan; it was oxygen for a joint team.

Riyadh himself embodied another leadership lesson the generals' report only hints at: Professionalism outlives regimes if you let it. As a lieutenant colonel, Riyadh fought against us in 1991 as a tank battalion commander in the Hammurabi Division. Sixteen years later, he fought beside us to clear Mosul. We broke Ramadan fasts together, traded stories about our sons—both new lieutenants—compared scriptures and tactics. He taught me how faith and patriotism coexisted for him; I watched him lead from the front of a mixed force of Sunni and Shia Arabs, Kurds, and Yazidis. And then I watched, and even argued with, Prime Minister Maliki as he removed him—mid-fight during a major operation—because Riyadh was a Sunni and Maliki used sectarian politics to trump competence. It was a purge that helped hollow out the Iraqi army and set conditions for ISIS's later sweep in 2014. You can write exquisite doctrine, but if leaders install loyalty over merit, they can undo an army's capability in a New York minute.

One more leadership truth sits slightly off the battlefield but matters just as much: Who tells the story shapes what your people learn. In early 2003, we walked the marble corridors of Saddam's palaces and found murals that recast 1991 as an Iraqi victory—an Arab narrative of noble resistance that "drove the Americans away." The POW generals' candor about being surprised, out-ranged, out-coordinated never made it to those walls. That propaganda wasn't art appreciation; it was a strategy to immunize a nation against hard lessons. The reminder for any leader is simple: Curate and tell your organization's story with the same rigor you curate your balance sheet. Celebrate truth, not myth, or you will train your people to fail the next test. As the *Hamilton* lyric suggests, we have no control over who lives, who dies, who tells our stories. You control what you model and memorialize while you're in charge.

Finally, a word about the limits of victory. Those nine generals admired the discipline and magnanimity of American soldiers. So do I. But admiration from an adversary should never blind us to future adaptation and the hard work that is always ahead. The transformation that won 1991 had to be renewed for 2003 and 2007 . . . and it will need continuous renewal again for whatever comes next. That's the real and final leadership lesson threaded through the intel report from a bunch of defeated generals: Learn fast, invite friction, plan past the first success, and reinvent on schedule. If you lead a brigade, a hospital, a classroom, or a company—it's good to continuously build those habits when things are quiet. That's the difference between a force that wins once and a team that endures.

HAVING SEEN THE FIRST ELEPHANT

Post-Combat and Views of the Future

17 MAR 1991—The Commanding General, Iron 6

The Commanding General, MG Griffith, came to talk to our Soldiers today. We immediately fell back into the peacetime "dog and pony" mode—the SCO directed we place all our Bradley's in a U-shaped area in an open area in the desert, soldiers would be formed up in the middle in Troop and Squadron formation. While I kept my thoughts to myself, I found this a bit disgusting; the kind of thing that I hate and newly battle-hardened soldiers see right through. Oh well . . .

But General Griffith handled it all very well. He arrived on his helicopter in a field far enough away so the troops wouldn't get blasted by the prop wash of the blades. The SCO met him and walked him to the formation. The general then said some nice things, and he told the soldiers how well they had performed under some tough circumstances. He told them they would all receive a bunch of medals (I remembered back to my SAMS days when I read how Napoleon had said, "Give me enough ribbon and I will conquer the world") and he told them that as soon as we get the word to move back to Saudi Arabia that we would be back home to Germany within 37 days after that. I hope he's right, that it's a timeline we can keep, and I hope we get the word to move to Saudi Arabia soon.

There are some problems in Iraq. Hussein is trying to prevent an overthrow of his government and a takeover by the Kurds in northern Iraq. He's using his army—the ones that got away—to suppress his people. We've heard he's shooting at civilians with tanks and artillery in the north. In Basra, just about 20 miles to our north, there are about 1,000 people dead in the streets. Some dictators never learn.

Love ya,

Dad

Reflection

When I wrote that entry, I was captured more by the choreography than the meaning. Major General Ron Griffith wasn't just "the general" to me. When I served on his staff, I knew him as my new commander in Germany, taking over from someone whom I truly admired after working for him for almost two years, Major General Fred Franks. Soon after the change of command, when Franks was promoted to three-star lieutenant general and went to Stuttgart to take command of VII Corps and MG Griffith had only been in command a short time, the Berlin Wall fell, and the routes we'd studied for a potential Warsaw Pact invasion suddenly opened for ordinary people carrying shopping bags instead of rifles. I drove those roads into Czechoslovakia soon after the opening of the Iron Curtain, before I was reassigned to 1-1 Cav and saw the cracked pavement, the bleak barracks, the stained riverbanks near garrisons, the concrete apartments that had worn a generation thin. Griffith was new, and he had to face a lot of different challenges and lead a heavy division built for the Fulda Gap and Meiningen Gap into a world that was shifting under all our boots—and was then ordered shortly thereafter to take that same division into an offensive war in the desert. He had one foot on the dock of history's closing chapter and the other on the boat of what would happen during its next phase.

That's why what happened after the helicopter dust settled in our squadron laager area mattered. We had staged the usual U-formation of Bradleys—an armored proscenium arch—but Griffith gently set the theater aside and became a human being. He told nine hundred soldiers to fall out and crowd around. He climbed onto a box so every set of eyes could find him, and he spoke in that steady cadence soldiers lean toward. He started broadly—how the division had trained, how we had performed, how the brigade fights and the cavalry advance guard mission fit together—and then he narrowed the aperture. "How are you all doing now?"

A young soldier yelled out from the rear, "We're doing great, sir, how about you? And when are we going home?"

Everyone laughed. Then, General Griffith started picking out soldiers in the crowd: "Sergeant, where are you from?" "Specialist, how far did you drive that first night?" He asked and listened, then repeated and yelled the soldiers' answers so the whole formation could hear. The rank on his chest didn't change—but the distance between him and the young men in front of him did. The soldiers began to see who this person was, this man who held our fate in his hands, who was relatively new to the job of our division commander. In a war zone, that kind of presence is not cosmetic; it is connective tissue.

I would find myself in that same role, that same position, sixteen years later. I would be that new division commander who hadn't been a division commander before, taking thirty thousand soldiers I didn't know into combat, hoping they would put their trust in me too. But that day with MG Griffith taught me to think more clearly about the kind of leadership that was at play and the kind of leader I wanted to be. Formal leaders are charged—by rank, charter, responsibility—with outcomes. They hold the colors, own the mission, have their names on the signs outside the headquarters and maybe on a personal parking spot in front of the building, but they are accountable for results. Informal leaders may not have a hefty title or a big office; they are the soldiers, the medics, the mechanics, the cooks, and the clerks who knit a unit together in spirit and in practice. They carry the kind of influence that is earned by competence and care, and they make formal leadership possible, just as the formal leaders support them. I've told doctors and MBA students since then that all people should strive to be leaders. Whether or not you have a designated parking spot outside your building or your name on an office door, you must contribute to establishing a vision and a culture for your team, in support of the formal leader.

There's also a third category that every organization must be honest about: toxic leaders. These are not simply demanding leaders; they are corrosive ones—self-focused, fear-dependent, transactional in the worst sense. They can produce short-term compliance at the cost of long-term trust, initiative, and truth. Soldiers, nurses, junior analysts—people in any field—sometimes see these people, feel the difference in their bones, and know that they will never be willingly followed.

Griffith—as the formal leader of a large organization—understood that a senior leader must wear authority without hiding behind it. Presence must be both formal and authentic: formal enough to signal responsibility, authentic enough to invite candor. If you want to lead, you can't remain a distant silhouette on a reviewing stand. You must walk the lines, get mud on your boots, be in places where your soldiers don't want to be, and ask and answer questions with genuine curiosity. That's how you pull people together and establish trust.

Sixteen years later, when I returned to the division and then to Iraq as the commanding general of the same 1st Armored Division, Griffith's box-top talk was still in my head. The army had alerted our headquarters—about four hundred leaders and staff—to deploy during the surge but told me that the rest of our division would not come with us, as they were scheduled for deployments to other areas. Instead, I would receive brigades, battalions, and teams from across the force, from twenty-seven different states, to form a new team called "Task Force Iron." And with them would be a few allies and five Iraqi army divisions. Most of those soldiers and their leaders didn't know me from Adam, and I didn't know them. But I would be their task force leader.

Later, in Iraq, during a battlefield circulation, I heard a young lieutenant whisper to his commander, "Who is this guy?" The answer—"That's the division commander"—made me smile, but it was also a reminder and a warning. Most soldiers do not live their lives inside a general's staff brief. They live them at their squad and platoon levels, following the people who check their weapons, square away their leave forms, knock on their hooch at 0430, and lead them into hostile situations. Joshua Chamberlain's line from the movie *Gettysburg*—"There's nothing so much like God on earth as a general on a battlefield"—can go to your head if you let it. The cure is to show up in a human way and to show increasing humility the higher you go in the organization.

Our small command group built a rhythm that balanced presence and performance. We still did the formal things—after-action reviews, battle updates, ceremonies that mattered—but we tuned our visits for listening. My aides, first Captain Eric Vetro and later Captain Jason Wright, mapped an aggressive circulation plan to fly all over the northern provinces of Iraq where our soldiers were on dozens of different FOBs, COPs, and patrol bases. We dropped into outposts unannounced, did patrol with sergeants and lieutenants, received updates from captains and battalion commanders, sat on ammo cans, asked what was working and what was broken, and took notes that we would act on. I learned more in ten minutes with a squad leader who had just done a patrol than in an hour of polished slides with a lieutenant colonel back at headquarters. These visits became so important that I started taking the intel analysts who covered different areas with me on these "battlefield circulations." I've always believed that kind of approach also works in hospitals and corporate businesses: The surgeons and charge nurses, the line supervisors and customer service reps—they can tell the administrators where their plan collides with reality, if that executive is patient and present enough to hear it. A long time ago, the *Harvard Business Review* published an article entitled "The Effectiveness of Management-By-Walking-Around." Well, leadership by walking around—being present—is a lot better.

That March day in the desert also sat on a longer arc of mentorship that tied Griffith to Fred Franks and tied both to me. Before Desert Storm, I'd served as the division's G-3 operations officer while Franks commanded 1AD. He was quiet, exacting, and brilliant—a Vietnam amputee who never made his injury anyone else's burden and who later led VII Corps with the left hook that broke the Republican Guard. After the war, Griffith became the army's inspector general, then the army's vice chief. One day in 1994, I was traveling with four-star General Franks, who had asked me to be part of his initiatives group at

US Army Training and Doctrine Command, and we were visiting the Pentagon for some meeting. General Griffith, serving there as the IG, sent me a message saying he wanted to talk to me, not General Franks, and told me to come to his office when I could find some time. Well, it's not a good day when you get called to the IG's office, so I was expecting the worst. What I got instead was a conversation about troopers, our time together in Germany and Iraq, and the strange way memory keeps returning to certain nights in the desert. While I was expecting to leave with tasks to pass to my boss, the general just wanted to relive our time together. Years later, at the VII Corps twenty-fifth anniversary, or what we called the annual "Jayhawk Reunion," the four former 1st Armored Division commanders—Franks, Griffith, Marty Dempsey, and me—stood shoulder to shoulder for a photograph. We had all once been subordinates to General Franks, our corps commander, during Desert Storm; now, we shared a singular honor: We all had, at one time in our lives, had the privilege of commanding America's tank division. The picture means more to me with each passing year. It captures succession and stewardship—how one generation carries the colors for the next. How senior leaders look for talent, then build a bench with those they think have the most potential to take on the toughest of assignments., then build a bench with those they think have the most potential to take on the toughest of assignments.

If Griffith gave a lesson on how a senior leader closes the distance with his soldiers that day, he also reminded me to beware of the distance that rank creates even when you don't intend it. A general's helicopter, the convoy, the aides, the security—those trappings can smother candor before a leader says a word. The antidote is deliberate humility. Ask a private to explain a checklist. Invite a specialist to show you how the new software works. Praise the mechanic who found the hairline crack no one else saw. Talk to a lieutenant about what they've found during pre-combat checks. Make eye contact with the soldier whose name tape you mispronounced and try again. Laugh with the soldier who yells out, "When are we going home, sir?" Or, if you're working with health care providers as I did later in my career, accept the invitation from an emergency department physician to spend a shift with her (as I did with Dr. Omayra Mansfield, whom I introduced earlier in this book), or watch a cardiovascular surgeon and his team perform a heart valve replacement on a patient, then go with him as he informs the family about the positive results of the surgery (thank you, Dr. Kevin Accola!). These aren't gestures; they are investments in the only currency that buys performance under pressure—shared trust.

There's one more thing that day taught me, which I now share with physicians and MBA students: Everyone is a leader. Some are leaders by appointment, with explicit responsibility for outcomes and for people. Others are leaders through capabilities and skills—the ones peers gravitate toward when things get hard. Both must know the work, the purpose, and the people. Both must understand that influence is not a speech; it is a series of consistent, competent, decent actions that can only be applied when you know another individual's motivation for doing things. And both must guard against the habits of toxicity: the shortcut that erodes standards, the sarcasm that shames a junior in public, the hubris that stifles listening, the rigid certainty that squeezes learning out of a team.

The backdrop to Griffith's visit was itself a leadership lesson. Even as he spoke, the region was convulsing: a Kurdish uprising in the north, Shia demonstrations in the south, Saddam's forces turning their remaining guns inward against fellow Iraqi citizens. We were still young enough not to know how unfinished that story would be. Griffith was also a Vietnam veteran, so he had a feel. He had lived through the end of one era and the violent birth of another. His message—part praise, part promise, part warning—wasn't just about medals and timelines; it was about stewardship. You train hard, you fight well, you treat people decently, you develop a team in myriad ways, and then you hand the division to the next leader a little better than you found it.

That is where—looking back—I see this particular through line from Germany to the desert to Baghdad and beyond. Leadership matters. The kind of leader you choose to be matters, and the kinds of leaders one chooses to emulate matter as well. All that matters most when the stakes are highest. Formal authority gives you the microphone, but methods of influence give your words weight. Presence—real, human, prepared, and curious—turns a speech in a dusty field in the middle of nowhere into a moment and a memory people carry with them for years.

I learned that from Griffith. And Franks. And Dempsey. And so many others whom I saw as true leaders. I tried to practice their style, with my own added personal brand of authenticity, that I had learned by watching them with my soldiers. I teach all this now to people in suits and scrubs who will never command a tank but who will face their own versions of uncertain skies, tight timelines, and tired teams looking for a leader they can trust.

19 MAR 1991—Misty

Had the chance to use our satellite phone to call home today for the first time since mid-February, before the war started. Got to talk to Mom for about 10 minutes—it was well worth it. It was great to hear her voice. Sorry you guys weren't home, but I sent you my love through her.

Mom gave me a lot of good info in that ten minute stretch: how you guys really miss me and can't understand why, since the war is over, I can't come home; how LT Clark reported my being a casualty almost two weeks after the war ended; how our scheduled move back to the US may be postponed by as much as six months; and, though it happened on 10 January, how Misty had to be put to sleep.

Mom was right in not telling me about Misty in a letter back then, because I would have thought a lot about it. It's probably hard for you guys to understand, but I really loved that crazy dog. You guys probably don't remember her crazier days when she was younger, but her personality was unique for a dog, one which always made me smile.

You've heard the story about our purchase of Misty many times: A rainy day, a little puppy who nuzzled Mom's knee when the rest of the litter cowered away, and a wet trip home with a little puppy in September of 1978 at Fort Polk, Louisiana. What we probably did not tell you is that both of us had some unspoken ideas about this dog—we were told by a good friend before we brought her home that if you want to be a good parent, get a dog! So, Misty was the thing that was going to help us become a better mom and dad for when we had you guys.

You see, moms and dads don't have any schools to go to that teach how to be good parents; it's a complete trial and error sort of thing. By making some mistakes on a pet—and believe me, we made some mistakes with Misty! —we learned about what works with discipline, love, and caring. Don't get me wrong, we certainly don't think there is a 100% carryover between dogs and little boys. But we sure did learn a lot about how to treat and teach you guys from our very first family pet.

I can also remember the fun times with Misty. How when we first tried to teach her to swim, she wouldn't go near the water ("But Sue, she's a Labrador. She's supposed to love the water!"). How she used to pull her little "wonder-dog" trick through our house in Rosepine, Louisiana. How I once put glasses, a cap, and a shawl around her to make her look like a person, and how that picture of her is one of our favorites now. Her looks over her shoulder at Mom right before she would run away. Her sad eyes when she was in the kitchen begging for food or when she was about to go into her shipping crate as we prepared to make another move, or another flight to Germany. Her joy at seeing Grandpa Schmutz and anticipating the many walks he would give her to wear her out (he loved that dog as much as we did). The joy at seeing Grandpa Hertling and the time he would spend scratching behind her ears. Her laying under the coffee table, constantly! Her chewing of flip chews or bones until her teeth bled. Her cuddling with us when we would watch TV. My loving walks with her—a chance for me to think and a chance for her to piddle—in all our assignments when she was with us: Louisiana, Indiana, West Point, Leavenworth, and especially here in Germany. And her Christmas letters, which always made me emotional and seemed to elicit a lot of joy from our friends that a dog would give her perspective on what the Hertling family was up to.

I'm gonna miss that pain in the ass dog. And I sincerely hope you remember all the good times we had with her. Try very hard to forget this last year, as she failed in health, couldn't see or walk very well, and constantly had accidents, which Mom so patiently cleaned up. Think instead of the puppy who gave us lots of laughs and lots more love, the one who got muddy on the Volksmarches in Germany and constantly had puppy breath and hated to be bathed in the bathtub. That Misty "loved us all proudly," just like we loved her. And now, just like we love you. Maybe dogs do teach people how to be good parents.

Love,

Dad

Reflection

That phone call in March 1991 was a gift—but also a gut punch. For ten minutes, I felt the joy of hearing Sue's voice but also the heartbreak of learning that Misty—our first dog, our first shared "trial run" at parenting—was gone. Months had passed since her death, and I had no chance to be there, no chance to say goodbye. That is the reality for military families: Grief and milestones do not wait for deployments to end.

What I didn't put in the journal was the dread I carried before leaving for the Gulf. Misty was already failing; the army's veterinarian had found cancer, and her decline was obvious. On cold German nights, I walked her up Hauptstrasse, watching her rally during those moments outside even as her body weakened indoors. In my mind, those walks became symbols. If she could push through pain for me, I could push through for my family. Yet I also carried the fear that she and I would both die while I was away—two losses Sue and the boys would be forced to absorb alone. That weight is something many soldiers carry—not only fear for themselves but fear for what their absence will mean at home.

Sue bore that burden with quiet courage. When the time came, she made the decision to put Misty down while the boys were at school. When Todd got off the bus, he asked simply, "Is it done?" The three of them hugged and walked home hand in hand, a family diminished but bound even closer. Scott, younger, asked for Misty's red collar as a keepsake. Sue, thinking earlier in the day it would only deepen the wound the boys might experience, had thrown it away. But when she saw what that symbol meant to him, she climbed into the neighborhood dumpster, fished it out, scrubbed it clean, and gave it back. That moment taught her—and me, when we talked about it later—something profound: Grief is not uniform. Some need to let go; others need something physically tangible to hold on to. Families learn, in the hardest moments, that mourning looks different for everyone.

We promised the boys another dog when I returned. In 1993, at Fort Knox, we found another black lab, full of life and love and chaos. Scott suggested "Spot" as the name—for a completely black dog—but we settled on "Shadow," for how she followed us everywhere. She became another part of our family story, another teacher. And again, later, war intervened. In 2004, while I was in Baghdad, Shadow was also diagnosed with cancer, the same kind that had struck Misty. Sue was also battling Lyme disease at the time. Scott, home from West Point during a vacation, shouldered the grief and the chaos but could not bear to go into the vet's office when it was time to let go. Another loss, another strain borne by the family at home while I was away.

These stories may seem small in the context of war—dogs, collars, vet visits, maladies—but they are emblematic of what military families endure. Soldiers carry rifles; families carry burdens that are quieter but no less heavy. The absence of a parent leaves one to handle tragedies alone, to shield children from pain, to manage crises without a partner. For me, these stories of Misty and Shadow are inseparable from my memories of Desert Storm and Baghdad. They are part of the same ledger of sacrifice.

And there is another lesson. We were told, back in 1978, that if you want to prepare for parenthood, get a dog. Looking back, that advice still rings true, and I offer it to young couples wanting to be parents. Dogs teach patience, consistency, and, most of all, unconditional love. They expose us to mistakes and forgiveness, and they give us constant joy. They reveal differences in how people show love and process loss. And they prepare us, in ways subtle and profound, for raising children. Today, our sons' families both have dogs of their own. I see in their homes the same combination of joy and chaos, and I smile knowing the tradition continues.

But above all, the lesson is this: The sacrifices of war are not only measured in battlefields and casualty lists. They are measured in empty collars, missed goodbyes, and families carrying grief alone. They are measured in the resilience of spouses who climb into dumpsters to honor a child's way of mourning. They are measured in the next generation, who inherit not only the stories of war but also the stories of love and loyalty that carried us through.

20 MAR 1991—The Environment

Today, at about 9:00 am, it looked like midnight. It stayed dark—very dark—all day long. The reason: the soot from the burning Kuwaiti oil fields, combined with a strange temperature inversion, put a black sky in the air all day long. It was hot, muggy, and very scary. I was using my flashlight at noon.

I decided, after viewing this display, that I am gonna be like Mom—maybe even better—in terms of how I treat the environment. I'm going to concentrate on ecology, and I'm gonna make every effort to help you guys do the same thing.

This is a beautiful world we live in. I guess I've been here too long, because there are even parts of the desert that are beautiful. But in the last few weeks, I have seen thousands of rusting and destroyed tanks, PC's, trucks, and other vehicles strewn throughout this desert (I am sure they will be here for years), trash and more trash, and now darkness in the middle of the day. It's too much . . . I want to go someplace that is pretty.

Let's try our best to keep the world a pretty place.

Love ya

Dad

Reflection

At the time, I promised myself I would treat the environment differently. I didn't yet have the vocabulary of "climate change" or "climate security," but we were living in the middle of a world that had been poisoned by one human's decision.

That day in the desert, when noon looked like midnight, marked the first time I truly grasped that the environment itself could become a casualty of war. Saddam Hussein had set over six hundred Kuwaiti oil wells on fire as his forces retreated, and the result was apocalyptic. Soot blackened the sky, the air was unbreathable, and even the simplest tasks—like flying a helicopter—were suddenly dangerous. That day in 1991 felt apocalyptic. At nine in the morning, it looked like it was midnight. By noon, we required flashlights to see our way around. Saddam Hussein's torching of those Kuwaiti oil wells created a man-made eclipse that turned day into night. The smoke, the heat, and the suffocating air made it impossible to ignore: The environment was not a backdrop to war—it was part of the battlefield itself. We couldn't control what dictators did, but we could be a part of some fixes.

The lesson was clear: Over the next few years, we would need to adapt to a rapidly changing environment. As the chief of staff of the army, General Ric Shinseki once told all of us that if we didn't like change or adaptation, we would like irrelevance even less!

Years later, serving as the Joint Staff J7 at the Pentagon, I would connect those 1991 images with emerging studies warning of climate change's effect on security. We saw RAND studies on climate change that were sometimes written in scientific language that also had blunt military assessments. Rising seas would flood naval bases like Norfolk. Droughts and food insecurity would fuel instability across Africa and the Middle East. More missions for the National Guard would be domestic, responding to hurricanes, wildfires, and floods. In other words, climate wasn't just a political debate. It was a threat assessment.

It was easy to make the connection even when ignoring scientific jargon. We'd already seen how a single man's decision to torch oil wells could change the skies, the land, and the health of thousands. The RAND and DOD reports merely reinforced what my eyes had shown me in Kuwait: The climate was changing from an abstract issue into a national security threat multiplier. Drought meant hunger and thirst. Hungry and thirsty people migrate. Migration often leads to conflict.

In 2003, we saw new variations of the same theme again. In Baghdad, during the early days of Operation Iraqi Freedom, the destruction caused by "shock and awe" was everywhere. Bridges, factories, power stations—necessary targets to disable Saddam's ability to fight—were replaced by generators and irrigation workarounds. These became daily reminders of the damage the Iraqi citizens would be living in for a long time. Driving around the city in a Humvee, we passed cratered roads and gutted infrastructure that left entire neighborhoods without reliable power or water. And our soldiers had to operate inside it.

Later, in 2007, up north in the Salah ad Din province, we faced an even older enemy: the environment itself. Iraq had once been part of the Fertile Crescent, but drought and damaged irrigation canals, as well as a lack of Hamrin Mountain snow runoff in the Kurdish region, had left fields barren in the Diyala province. With the land stripped and water redirected and reduced by terrorists and the Kurds against their Arab brothers, the winds created massive dust storms—what the Arabs call haboobs and shamals—that lasted for weeks. Red dust filled the air and settled into everything. Helicopter engines clogged. Precision optics, especially our night-vision lenses, were scratched beyond use. Soldiers coughed constantly, our operational tempo slowed, and in some cases, entire missions were halted. I realized then that nature was not just scenery to consider—it was a force with as much power as an enemy army. As the climate continues to change, that power will certainly reshape not just our lives but every future battlefield.

Commanding in Europe drove the point home. When I visited our northern partners, they raised the issue of the changing Arctic as their primary security threat. The Nordic and Baltic generals spoke of the Arctic ice melt not as an environmental debate but as an operational reality. Melting sea lanes meant other nations could push more warships and submarines into areas that had once been locked by ice. They were shifting resources, redrawing defense plans, and urging NATO to think twenty years ahead. The conversation made me realize the melting ice wasn't just about polar bears—it was about Russia. As sea lanes opened, Moscow could project naval power further north and west than ever before. For Norway, Finland, and Sweden—nations that knew Russia as a neighbor who also used those waterways—the melt was a military challenge.

In southern Europe, the concern was different but no less urgent. Italian, French, Spanish, and Adriatic leaders described the rising tide of migrants from Africa and the Middle East, driven by conflict, hunger, and drought. "Climate is already at our doorstep," one Italian officer told me, and he was right. For them, this wasn't a hypothetical "future war" scenario. It was happening in real time. Drought in North Africa and famine in the Sahel had driven waves of people north. For them, climate was not a "someday" issue—it was arriving on their beaches in boats filled with immigrants. They had to plan not only for conventional threats but also for humanitarian missions, border control, and the strain of resettlement.

The message was consistent across the continent: Climate was reshaping the security map of Europe.

But it wasn't just Europe. Back home, US military planners were warning that coastal bases—Norfolk, San Diego, even parts of Florida—could be at risk of flooding in coming decades. Naval leaders understood what that meant: fewer secure harbors and more contested operating environments. National Guard units saw it too, as their callouts for floods, hurricanes, and wildfires multiplied year after year.

The environment was not just a black sky resulting from oil well fires in Iraq. It was expanding to become a matter of security, of economics, of migration and borders, of life and death. When I drove through the black skies of Kuwait, when I coughed through weeks of red dust in Iraq, when I sat across from European generals worrying about Arctic ice or migrant flows, it all came back to the same truth: The world we shape will shape us in return. And it will certainly affect military leaders in the future.

But adaptation was also happening in ways both big and small, for those who were paying attention. At one of my favorite places in the world—the National Training Center in California—the garrison commander told me that he realized he could save money for soldier training if he cut energy bills. In the middle of the desert, solar energy wasn't "woke." It was—in his words—a no-brainer because it freed dollars for readiness instead of utilities.

Translated to combat, that same kind of approach to energy efficiency could mean lives saved. At the War College, we used to repeat a hard truth: "Amateurs study tactics, but professionals study logistics, because logistics determine the art of the possible." Every gallon of fuel we saved meant one less truck convoy on the road, one less chance of an ambush, one less family grieving back home. That connection between energy and human lives was real.

That dark day in March 1991 started me on an intellectual journey. By the time I retired, I understood that climate change wasn't someone else's issue. It was my soldiers' issue, my allies' issue, and my grandchildren's issue. It was, and remains, a matter of security.

That's why Sue and I drive electric vehicles. It's why we try to make energy-conscious choices. Not because of politics. But because stewardship is a form of service. The world is beautiful—and fragile—and our children and grandchildren will inherit what we leave behind.

21 MAR 1991—The Victims

Made another move today; to the north, about 100 kilometers deeper into Iraq. We (1st Brigade, 1-1 CAV) are taking over the sector previously held by the 82nd Airborne Division. We are about 20–30 kilometers south of the Euphrates River, near the towns of An-Nasiriyah and Basra. The Demarcation Line is about 5 kilometers to our front. I can't believe we're still moving away from Saudi Arabia. We should be going home.

After we set up our northern screen line, I went to visit the two troop commanders—CPT Roger Alford and CPT Greg Heck. Both had some interesting stories about the first few hours in this new sector. Roger had already taken eight prisoners—all of whom had gotten off a bus when one of his scout teams started searching it. They said they would rather become POWs of Americans than go back to Saddam, who would probably kill them. They looked well-fed, clean, and rested. They obviously weren't part of the Iraqi front-line forces.

Many soldiers and civilians approached our scouts for humanitarian and medical aid. Many of them told stories of the fighting in Basra between loyalists and insurgents who were trying to overthrow the government. One injured woman said troops were taking women and children and forcing them to ride on the outside of tanks, so the rebels wouldn't shoot them. Another woman showed burns on her arms and legs from where napalm had been used against civilians. Among these people were others with bullet wounds, and children who had stepped on—or played with—cluster munitions that had been dropped, now missing an arm or leg. (One six-year-old, we were told, had been killed by a cluster bomb.) Many, many other horrible stories were related to us.

In the past few weeks, I've felt sorry for our soldiers who died or were injured; I've also felt sorry for the Iraqis (remember the tank crewmen) who we killed because Saddam wouldn't wake up. Now, I'm feeling very sorry for the women and children who have lost husbands and fathers and now must continue against great odds. It's very tough to look at that and not feel for them with a heavy heart.

I saw a herd of camels today; further from the road I saw a camel that had stepped on a cluster bomb and had lost its leg. It was dying in the sand. There will be a lot of three-legged, dead camels in the Iraqi desert.

Love you,

Dad

Reflection

Executing a combat operation was one thing; facing its aftermath was something altogether different. This wasn't the first journal entry where I confronted death, and it wouldn't be the last. As we drove through the desert, what initially weighed most on me were the burnt-out and rusted tanks that had been destroyed and the soldiers killed in action. But then came other images: women burned by napalm, children maimed by unexploded bomblets, civilians begging for medicine, and even camels—symbols of resilience in the desert—reduced to three-legged shadows of themselves. These images forced me to confront the true cost of war, one that no battlefield victory can ever erase.

In combat, we had focused on soldiers, on the enemy, on our systems, and even on our own self-preservation. But here, in the villages and highways south of Basra, it was women, children, civilians, and even animals who were burned, broken, or begging for medicine that made the war real in a new way.

I happened upon the medics in A Troop, who were administering aid to the victims. I observed them handing out "pills" to several

Bedouin women who were begging for help for their wounded children. When I asked them where they had received the right medicine for treatment, one of them pulled me aside. "Sir, we didn't have any pills, but we wanted to give them something that they might think could help. So we merged Skittles from the MRE packages, separated them into different colors, and put them in pill bottles. I heard in medic training that placebos could make some people feel better, and it's all we got." Simply amazing innovation by a young army medic. It was the same kind of care and dedication to patients I would see much later in life, when I started a second career working for AdventHealth hospital in Orlando. Doctors and nurses live by the Hippocratic pledge of "do no harm," and the doctors, medics, and pharmacists at times recite the beautiful Oath of Maimonides: "The eternal providence has appointed me to watch over the life and health of Thy creatures. May the love for my art actuate me at all times; may neither avarice or miserliness, nor thirst for glory or for a great reputation engage my mind; for the enemies of truth and philanthropy could easily deceive me and make me forgetful of my lofty aim of doing good to Thy children. May I never see in the patient anything but a fellow creature in pain." These young medics and our squadron surgeon were certainly living true to these words as well.

Seeing the damage done by the massive amount of cluster munitions we had fired into the area left a mental scar for me. Designed to shred armored columns, they were effective in the short term. But their "dud rate" left fields littered with small, deadly bomblets indistinguishable from a child's toy or a small can, and children were picking them up. Those who weren't killed were horribly maimed. I remember talking years later about this in interviews, when cluster munitions became a subject of heated debate in Congress and among our allies. Princess Diana's work in Bosnia and later the international campaign to ban these munitions—as well as anti-personnel landmines—shined a spotlight on what soldiers already knew: These weapons often outlived the wars they were meant to win. During my later travels in Europe as

USAREUR commander, I visited Balkan states still scarred by landmines and cluster munitions, with entire woodland areas taped off and demining operations projected to take decades. Leaders there didn't need lectures on humanitarian costs; they lived with them every day.

As our medics and cavalry scouts talked to these men and women who had lived in tents in the desert, we didn't realize that what we were seeing foreshadowed future wars in this same nation. Twelve years later, in 2003, US forces would again drive through An-Nasiriyah, Basra, Hit, and Karbala. These cities were infamous not just for what Saddam had done to his own people in 1991 after our victory but for the resulting chaos that followed the American departure after Desert Storm. An-Nasiriyah became a bloody fight for marines pushing north in 2003. Basra became a swirl of sectarian tension. Hit and Karbala became our area of operations in 2004, when the division was extended during the Sadr uprising, moved from Baghdad to the south to replace the European armies who had decided they had had enough. In these insurgencies and uprisings—different from 1991 when Saddam's armies had worn uniforms distinct from the people—fighters blended into the landscape, and civilians once again bore the brunt of the fighting and the "collateral damage."

Civilians in the Pentagon, the nascent Coalition Provisional Authority, and even some military planners who hadn't experienced Desert Storm had faulty expectations. They underestimated the complexity of Iraqi society and how religious fervor, nationalism, violence, and destruction could overshadow any welcoming gratitude from people just wanting to live their lives. The problems were exacerbated when planners deleted critical US forces—civil affairs teams, military police, governance specialists—from the deployment list because the invasion had been designed for speed, not stability. The Coalition Provisional Authority compounded the error by disbanding the Iraqi Army and banning Ba'ath Party officials, stripping the country of the very leaders and bureaucrats who might have helped stabilize society.

Later, in 2007, during another deployment in northern Iraq, the war was no longer about waging offensive maneuvers against a conventional force, supporting a regime change, or liberating a population from oppression—it was about stabilizing areas, working with tribes and religious communities, and providing security for neighborhoods and families. Our division's fifteen-month tour was defined by tactical firefights, special operations strikes, and the complexity of various groups: sectarian militias, tribes, religious factions, foreign extremists, and everyday Iraqis just trying to survive. Each had its own wounds and grievances, and each was susceptible to manipulation by insurgents or extremists. At times, we took three steps forward to advance trust, but at others, we took two—or more—steps backward.

There was one exceedingly painful moment in Salah ad Din province that I would consider my second-worst day in command of the 1st Armored Division. In the dead of night, while sleeping in my hootch next to headquarters, I received a call on the landline from the shift officer in the operations center. The Joint Special Operations Command (JSOC) liaison said his boss wanted to talk to me. While it wasn't unusual to get late-night calls—usually asking permission for strikes in our area—I had never been asked to coordinate directly with the JSOC commander, who commanded the Seals, Rangers, and all the special operations forces that "worked" the major counterterrorism missions. I knew it must be something special.

It was. JSOC intelligence believed that a key al-Qaeda leader was in Tikrit. They were pinging an active location and wanted immediate permission to strike inside the city. While I was on the line, our division G2 came through the door of my hootch—I was still in my sleeping bag—and waved for me to put the call on mute. The G2 reported they weren't sure the target was the right individual; the name was common, and the folder was incomplete. When I relayed that to JSOC, the commander insisted they had the right man and that it was a time-sensitive target. If they didn't strike now, they might lose him. It was a hard call.

Considering the circumstances, I overrode our division G2 and gave permission.

JSOC has two terms after an operation: "dry hole" or "jackpot." A dry hole means the target wasn't there. A jackpot means they had captured—or killed—the intended target. Within an hour, about 4 a.m., I received another phone call. Jackpot. No details. I'd get more at the morning update.

When I walked to the operations center early the next morning, the G2 and the shift officer were waiting outside for me. Yes, it was a jackpot—they had killed a man during the operation—but he wasn't the right target. JSOC forces had rappelled onto a roof in the middle of Tikrit, conducted their search, and found someone sleeping with a rifle where they had expected. Unfortunately, the young man reached for his AK-47, and the SEAL team "neutralized" him with a double-tap, two shots to his head. They later found that while the man they'd killed had the same name as the terrorist, albeit with a slightly different Arabic spelling, the biodata they took didn't match their intended target. Worse, he was the son of the governor of Salah ad Din province—a man who had once been close to Saddam but whom we had worked with for months to establish new governmental processes. Worse still, the governor had already lost his wife to a roadside bomb and another son earlier in the war. The JSOC liaison then showed me photos of the bedroom where it had happened; the scene was horrific, as one would suspect.

I immediately authorized a large solatia (condolence) payment to the governor, a typical first step in Arab culture. But when I went to his office that morning, there was an obvious and expected chill. He looked me in the eye, silently, and through my translator, I heard his words: "You were my friend. I trusted you. Why did this happen? Why did your forces come into this house and kill my son?" Of course, I couldn't tell him. I couldn't share the details of the raid, the mix-up between headquarters, or that I had personally authorized it. We lost the governor's trust and his support, and during the final few months of our tour, insurgent violence surged in that province. It didn't matter that intelligence was faulty; the result was the same. No amount of condolence money could undo that. In counterinsurgency, trust is the real currency, and we had just bankrupted ourselves in that province.

These experiences forced me to widen my understanding of combat leadership—to the context. As a young officer in 1991, my circle of responsibility was narrow: my troops, my mission, my equipment. By 2007, it included not just thirty thousand American soldiers but fifty thousand Iraqi security forces, provincial leaders, tribes, and civilians whose fates were bound to our success or failure. I learned that leadership is not just defeating enemies—it is caring not only for your soldiers but also for those who become victims, whether they wear your uniform or not. During this third tour, it became clear that my responsibility as a commander in a complex insurgency extended beyond American soldiers. By 2007, I was accountable for the thirty thousand troops under my command, the fifty thousand Iraqi *jundi* (soldiers) we were training, the police and border forces we were helping establish, and the civilians whose lives were shattered daily by bombs, raids, and reprisals. At this point in my career, leadership meant widening the circle of responsibility, even when those civilians didn't wear our uniform, weren't our supporters, and weren't in our chain of command. We had to focus on building trust, not wreaking violence.

The focus on combat actions—kinetic activities—also shifted. We not only had to fight with our forces and coordinate with JSOC during their nightly raids in 2007–2008; we also had to work with State Department Provincial Reconstruction Teams and USAID teammates to bring governance, essential services, and economic hope into communities where despair bred violence. Our four lines of effort centered on security, but as soldiers, we also contributed to economic development, political progress, and the growth of Iraqi security forces. Without all four, none would endure. Compared to this, our actions during Desert Storm seemed simple.

Looking back, the lesson for leaders is sobering but vital. Leadership is more than maneuvering forces or defeating enemies—at times, it also requires recognizing and protecting the potential "victims" of conflict. Often, those are civilians caught in the middle, whose suffering shapes the future far more than any tactical battlefield victory.

While most researchers say the three key elements of leadership are defined by a leader's attributes, competencies, and influence methods (which I'll address in a later reflection), a leader must also incorporate the **context** in which he or she is leading. Context requires understanding the scope and scale of the issues, the culture of the organization, and the growing responsibilities placed upon you. It requires widening the aperture—recognizing that a broader, more diverse group of followers depends on you. This hit home in the counterinsurgency and counterterrorism environment of the early twenty-first century and forged a degree of difficulty far greater than what I had experienced during Desert Storm.

22 MAR 1991—Sensitivity

I got letters from both mom and Grandma Schmutz about the maturity of my two guys when the ground war started. They said that Todd and Scott, on 24 February, were very clued in to what their mother was going through: the stress, the depression, and the hanging on every word of the newscasters. Your solution, from what I understood, was to tell Mom that she needed to get away from it all—"Let's go on a Volksmarch to Rothenberg and try not to think about it." WOW.

To top that off, I understand Todd said, "Mom, don't worry about Dad. He's smart and he knows what he's doing. He'll come home safe!" While I'm not sure about his judgment of my intellect, I appreciate the compliment, and I feel like I know what I'm doing most of the time!

Guys, you don't know how much your support of Mom means to me. You were sensitive to her feelings, and you put her needs above your own. That's empathy, and it's a true mark of a good person. Please keep that quality as you continue to grow. It will serve you well in a dog-eat-dog world, when the nice guys usually wear Milk-Bone underwear.

You guys were also smart in advising Mom to get away from her problems. You know her like I do; the only way she brings down stress is exercising and praying. Keep telling her to do that, to back away when things get rough—and you guys should do that too. Because things will always look better when you take a deep breath, back away for a while, and then return to tackling the tough problems.

Love you guys, and I'm proud of you, too!

Dad

Reflection

After days and weeks of my journal recording only war, violence, and the consequences of combat, here was a moment of pure humanity in a letter I received about the actions of my boys. According to that letter from my mother-in-law, Betty, Todd and Scott didn't just comfort their mom—they modeled one of the greatest leadership traits of all: empathy. As young boys, they saw her stress and sadness, and instead of adding to her worries, they offered her their own kind of counsel: Take a walk, get outside, don't dwell on the news, trust that Dad will be okay. That is the difference between sympathy and empathy. Sympathy says, "I feel bad for you." Empathy says, "I see you, I feel with you, and I'll help carry the load." Even at a young age, my sons understood that.

Their words also reflected another truth about resilience. Sometimes the best way to tackle a problem is to take a step back, breathe, and regain strength. As a soldier, commander, private sector executive, and professor, I've seen and tried to use that same wisdom. When fatigue and stress cloud judgment, step away—pause, re-center, maybe exercise a bit and think while running or swimming, then return with focus. This often makes all the difference. Leaders who push endlessly forward without pause usually miss the bigger picture and never take a break to refresh their minds. My boys were giving their mom that lesson, framed in love.

This entry also reminded me of advice I've repeatedly told my students and subordinates: Take your job, but never yourself, seriously. And have fun when others least expect it! The mission, the work, the responsibility—all of that requires gravity and focus. But I've found that those who carry themselves with too much self-importance lose the ability to laugh, to learn, and to connect with others. What I loved about our boys' words to their mom was that they gave her confidence in me, but they also gave me humility. Todd's reassurance—"He's smart and he knows what he's doing"—made me chuckle then, just as it does now. It reminded me not to overinflate my own role but to stay grounded, approachable, and human. And it reminded me that sometimes people put their trust in you when you don't even know it!

Then there was the "Milk-Bone underwear" line—a quip I haven't used in decades but one that made me laugh as I reread it from years ago. It was a reminder that this journal shouldn't be just about reporting the trauma and death of war. At the time, I wanted this entry to be a break for my sons when they someday read it—a chance to smile, to breathe, to step away from the candid reporting about what I was going through, and to see their dad as more than a soldier cataloging disaster. War leaves scars; humor, warmth, and levity leave their mark in a much different way.

The lessons that I took away when rereading this entry are straightforward but powerful. First, empathy is a mark of strength, not weakness, and it will carry you further in life than hardness ever will. Second, resilience often comes not from constant forward motion but from knowing when to pause, step back, and return to the problem with clarity. And third, balance matters: Leaders must take their jobs seriously, but never themselves. The ability to laugh, to lighten the load, and to offer hope is as much a part of leadership as strategy or decision-making.

23 MAR 1991—Thanks for Your Service

I gotta admit, I don't feel much like writing to you guys today. You see, I've just finished writing about 15 letters to people who had written to me during the operation. Most of them were quickies—letting them know how much I appreciated their thoughts, prayers, and support, and a little bit about what we're doing now and what we had done over the last few weeks. I wrote to the Nojis, Wantys, Anschutzes, and about ten others. I'm sure they might appreciate getting a description of what happened from someone who was/is there, but I gotta tell you it got tough writing those letters and trying to make each one of them a little different, because I know they might share and compare.

I also wrote to you guys and Mom last night. I hadn't written in a while, and I needed to just say "hi." It's difficult to write a letter when all you must talk about is Army stuff—which, you guys know, I don't like to talk about anyway. So, what I did was basically tell you how much I love you and miss you. Which I do, a lot!

Love,

Dad

Reflection

I remember writing this journal entry after I had finished fifteen letters home—short notes to neighbors, friends, and extended family who had sent prayers, letters, or care packages during the months we had been in Iraq. To be honest, I was exhausted from trying to be clever and different with each addressee. If the day of word processors and cut and pastes had been available, it would have been a lot easier, but all these notes were individualized, and I felt I had to get them sent off. It would have been easier to procrastinate, to dash off a single general note, or to let the gestures pass unacknowledged, but I believed then, and still believe now, that a personal "thank you" is more than good manners: It is a form of respect. It tells the person who took the time to care about you that their effort mattered.

I was proud then, and even prouder later, when our boys began to understand this human requirement. Both of our boys, and now our grandchildren, learned early that writing a thank-you note was not optional. Whether it was a "thanks for the birthday gift," an acknowledgment of a wedding present, or appreciation for a Christmas surprise, they all learned the right response was gratitude . . . in writing! Don't get me wrong, we sometimes had to nudge, remind, or insist, but they learned that a few sentences of appreciation sent in your own handwriting meant far more than silence. We taught them those notes didn't just acknowledge a gift—they strengthened bonds of relationship, reminded others that their kindness was seen, and made them stand out in a world where fewer people bother to say thanks. It reflected their character, and it was a show of their presence.

Courtesy extends beyond thank-you notes. It's found in the way we treat others in everyday life. Opening doors for people. Standing when someone enters a room. Making eye contact when you converse. Saying "please" and "thank you" without fail. Even the old standby that I use: When walking with a woman, I am always on the street side, nearest the traffic (learned at West Point from the women who act as cadet hostesses!). These small courtesies don't cost anything, but they convey respect, humility, and presence. They build trust with strangers and deepen connections with friends.

That is how truly good people are raised—to exhibit character in small, tangible ways that others feel. Character is the sum of our values and beliefs, our conscience, and the moral compass that governs us when no one is looking. Presence is how others experience that character: the bearing, the tone, the confidence, and the steadiness we show in public. Character is who we are; presence is how others see us. One without the other doesn't work. Character without presence is invisible. Presence without character is hollow. When the audio matches the video, when the walk matches the talk, people trust you enough to follow.

I laughed out loud when I first saw a copy of George Washington's *Rules of Civility and Decent Behavior in Company and Conversation*. For his day, he was astute, and he understood protocol and manners long before leadership manuals defined them. As a teenager, he copied into his notebook the manners he wanted to display in his life. In reading it today, some are almost comical: "Spit not in the fire, nor stoop low before it, neither put your hands into the flames to warm them," and "In the presence of others sing not to yourself with a humming noise, nor drum with your fingers or feet." But others cut to the heart of leadership and representing yourself and your values in the presence of others: "Let your countenance be pleasant but in serious matters somewhat grave," and the final one, "Labor to keep alive in your breast that little spark of celestial fire called conscience." Silly or solemn, all pointed toward the same truth: The small courtesies and self-disciplines shape how others see us, and they reveal what lives inside us.

Some might call these habits old-fashioned, but they have never been more necessary than today. In a noisy world where too many voices prize cleverness over kindness and ego over humility, those who say "thank you," who hold a door, who look others in the eye, who live consistently by their values and what they profess to believe—these are the people who really stand out. Simple courtesies may seem minor, but they are the threads that stitch character, presence, and our civility together. When those threads hold, trust follows, and where there is trust, there is true leadership and forward movement.

25 MAR 1991—Music

We have a new guy (not new, as he was a "reinforcement" that came to us before the war) in our TOC. His name is CPT Buddy Carman. Funny, upbeat guy, and I like him a lot. He was really a great addition to the team. Smart guy, too. It appears to me that he has a hobby that he loves—music. Which brings me to today's lesson: No one likes your music like you like your music! What I mean is this: don't try and push the music you like on other people, because they will not hear the same things you hear, whether that be a great percussion, and melodic guitar, a great bass movement or a unique voice. Only you can pick up the things you like in music.

CPT Carmen doesn't push his music on others; he just enjoys it. And when a song comes on his tape player that someone else likes also, they enjoy it together and they have fun, for a short period of time, talking about why they like that song. Then it's on to something else.

Not to get too deep here, but there are a lot of things in life like music. You shouldn't try to push your likes and dislikes on other people. Just let them enjoy your "likes."

And I'll just end with this . . . I know both of you are fans, but I'm sorry, I really don't like New Kids on the Block!

Dad

Reflection

When I look back at this short journal entry from March 1991, I can almost hear the soundtrack of those years. While I was in the desert writing letters and leading soldiers, back home, the sounds of boy bands and bubblegum pop were beginning to spill out of small bedroom radios and cassette players. Our boys were finding their own musical identities, and like most fathers, I sometimes poked fun at their tastes. That's why I ended the journal with the half-playful, half-serious jab about New Kids on the Block. They loved that group's catchy hooks and coordinated dance moves. Me? Not so much. But that was the point: We were already living in a household where musical tastes diverged, and those differences said something about individuality, generational shifts, and the way humans find connection through sound.

I wrote that entry because of CPT Buddy Carman, whose love for music was obvious. He didn't force his favorites on others, but he enjoyed them deeply and passionately. And when overlap came—when someone else liked the same song—it became a short moment of community. But then it passed, and no one tried to insist that their musical taste was the only valid one. That struck me as a metaphor not just for music but for life.

Humans have different tastes in nearly everything. Music, food, art, literature, clothing styles, sports teams (I like Seinfeld's description of sports fans: They root more for the uniform—the "laundry" as he says—than the players), even news sources. Those differences don't divide us; they make us interesting. What we choose to listen to, read, watch, and admire reveals something unique about our inner wiring. If everyone liked the same bands, read the same authors, and thought the same thoughts, the world would be gray and flat. Diversity of taste gives it color, texture, and harmony—even if sometimes that harmony sounds more like dissonance to the untrained ear.

For me, music has always been more than background noise. It has been a companion through long drives, long deployments, and long nights of thinking. And my tastes reflect my stages of life. The musicians and groups I've gravitated toward are not just artists—they are storytellers, craftsmen, and emotional guides.

I have always loved the Eagles. Their harmonies, their blend of country-rock and California cool, and their ability to capture an era of sound have always resonated. Songs like "Hotel California" or "Lyin' Eyes" have layers: on the surface, catchy melodies; underneath, sharp lyrics about freedom, temptation, and identity. What I like most is the way they balance technical precision—tight guitar work, perfect harmonies—with a laid-back presence that makes you feel like you're on a long drive down an open highway singing along with them (usually off-key). The Eagles taught me that music can be both serious and easygoing, sophisticated and accessible.

Billy Joel is another favorite. Joel has an uncanny ability to turn everyday life into an anthem. His style—equal parts piano man, street poet, and rocker—bridges so many worlds. A song like "Scenes from an Italian Restaurant" tells a whole novella in under ten minutes. "Piano Man" makes a bar full of strangers into a choir. "We Didn't Start the Fire" turns history into rhythm. Joel's music teaches that storytelling doesn't always have to be linear—it can change as you do and just as your audience does. And it reminded me that a musician's presence, his willingness to share his New York bluntness and his blue-collar poetry, can make millions across the nation feel a part of the Long Island experiences.

Gordon Lightfoot captures me for different reasons. His folk ballads—"If You Could Read My Mind," "Sundown," "Canadian Railroad Trilogy"—are quieter, more reflective, rooted in narrative. Lightfoot had a gift for taking lost love, landscapes, and history and turning them into song. He was Canadian to the core yet universal in appeal. His music taught me about the power of restraint—how a soft guitar and a haunting lyric can sometimes be louder than a crashing drum. You really gotta be in the right mood to listen to Gordon.

P!nk is a more modern favorite, and she represents something else altogether: grit, authenticity, and power. Her voice is raw, unvarnished, and unapologetic. She sings about pain, resilience, and self-definition. Songs like "Just Give Me a Reason" and "What About Us" cut straight to the emotions of brokenness and rebuilding. She is as comfortable hanging upside down on stage as she is belting out lyrics that challenge norms. P!nk taught me that strength can coexist with vulnerability and that presence is as much about honesty as it is about polish.

Jason Mraz brings optimism. His style is acoustic, sunny, playful, optimistic, joyful, and full of wordplay. Songs like "I'm Yours" and "Lucky" and "93-Million Miles" are reminders that music doesn't have to be epic to be powerful. It can be lighthearted, hopeful, and fun. I've always admired his ability to lift spirits with a simple chord progression and a smile in the lyrics.

Ed Sheeran is another artist I've come to admire. He combines lyrical storytelling with an almost mathematical precision in his loops and arrangements. His acoustic ballads like "Thinking Out Loud" and "Perfect" and "Galway Girl" are modern love songs with a timeless feel. But his versatility—moving from folk- to pop- to hip-hop-inspired rhythms—shows how music crosses boundaries. Sheeran demonstrates the value of adaptability, of being able to surprise audiences without losing your essence.

And I appreciate hard rock bands. The energy, the distortion, the defiance—they speak to a different part of the human spirit. Sometimes you need volume! Sometimes you need noise that shakes the walls. And in that noise, there is release, catharsis, and even a strange kind of order.

As I've grown older, I've even found delight in expanding beyond these favorite genres. The soundtrack of the Broadway musical *Hamilton* pulled me into understanding hip-hop and rap in a new way. Lin-Manuel Miranda didn't just write songs; he wrote characters into rhymes. In the libretto, Miranda tells how each historical figure in his play uses a different rap style—Hamilton's quick, relentless bursts of syllables reflect his ambition; Jefferson's old-school, jazzy, showboating rhythms reflect his youthful swagger as he returns from France, then transform later into a more mature rap style as he finds confidence in being a member of the cabinet; Washington's measured cadences reflect authority. Reading the libretto, I realized how rap is as nuanced, technical, and poetic as Shakespeare and how its artistry has often been overlooked because of bias or misunderstanding. I was one who misunderstood hip-hop at its beginning, but recently, my ears have been opened to a genre I once ignored. All this reminds me of a larger truth: Curiosity is the cure for prejudice, even in music.

But of course, this reflection on a journal note to our boys isn't just about playlists. It's about people. Just as no one likes your music quite like you like your music, no one sees the world quite like you do. And the civil thing, the respectful thing, is not to insist that others adopt your taste but to allow them to delight in their own. That's not just tolerance—it's appreciation. When someone tells you why a song, a book, or a painting moves them, the generous act is not to dismiss it but to listen. Listening doesn't mean you have to convert (if someone tells me they're a Cubs fan, I'm still a bit prejudiced toward them!). I've never liked New Kids on the Block, and I'm sure my boys knew it, but by listening with them for a moment, I could enjoy *their* enjoyment. I could feel their excitement when the songs came on, and that was enough to create connection. But only for a short time!

There's a leadership lesson here. Leaders, like music lovers, must resist the urge to impose taste. The temptation is strong: to assume that what we like, value, or prioritize is self-evidently best. But great leaders learn that influence doesn't come from pushing your preferences onto others. It comes from listening, appreciating, and finding the overlap—the moments when your "song" or your idea may resonate with theirs. And then, once the overlap fades, moving on respectfully without forcing it.

The world is filled with dissonance right now. People divide themselves not just by politics or ideology but by tastes in news, culture, and identity. But dissonance is not the enemy; it is part of the composition. Back when I was younger and playing the guitar, I realized that unresolved chords create tension, and tension sometimes makes the resolution sweeter. Likewise, diversity of taste makes a community richer, if we have the civility to hear each other out.

So hopefully you'll see that the lesson of that small journal entry is bigger than music. It is about individuality, respect, and curiosity. Music gave me a metaphor for this reflection, but life has given me the examples: Our sons growing up with their boy bands, me discovering rap through *Hamilton,* my wife rolling her eyes at some of my playlists as we drove down the road, my soldiers sharing cassette tapes in a TOC in Iraq way back when. Each taste tells a story. Each preference is a window.

In the end, leadership and life shouldn't involve pushing our playlists on others. Instead, we should create enough space in our heads to at least listen to everyone else's songs just once. And we should have enough humility to know that sometimes the best music is the joy someone else feels when their favorite song is playing.

28 MAR 1991—The Media

Received a call early this morning that an NBC News crew was located at A Troop's checkpoint and was told to head out there. We had received guidance from Division not to let unescorted news people into our sector. Well, I went to the checkpoint and found an NBC newsman, who I recognized from television, and a camera crew. They were already filming some Iraqi POWs that Roger's Troop had taken, without any American soldiers nearby to explain what was going on. I asked them if they had an escort, they both said no. They told me they had checked in at Safwan (where the peace talks are taking place), received their passes, and were given permission to move through the countryside, and they were now freelancing. That seemed a little dangerous to me. They then asked Roger and I some questions and then requested an interview for use on the NBC Nightly News or the Today Show—they said the things we were telling them about the atrocities we had seen had been the most info they had received so far. We agreed, but only after we had received the okay from the Division Headquarters.

The interview went well. They seemed to think the info we had given them—stuff we had been experiencing for a few days—was fascinating news. I guess it's a little different from "news" when you're the one viewing it up close.

I tell you this story for a couple of reasons. First, a lot of military guys are afraid of the press because the press has a reputation of "using" sources—by this I mean twisting a question, so it gives the answer they want or only using part of an answer to convey the wrong meaning. Maybe I'm naïve, but I think if you're totally up front and honest with the press they will respect your honesty and treat it wisely. Additionally, you can usually tell when someone has a hidden motive and is "pumping" you for information to suit his or her purposes. Those are the people you want to avoid. All others, give them the facts.

Secondly, don't be intimidated by someone's credentials. The Today Show is heady stuff, but our purpose in giving this guy the information was because we felt strongly that this story of the atrocities was a story that needed to be told. I wasn't concerned about showing up on TV in either a good or bad aspect; rather, I thought there was something here that the American people should know about.

Finally, whenever you're asked to talk to a journalist, try to be honest with them and don't be afraid to relate the facts when asked. This will help other people understand your situation.

Love,

Dad

Reflection

When I wrote that short journal entry in March of 1991, I downplayed what was really happening. I told a simple story to our boys about NBC News showing up unannounced at one of our troop checkpoints, about me and the troop commander, Captain Roger Alford, giving them an impromptu interview, and about my thoughts and philosophy of being honest with journalists. I did not record what we had been living through in those days and what led those journalists to find us in the middle of the desert—the discovery of torture sites, evidence of cruelty that still sears my memory.

During our movement through the area to continue to destroy weapons of war and gather intelligence, we had uncovered sites that had iron beds with jumper cables attached, where human beings had been shocked for information or punishment. In some of those locations, we'd also found industrial-strength dryers with bodies inside, as though people had been tossed around like laundry until dead. Hooks dangled from ceilings and walls, where others had been hung and beaten. These were obviously torture chambers, displaying man's inhumanity to man, stark and unapologetic.

In those days, I chose not to write those details to my sons. They were too young, and I was too raw. Instead, my journal entries just before this one were about music, about writing thank-you notes, about being sensitive to others. Those lighter entries were my escape from the darkness. They were my attempt to put down something life-giving after spending all day in the presence of death and depravity.

But when NBC showed up, the truth had to come out. I did not yet realize it, but that impromptu interview—the first time I ever faced a national journalist's camera—was the beginning of a long relationship with the media. It would grow in ways I never imagined: as a commander briefing embedded reporters, as a general officer holding weekly press conferences, as a writer publishing alongside a true professional and an admired *New York Times* journalist, and later as an on-air military analyst for CNN.

This reflection is about that journey. It is about what I learned from those first moments in 1991, how those lessons shaped my leadership in Iraq more than a decade later, and how they influenced my second career telling America's military stories through television and print as a cable news analyst. It is also about truth, trust, and the role of two professions: the military and the media.

Standing at that checkpoint in 1991, I felt a mixture of suspicion and respect. Suspicion, because the NBC crew had no escort, and it was dangerous for civilians to be roaming the battlefield without protection. Respect, because I recognized the correspondent from television, and I knew he was doing his job.

When he asked for an interview, my initial instinct was to say no, but at the same time, I realized it was important for him to tell people this story. Not to shy away. My instinct was to tell the truth. That, I believed, was the only way forward. I had seen too much already to believe in sanitized accounts. The American people deserved to know what their soldiers were confronting, how horrible this regime was that we'd just defeated—not just their tanks and trenches but their application of tyranny.

I told NBC what we had seen. They were fascinated. For them, it was "news." For me, it was a report on yesterday's patrol. I was struck even then by the gap between what soldiers live and what civilians can imagine. And I learned a lesson that day: If you are up-front and honest with reporters, most—not all—will treat your honesty with respect.

At the time, I thought of it as a one-off. I was just a major, one voice among many. But looking back now, I see it as the start of something much bigger.

Fast forward twelve years to 2003. I was back in Iraq, this time as an assistant division commander in the 1st Armored Division. My commanding general, Marty Dempsey, handed each of his subordinates a one-page memorandum describing their responsibilities. Mine included tactical tasks, but one stood out: "Expand information operations, public affairs, and command information."

At the time, those three terms had distinct doctrinal meanings. Information operations referred to the full spectrum of activities designed to influence our enemies and protect our own decision-making. IO consisted of psychological operations, electronic warfare, deception, and information security. Public affairs was the communication of facts to the public, usually through the media, and it focused on telling the army's story truthfully and effectively. We were not allowed to use information operations against journalists. Finally, command information referred to internal communication within the force: that is, messaging that kept soldiers, families, and the army community informed so rumors didn't fill gaps.

Dempsey understood something few others did: In modern conflict, these three were interconnected. If we wanted to stabilize Iraq, we couldn't just fight insurgents; we had to protect information from the enemy, but we also had to win narratives, build trust, and tell the truth. His guidance was clear and written as a subparagraph—which I still have in my files as an example of how bosses should give directions. Words are important, and he was precise: "Find ways to get good news to the Iraqi people that will help the task force meet the tactical mission. Maintain themes that synchronize with the operational plan and civil-military activities. Drive public affairs and public diplomacy. Get more media involved in telling the 1AD story. And develop the young professionals we have in public affairs."

That guidance shaped how I approached what he wanted me to do, not just then but for the rest of my career. In Baghdad, we instituted weekly press conferences at our division headquarters. And while our public affairs officers were highly competent—young Captain Dave Gercken, who would eventually become one of the army's best PAOs, was savvy and smart—I quickly learned that reporters wanted to hear from and quote generals, and Dave knew that too. The press wanted context, details, authority, and a high-ranking name to slap behind their story. So I stepped forward, and Captain Gercken taught me and prepared me well.

It was awkward at first, but it became one of the most important things we did. Additionally, those conferences introduced me to journalists who would become lifelong colleagues and, in some cases, friends.

One of the first was Jane Arraf from CNN. Jane was fearless. She seemed to have a nose for where the action would be, and she was relentless in getting stories right. She was very pushy, but she also had flair, something soldiers deeply respect in reporters. She also had a young intern named Arwa Damon, who would soon become a dogged reporter in her own right.

Late in our 2004 tour, a tragedy struck Jane's team. A CNN stringer—a locally hired freelance journalist who provided ground reporting—and a CNN cameraman were killed by insurgents while covering a story south of the capital. CNN's bureau in Baghdad was based in the Palestine Hotel, a building well-known for housing international journalists, and CNN's president of news, Eason Jordan, was coming to Baghdad to comfort his shocked team and see how he could help them. Another great example of leadership.

Jane asked if I could give her boss a ride from the airport to the city so he would not be in danger when riding along the notorious "highway of death." I agreed. During that ride, he expressed appreciation for the support we had given CNN's team under such dangerous circumstances. I told him how tough his reporters and their bureau were and how accurate they had been in covering our operations. That short convoy fostered an immediate friendship. After we redeployed, Eason wrote and offered my wife and me tickets to Ted Turner's box to see the Braves play. I told him I'd only take him up on it if Atlanta was playing the Cardinals there. He laughed and said it was a deal . . . but then warned me not to wear a St. Louis hat in Turner's box! Years later, I believe that friendship was part of the reason CNN asked me to become one of their military analysts.

In 2007–2008, during my next Iraq deployment, the great Thom Shanker of *The New York Times* was one of our early embeds. Thom was a consummate professional—fair, rigorous, respectful of boundaries, and a phenomenal writer. A wiry and smart guy, whose small frame was rife with personal courage, he was also very tough, following our soldiers and units into some of their most dangerous missions. We gave him unprecedented access, even inviting him into some classified discussions about upcoming operations, with the agreement that he would not report until after the execution of those missions. He would always go on those missions, for context, but he also always kept his promises. Trust worked both ways.

At the end of that tour, Thom and I met in Germany, and he had the idea to co-author a piece titled "The Military-Media Relationship: A Dysfunctional Marriage?" In it, we wrote about our respective views of each other. Not all of what we wrote was complimentary, but it was respectful, and it did show a shared understanding of the other's professional responsibilities. In our closing, we said this:

"The military and the media are like parents who stay together for their kids. Neither is entirely happy with the arrangement. Both sides often think the other doesn't understand them, or worse, doesn't respect them. But we stay in it—because the kids, in this case, the American public for the journalist and the American soldiers in the field for the military, deserve better than divorce."

That metaphor captured what I had been learning since 1991: The relationship between the military and the media is often tense, but it is essential. Soldiers fight wars; journalists explain them. Neither can do the other's job. But both serve the same democracy. Thom Shanker remains one of my best friends, and we agree on more things than we disagree on.

During that same 2007–2008 period, Australian Michael Holmes, a CNN correspondent, also embedded with us for several months in northern Iraq. Michael's stretch with our division was one of the longest of any reporter, and he reported not just on operations but on the climate of the command. He had an eye for the human side of soldiering, and he told stories that captured both grit and humor.

Michael and I became close friends. We had similar personalities and senses of humor. We both took our jobs, but never ourselves, seriously. Instead of calling me "sir," he would always refer to me with the Australian caveat of "mate," and I did the same to him. Michael was with me during a particularly dangerous adventure in the Diyala province. He reported on our unit's difficult fights in Mosul and Kirkuk and also covered Carolyn Blashek delivering her two millionth Operation Gratitude care package in Tikrit. I later learned that Michael had been the one pushing my name to CNN leadership to become a military analyst, and I learned it'd been his recommendation that had ultimately tipped the network into reaching out to me after I retired from the army. But it was his reporting that showed me how good journalists don't just cover battles; they reveal the character of a unit and its people. We are also still friends to this day.

When I retired from the army in 2013, CNN called. At first, I said no. I was ready to put war and the army behind me; I wanted to do something else. But friends and colleagues reached out to influence me to sign on with them. They argued that I could bring something rare to the media: senior leadership experience in combat, honesty, clarity, context, and care for soldiers. I reconsidered. In 2014, I joined CNN as a military analyst.

Over the next decade, I covered everything from the strategically important to the tactically ridiculous. The rise of ISIS in Iraq. Russia's invasion of Ukraine. The war in Israel and Gaza. Humanitarian missions, military ceremonies, and changes in Pentagon leadership. The crazier ones, I won't mention. There were occasions when I would tell a producer, "You know, this story isn't all that important. You shouldn't cover it." Once, I even said, "You give airtime to this story, and your viewers in the military will really think you're stupid, and I'm not going to provide you any analysis." They killed that story.

But covering ISIS brought me back to familiar ground. I told viewers that ISIS was not a "new" threat but rather the outgrowth of many mistakes made after the 2003 invasion, as well as the incompetence and sectarianism of the Maliki leadership in Baghdad. The US had disbanded the Iraqi Army, marginalized the Sunnis, and created a power vacuum that extremists exploited. Prime Minister Maliki had replaced competent leaders like General Riyadh with his friends who had little operational experience, had not paid his soldiers in months, and had used his army as pawns and palace guards instead of the professionals that they were becoming; he was almost as bad as Saddam. I suggested that even the gold-standard US 82nd Airborne Division would likely cut and run from a government that was treating them like Maliki was treating the Iraqi *jundi*. I put it plainly when ISIS was rolling across the Ninewa plain toward Mosul: "You can bomb their convoys, but unless you address why they are recruiting so many and why the Iraqi army is cutting and running, this fight will continue for years, and all the advances that Iraq has made will be destroyed."

Ukraine was different. When Russia invaded in 2022, my years of working with Ukrainian forces as USAREUR commander became invaluable. I knew their strengths and their challenges, and I had seen Russia's weakness up close during visits to that country. On air, I said:

"Don't underestimate the will of the Ukrainian soldier. They are fighting for their homes, their families, their land. They are a unique culture that isn't like Russia at all, and they do not want to be under Putin's thumb again. That's a different kind of power than what Putin's conscripts bring." That message resonated, and viewers began to understand why Ukraine could hold on.

Israel and Gaza were wrenching to cover. Having had Israel in our USAREUR area of responsibility (that has since changed), I had visited and worked with the Israeli Defense Forces and knew the terrain, the politics, and the stakes. When the October 7th attack occurred, I recognized the Gaza Division headquarters, as I had spent a lot of time there with Israeli General Schlomo Turgemann. On CNN, I emphasized the human cost of continuous war and the need for a political solution as well as a military one. I reminded CNN's audience that security is important—but long-term stability and absence of war require trust, political legitimacy, and hope for the future.

And then there were the Memorial Day commentaries. Those were closest to my heart. I often ended with the phrase from *Saving Private Ryan*: "Earn this." I told viewers that living lives worthy of our soldiers' sacrifices requires more than just saluting the flag—it requires us to continuously contribute to our nation's future because those who died cannot. I also reminded them that America's strength is in its diversity, no matter what some people say: "In our cemeteries rest every race, creed, and faith, side by side. They did not die as demographics. They died as soldiers defending our nation." Those were the moments that mattered most to me: when I could use a platform to remind Americans of the humanity behind the headlines.

In 2024, CNN offered to renew my contract, but I declined. I had been with them for ten years, but it was time to leave because the network I joined in 2014 was not the same network I was working for a decade later. Many of the journalists, anchors, producers, and crew had become my friends, and I'd learned so much about what happens in front of and behind the cameras and in the production rooms. Reporters have an extremely tough job, and we need them to inform the citizenry, just like our Founding Fathers intended.

As Thom Shanker and I had written, both the army and the press were important enough to be named in our Constitution. One is charged with security for the people, the other with informing them. Both owe the American public their best. I loved serving in both roles: defending the people as a soldier, informing them as an analyst. But my West Point and army values, and the desire to always do the harder right instead of the easier wrong, said it was time to put that part of my life behind me.

Looking back across those decades in this "career in the news," I see a thread. From that NBC interview in 1991 to Dempsey's one-page memorandum in 2003 to observing and admiring Shanker's and Holmes's reporting to my decade at CNN with many terrific people—the theme has always been truth.

Truth, even when it is ugly, like the torture chambers we found in the desert. Truth, even when it is dangerous, like admitting the challenges we were facing in Iraq. Truth, even when it is inconvenient, like telling American audiences that wars aren't video games and that they never end neatly—and, as importantly, that it's relatively easy to start a war but much harder to end one.

Presence matters too. A leader's presence—bearing, tone, words, knowledge—shapes whether others believe what you say. In the media, as in command, if the audio doesn't match the video, trust is broken.

In 1991, I wrote about the NBC reporter's visit in simple terms. I had no idea that moment was the beginning of an eventual larger connection to the media that would influence my life and the lives of those I spoke to through the camera's lens. From escaping horrors by writing about music and thank-you notes to briefing generals and journalists alike to analyzing wars on national television, I have learned that leadership is always about trust.

For soldiers, that trust is life or death. For journalists, it is credibility and truth. For citizens, it is their connection to the institutions that make up our democracy.

And for me, these particular connections all began on a dusty road in Iraq, when a young major decided to tell NBC the truth about what he had seen.

29 MAR 1991—Cursing

I'm gonna address a subject today that is near to my heart—using bad, profane or obscene language. Unfortunately, sometimes I use these words, especially when I've been out in the field for a long time (it's been three plus months now since I've been on this deployment), and it seems my cursing has increased with time. I don't like myself when I do it, I try to prevent myself from doing it, but go figure, sometimes it just slips out. I hate it when that happens!

As you guys grow up, a lot of your friends will use curse words and foul language to fit in as part of the group. The funny thing is language—good or bad—won't make a difference as to whether you're accepted by your friends. Bad language can only turn people off (the ones who don't like it) and it will never turn people on (gee, he's cool because he curses).

Foul language is also an indicator that you don't have the smarts to use a better word. So, my advice today? Try not to use foul language. Keep your speech clean because that is acceptable to everyone. A good test: would you want Mom or Dad listening to you when you used some specific words? I bet you wouldn't.

Love,

Dad

Reflection

Every soldier I've ever known has struggled with language. After three months in the desert in 1991, I found myself swearing like every other trooper around me. The "f-bomb" slipped out without thinking—a verbal shortcut, a release of frustration, and, if I'm honest, sometimes just a way of sounding like "one of the guys." But I knew then, as I know now, that it wasn't the best way to communicate.

Mark Twain had plenty to say about profanity. He once admitted that "profanity provides a relief denied even to prayer," and in that he was right: A well-placed curse word can release tension in a way nothing else can. But Twain also understood that overuse is a sign of laziness. If every other word is an expletive, it's no longer sharp or funny; it's just background noise. Another observation—echoed by more than one thinker—is that bad language is often the mark of someone who doesn't have the vocabulary to say it better.

That's the real lesson: Language is a tool. Leaders especially must use it carefully. Words can inspire, teach, encourage, or wound. They can make people laugh or make them walk away. A curse word here and there might have its place—in the field, at moments of high stress, or even to jolt a listener's attention. But it loses power when it becomes a habit.

And here's where communication, in its full sense, matters. Communication is not just what you say—it's what others hear and see. It includes tone of voice, facial expressions, posture, gestures, and the medium you use: a face-to-face conversation, a phone call, an email, a text, or even a smoke signal or carrier pigeon. Each of these channels shapes how your words are received. Profanity—or any kind of foul language—changes the meaning of the message because it colors all those other dimensions. A sharp curse delivered with a smile may come across as humor. The same word shouted in anger, with clenched fists or a red face, can wound deeply or destroy trust. Leaders don't just transmit words; they transmit meaning, and foul language can become a filter that shapes that meaning, for better or worse.

In my own career, I tried to hold myself to the test I wrote to my sons in 1991: *Would I want my wife or my kids to listen to the words I just used?* If the answer was no, then it probably wasn't language that built trust, respect, or confidence. Now, truthfully, I knew that deep in my heart. But I've failed many times by using profanity in front of people when I should not have used it. So, this reflection is a good reminder to me too. Let's try to keep it clean!

The truth is, Twain was right again: "The difference between the almost right word and the right word is really a large matter—'tis the difference between the lightning bug and the lightning." Good leaders know how to find the lightning, not just fall back on the easy spark.

31 MAR 1991—Easter

It seems strange that this day would start like so many others—up at 0500, run to the piss tubes, brush my teeth, shave, then go into the TOC to see if anything happened during the night (it didn't). What was becoming a typical morning in post-war (sorta) Iraq, until the soldier manning the radio said, "Happy Easter, sir," and I realized that this was the most important holiday on the Christian calendar. We're here in the desert celebrating the risen Christ just like we were here in the desert a few months ago celebrating the birth of Christ.

I once thought, when I was going through my cynical high school days, that all the trappings of Christmas and Easter (lights on all the houses in the neighborhood and everyone worrying about what gifts they were getting/giving at Christmas; new suits and dresses and all the chocolate candy at Easter) were feeble attempts to commercialize a profoundly important Christian event. Now, knowing that today is one of those special days but not really feeling special, I realize that all the things that make up the surroundings of a holy day contribute to the mood—helping us all see the spirit of the season.

It's 8:42 am right now, and the makings of a VERY HOT day are already upon us. I wish I could enjoy an Easter Sunday afternoon bike ride with you guys in the very cool weather of southern Germany.

Love,

Dad

Reflection

Missing Easter in the desert in 1991 was as painful as missing Christmas with the family, perhaps more so because I began to have Catholic guilt about forgetting the day altogether. But we had been extremely busy in "post-war (sorta)" Iraq, and in hindsight, the thoughts about "missing" this holy day were just the beginning of something that deepened over the next two decades of deployments: my exposure to the world's religions in their original settings. I would experience faith, theology, and worship not as abstractions or lessons in a textbook but as lived faith among the people we served alongside, fought against, and tried to protect.

It was especially interesting because during our mission the day before, we had passed a large thing in the desert near the town of An-Nasiriyah. I remember asking, "What the hell is that?" and later found out that we'd been about five hundred meters from the Ziggurat of Ur, rising suddenly from the flat desert. Built around 2100 BC by King Ur-Nammu of ancient Sumer, the huge, man-made temple honored Nanna, the moon god, and had been a center of worship and trade in Mesopotamia. I later discovered the Bible mentions Ur but proclaims it as the birthplace of Abraham, seemingly making it holy for pagans, Jews, Christians, and Muslims alike. Seeing its massive, mudbrick terraces after millennia of those steps being worn by winds and sun reminded me that Iraq is not just a battlefield—it is the cradle of faith itself.

Returning in 2003, our soldiers were once tasked to guard the first free Ashura pilgrimage to Karbala in decades. Our team drove to one of the checkpoints that the pilgrims would pass to check the movement, and it was there that I watched rivers of Shia faithful mourn Imam Hussein, killed at the Battle of Karbala in 680 AD, as they marched. I later learned that this important Shia holy day of Ashura is at once grief and defiance—millions chanting in their neighborhoods and mostly young men marching the long route between Baghdad and Karbala with chains across their backs, cutting their foreheads so blood streamed down on the white shrouds they were wearing, all with anger in their eyes and faces. For Western soldiers watching, it was incomprehensible. For Iraq's Shia, it was liberation of the spirit after years of Ba'athist suppression. The Imam Hussein Mosque in Karbala—second only to Najaf as a holy site—was their heart.

During our time in Baghdad, General Dempsey made friends with one of the Sadr family clerics, Imam Mohammed al-Sadr—the brother of Ayatollah Muhammad Baqir al-Sadr, namesake of Sadr City, who led a Shia uprising in the late 1990s before being assassinated by Sadam, and the uncle of Muqtada al-Sadr, who was rising as a political firebrand during our time in the city. The conversations with Muqtada's uncle Imam al-Sadr gave us glimpses into the theology of Shia Islam but also revealed how faith, politics, and insurgency are intertwined. What for us was intelligence or "stability operations" was, for them, part of a centuries-long struggle for identity and survival.

Later, when we were kept in Iraq with a three-month extension and moved to the cities of Najaf, Karbala, and Hit, our soldiers would see the ruins of the Gardens of Babylon and the reconstructed Tower of Babel. Though much of it was Saddam's heavy-handed restoration, standing amid those walls recalled one of the world's great wonders. Empires had risen and fallen here, and each had left its mark on the people and their beliefs.

When I returned with the 1AD during the 2007–2008 surge, some of our toughest operations were in Ninewa. But that province and its peoples also exposed me to an extraordinary tapestry of religions. In Mosul's old quarter, I discovered a Jewish community that had endured quietly for centuries. A few dozen miles outside the city, toward the Kurdish region, was Archbishop Paulos Faraj Rahho's congregation, and I met with his Chaldean Catholic leaders after he was murdered for his refusal to yield to extremists. His death was a reminder that even in ancient Christian strongholds, faith carried risk.

Besides the Chaldeans, there were also Turkmen, Assyrians, and Yazidis of Mount Sinjar. Visiting the Yazidis introduced me to their traditions rooted in Zoroastrianism, Sufism, and ancient Mesopotamian belief. As anyone might imagine, their reverence for Melek Taus, the Peacock Angel, puzzled all outsiders, but their hospitality and resilience were unforgettable. When they were terrorized by ISIS, their plight helped unite others into fighting that scourge years later, and I understood who they were and what they were fighting for. These were not just faiths—they were survival strategies woven into centuries of persecution.

That same year, the governor of Ninewa asked our civil affairs and engineering units to help open Mosul International Airport in time for his citizens to travel to the Hajj. The airport had been closed to civilian traffic for years due to the war, but things were starting to return to normal. Helping the local government restart flights for the pilgrimage to Mecca, a faith journey required of Muslims at least once in their lifetime if they are able, seemed like an opportunity for them and for us. Our engineers, alongside USAID and the State Department, worked day and night to make it happen. When the first planeload of pilgrims boarded, the Iraqi 2nd Army Division commander and I stood side by side and watched the waves of Hajjis as they boarded the flight. Seeing ordinary Iraqis, wrapped in simple white robes, boarding a plane to fulfill one of Islam's greatest obligations, was one of the most hopeful moments of that long deployment.

My religious exploration didn't end in the Middle East. Later, as US Army Europe commander, I traveled to Israel, where the world's great religions sit within walking distance of one another. During my first of many visits to Israel, the US ambassador to Israel escorted our small group to the Temple Mount, Judaism's holiest site, where the Western Wall remains a place for Jews to pray and put written petitions between its stones. I was able to place a torn piece of paper with my prayer in one of the cracks. Just above this site are the Al-Aqsa Mosque and the Dome of the Rock, where Muslims believe the Prophet Muhammad ascended into heaven. I could not enter that site, but it amazed me how close all the places of worship were in this area. A short walk away stood the Church of the Holy Sepulchre, revered by Christians as the site of Christ's crucifixion, burial, and resurrection and also opened daily by a Muslim as part of the tradition of the structure. The proximity of all three sites is awe-inspiring, a tribute to shared sacred space. But it is also combustible: three faiths, side by side, with centuries of tension that still flare into conflict.

On three of my visits to Israel, I had the honor of placing a wreath and praying at Yad Vashem. On one visit, I walked the Via Dolorosa, and on two visits, I was able to meet with an IDF soldiers at Masada, where Jewish defenders chose death over Roman enslavement. Standing there at sunrise, I understood when the Israeli Army commander explained their tradition of requiring newly commissioned armor officers to walk up the mountain for the sunrise. There, these new lieutenants swear an oath to put themselves between the people and the sea, before chanting in Hebrew, "Masada shall not fall again." Faith and sacrifice, duty and memory, fused together.

While Sue and I have visited many cathedrals in Europe, this narrative reflection would not be complete without mentioning one of the most memorable Christian experiences shared. One year, we received an invitation to attend midnight mass in a cave from one of our commanders who oversaw the BENELUX (Belgium, the Netherlands, Luxembourg) garrison. "Come up, as I think you'll enjoy it," he said. We drove up to attend Christmas Eve midnight Mass in the Groeve de Schark cave near Maastricht. The limestone cavern, known as De Schark, sits just a short distance from the Netherlands American Cemetery at Margraten, where thousands of US soldiers killed in World War II are buried. During the winter of 1944, American troops who were about to fight in the Battle of the Bulge had gathered in that same cave for prayer and carols before marching to the front lines. Sitting in the flickering light of candles, we were surrounded by Dutch worshippers and American families, all present for a midnight mass offered by a priest who'd been a young altar boy in 1944. Above our heads was a wall filled with American signatures written in charcoal of the men who later fought and died at Bastogne and St. Vith, right up the road. We felt the weight of sacrifice and the continuity of faith, as that night was a reminder that the sacred is not always found in grand cathedrals or ornate mosques but sometimes in cold, stone caves where soldiers once knelt together, clinging to hope before battle.

What I took from all these opportunities and encounters, and what I hope the reader takes from my descriptions, is this: While Easter 1991 reminded me of what I was missing, the decades since have given me an expanded view of what faith can mean. It is repentance expressed in chains at Karbala, hope embodied in Hajj pilgrims boarding a plane, resilience preserved in the Yazidis of Sinjar, defiance enshrined at Masada, prayer whispered at the Western Wall, and the faith and remembrance found in a limestone cave.

As a soldier, I missed my share of holy days, holidays, and events at home. But in return, I saw the world's faiths in their own sacred spaces. That perspective became a gift—not just to me but to my family and to those who now hear these stories. Belief, I came to realize, is humanity's common inheritance, and the chance to glimpse it across traditions was one of the greatest privileges of a career spent in uniform, even when, at times, it was far from home.

1 APR 1991—Iraqi Volleyball

A Troop continues to mystify me. Their Troop Commander, Captain Roger Alford, has an incredible ability to see the best in any situation (a trait that I hope both of you boys acquire), inspire his troopers to accomplish their mission with aplomb, and ensure his Soldiers are always upbeat and have fun (also, something I hope you boys always have). I drove out to his site early this morning, and his soldiers had made a "gym" in the middle of the desert out of sandbags (weights), tent poles (parallel bars and chin up bars), and used, destroyed auto parts (more barbells). It was keeping his guys busy (to avoid boredom), but it allowed them to work out.

After I talked to him for a while, and "inspected" his new gym, I came back to the Squadron TOC, only to get a frantic call from him asking me to come back to his location. It seems that a group of refugees had come to their location looking for food, saw their volleyball net (made from tent poles and camouflage net) and challenged them to a game. They had one big guy (about 6'7") who stated he was the coach of the Iraqi national volleyball team who had a potential scholarship to a U.S. university. When I arrived, Roger told me he needed me to counter this guy at the net because none of their troopers were as tall as me!

So today, I played volleyball against a group of Iraqis—most of whom freely admitted they had deserted from the Iraqi army a few weeks ago. Most of them looked young, professional. (A few were teachers, college students, and one was a doctor) and they stated they were heading toward Safwan to get aid.

We had a lot of fun, though it did seem very strange, playing with these Arabs that a few weeks ago we could have very easily been fighting, even killing.

We talked to them afterward, and they seemed very pleasant. They were probably not hardline soldiers (probably draftees), and they also were not amateur athletes (even the coach was not that good). They were well fed, informed, and interesting. Just as the Nazis who were met by Americans after WWII, all of them claimed they had fought the Russians, none of them admitted they fought the Americans. The same was true of this group—all of them hated Saddam, loved Bush (one even said he loved VP Dan Quayle), and they all just wanted peace.

It was an interesting, and fun, afternoon.

Love,

Dad

Reflection

Memories! Roger Alford sure knew how to create them. I am convinced many of his soldiers still tell stories about their time in A Troop—yes, about combat, but also about volleyball games with Iraqi refugees and makeshift gyms built from scrap metal and tent poles. Those moments, equal parts absurd and profound, carried the unit through long stretches of tension and monotony.

Leaders like Roger understand that memories are part of the mission. Memories give people a reason to smile when the circumstances are unbearable. They create bonds that last long after the dust of deployment has settled. They provide resilience. They make stories you can tell, and embellish, for decades. This principle applies well beyond the battlefield. Since we've come to live in Orlando, we've also come to admire the culture of Disney, a company built on deliberately creating memories. At Disney parks, nothing is left to chance: the smell of popcorn on Main Street, the hidden details in architecture, even the placement of trash cans within thirty feet so the grounds remain spotless. Sometimes, those trash cans even move, following guests around; it's one of my favorite things to watch guests react to these robotic bins. In the "land of the mouse," the point is this: Every detail is engineered not just to provide service and an experience but to create moments that endure in a guest's memory long after they leave.

Roger Alford, without any corporate manual or team of imagineers, was doing the same thing in the desert. His soldiers may not remember the exact coordinates of their defensive positions, but they will always remember the time they lifted "weights" made of sandbags and wreckage, or the day their commander brought the squadron S3 into a volleyball game against a self-proclaimed Iraqi national team coach. Like Disney, Roger understood that memory-making is not a byproduct of leadership—it is a core element of organizational culture and longevity with a team.

Leaders build memories in all kinds of ways. They especially celebrate victories—big or small. Not every day ends with a captured objective or a signed treaty, but every unit has moments worth honoring. I've seen and been a part of units that use "gag awards" to highlight mistakes with humor rather than shame—turning an embarrassing stumble into a humorous roast and reminding soldiers that failure is survivable. Others use formal occasions, like celebratory balls or military dining-ins, where there's a mixture of tradition and levity. I'll never forget one ball where the leadership all had special dress shirts made in Korea. From the front, they looked perfectly formal—stiff white pleats, black studs, bow ties. But when the dancing started, the jackets came off, and the sleeves and backs of those white shirts revealed wild patterns—plaid, polka dots, paisley, even one with a jalapeno pepper design—signaling that the serious part of the evening had ended and it was time to party. That single act said more than any speech: We take our duty seriously, but we take ourselves lightly.

Sports are another way to etch memories. All units I was a part of scheduled "sports days" where units faced off in athletic competition to see which organization was the "best." But I also liked to include a commanders competition that the young soldiers and their families could come watch. One favorite was 9-ball soccer: multiple balls in play at once, chaos everywhere, no real defense or offense, and no one able to hide behind the slow pace of a single-ball game. Another favorite was one my staff officers invented, knowing I loved baseball but loathed golf. The sport? "Balf," a hybrid of baseball and golf, turned the base golf course into a winter playground. A baseball bat with a putter head drilled into the end was the required tool of choice. Soldiers swung the bat against the small golf ball, then sprinted after each shot to the ball's location, swinging again furiously until they reached the green. When it was time to putt, they used the bat like a golf club for the final stroke before sprinting to the next hole. The winners weren't just those with the lowest "score" and the fastest run time but those who laughed hardest in the process. It was a ridiculous game, and I still hear from those who played it with me.

These activities weren't frivolous—they built cohesion, gave people release, and ensured that when stress came, everyone had something light to remember and hold on to.

Some of the most powerful memories are educational ones. I love staff rides and always find veterans—and recently more health care providers and students—who tell me how much they gained from the experience. When executed correctly, staff rides combine history, leadership, and camaraderie in unforgettable ways. I've led commanders across the fields of Shiloh, Gettysburg, and Custer's Last Stand. As the commander of the US Army Europe, using unit funds for professional development, I had us bused to Normandy, Anzio, Bastogne, and the Hürtgen Forest in Europe. These were not just battlefield tours. Each soldier or officer would take on the role of a historical figure, study their style and their decisions, and stand on the very ground where those decisions were made. On these educational trips, the lessons of leadership, chance, and consequence come alive in ways no classroom could match.

Even after retiring, I continued that tradition. Physicians from our health care leadership courses walked the fields of Gettysburg, reflecting on courage, mistakes, and resilience. MBA students from Rollins now do the same, joining the ranks of just a few institutes of higher learning—the Johns Hopkins SAIS yearly rides are the gold standard—who take part as well. This isn't just a study of history; it's leadership training wrapped in memory making.

What has struck me most in recent years is how these memories endure. Soldiers I haven't seen in decades still reach out to remind me of those moments: the crazy shirts at a ball, the absurd rules of "Balf," or the time a volleyball game with Iraqis turned enemies into teammates for an afternoon. They rarely mention the endless hours in TOCs or the detailed orders we agonized over. What they remember are the moments that lifted them up, made them laugh, and helped them feel alive.

That's a lesson I share with students and young leaders today: Success is not measured only in objectives achieved but in the memories that your people still remember years later.

So why do old generals tell so many stories? Because orders and missions and operations often fade, but what is left provides a memory of something good. The laughter of a ridiculous game or crazy experience, the seriousness of history found standing on the same spot as your predecessors during a staff ride, or the pride of an unexpected celebration—these endure. "Hey, let me tell you a story . . . this really happened!" is often the start. Over the years, the story grows, and that's okay. Soldiers tell those stories and relive those memories at reunions. Families hear them at kitchen tables. Leaders pass them down as lessons.

In 2012, I was at the anniversary of the Normandy D-Day invasion when I was introduced to a group of veterans from that campaign who had all served together in the 82nd Airborne Division. The four nonagenarians—all wearing the uniforms of sergeants with their awards and combat airborne insignia except one, who wore the rank of major—gathered around me and wanted to tell me their stories, their memories, of their combat jump into the area near Sainte-Mère-Église. The stories started with descriptions of the fight, the insanity of that jump into enemy territory. But soon, the stories turned into memories: how they'd found each other in the marshy field at night, the eventual "liberation" of bottles of wine from a farmhouse, the injury to their major (who was standing there with them, smiling wide as could be, as his three NCOs described the folly of him limping along on a sprained ankle). They loved how I laughed at the memories, and they were kind enough to invite me for drinks that evening after the formal ceremonies were over. I joined them, and they treated me to more of their memories—some serious but most humorous—about their other jumps, their journey across Europe together, and how they had stayed in close contact all these years.

One of the four was accompanied by his granddaughter, and during the evening's revelry, she stayed in the back, smiling but saying nothing. As I was leaving, she approached me with tears in her eyes, telling me she had often asked her grandfather about his war experiences, but he would never tell her. That night, she said, gave her a completely different view of the grandfather she had always admired, and the memories he shared with his buddies made her love him even more. She thanked me for being there, for allowing him to relive his time with his friends for an evening, and for allowing her to hear about his youth. It was a night to remember, to be sure.

Great leaders, like Roger Alford, know that their legacy isn't just in the missions accomplished—it's in the memories they leave for their people. Memories are the glue of trust, the anchors of resilience, and the currency of leadership.

And maybe that's the truest test of leadership: not just whether your team accomplished its mission but whether they have stories worth telling.

2 APR 1991—War Buddy

A very tough day today as CPT Scott Milliren, the fire support officer and someone who has become my good friend in the squadron, left for home. You see, he was scheduled to leave the Army way back in January, but the deployment postponed that. He put aside his new, anticipated civilian life to spend a few months in the desert, doing his duty. I was very glad he was here with us, for besides being a very loyal member of the Squadron (he came here with us when he didn't have to) he was also someone I could talk to about many different things. He was my best friend while he was here, now he's leaving before the rest of us to start a new life. I'm a little jealous, but very happy for him.

As you guys know (because I wrote about it in one of my first entries in this journal) I hold a very high price on friendship. With that in mind, there is also a concept called "war buddies" which defines the friends you make in a pressure situation. Those friends truly understand the deep fears, the emotions, and the hard times you've gone through, together. I've never understood this concept before, but I do now.

Scott Milliren is now another on my list of "friends;" being a "war buddy" also makes him special. I'm hoping he has all of life's best.

Love,

Dad

Reflection

Scott Milliren wasn't just another officer in the squadron; he was our fire support officer (FSO), the person who—along with our air liaison officer (ALO)—orchestrated our artillery and air support as we maneuvered against the Iraqi Republican Guard. While the squadron commander and I were each in our Bradleys, commanding and leading the fight, Scott and the ALO were right there next to us in their box-like M113 personnel carrier. This was our squadron tactical action center (TAC), a small command post that provided command, control, maneuver, and firing orders and determined the placement of indirect fires. From their position, Scott and the ALO requested not just the long-range artillery batteries far behind us but also the fast-moving A-10s and jets overhead, all while coordinating our own air cavalry troops that patrolled the sky above the ground troops. In essence, Scott was the hinge between earth and air, between the thunder of artillery and the precision of close-air support. It was delicate work, dangerous work—and it required trust.

For me, Scott became much more than just a fire supporter. He was a "near peer" I could confide in—a voice of reason, a sounding board, and a friend when the pressures of combat felt heavier than steel. We would sometimes use the radios to request missions from him and the ALO, and we would often yell across the noise of our engines to provide direction during movement. But it was off the battlefield that Scott provided me with friendship and advice, and his departure reminded me of how precious war buddies are and how different they are from any other kind of friend.

Early in this journal, I provided our boys some advice on friends and reflected mightily on that topic because in a tough world, friends are critical. There are friends from childhood, from college, from neighborhoods, and from family gatherings. But war buddies are different. They share an understanding of the smell of cordite and vehicle fumes in the air, the tension of the fight and the waiting for the next move, the fear you don't always admit to yourself, and the relief that comes when you survive.

Those friendships are compressed by urgency yet deepened by risk. And while years may pass, I've since found that war buddies can pick up a conversation a decade later as though they were still in the desert together. I'm also amazed at how both our combat veteran sons stay in close contact with their war buddies, scheduling reunions long after their fights.

I admitted in my journal that I was jealous of Scott heading home while we remained behind. That seems selfish, but it's a very human response. Soldiers often feel the tug of envy when comrades move on—out of danger, on to the next chapter. But leadership requires celebrating those departures, too, recognizing the sacrifice made and the duty fulfilled. In that moment, I learned that even as I envied him, I also admired his courage to serve, then step off into civilian life.

Every leader needs at least one or two people with whom they can drop their guard. Scott was that person for me during Desert Storm. In 2003, Brigadier General Mike "Scap" Scaparrotti, my fellow assistant division commander, would become my battle buddy in that conflict. In 2007, my battles buddies were primarily our division command sergeant major, CSM Roger Blackwood; our assistant division commanders, BG Jim Boozer and BG Tony Thomas; and our division chief of staff, Colonel Bryan Watson. All were "battle buddies" but also strong friends. And there were others—staff officers; trusted peers; my aides, Eric Vetro and Jason Wright; security and communication team members, Sergeant Andrew "Smitty" Smith, Sergeant Rodriguez, and Sergeant Ramos; and even Iraqi counterparts like LTG Riyadh. Confidants like these continuously remind leaders that they cannot carry burdens alone. Leadership is lonely work, but it doesn't have to be solitary if you have people around you who understand both your responsibilities and your humanity.

And then there was Marty Dempsey. Marty was not only my friend but often my boss—someone who outranked me for most of our careers, including during the tough days of OIF I in 2003–2004. That could have made our relationship purely hierarchical, but instead, it deepened into one of those rare bonds where trust crossed both professional and personal lines. I never blurred the formality of his position; I respected his authority as my commander. But he was also a friend and mentor, and when I asked him tough questions or shared personal reflections, I knew his feedback would help me grow as both a professional and a person. That kind of mutual trust—between commander and subordinate, mentor and friend—is rare, and it is one of the reasons Marty and I always remained close. War buddy doesn't always mean peer; sometimes it means having a commander who shows you the dignity of friendship even in the hierarchy of command.

Those kinds of bonds are timeless. Civil War soldiers wrote about them in letters. In fact, once, while visiting the Gettysburg battlefield, I learned how the Eternal Peace Monument there was dedicated in 1939, with soldiers from both the North and the South who'd fought there coming together in a grand reunion. WWII veterans spoke of these deep friendships (as I mentioned in a past reflection), and young soldiers from Iraq and Afghanistan still speak of their brothers and sisters in arms the same way. The common thread is hardship, fear, and shared responsibility. Civilians experience glimpses of this too—in medicine, firefighting, disaster relief, and even high-pressure start-ups—where shared stress builds lifelong ties. But in combat, those bonds are unshakable. I hate to be biased, but they're just different from all the other groups I mentioned.

Scott's departure was also a reminder of the countless goodbyes military life demands. Families say goodbye at airports, friends move away every few years during constant reassignments and rotations, and comrades rotate home on staggered schedules. Each goodbye carries a cost. For leaders, part of the role is helping their teams navigate those goodbyes with dignity and gratitude—recognizing that love and loss, envy and pride, all mix in the churn of military life.

Military leaders are not just defined by their positions, their rank, or the missions they lead but by the friendships they form and the ways they sustain them. And truthfully, I've seen military leaders throughout my military career who want to "stack the deck" by bringing friends they have served with in the past, who they know and trust, into their units. There's wisdom in that approach—it builds immediate cohesion and predictability. But I've been more of a "play the hand I'm dealt" kind of commander, knowing there are new friends to meet, new buddies to bond with, new talents to discover. It's a riskier path but one that creates opportunities for surprise alliances and lifelong bonds I might otherwise have missed. Scott Milliren was one of those bonds—unplanned, unexpected, but invaluable.

War buddies are unique—they are a human necessity beyond the constraints of command. They provide grounding throughout life, holding up the mirror when it's required to help their friend. Because if they're good, they make sure that their battle buddy stays human in the most inhuman circumstances.

Scott Milliren left the army that spring, but he never left my memory—or my list of treasured friends. And perhaps that's why I've always preferred the German farewell, *auf Wiedersehen*. It doesn't mean "goodbye" in the final sense; rather, its literal meaning is "until we see each other again." That's the way I choose to remember every departure, whether from a battlefield, a post, or a friendship: not as an ending but as the hope of an eventual reunion.

5 APR 1991—The Human Condition

It's been over a month since the end of the war, but I found myself firing my personal weapon at several Iraqis again today. They were not soldiers (they may have, at one time, worn an Iraqi uniform). Rather, these were individuals trying to make money off other's hardships.

As I've mentioned, we are about 20 kms south of the main road between Basra and An-Nasiriyah—two towns that have seen a lot of hard times, and whose people are suffering under the hand of Saddam's henchmen. To our rear is a pipeline through which flows gasoline.

Over the last several days we have seen Iraqis drilling into these pipelines, putting holes in the pipes and stealing gasoline. Our medics even treated one of these individuals when the pipeline blew up and burned him badly. We thought these people were stealing gasoline to run their trucks and help their farms get started again. Not so. We found they are stealing the gas and taking it to the two towns to our north, where they are selling it for 500 Dinar (about $150) a barrel, to folks who are dying because of Saddam thuggery.

Today, we ran them off. They came back; we ran them off again. On the third go, I approached in my Bradley, yelled at them to leave, and when they refused, I shot out their trucks' tires and told our crews to puncture all the 55-gallon drums they had in the back of their trucks with an ax (probably about $3,000 worth of gasoline).

They didn't like it, but they couldn't do much about it. They were "feeding" off a poor human condition. After reading the reports of the atrocities occurring to our north, it didn't bother me a bit that I had lost my temper.

I'm sure they may be back, so we'll have to run them off again. War, and bad times, do strange things to people.

Love,

Dad

Reflection

That day was another reminder to me that war strips away normal rules and leaves only the raw edges of the human condition. Those men we saw stealing from the gas pipes weren't freedom fighters, nor were they farmers trying to survive. They were profiteers exploiting chaos, drilling into pipelines, and selling stolen fuel while their neighbors suffered. What I didn't know then was how familiar I'd become with this behavior in a variety of places and just how corrosive it was to building trust in a society.

In 2003, when Baghdad erupted after Saddam's fall, we saw looting on a massive scale. Some of it was understandable—people taking food or medicine to survive—but much of it was the same opportunism I had witnessed a decade earlier. Museums were ransacked, hospitals stripped bare, universities burned. Iraqis were looting their own future. And the coalition had known it might occur, but we hadn't planned to address it; law and order is always a requirement during the turmoil and chaos of war, especially during periods of "regime change." Later, in 2004, when 1AD was told to go to southern Iraq, we watched in dismay as Sadr's rebellion also created that kind of atmosphere. What made it worse, Ukrainian soldiers who had been in those areas as part of the "coalition of the willing," not leaving their bases for over six months, had sold Iraqi army artillery shells found on those bases to insurgents who would use them against Americans, Iraqis, and other coalition partners. That was not desperation—it was criminal behavior and outright corruption, the kind I would later learn was inherited from decades of the Ukrainian soldiers modeling what they had been taught as part of Soviet military culture.

Years later, I came to know Colonel General Henadii Vorobiov, a Ukrainian officer of extraordinary professionalism who had once been a part of the Soviet army and who knew their culture. He recognized that the Soviet legacy had hollowed out his army and his newly independent nation's culture, leaving behind communistic and oligarchic habits of graft, exploitation, and indifference. His personal mission became nothing less than the transformation of Ukraine's military into a professional, Western-standard force; he wanted to turn around Ukraine's military culture and profession. In many conversations in Kyiv, Yavoriv, and Heidelberg, he shared with me that he had also observed what I had seen in 2003—that his army was without integrity and was not a shield for the people but rather another predator of the Ukrainian citizenry. He began making changes. Vorobiov purged corrupt practices, embraced training with NATO, and insisted on building a culture of trust and professionalism. Looking back, I shudder to think where Ukraine would be today, facing Russia's invasion, had Henadii not begun that work two decades ago. In my view, his reforms saved his country.

What I learned from both Iraq and Ukraine is that opportunism thrives in the vacuum left by failed institutions. People who have no faith that their government will provide food, water, fuel, or security will take matters into their own hands. Sometimes that means stealing fuel from a pipeline; sometimes it means rioting in city streets. In America, we've seen moments when institutions faltered and riots turned cities into places of fear and lawlessness. In those moments, ordinary people are swept up in mob behavior that tears at the fabric of community and civility.

The lesson is stark: Without trusted institutions, the human condition bends toward chaos. Leaders—whether military or civilian—must not only prepare to confront that chaos but also work tirelessly to prevent it by ensuring their people are cared for, protected, and respected.

A government that cares for its people will always be more resilient than one that leaves them desperate.

For me, the memory of shooting out those fuel trucks' tires south of Basra was not about anger but about clarity. Chaos, if left unchecked, will consume everything. But with strong leadership, institutions built on trust, and the kind of professionalism modeled by leaders like Henadii Vorobiov in Ukraine, and later Barham Salih in Iraq, societies can resist the pull of opportunism and corruption and instead move toward stability and hope for the future.

6 APR 1991—Mass Burials

Two days ago, CPT Alford and LT Silverman found a car on the median of Highway 8 (the main highway between Basra and An-Nasiriyah—it was designed by the Germans, and this 6-lane highway looks a lot like an autobahn) with two dead bodies. Both were still in the front seat of the car, and the car had evidentially been hit by something that made it burst into flames. The bodies had been there for quite some time (saw them before they took them out of the car—it was not a pretty sight), yet traffic had passed these vehicles for a month plus without doing anything about them. Roger's guys took them out, put them in body bags, and buried them.

Yesterday, the CG flew over Roger's sector from the air and noticed two more bodies lying in the desert. He called our TOC (since they were in our sector) and told us to police them up and bury them. From the grid he gave me, I could tell that CPT Alford had another task to perform. I gave A Troop the mission for today.

Roger Alford, like any good leader, accompanied his men on this mission. When they arrived at the grid, they found not two but rather twenty-five bodies, all in various states of inaction, most looking like they had been caught in the act of running and then felled by some unforeseen explosion—possibly napalm or a very high explosive bomb. Expressions of terror were still on faces; arms were raised in a running motion, legs flailing, eyes open (though they had been plucked out by birds). I don't tell you all these things to gross you out, although I'm sure it will. I will tell you instead because it sets the tone for the rest of the story.

We've been tasked to write a history of our actions during the conflict by the Division Staff. I've tasked various people to write about various topics, and I'm in the process of compiling these. LT Steve Hill, who accompanied Roger to the site, wrote a very moving story about the trip.

Steve talked about almost throwing up from the smell and the sight of a score of long-dead Iraqis. He wrote about some soldiers he approached, suggesting they receive a medal for doing that type of dirty work. The soldier replied, "We don't do these things because we want medals, we do this, without complaining, because it's the right thing to do." A very good answer.

Finally, he describes in very moving detail the reaction of Roger Alford to the site. He tells how, after the bodies were marked, put in body bags, and put into a mass grave, CPT Alford stood alone, for a very long time, over the grave with his hands folded looking off into the distance. This is Roger Alford, the crass, boisterous, maverick, fun-loving troop commander who was always rollicking along. Roger Alford, who always had a smart-aleck remark for everyone to make them laugh. The Roger Alford who just a few days ago was hosting Iraqis in a volleyball tournament at his laager site. His comment to LT Hill when Steve approached him to ask what he was thinking. "I have no respect for any military force that doesn't bury their dead."

It was a long, tough, dirty day for the troopers of Alpha. It's strange, boys, but it takes a long time for the smell of death to leave your nostrils after you walk away. The times that I've seen dead people since I've been out here, I've smelled the distinct smell of death even as I've zipped up my sleeping bag. It's nothing you can describe; it's only something you can experience.

I hope you guys will never experience that smell.

Dad

Reflection

What Roger Alford and his soldiers did that day was more than a battlefield chore. It was a timeless act of humanity, carried out in the most inhumane of circumstances. Their job wasn't glamorous; it wasn't something that would ever appear in an official battle streamer or citation. Yet it was profoundly important. They bore witness to the aftermath of war, and they shouldered the responsibility of honoring the dead—enemies or not—because failing to do so would diminish us as soldiers and as men.

As Roger, XO Mike Silverman, and their troopers gathered those bodies from the desert floor, they weren't thinking about geopolitics or military strategy. They were thinking about dignity. About respect. About the quiet obligation to see that no human being was left to rot under the sun like discarded trash. And they did it as soldiers always have: without fanfare, without complaint, without medals. They even marked the spot carefully, recorded the coordinates, and sent them up in their mission report so that history would know where the dead lie. That act alone separated them from the atrocities of the twentieth century, when armies in the Balkans and in Nazi-occupied Europe filled mass graves and tried to erase them. Roger's men buried the dead not to conceal but to acknowledge. To bear witness.

For soldiers, these moments test not just stomachs but souls. LT Steve Hill wrote that some of the men nearly vomited from the sight and smell, yet they did their duty anyway. Duty, of course, was one of their values; respect was another one. One soldier, when offered the idea of a medal, dismissed it outright: "We do this because it's the right thing to do." That is soldiering at its purest. Honor is not found only in the clash of battle but in the quiet, awful work of decency after guns have gone silent.

Roger himself, usually so loud and irreverent as I pointed out earlier, stood silently over the grave when the work was done. Hands folded, eyes fixed on the horizon, as if holding vigil for strangers. When LT Hill asked him what he was thinking, he simply replied, "I have no respect for any military force that doesn't bury their dead." His answer cut to the heart of what it means to be a professional. We fight, but we do not desecrate. We kill when necessary, but we do not strip humanity from the fallen, friend or foe.

I remembered a play I had once studied in a West Point English class: *Antigone*. Sophocles's heroine defies the king's edict to leave her brother's corpse unburied because she believes there is a higher law, a moral duty to honor the dead. For that act, she risks—and ultimately gives—her life. That ancient Greek tragedy echoed in my mind when I thought about Roger Alford standing silently over that mass grave. Across cultures and centuries, soldiers and civilians alike have wrestled with this same obligation: whether to respect the humanity of the fallen or to erase it. Roger, in his boisterous but deeply moral way, knew where he stood.

During the time in my West Point studies when we were reading *Antigone* in English class, we were also reading about Eisenhower's campaigns in World War II. Serendipitously, we were studying Ike's actions when his troops found the unnerving death camps in southern Bavaria. Upon discovering the horrors, Eisenhower ordered them to be filmed and meticulously documented. He knew that future generations would doubt the horrors if they weren't preserved in evidence. His words still echo: "Get it all on record now—get the films, get the witnesses—because somewhere down the road of history some bastard will get up and say that this never happened." I suspect Eisenhower had seen enough of carnage and man's inhumanity against man that he suspected the worst might come, the facts might not be believed, if those sights weren't recorded.

Don't misinterpret what I'm saying. What our soldiers found in that Iraqi desert was not nearly the same scale of atrocity as Auschwitz or Dachau, but the smell, the gore, the sense of abandonment carried the same universal message: Leaders who neglect the dead neglect their humanity. That is why Captain Alford's troops marked the site, bagged the bodies, buried them, and reported the coordinates up to division headquarters. They weren't hiding the crime. They were doing their duty. The contrast with the deliberate concealment of massacres in the Balkans during the 1990s and the orchestrated exterminations of WWII could not have been starker.

One of my favorite stories about soldiers adhering to their army values came years later, with another soldier—Private Green. I was on a patrol with the platoon Green was a part of in northern Iraq. I told the platoon leader that I wouldn't interfere with their actions but that after the mission I would give them my assessment of how they had conducted their mission. While entering the FOB, I asked my go-to opening question of soldiers: What made you all join the army? They all started giving me their responses—they joined because of 9/11, they needed college money, their uncle told them they needed discipline, and so on—until one soldier told me I ought to ask Private Green why he'd joined the army. Green was manning the .50 caliber machine gun, standing next to me as I sat in the "shotgun" seat of the MRAP. Because I could only see his legs and could only hear his voice over the intercom, he said his colleagues were just screwing with him and that he didn't want to relay why he had joined the army.

With a bit of encouragement from his fellow soldiers and an order from me, Green laughed and admitted he had once been a male model. He had enlisted not to get away from the glamour but because he believed in serving something bigger than himself. When we entered the base, dismounted the truck, got down on the ground, and cleared our weapons, I saw what a handsome young man Green was and pushed him to tell me more while we were all standing around the cleaning barrel. Green responded that while he'd been making a lot of money as a model, he hadn't felt he was growing. Stepping into a recruiter's office one day, he'd become interested in the army's values—loyalty, duty, respect, selfless service, honor, integrity, and personal courage. When I turned to his patrol mates and asked which of those values mattered most to them, they all answered differently. Some chose courage. Others chose duty. I saved Green for last, and when it was his turn, he said quietly, "Sir, all of them. Those values changed my life for the better, and I realized a long time ago that if you take away one, all the rest of it falls apart."

The other soldiers didn't laugh. They grew solemn, looked down at their feet, kicked at the sand as soldiers do when they're thinking about truth. These men had been together under tough combat conditions, had lost one of their own in combat action, and deep in their hearts, knew Green wasn't parroting doctrine; he was living it. Just as Roger's soldiers buried the dead and didn't want any medals because it was "the right thing to do," Green reminded me that values only matter when they are whole and lived.

The same values were embodied by our army doctors who, in both 2003 and 2007, worked hand in hand with Iraqi physicians to rebuild broken hospitals and clinics. These weren't just medical missions—they were acts of restoration, of handing back dignity to a society whose systems had collapsed.

Our military police, too, trained Iraqis not just in tactics but in philosophy: that police exist to *protect and serve,* not terrorize and extort. In classrooms and dusty camps, young Iraqi recruits were taught how to interact humanely with their fellow citizens. It was slow work, sometimes frustrating, but it was an antidote to decades of fear.

Generating trust through the exhibition of values was a big deal for LTC Chris Vanek, one of our battalion commanders. In 2007, Chris was commanding an infantry battalion in northern Iraq and decided to set audacious goals in one of our toughest areas. He told his brigade commander, Dave Paschal, that in fifteen months, he would tame the violence, engage with local leaders, and bring enough trust that someday he could sit outside the police station without body armor, playing checkers with Iraqi officers. He also vowed to form a battalion soccer team and play against locals, not as occupiers but as neighbors.

Fifteen months later, he had done exactly that. Vanek's story was the mirror image of Roger Alford's volleyball match years earlier: soldiers doing their duty under tough conditions, building bridges by generating respect and loyalty among their teammates, and showing that peace is possible when leaders exhibit their values and define success in human terms.

What ties all these stories together—from Roger Alford's burial detail to Private Green's articulation of values to army doctors and MPs to Vanek's soccer game—is why I loved being with soldiers throughout a four-decade career. Young soldiers are both formal and informal leaders in everything they do, and they accomplish the toughest missions, but they also incorporate the moral weight of context.

In 1991, the context meant burying the enemy's dead with dignity. In 2003 and 2007, it meant realizing that Iraqi civilians, police, and soldiers were also part of our collective circle of responsibility. Context meant recognizing that kinetic action alone—bombs and bullets—does not win the war. Trust, respect, and human dignity do.

As I provide this reflection thirty-five years after the event, the smell of death on that day still clings to memory. But so does the sight of Roger Alford standing silently, head bowed, over a mass grave of enemies. That juxtaposition—affable and boisterous Roger, suddenly solemn—reminds me that leadership is not about always being loud or tough. It is about knowing when to be serious, when to show respect, when to set an example by living your values.

9 APR 1991—Unique Personalities and Leadership

I've realized that I've spent the last few entries talking about the adventures and misadventures of CPT Roger Alford and A Troop. I've failed to mention some of the other leaders—officers and noncommissioned officers—in the squadron, so I will do that now. I've judged them on various leadership qualities, and I will be candid so you both get to see how I evaluate and assess members of the team . . .

Reflection

From the beginning of this project, I promised myself I would keep these journal entries intact, exactly as I wrote them in 1991. With this one, though, I'm going to make an exception. The reason is that the original journal entry was a commentary on what I saw as the personalities and leadership traits of many of the officers and NCOs in the squadron, both good and bad. My words reflected an honest assessment at the time, but to showcase them here with their names attached—three decades later—might expose and maybe even embarrass those leaders whom I admired and served alongside. Many of them went on to have distinguished military and private sector careers, and a few have since passed away.

So rather than revisiting the dated and raw entry, I want to use this reflection to describe how I now assess leadership traits. That's what I was really doing back on April 9, 1991—analyzing our fellow leaders of the Blackhawk Squadron.

But first, a story.

In 2016, after designing and executing a leadership development course for doctors, nurses, and administrators in the health care organization I joined after retirement, the chief medical officer asked me to write a book about what we were doing in those classes to develop others in our organization. In *Growing Physician Leaders,* I described that program. When the book was published, I was asked to speak to a variety of health care professionals, hospital systems, and even some schools. I spoke to a wide range of groups about the approach, as it seemed a lot of organizations wanted to develop leaders.

One of those invitations came from the dean of the Crummer Graduate School of Business at Rollins College. After my presentation, he asked whether I'd be interested in applying to the executive doctoral program they had recently created. I thought that might be fun and contribute to my private sector growth. I soon found myself as the oldest student in the class (and older than all the professors too!).

At a reception for new doctoral students, I met my student mentor, Rhonda Bartlett, a career nurse turned C-suite executive. When I asked her what she had learned so far in her time in the program, she immediately replied, "I've learned just how much I didn't know."

In just the first few classes, I soon realized this was true for me as well. I had commanded soldiers across the world, written orders in combat, and made life-or-death decisions, but when I began studying leadership theories and reading research others had conducted on the subject, I recognized how much of what I *thought* I knew was instinct, experience, and gut feelings, not structured analysis. There were similarities and differences in each leadership theory I dissected, and there were some common elements in each scholarly article I read. All of that shaped my learning, and it also evolved my thinking to consider what all those who study leadership realize. There are four elements that people should evaluate when they want to assess leadership: the individual's attributes, competencies, influence methods, and context.

Attributes are the inner qualities of a leader—cultural background, values, character, integrity, humility, resilience, empathy, personal courage, discipline, presence, and intellect. They form the moral bedrock of trust. It has since struck me that during Desert Storm, and in other jobs in both the army and the private sector, that model of sizing leaders up in the army doctrinal manuals contributed to how I assessed trust: *Can I trust them? Do their people trust them? Do they have a set of values that drives them and that helps them make decisions? Do they see the world in a clear way? And does their presence coincide with their character?*

As I've learned since, attributes don't just affect how others see you; they shape how you see yourself. Leaders who know and continuously evaluate their traits, their biases, their character, their personal values, their limitations, and their strengths are far more prepared to generate trust than others. After all, trust is the coin of the realm when we're talking about leadership.

Competencies are the skills and behaviors used by leaders—communicating, planning, decision-making, problem-solving, building teams, developing others, and accomplishing the tasks before you. The ability to do all these things and grow these competencies can be taught, refined, and practiced.

When I judged fellow leaders in 1991, I was first measuring their attributes, then measuring their ability to accomplish their mission effectively and efficiently, communicate effectively with their teams, handle ambiguity, and act under pressure. Could they devise a plan, communicate it clearly, execute it with discipline, and push to get results? Could they improvise when plans broke down?

One of the most practical truths I've learned is Yogi Berra's: "If you don't know where you're going, you might end up someplace else." Understanding and working on the right competencies associated with their assigned tasks gives leaders the tools to take a vision, turn it into concrete steps, communicate it effectively, and evaluate when it is accomplished so their team has clarity, not only about today's tasks but also about how accomplishing them contributes to tomorrow's destination as well.

Competencies without attributes are brittle—skills applied without moral grounding. But attributes without competencies are equally fragile—good intentions with no ability to deliver.

Then, there are methods of influence. How do you get others to do what you ask them to do? How do you tap into your team members' motivations and inspire them—influence them—to achieve that objective or goal? During one of our classes with physicians, a doctor once said to me, "General, you have it easier than we do. Soldiers follow orders because you order them to; we must be more nuanced." I laughed because anyone who has ever led knows there are no effective organizations that work that way, especially when you may be asking young soldiers to put their lives on the line.

Here's the truth: Many people think influence is just about motivating someone to do something. Unfortunately, those who study human psychology know motivation is internal to each person. Some do things for glory, money, advancement, or a sense of purpose. Leaders do not create motivation; it can't be injected into others. Instead, leaders **must first** come to understand others' motivations, then align an influence method with those individuals' needs to help them contribute to the organization as a whole.

That's why Lao Tzu's wisdom endures: "When the best leader's work is done, the people say, 'We did it ourselves.'" Influence is mostly about empowerment, and only on a few occasions is it about directives or coercion. Authority may compel compliance, but only properly applied influence turns motivation into true commitment.

Influence is not one-size-fits-all. Sometimes it's persuasion. Sometimes it's modeling calm under pressure. Sometimes it's participating in the action, and sometimes it's stepping aside to let others prove their talent. But the best leaders know their people well enough to influence each person differently—tapping into the motivation that already exists within them.

The soft influence techniques—trust, respect, listening, recognition—take longer but always yield deeper results. Leaders who rely only on authority may get things done, but they won't grow effective or resilient teams.

Context is the variable most leaders underestimate. Context puts leadership in perspective in different environments, where there are changing rules or expectations, especially when different cultures come into play. A garrison leader may stumble in combat; a business executive brilliant in one industry may falter in another. Context is the battlefield or boardroom terrain that frames action and decision.

During Desert Storm, context meant a lightning-fast armored campaign where initiative mattered less than overwhelming firepower. By 2003, in Baghdad, I held a different rank, with more responsibilities and requirements, and the context had shifted to insurgency, sectarian violence, and nation-building. Then, in 2007, with even more responsibility and a wider spectrum of obligations, the context was a counterinsurgency, where I was required to influence tribal leaders, State Department teams who hailed from a different culture than mine, allied teammates, and fragile Iraqi security forces who were now our teammates. Each required different leadership approaches—not abandoning core values or leadership skills learned and practiced throughout the years I had spent at other organizations but adapting the methods and approaches I used.

The average person changes jobs and positions many times during their life and career, so leaders should never ignore context. Parents of growing families also might consider context, as the ages of children and a growing number of young people in a family certainly change parental leadership!

Years after Desert Storm, I was seated on a long international flight—those trips when I like to sleep—next to a man who wanted to talk. I was trying to be polite, but I was truthfully listening half-heartedly. Until he started telling me a story that he had read about diamond polishing. He was in the jewelry business, and he wanted to describe the smallest detail of his craft.

For eight hours, as we flew from Frankfurt to New York, he explained the art of polishing a diamond: In the beginning, raw stones are cloudy, flawed, and unremarkable. But it is only through the polisher's patient, careful shaping, using a variety of techniques, that brilliance and the true value of the stone are revealed.

I was glad I stayed awake for his tutorial, as his metaphor was pertinent. I applied his story to an issue I was having with a subordinate whose character was raw, cloudy, flawed, and unremarkable. In this metaphor, that individual was the proverbial diamond in the rough. How could I help polish that subordinate to become the best version of himself?

That experience has never left me. Leadership takes the same approach. Soldiers, doctors, students, employees—all of them come with raw potential. A leader's job is not to force brilliance upon them but to carefully polish, refine, encourage, and shape what already exists within them. A leader's art is to help people uncover their internal motivation, see their own strengths, and confront their own weaknesses. It is diamond polishing. Done poorly, people scar. Done well, people shine and realize their value.

Back in April 1991, my instinct was to size up the "different personalities" in my squadron. Today, I see that I was fumbling toward a framework I didn't yet have words to describe. Now, I know leadership can be defined by attributes, competencies, influence methods, and context—woven together by trust, adapted to different people, sharpened by time, and shaped by reflection.

Just to be clear, though, I'm also mindful of the times when I failed in one of these elements, where I fell short. I failed to persuade the army chief of staff to adopt the new physical fitness test we had carefully designed, but I can now see that it wasn't the merit of the test that doomed it but my own approach. There was defensiveness in my sales pitch, and it hurt the outcome. My influence method had fallen flat, undercutting my ability to shape his decision-making.

I failed to convince members of Congress to maintain troop levels in Europe in 2012, despite intelligence that showed the dangers of further cuts, but I now recognize that my approach and methods of communicating the issues were flawed. I relied on blunt argument rather than building trust, context, and a shared vision with the committee decision-makers. My values were sound, my analysis was accurate, but my leadership execution was flawed.

Notice I didn't address all the other leadership action failures that were also part of my career. But trust me, there were many.

Failures sting. But they also teach. Without a deeper understanding of how attributes, competencies, influence methods, and context might better shape interactions, I often felt frustration. But with that appreciation, I now feel I can diagnose my own leadership lapses and learn from them while also helping others to do the same.

Michael Jordan once said that leadership has a price. He was right. Yogi Berra was also right that vision matters. Lao Tzu was right: The best leaders leave their people saying, "We did it ourselves." And my seatmate on that long flight was right: With patient work, leaders polish the diamonds entrusted to them so that brilliance emerges.

That's why, as a teacher of leadership today, my passion is to be the best damned diamond polisher around. Every student, every physician, every MBA candidate, every soldier carries raw potential—cloudy, imperfect, but with brilliance waiting to shine. I wish I had known much earlier that my task isn't to make them into something they're not but to provide advice that will help them refine what's already within them, to help them avoid the scars I carry, and maybe to give them a bit more clarity so that they can shine a bit brighter.

That's the mistake I made when writing about different leaders in the squadron in that desert journal back in 1991. I didn't see leaders for their potential; I saw some for their gifts, others for their flaws. I didn't see them as people, with complex combinations of values, skills, influences, and environments that they might someday shape into something great. I only saw them on that mission, in that period of time. That's the reason I didn't name names in this section but instead focused on what I've learned about leadership and all its complexities since.

13 APR 1991—Back in Saudi Arabia

Sorry I haven't written recently, but over the last three days, our 1st Armored Division finally moved back to Saudi Arabia from our position along Highway 8 on the Kuwait-Iraq border. The move was over 300 kms long, we traveled at 15 mph (max) across the vast desert that we passed only a few weeks earlier, and the conditions were radically different. My face is burned, my uniform is sweat-soaked and marked by salt perspiration and filled with dust, and I have a thirst now that I know will last for days. The temperatures during our move ranged from 90-115 degrees, and the dust was so thick we had to stop every two hours to allow the M1 tanks that were following us to blow out their engine air filters.

This made all of us think how the conditions could have been radically different had it not been raining and cool during our march into Iraq during the 100-hour war just a few months ago. If we had been wearing our chemical suits now as we were back in February, or if we had expected to "sneak up" on the Republican Guards with the clouds of dust and smoke that our vehicles were generating, the results could have been very different. Thank God they were not!

During the movement back to Saudi, some very interesting incidents occurred. One tank that was towing another tank generated so much heat that the towed tank caught fire—it proceeded to cook off for hours, rounds exploding everywhere. An ammunition carrier for an artillery unit also caught fire, with the resulting cook offs scaring everyone around it. My HMMWV, again with SFC Tim Bretl driving, hit a cluster bomb that U.S. forces had contributed to the desert landscape and blew out another tire. SFC Bretl got it fixed within minutes and was back with the convoy before we even knew we had lost him at the back of our formation. I had my dust goggles on to protect my eyes from the dirt and the ever-present heat exhaust from the Bradley's engine that was off to the side of the turret, and as a result I now have "raccoon face" (white around my eyes, my face burned by the sun and exhaust).

The most interesting part of the trip, though, was then we crossed the berm back into Saudi Arabia. It was getting dark, and we could see the berm way in the distance as we approached. When we finally crossed, someone keyed the radio net and proclaimed, "We're finally back in friendly territory." We all felt very relieved to have that Iraqi part of our life behind us.

I'm one step closer to being home with you.

Love,

Dad

Reflection

Crossing that berm back into Saudi Arabia was a moment of euphoria. We believed—naïvely, as it turned out—that Iraq was behind us. The soldier's announcement on the net that we were "finally back in friendly territory" gave us relief and felt like the truth. But hindsight makes it clear that it was only a pause in what would be a much longer story.

I ended that journal entry with "one step closer to home." It was true in 1991; within weeks, we were back in Germany. But Iraq was not finished with me—or with America. Forces would cross that berm again in 2003. Soldiers and families—ours included—would spend decades living with the consequences of a war we thought was over when we crossed that berm back into "friendly territory."

That April movement reminds me how much the environment determines outcomes. Dust clogged air filters and forced tanks to halt every two hours. Heat turned steel into ovens and, in several cases, even caused vehicles to catch on fire and explode the rounds that were inside. Uniforms became salt-encrusted rags, and men turned into husks.

I remember thanking God for the February rains of the one-hundred-hour war because had those conditions mirrored April's, our mission could have gone much differently. Soldiers can outmaneuver enemies; they cannot outmaneuver climate.

Later, in 2007, I traveled around northern Iraq with helicopter doors open. One day, going from Mosul to the Syrian border, the same kind of heat was pressing like a furnace on my skin. Our UH60 crew chief joked it was like sitting in a sauna with a giant hair dryer aimed at your face, and he didn't know if closing the aircraft doors would help. We never resorted to that. The soldiers on the ground had it worse, walking patrols in the heat and dust of the desert or driving MRAPs and up-armored HMMWVs with vehicle air conditioners that weren't always reliable. Heat and dust were constant. And everyone was wearing seventy pounds of Kevlar body armor and carrying loads that contributed to relentless fatigue.

Of course, in 2003, we didn't even have the protection of those MRAPs. As Secretary Rumsfeld bluntly said, "You go to war with the army you have, not the army you might want." For us, that meant thin-skinned HMMWVs vulnerable to every roadside bomb. Soldiers improvised, welding steel plates, bolting scrap to doors, or sandbagging the floors. It echoed the ingenuity of WWII tankers welding "Rhino tusks" to Sherman tanks in Normandy to cut through hedgerows. Different century, same instinct: Survive with what you've got.

That same year, insurgents showed their own ingenuity. On one August day, driving from our Log Base Dogwood into Baghdad, my HMMWV was hit by an IED hidden inside the body of a dead dog. The blast cracked the windshield in front of where I sat in the front passenger seat and blew off the right-side mirror. Luckily, none of us were hurt, but for the rest of that year, riding in that scarred vehicle was a daily reminder of insurgent cunning and of our own need to stay alert every second. The cracked glass in front of me became a symbol: Even when you survived, danger was never far away.

Back in 1991, we knew—because we had been told by MG Griffith just a few weeks earlier during his visit to our squadron—that crossing the berm truly was the beginning of redeployment. Vehicles would go to ports, planes would be lined up, and families would be waiting. But then we realized our twenty thousand 1st Armored Division soldiers were competing with over one hundred thousand from the other units that were part of the Desert Storm force for a ride home. But at least we knew it would come.

In 2004, 1st Armored Division would experience a crueler story. We were at the end of our tour, and we were ready to go home. As the assistant division commander for support (ADC-S), I was down at the ports supervising the flow of equipment back to Germany while the commanding general and the ADC for maneuver were still in Baghdad, conducting the transfer with the 1st Cavalry Division. We had already shipped about a third of our thirty thousand soldiers back to Germany when we started hearing rumors of our extension. Equipment was staged at the port, and helicopters were bubble-wrapped and ready to be loaded on ships. From the soldiers who had already returned home, we were hearing news of families cheering and shedding tears when their soldiers arrived at the various theaters and gyms at our *kasernes* in Europe. LTC Jay Larson, one of our aviation battalion commanders, was photographed kissing his wife Liz in the Hanau gymnasium as a local paper captured the "welcome home." The picture ran on the front page Monday morning—and that same morning, Larson was already back in Baghdad.

The whiplash was brutal. Soldiers were pulled off airplanes and told to gear up again. Families who had celebrated reunions were forced to say goodbye again. Equipment was unpacked from ships and returned to the fight in a new area of operation—southern Iraq. For the command teams, it was one of the most difficult orders to relay to the soldiers: return to combat. This time, the lines soldiers cling to, the kinds of berms and boundaries they cross to go home, had evaporated overnight.

These events taught me something we all already knew. Thresholds—crossing a berm, boarding a plane, embracing your spouse and children on a gym floor at a welcome home ceremony—carry enormous symbolic weight. They matter to morale, to fighting spirit, to the sense that sacrifice has purpose. But leaders also must prepare their people for the possibility that thresholds can be false ones, as 2004 proved in such a devastating way.

That April night in 1991, crossing the berm, we all thought Iraq was behind us. The front-page photo of LTC Larson and Tammy in 2004 showed me that "homecomings" could vanish in a heartbeat. The continuous ebb and flow of the terror attacks and the creation of better Iraqi governance in 2007 was a constant indicator that we were taking three steps forward and two back every single day.

The two young boys I was writing this journal for would experience those same emotional rollercoasters over the first two decades of the twenty-first century. Crossing that berm gave me some initial relief, but the real lesson was that there's always another berm ahead.

19 APR 1991—Camp Kasserine

It's our final place of encampment in this long adventure. Named after a famous WWII battle that the 1st Armored Division was involved in (which, by the way, they lost), Kasserine is a site just to the west of King Khalid Military City, in the middle of the desert. The division built a town hall about three miles from the Cav's location, and it contains a small PX in a tent, a hamburger stand, a movie theater (where they are playing VCR tapes of old movies) and a telephone tent (I called Mom from there just yesterday to tell her I was back in Saudi). It ain't much, but it's home.

The atmosphere is different from all the other places we've lived in, as the entire squadron is together. Six hundred soldiers living in tents all in a row depending on which troop you're in. It's neat to have everyone together, eating at the same mess tent, taking daily showers (which are sometimes even filled with water!) and not having to travel anywhere by vehicle to talk to one of the units.

It's very hot—over 110 in the daytime and hovering around 95 at night. We stay in our tents between 1000-1600 because it's scorching. We had a detail just the other day to pull up the aircraft matting that Fourth Brigade was using for its helicopters. We had to wait until 7:00 pm—after dark—to begin to allow those mattings to get cool enough that we could touch them. Everyone drinks between 6 and 10 liters of water per day. But you know what? It's all bearable because we know we'll all be going home soon.

My last adventure consisted of going to a Saudi Arabia "souq" or "souk"—an Arabian shopping center or marketplace—to buy you guys and Mom a present. Bought Mom a 21-karat gold necklace (gold is very inexpensive in this part of the world, but a high quality) and I bought you guys each an "abaya"—the traditional camel bit that Arabs use to keep their headdress on. It's the only thing that looked worthwhile, and really the only thing I want to bring home as a souvenir.

With the rest of my Saudi riyals, I bought some non-alcoholic beer. In a few days, I'll be able to give you your presents and drink a real beer.

Love,

Dad

Reflection

Over the years, I had forgotten how bad Camp Kasserine really was. An awful place, thinking back on it, but an oasis during that period. We were going home, and nothing could detract from that because nothing else mattered. The war was over. The Republican Guard had been defeated, and our division was back in Saudi Arabia. We were hot, tired, and coated in dust, but the promise of home was finally within sight. The PX tent, the hamburger stand, the VCR tapes playing old movies, the grueling work of pulling up 4th Brigade helicopter mats—nothing mattered to any of us. In our minds, Iraq was behind the Blackhawks.

But history has a way of humbling soldiers who believe in clean endings.

The name "Kasserine" itself, though we didn't admit it, should have been a reminder of humility. In February 1943, American forces—indeed, our very own 1st Armored Division—suffered a crushing defeat at Kasserine Pass in the desert of Tunisia. The US Army was green, poorly coordinated, badly led, terribly equipped, and untested against the battle-hardened German Afrika Korps. Units broke under fire. Leadership faltered. Sherman tanks became "Purple Heart boxes." The press back home reported a humiliation.

And yet, out of that defeat, the army learned important lessons. Leaders were replaced, doctrine was refined, equipment was strengthened, training was intensified. The sting of Kasserine would eventually become the steel of Italy and later Normandy. From failure, the army built resilience. That is the story of American arms: what Heller and Stofft call the lessons of all our wars in their phenomenal book *America's First Battles: 1776-1965*. Those authors proclaim the US had a 3-5-1 win-loss-tie record in the first fights of each war in our history. The Battle of Kasserine Pass was the authors' example of the first "loss" of World War II. But they also note that the path from Tunisia to Berlin was forged in that early crucible.

When the 1st Armored Division established its final encampment of Desert Storm in Saudi Arabia at a camp named after that same battle, there was more than a touch of irony. There we were, the inheritors of Kasserine, victorious in a modern armored campaign. We had not erased the defeat of 1943, but we had shown what a military can become when it refuses to repeat its mistakes. Humility, as the wise historians often say, teaches us more than triumph ever will.

But if humility in 1943 made us stronger, I now wonder, as I reflect on this journal entry with the advantage of the passage of time, whether hubris in 1991 infected us and made us weaker. Desert Storm was swift, decisive, and overwhelming. It shouted that the US military was not only the best in the world but capable of solving nearly any problem, anywhere. Politicians began to see the US armed forces as a tool of first resort. Why wrestle with the slow grind of diplomacy when precision munitions and armored thrusts delivered results in days?

That overreliance came at a cost. We moved toward the twenty-first century with confidence that our power could remake nations quickly, decisively, and cleanly. But war, as Iraq and Afghanistan showed us, is never simple. Toppling a dictator is not the same as destroying an army. Desert Storm conditioned us to expect lightning victories. What followed in 2003 and beyond in Iraq reminded us that lightning does not last; it flashes, then it fades.

In 1943, humility taught us to grow. In 1991, victory taught us to believe perhaps too much in our own strength. That distinction matters because it helps explain how our stumbles contributed to some of the challenges of the next decades.

There's another lesson that Camp Kasserine makes me think about now. In 1990, Saddam Hussein invaded Kuwait, and the world responded. The United States, leading a coalition of dozens of nations, acted decisively. We deployed half a million troops, liberated Kuwait, and declared that the principle associated with one large nation's aggression against a peaceful smaller nation would not stand.

Fast-forward to the twenty-first century, and the contrast seems stark. Russia invaded Ukraine in 2014 and again in 2022. But this time, the response was slower, more hesitant, more cautious. We supported Ukraine with weapons, intelligence, and training—but there was not an equivalent kind of immediate, overwhelming response that had defined Desert Storm. We debated, hesitated, and parsed words.

Why did we act so quickly for Kuwait but so carefully for Ukraine? Geography, alliance structures, nuclear deterrence—all these matter, and they contribute to action. But history might ask whether we forgot the urgency of countering authoritarians before they grow stronger. Saddam in 1990 and Putin in 2022 were not so different: Both sought to swallow a neighbor, to erase sovereignty, to destabilize international order, to rape land and people. One dictator was stopped in months. The other still fights as I'm writing this, with an undetermined outcome.

The legacy of Desert Storm is complicated. It showed what decisive action can achieve. But perhaps it also conditioned us to see wars of aggression as solvable by force alone, while leaving us hesitant to act boldly when the stage shifted to Europe.

Another thought. As I've paged through the entries of this journal, looking back at those days and reflecting on what has happened in my life and to my outlook since, what strikes me most is how I began it in December 1990—uncertain, pragmatic, philosophical, advising our sons on how to live their lives in case I didn't return to give the guidance later. Looking back, I was sometimes almost clinical and used doctrinal terms in describing the movements of men and machines in our fight.

I wrote to explain things to our sons in a way they might understand if I wasn't there to explain. It speaks to their age, but it also confirms my immaturity as a young officer. I was still growing as a soldier and as a man, still trying my best but sometimes failing to translate experience into words.

By April 1991, as we moved into a post-war era and got closer to leaving, my writing changed. The entries were no longer just tactical notes; they were reflections on humanity, leadership, values, and death. The war matured me. It deepened my understanding of responsibility, trust, the human condition, people. Being given the opportunity to read that journal now, with the request to provide further insight, is like watching a young officer grow into a seasoned professional, page by page.

There was a favorite book among young officers back in the 1980s that was on everyone's bookshelf: *Once an Eagle* by Anton Myrer. The novel is the story of a young man, a maverick with a great deal of leadership skills, from Nebraska who enters the army prior to World War I. He's given a battlefield commission for heroism in the trenches of France, then continues to grow through the ranks during the tough interwar years before becoming a division commander in the Pacific. It's a great story, but there's one line that always guided my life as a soldier. It comes when the main character, Sam Damon, is talking to the son of an old battle buddy who was truly selfless and loved his soldiers. Unfortunately, the son has become a careerist and is focused on promotion and advancement in rank, so he asks Sam for advice on a particular issue. Sam offers an easy path for the younger man to consider. "Joey," he says, "when it comes to a choice between being a good soldier and being a good human being, be a good human being . . . as that will make you a great soldier."

Be a good human being. Key advice for anyone who wants to be a great leader, in any profession, in any industry.

That understanding and growth is what connects this penultimate entry to the one that will follow, the last one of this work. At Camp Kasserine, I believed I was closing a chapter. But what I was really doing was preparing for the next one—not just the wars that would follow but the life I would lead and the lessons I would try to pass on.

Kasserine was not just a camp in the desert. It was a symbol of history's continuity and of a soldier's growth. It reminded me that humility shapes strength, but hubris can blind us. It highlighted how victories can be fleeting if we fail to act decisively against aggressors. And for me personally, it marked the point where my journal shifted from tactical to strategic, from describing events to distilling lessons, from personal diary to legacy. To becoming a better human being.

The final entry, which follows, will not be about battles or camps or PX tents. It will be about our boys, about the men they have become, about the character and decisions that define life. This reflection, then, is the bridge—the reminder that war teaches us not just how to fight but how to grow and how to pass lessons forward.

In reading the history of Kasserine Pass in 1943, it's apparent that soldiers and leaders learned about humility. In reflecting back on Camp Kasserine in 1991, I was reminded that endings are rarely final, that freedom is always under threat, and that the real legacy of a soldier's journal is not memories of wars fought but lessons handed down.

25 APR 1991—My Sons

I once remember reading a passage of a prayer that was attributed to General Douglas MacArthur titled "Build Me A Son, O Lord." In this prayer, General MacArthur asks for a son who would be strong enough to know when he is weak, and brave enough to face himself when he is afraid. One who is proud and unbending in honest defeat, but humble and gentle in victory. One who is selfless, kind, and compassionate in the face of all challenges, and one who deals every man and woman he meets the fairness that other human beings deserve. The prayer of this famous WWII fighter has become my prayer also, for our two terrific sons.

Time was when a boy proved his manhood in many ways. He worked hard if he wanted food to eat or a fire to warm by. He milked cows, cut wood, killed the deer for supper. The art of growing was once determined by keeping your mouth shut when superiors spoke until you had learned something worth saying. To prove you were growing into a man, you had to be able to plow a straight row, build something useful, or whip the town bully.

Today it's different. There are many things around you persuading you to live up to a certain standard: sports figures who are making millions of dollars; peers taking drugs or talking in bad ways about sex; businessmen taking advantage of other people for a better deal, higher prestige, or more money. When you do these things (and others), some misguided person will tell you you're growing up. And you know what? They're all dead wrong. The reason I know this is because I've seen men doing what they're supposed to do, with maturity, over these last several months in the desert. And these men, surprisingly, are just a few years older than you two. A few months ago, many of them were also just boys.

It takes men to build men from boys, and that's where I come in. A real man, you boys need to see, doesn't need to bolster his ego or courage with alcohol, or treat others badly, or crow about how good he is at a sport, or job, or a particular task. A real man proves his masculinity by being considerate, protective, concerned, and confident—and by demonstrating it.

Boys also need challenge to become men, and I (and your Mom) will continue to try and provide that. You need jobs and chores and the chance to prove yourself in important things. And, at times, you need the opportunity to fail and learn from your mistakes. Believe me, those growing experiences will be the hardest for your Mom and me to provide. But we will provide them, nonetheless.

We will attempt to set goals and challenges for you two, and sometimes we'll even know that there are obstacles in your path. Know that you do not have to achieve the goal all the time, but just the fact that you're trying is enough for us.

We both want you to have happiness, but we will also attempt to help you through your sorrows. We will laugh with you and try to cheer you when you're sad. As you experience life and learn from it, know that Mom and I are always on your side.

This is my second to last journal entry for you guys, for tonight I wrap this in a waterproof container, put it in my duffel bag, and prepare to go to the airfield. My last entry will be entered some night within the first two or three days of being home, when everyone's asleep and I'm in my office with all its familiar surroundings. That will be a very sweet entry. What makes that entry so important is, at the beginning of this whole thing, I never thought I would be making it. I believed that this war could have taken its toll on one Mark Hertling, and that there was a good chance that I would not see you guys again when I left our house in Lehrberg on 20 December 1990. I had told my friends to ensure that, if anything happened to me out here, that you guys would get this book. My thought was that it would at least give you some idea as to who your old man was. I was brave enough to face the possibilities when I was very, very afraid.

The good news is that now I can help you guys grow to be men. I will relish that work. From what your Mom has relayed to me about both of your actions over the last several months, you are well on your way to being considerate, protective, concerned, and confident. I will do everything I can to assist in your further development, so one day both of you will be able to say, "Thanks, Dad, for helping me to become a man."

I love you,

Dad

Reflection—"Build Me a Son"

This reflection will be the last in this book, and it expands on MacArthur's prayer that I wrote about in this journal entry, not because I admired the general's fame but because I admired the honesty of his petition. The prayer is longer than the few lines I captured that night before sealing my journal in a waterproof bag to go in my soldier's duffel. It's a father's litany of hopes: strength with humility, courage with self-knowledge, pride only in honest work, a sense of justice, a reverence for truth, a ready laugh, and a steel-core willingness to serve something larger than self. It asks not for a paved road made easy but for character strong enough to walk any path.

That prayer has always been close to me, and Sue loved it, too, when I first showed it to her after Todd was born. She had a friend of ours write it in beautiful calligraphy and frame it, and now, each of our sons has it hanging in a place where it can interrupt the noise of a busy day and remind them of what "right" looks like as they raise their own sons. Each time I see it in their homes, I am reminded that it has become more than MacArthur's words; it has become our family's constitution. And now, looking back across years of war, teaching, medicine, leadership, and family life, I can see how each line has taken root in our lives. Throughout the years, I've learned that the prayer isn't just about boys becoming men. It's a guide on how to live a life—man or woman, soldier or surgeon, chief executive or brand-new private. It certainly is a father's North Star for any child, but it's also a compass for living life.

MacArthur begins, "Build me a son, O Lord, who will be strong enough to know when he is weak and brave enough to face himself when he is afraid." That paradox—strength in admitting weakness, courage in facing fear—has proven itself to me countless times. On the battlefield, I saw it when talking with a young leader who admitted he wasn't sure how to execute a tough mission. That shows real strength. In a hospital, it was the physician who, while revealing his expertise in the science of medicine, confessed his inexperience in the art of leading his team. That was a display of true courage. In the classroom, it was the student who said, "I don't know much about this subject yet, but I want to master it," who revealed the kind of character that lasts. The army names "personal courage" as one of its core values, and while it certainly applies during combat, I've found it is just as critical in daily life. The most effective leaders practice courage in their words and actions: weighing what they say and ensuring it is ethical and logical, not simply emotional. Strength isn't swagger, and courage isn't bravado; both are honesty in action.

The prayer continues, "One who will be proud and unbending in honest defeat, and humble and gentle in victory." Defeat, I have found, is often the best teacher. In sports and in war. Our army's humiliation at Kasserine in 1943 prepared it for triumphs that followed, but our swift victory in Desert Storm tempted us into overconfidence that would cost us dearly later. And in my own life, I can recall seasons when everything seemed to be going right—when a new plan or initiative looked brilliant—only to watch things unravel. Those moments became cautionary refrains. As I grew older, the line "don't spike the football just yet" repeated itself in my head more and more. The leaders I have trusted most were those who carried defeat with dignity and wore victory with humility. Both moments—failure and success—reveal who you really are.

MacArthur next prays, "Build me a son whose wishes will not take the place of deeds." Empty promises and noble intentions mean nothing without the weight of action. I have seen this not only in individual lives but in organizations. A strategy or vision statement can sound inspiring, but unless leaders provide the path and means to achieve it, that vision often remains just a wish. Real leaders do more than articulate goals—they act, they plan, they participate, and they communicate the next steps to make the vision real. Over time, I've come to believe that words are wind, while deeds endure.

He adds, "A son who will know Thee—and that to know himself is the foundation stone of knowledge." Without those anchors, we drift. Leaders who lack faith or self-awareness chase applause and position; sons who lack them chase the crowd. What I learned is that when you know who you are, when you know your values and your beliefs and who you really serve, you can face any storm without losing your course.

MacArthur then pleads, "Lead him, I pray, not in the path of ease and comfort, but under the stress and spur of difficulties and challenge." That request may seem harsh to a parent, but it is a truth every father comes to understand. It is hardship that shapes resilience, trial that forges maturity. I often found myself wishing for ease for my sons, then realizing that if they never had to struggle, it would do them no good. Stress builds the muscles of character. I came to understand that we grow most when our path is steep.

He continues, "Here let him learn to stand up in the storm; here let him learn compassion for those who fail." The two belong together. Hardship without compassion produces harshness; compassion without hardship produces sentimentality. In war, I saw soldiers bury their enemies with dignity and medics treat civilians with the same care they gave comrades, living up to their professed values. In health care, I watched teams prepare for hurricanes by standing shoulder to shoulder when the rest of their fellow citizens were hunkering down, watched doctors and nurses rehearsing how they would protect their communities when storms struck. Years later, those same lessons carried into something even greater: When COVID came, the literal practice of standing together, facing the crisis, became the foundation for remaining strong in the face of a disease that brought fear and death to colleagues and patients alike. What endures for me is that resilience and compassion, when held together, make us fully human.

The prayer then looks forward: "Build me a son whose heart will be clear, whose goal will be high; a son who will master himself before he seeks to master other men; one who will reach into the future yet never forget the past." Those lines have carried me through crises in every stage of leadership. Integrity provides clarity, vision gives direction, self-discipline grants authority, and memory teaches humility. I have seen organizations crumble when they forgot one of those pillars. What I see now is that leadership begins inside—with self-mastery—and only then reaches outward to others.

The general does not forget joy: "And after all these things are his, add, I pray, enough of a sense of humor so that he may always be serious, yet never take himself too seriously." That line, more than most, rings true to me. I have watched humor sustain soldiers after tough combat, physicians during long hospital nights, journalists trying to get a story just right, and students in grueling courses. Laughter builds trust, restores balance, and reminds us that even in the gravest work, joy remains a necessity. I came to treasure humor as resilience in disguise—it allows people to carry burdens that might otherwise break them.

Finally, MacArthur offers this: "Give him humility, so that he may always remember the simplicity of true greatness, the open mind of true wisdom, and the meekness of true strength." That line is the key that unlocks all the rest. Humility prevents power from becoming arrogance, wisdom from becoming pride, and strength from becoming cruelty. I can recall times in my own life when I believed everything was going just right, that I had been part of a brilliant plan or a wonderful innovation—only to watch it fall apart. Those experiences reinforced the truth that hubris is always waiting to ambush those with egos that can't be satiated. "Don't get cocky" should be an inner warning for all of us, echoing again and again. I have watched nations falter when leaders abandoned humility, and I have seen communities flourish when they embraced it. What I now know is that humility is not the absence of strength—it is strength under control.

The prayer ends with the father daring to whisper, "Then I, his father, will dare to whisper, 'I have not lived in vain.'" When I first went off to war in 1990, I feared I might not return. I hoped my writing would help my sons know who I was. Now, years later, I see that MacArthur's words shaped not just our sons but our grandchildren, my students, and perhaps even the soldiers and colleagues I've had the privilege to lead. This whisper has become a truth: A life lived by this prayer is never in vain because it is carried forward in others.

When I began the journal in December 1990, I wrote as a young officer who did not know if he would come home. I wrote to give two little boys a picture of their father. I wrote in simple language because I wanted them to understand it when they were older. Decades later, they brought the journal back to me and said, in effect, "Dad, add the footnotes. Tell us what you learned after the entries ended."

What I learned is what MacArthur's prayer was asking for all along: You need character that tells the truth and relies on values. Competence that learns, practices, and develops yourself and others until good becomes a habit. Influence that privileges trust over intimidation. Context that reads the room, the culture, the faith, the history, and the human involved before acting.

During my life, I've often fallen short. There were moments when I allowed defensiveness to replace curiosity, when I mistook position for persuasion, when I pushed too fast for a change I hadn't yet earned. I can see places where, had I further polished my character and competencies, I might have built more trust, won more allies, and preserved more energy to achieve longer-term visions. The scar tissue from falling short reminds me to teach to others what I had to learn the hard way.

Our sons are no longer the boys I wrote to way back when. They are husbands and fathers and professionals with their own scar tissue that no one can avoid in life, but they also have their own light to provide to others. They each reflect the prayer in ways that are distinct but exactly right for them as individuals. They are strong enough to name their weaknesses and brave enough to face themselves. They are proud in honest defeat and gentle in victory. They are selfless in the small things that matter more than the big ones. They are fair. They tell the truth. They laugh easily, and they serve others.

If you have traveled through these pages with our boys and me—from the burning skies of Kuwait to the volleyball net in the desert, from the staff rides at Gettysburg to the staff meetings in a hospital, from CNN studios to MBA classrooms—then you have seen me revisit many of the same lessons repeatedly in many different uniforms. But what I'd really like everyone to take from this is that leadership is love in public. It is the steady choice to put people and purpose ahead of ego. It is the discipline of humility and the courage of beliefs. It is the willingness to widen the circle of responsibility until it includes not only "your" people but the ones you once called "other."

To our sons: You asked me to add reflections to a book I once sealed in a duffel bag to ship home to you. I did not know when I started that journal that I would get to teach you the lessons in person, then watch you grow and eventually teach them to your own children. That prayer that is framed on your walls is now a reflection of how your mother and I see you live every day. Keep it there—not as decoration but as an examination. When the world is noisy, read it . . . and let the words pull you back to your first principles.

To my grandchildren: You were the audience I didn't know I would have. If you find yourself reading these pages, know this: You come from a family that believes that service is joy; that truth and humor walk together; and that every person you meet deserves fairness, respect, and dignity. The world will tell you that winning is the point. It is not. The point is to be good and to do good, together, for as long as you are given breath.

To anyone who has paraded through this book with me, please remember the prayer's quiet demands. Be strong enough to admit weakness. Be brave enough to face yourself. Hold your head up in honest defeat and lower it in victory. Be selfless, kind, and fair. Seek the truth and laugh often. Choose service over self. Draw out the myriad motivations that live in others. Polish diamonds—gently, patiently, precisely—until their brilliance helps others see. Our world needs all of that, from each of us.

I began my journal back in December of 1990 because I thought I might not return to my family. I finished this book because I did return and because I now want to offer these stories as my gift to others. So, I'll say now what I said a thousand times in uniform and what we still say as a family: *Auf Wiedersehen.* Not goodbye—*see you again.* Keep faith, do the next right thing, and if you have the chance, show others what right looks like too. And when it's your turn to tell your story, to reflect on your life, tell it in a way that helps someone else live their life a little better. That's what I've tried to do. I can only hope it matters.

AFTERWORD

Even after I finished this book, I found myself returning to it, not just to edit but to reflect on the events of war and the lessons of leadership, on the people and places I wrote about that shaped my life. I was determined to say "thanks" one more time.

First, to Sue: The builder of homes, giver of grace, and the love of my life.

Sue has been the constant. Best friend, lover, confidante, partner, sharer of adventures. In the thirty-eight years of my service in uniform, we moved twenty-four times. Each new small set of quarters or rented house was simply walls and floors when we arrived, but Sue had a gift for quickly transforming them into a home for all of us, usually within the first forty-eight hours. While the rest of us slept, she unpacked boxes, hung pictures, placed furniture, and—more than anything—filled each room with her special kind of warmth and love so that when we awakened, we marveled at her work and our new home. Though it was often tough, she always embraced the adventure of our marriage, eager to see what the next posting, the next community, the next challenge, and the next group of friends would bring. Yet for all her sense of adventure, what she cherished most were the quiet nights when her family gathered close.

She has endured deployments that stretched for months and years, forgiven me when I've fallen short, and anchored our family in grace and love. She raised two beautiful boys largely on her own when duty carried me elsewhere. Her friendships, too, have been remarkable: She has a way of opening herself to others with complete transparency—sharing her soul, her compassion, and her laughter. Many people over the years have told me that Sue was their closest friend during a difficult tour. That is who she is and why she is so deeply loved—by others, but most passionately by me.

Then there are our sons, Todd and Scott, now husbands and fathers themselves. They grew up as "BRATs" (an acronym most don't know came from a British term, British Regiment Attached Traveler). They grew up in the shadow of deployments, living in Germany, in America, and in between. When playing baseball or soccer at one of our many posts, they would stop—like all military kids do—when retreat was played and the flag was lowered. They adapted with resilience, carried on with courage, and never failed to bring joy to our family and to others they met. Today, they both continue to serve this nation in different ways, building families and communities while embodying the values their mother and I prayed they would embrace and that the MacArthur prayer instilled in them. They are living proof that character endures across generations. They are truly good men.

I must also thank the United States—the nation that allowed me to serve my fellow citizens while wearing the cloth of this country, that gave me the privilege on dozens of occasions to swear the beautiful oath to that remarkable document we call the Constitution, and that encouraged me to live the values that define who we are. That oath was never to a person, a party, or an institution but to the idea that liberty and justice are for all, that all men are created equal, and that all people should have the respect of their fellow citizens. It has guided every decision I made in uniform and in civilian clothes.

Our service to the nation carried Sue and me to nearly every part of this country and most of the world—Virginia, Kentucky, Louisiana, Kansas, Indiana, Texas, Washington State, as well as Europe, Asia, Africa and Latin America. For an eighteen-year-old boy who'd never left St. Louis or experienced flight until he boarded a plane for New York and West Point in 1971, that journey was extraordinary. I saw landscapes that inspired awe, experienced traditions that amazed me, ate food that represented a region, and, most importantly, met people whose stories became part of my own. Farmers, teachers, mechanics, cooks, doctors, immigrants, lifelong patriots—all who made this country real to me in ways that no book or classroom ever could.

The army carried us across oceans. I walked the streets of Baghdad, Mosul, and Basra. I met leaders in Israel, Jordan, Lebanon, and Egypt. I traveled to China and South Korea and visited nearly every European nation. Sue and I have continued to travel since retirement, and everywhere we've gone, we have been struck by a universal truth: Governments and armies may concur or clash, but people—ordinary people—share far more than what divides them. The meals, the customs, the greetings, the drink of choice, the songs, and especially their families—all different, yet all familiar. As I wrote in one of the reflections earlier in this book, learning about other people's cultures and meeting other people's families are life's greatest blessings.

And yet, among all those places and all those people, besides our own nation, Germany holds a singular place in our hearts.

There is a German phrase that captures what Sue and I felt during our many years in that country: *gemütlichkeit*. It is a word without a precise English translation—warmth, comfort, a sense of belonging—but it describes perfectly what Germany became for us. It was not just the place where we lived; it was our second home.

When I retired from USAREUR, the German army pinned a medal on my chest but also gave me the honor of a *Großer Zapfenstreich*—the German torchlight ceremony of farewell—and that remains one of the most humbling moments of my career. The ceremony itself is deeply moving: the precision of the Bundeswehr soldiers, the solemnity of the torches at midnight, the music chosen with care, the silent closing of ranks as the honored officer departs. It speaks to centuries of tradition and respect. To stand there as an American, embraced not just as an ally but as a friend, was a reminder of the extraordinary bond between our two nations.

Our German story began in Schweinfurt in 1975. I was a new lieutenant with a young bride, a British sports car, and not much else. Sue and I arrived with lots more hope than possessions. Within twenty-four hours, I left her alone in a tiny apartment and headed to the "field" for training. She found welcome at the neighborhood bakery; I found my footing as an armored officer. From those early days, Germany began weaving itself into the fabric of our family.

We would return again and again: Lehrberg, Ansbach, Hanau, Grafenwöhr, Heidelberg, Wiesbaden. Each assignment added friends, places, and chapters to a story that became less about duty stations and more about a second home and a second family. After our time during the Cold War, we came back for another tour and saw the Berlin Wall come down. We celebrated with our German neighbors as their country reunited. Later on during that tour, German police and Bundeswehr stood guard over our children as they walked to school when our soldiers deployed to Iraq for the first time. On our next tour, Sue moved into yet another new house all by herself because I deployed again before even seeing where she would live. It was our German neighbors in Hanau who welcomed her to a home I would never live in.

Germany never treated us as temporary residents. Germans treated us as family. That's what allies do.

All told, Sue and I spent twelve of our thirty-eight years of service in Germany. They were the most formative years of our lives. Our children grew up in their schools and neighborhoods. They became fluent in the German language, even as Sue and I struggled with the simplest phrases. But we understood the most important word: *Freundschaft*—friendship.

Just like I usually wore the Iraqi and US flags on my sleeve when deployed, we always flew both the German and US flags from our porches in Germany—because we wanted to show respect. We sang both anthems with equal conviction. We learned to love the traditions, the fests that seemed to be sprinkled throughout the year, the Christmas markets, the crazy New Year's Eves, the towering cathedrals, the rolling hills, the quiet lakes, and the bustling cities. But more than the landscapes, we came to love the people. They welcomed us into their homes and favorite gasthauses, trusted us as neighbors, and shared with us their joys during unification and sorrows when their favorite football team lost. I am especially thankful to our friends Rita and Wolfgang and Siegrid and Norm, Kristin, and Herr and Frau Wachter.

So let this afterword also serve as a thank-you, Germany. Where I deployed from, and where Sue stayed, walked, and prayed. Thank you for embracing and guarding my family when I could not. Thank you for giving Sue community and friendship throughout long deployments. Thank you for raising our children alongside your own. Thank you for welcoming us not as visitors but as kin.

Finally, to friends. Throughout this book, I have mentioned many of them—fellow soldiers, commanders, sergeants, colleagues, and peers who shaped me. Some are no longer with us; others remain lifelong companions. But what's great is that there are many more friends we haven't met yet. I look forward to meeting them—in classrooms, in boardrooms, during future travels, at church, in quiet conversations at a café, and in the laughter of a shared meal. Because friendship, like service, is never finished. It continues as long as we live and as long as we are willing to open our hearts.

This book began with a journal written in fear that I might not return from war. It became, years later, a springboard for reflections for our sons, our grandchildren, and anyone else who is interested. Along the way, it turned into a story not just of one soldier's journey but of the enduring lessons of leadership, faith, conflict, love, life, and friendship.

I'll end where I began in that first entry: with emotion and gratitude. Gratitude for a wife who built homes, for sons who became men, for a nation that entrusted me with command, for allies and friends across the globe, and for all those who will join me on the road still ahead.

This story isn't finished. But it has been, and remains, a great honor to have come this far.

GIVING BACK: IN MEMORY OF PETE WAY

Fifty percent of the proceeds from this book will be donated to the National Ability Center (NAC) in Park City, Utah—an organization dedicated to helping individuals with disabilities discover their strength, independence, and purpose.

Founded in 1985 as an adaptive ski program for disabled veterans, the NAC has grown into one of the nation's leading centers for adaptive recreation. Today, it serves people of all ages and abilities, with service members, veterans, and their families making up nearly a third of all participants. Through sport, recreation, and education, the NAC empowers those it serves to build confidence, self-esteem, and lasting skills that restore not only mobility, but meaning.

These contributions are made in memory of US Army veteran Pete Way, a friend who was grievously wounded in Afghanistan but found healing, hope, and renewed purpose through the programs of the NAC. Pete's courage and resilience reflect the very spirit this book seeks to honor—the will to endure, to grow even through adversity, and to live fully.

If you would like to join in supporting this remarkable organization and the veterans and families it serves, please visit https://discovernac.org/support/.